ANTHEM
OF A
RELUCTANT
PROPHET

JOANNE PROULX

ANTHEM OF A RELUCTANT PROPHET

PICADOR

First published 2007 as a Viking Book by Penguin Group (Canada)

First published in Great Britain 2008 by Picador
an imprint of Pan Macmillan Ltd
Pan Macmillan, 20 New Wharf Road, London N1 9RR
Basingstoke and Oxford
Associated companies throughout the world
www.panmacmillan.com

ISBN 978-0-330-45296-0

The acknowledgments on page 358 constitute an extension of
this copyright page.

1 3 5 7 9 8 6 4 2

A CIP catalogue record for this book is available from
the British Library.

Printed and bound in Great Britain by
Mackays of Chatham plc, Chatham, Kent

Visit **www.picador.com** to read more about all our books
and to buy them. You will also find features, author interviews and
news of any author events, and you can sign up for e-newsletters
so that you're always first to hear about our new releases.

For Martin, my favorite flavor of everything

In memory of my sister Laurie Elizabeth Vasiga,
my heart is blue for you

One, one, one, one—you go up and down your note like a pup up and down a dune, until you don't feel your festering bites or your oozy eyes or sun-scoured neck, until you're not one moment empty, nor one bit lost or one breath scared. You're so damn far into ones you're not one anything. You're a resonating multiplication. You're a crowd.

—Tim Winton, *Dirt Music*

ONE

The first time it happened, I was bullshitting. At least, I thought I was bullshitting. I had no idea I was about to knock my world on its ass when I opened my mouth that night in Delaney's basement. It was October 7, 2002, and like most days in Stokum, the rank little pinprick of a town where I was born and raised, the seventh of October unraveled in a completely unmemorable way. Yeah, as I recall, it was a pretty Stokum kind of day. It wasn't until that night that things got weird.

I'd headed over to Todd Delaney's after dinner, was hanging with the usual crowd, smoking up and listening to the mindless techno shit Todd likes. I'm not going to say too much about Delaney except that his mother was never home, so by the time we were seventeen his basement pretty much reeked. (When I say his mother was never home, I mean she was *never* home. Last time I saw her, she was headed to a millennium bash with a magnum of wine tucked under her scrawny arm.) Another thing—so I don't go mental calling him Todd, he's been Fang since grade one when his adult incisors arrived extra-early and extra-large, leaving the baby teeth up front cowering like mini-marshmallows between two he-man tusks. It was a look that caused Fang a fair amount of grief during his formative years. And he still has a pretty lacerating smile, so the nickname has some staying power even if he doesn't.

Anyway, the night of the seventh, we were in *Fang's* basement and the air was thick, but we weren't all chilled out and laughing at nothing like usual. The weed had a nasty edge and the mood was sort of grim. I was sitting on the crap plaid couch Delaney's mom had rescued from some landfill, being violated by the techno throb, agonizing over just how *trying* it was to be friends with a guy who had such shitty taste in music, which should give you a bit of insight into where my head was at in those days. Another impediment to me getting anywhere near a comfortable high was Dwight Slater, the skank parked beside me on the couch.

I realized the cushions were soft. I realized they tended to roll toward the low-slung center. Still, I thought my buddy Dwight could have made a bit more of an effort to stay on his side of the furniture. But he just kept sloshing into me, his knee, his shoulder, bumping against mine. Instead of moving over, he'd just give me a real loose smile, pretending he didn't know he was pissing me off, pretending he didn't know that the only reason he was even permitted in the basement was that he always brought the weed. (I'd pretty much hated Dwight since the day he tried to strangle me. It was back in grade three and Mrs. McNulty, our teacher, had stepped out of the class for a smoke or something and *bam!* Slater's hands were around my neck. I don't remember if I'd been hassling him before she left the room or what. I do remember Dwight looking completely psycho and his grip being superman tight and my face getting really, really hot and thinking I was going to die— I mean, for the first time in my life truly believing I was going to die—and how, even with Slater squeezing the last breath from my body, I'd been worried there was something wrong with me because I was way more stunned than scared, which I was sure wasn't normal. Anyway, no big deal. Dwight didn't kill me. What he did was drop his hands real fast when Mrs. McNulty got back. And as the blood pounded its way into my head and I gasped for air, he'd acted like we'd just been fooling around, like the whole thing was all a big joke. Ha, ha. Slap me on the back. Very funny. *Asshole*.)

So Dwight. Yeah. He was definitely part of the lethal brew of bad dope, bad company and even worse music that got me going in Delaney's basement. Normally I lay pretty low and let conversations roll around me, occasionally tossing in a sarcastic comment or two just so people don't think I'm too slow to keep up. But that night I was fucking Chatty Cathy, man, and I started telling the whole room this dark tale about how one of us was going to bite it on the way to school tomorrow, get creamed by a van and be dead before they knew what hit them. The more I talked, the more details I spewed and my voice got all authoritative and shit and pretty soon everyone just sat back and let me roll.

Red van, out-of-state plates, license number BLU 369. There'd be a busted-up skateboard in the middle of the road and a dead kid on the sidewalk, head split open, eyes way wide, staring at the blue, blue sky from a puddle of red, red blood.

I made a show of looking around, let my eyes land on every sorry piece of gristle in the room, but the name had already settled into me, so I left the best for last. First I checked out Fang, standing in the bathroom doorway, one arm resting on the chin-up bar we'd mounted there a few years back to keep his pipes steely. Even stoned, Fang seemed nervous, panicked almost, like he'd just been nailed by the phantom spotlight he'd been running from all his life. In that light, exposed in a druggy moment of reckoning, we all considered him for the role of dead man.

Fang looked like a younger, more battered version of Steven Tyler—the fem lead singer of Aerosmith—but minus the strut. Totally minus the strut. Fang was all lips and teeth and long hair, all muscle and sinew and bone. I stared at him, slouched in the doorway, backlit by the glare of the bathroom light. I didn't get his retro rock star look. I didn't get his music. I didn't get him anymore.

Fang shook his head, bouncing the hair from his eyes, and for just a second we managed to connect. I could see him pushing the others out, holding them back, so there was just enough room for us to make contact. "Fuck off, Luke," he said. I gave him a knowing smile, a little nod of approval, before moving on to my next target.

I lingered on Chad Turner, Phil Stroper and a couple of the other guys, stretching the moment as far as the tension would take it. I skipped Dwight altogether because a) I couldn't be bothered cranking around on the couch to look at him, and b) I didn't want to stare into his gob anyway, because every time I did I'd find myself searching his face, trying to figure out why people, new to town and whatnot, always got around to asking us the same moronic question: "Hey, are you two brothers?" Jesus Christ. Me and Dwight? Retarded second cousins, maybe. But brothers? *Jesus.*

Stan, who looked nothing like either me or Dwight and was nowhere near retarded, was sitting in the corner opposite the computer, having claimed the basement's only decent chair. He was playing with the handle on the side of the La-Z-Boy, flipping the footrest up and down, apparently barely tuned in.

"Stan," I said, and I said it kind of loud so of course he had to look up. "Tomorrow morning. Eight thirty-seven. The red van with the out-of-state plates? You go head to head. You lose. You die." I looked him straight on, with my face all serious, and I may have even jabbed a finger in his direction, but he wasn't having any of my nonsense, Stan being Stan and all.

First he said something like, "Oooh, you're really freaking me out, *Luke*," and he gave the lever a final push. The La-Z-Boy springs snapped to attention. Feet up, fingers laced together behind his head, he assumed this completely relaxed posture. Real cool. Real Stan. "You want to know how I know your story is completely full of shit, *Luke?*"

I just shrugged and we locked eyes and had a bit of a smirk-off while he let his question hang out there. When he'd given everyone a chance to mull it over, he laid out his theory. "Your story is full of shit because no one from out of state ever comes to butt-fuck Stokum. Especially in October."

We all got a good laugh out of that and everyone called me on my bogus tale and fucking Slater punched me in the arm a little harder than necessary and then, thankfully, someone sane turned the music off and the TV on and we watched videos on MTV2 for a while before heading out.

On my way home from Fang's that night, I thought about why I'd stuck Stan in the middle of my man-versus-van scenario. I figured it was because I knew he would have a good comeback, or maybe it was because he wasn't a regular in the cast of misfits who hung out at Fang's. I think we all liked to see him squirm once in a while, just so he wouldn't get too comfortable thinking he was King Shit or something, who could drop by whenever he felt like getting high or hanging with the low-lying fruit or whatever it was that drew him in.

I will take a minute here to talk about Stan, because after what happened I think he deserves his dues, especially since the local media turned the whole thing into a two-minute community freak-of-the-week gig, aired in between cheesy car commercials at the end of the six o'clock news. The slick reporter with his great hair and white teeth practically forgot Stan altogether, clamoring to turn me into something I'm not. That definitely wasn't cool, but to him I was the kicker, the twist, the hype, but I'm telling you, Stan was the real deal.

He was one of those rare kids who could move in pretty much any crowd, a regular teenage chameleon who in theory everyone should have hated. But really, the only person I can even think of who wasn't big on Stan was Fang, which was weird seeing how Delaney wasn't all that picky when it came to friends. I mean, I'd been his best one for, like, ten years, which is a pretty good indicator of just how low his standards were. But whenever Stan was around, Fang was even quieter than usual, slung way back, arms folded across his chest, looking all pouty and unimpressed. Still, we both knew Fang would rather gnaw off his own knob than get into it, so if he had a problem with Stan he kept it to himself, which was fine by me.

When I consider just the basement dwellers, I'd have to say Stan was mostly my friend. We'd hooked up at school before he started showing up at Delaney's or spending his lunch hours with us stoners, cluttering up the school's back parking lot, passing around a spliff and doing sketchy tricks on his board to make us laugh. I have to admit, he was funny as hell, which was probably why so many kids liked him in the first place, although he was a lot more than just another pothead clown.

I remember this one time after lunch, when Stan and I went to class and Mr. Thorp, our math teacher with the huge head, sprang this surprise quiz on us. I'd sat there trying to make sense of the mess floating around on the page in front of me—you know, trying not to laugh about how unimaginative it was that a six was just a tipped-over nine or something equally brilliant—and I glanced over and Stan's like totally bent over the page, all intense and concentrated. I mean, he was just flying. He must have sharpened his pencil fifteen times during that test. Afterwards he chatted it up with the brains in the corridor, a big grin on his face. He ended up getting something like 95, only about 80 more than me.

After school, Stan usually shot hoops with the jocks, all buffed and shit, no shirt and his jeans just barely hanging on, boxers poking out the top the way the chicks dig it. He was a great ball player, but everyone knew he was just passing time, waiting for the drama group to wrap up whatever piece o' crap they were practicing so he could walk Faith Taylor, as in *the* Faith Taylor, home. Faith's one of the beautiful people at Jefferson, and even though she's in drama, she's also really cool, although I wouldn't have known it back then; back then I'd never been close enough to even get a whiff of what she was all about.

But Stan had been going out with Faith since freshman year, and from what I heard he'd definitely been on the inside. Man! Like most guys at Jefferson, I would have given my right nut to get anywhere with a girl like her, and fucking Stan was shagging her on a regular basis and she was probably loving the whole thing. I mean, they went out for like a year and a half, so you figure it out.

Anyway, not only was Stan dude enough to be with Faith, he was also smart and funny and athletic, just an excellent person from pretty much every angle, and unless you're a total brick, you've probably guessed that he died at 8:37 A.M., October 8, 2002, on his way to school. He was hit by a red van turning into the parking lot of the 7-Eleven he was ripping by at the time. He died of head injuries and was pronounced dead at the scene. (Later on, I overheard this kid at school whose dad is a cop telling some of his friends that the people in the van were from Windsor, Canada. They'd been tooling through Michigan, headed for New York City, got off the turnpike for gas, got lost on their way back to the highway and had headed into the 7-Eleven for directions. I thought Stan would have appreciated this bit of information, which proves he was right on. No one ever comes to butt-fuck Stokum, especially in October.)

Now, this isn't something I really like to rehash, but it's important and I have to lay it down once, so maybe people might understand a little better what was going on, I mean really going on, instead of buying the garbage they spewed on TV. The morning Stan died started out pretty much the same as every other day. I got up around seven-thirty, completely groggy from the weed the night before, grabbed a shower and some cereal and was on my way to school when I got this really weird feeling. I kept riding for a while, but I couldn't shake the weirdness, so I skidded out and picked up my skateboard. By that time the chatter of wheels on rutted pavement had moved past my feet, crawled up my legs, to settle in my belly. I actually went and leaned up against a tree, but it didn't help. The sun just kept getting brighter, and everything but the tremble in my gut got quiet, until all I could hear was playing on the inside—vibrations shifting and spinning, growing into something big and beautiful, something built on waves of sonic light. It was like feeling the bass moving through you when your favorite song is cranked and the music is right there inside you, threatening wonder, only it was so much cleaner and purer and it only lasted for a second.

I wasn't wearing a watch at the time, but it didn't matter. I was positive it was 8:37. I was positive Stan was dead. And I knew what a good, solid guy he'd been, an incredible guy, and what a loss it was that he was gone. I also knew that the life I'd lived until that moment was as dead as my friend.

TWO

I'm not sure how long it was before Fang came by and found me clinging to the tree, my forehead pressed up hard against the bark. He asked if I was humping the fucking thing or what, and when I didn't answer, he swung around the trunk, trying to get a look at me, asking what's wrong, dude, what's wrong, until I finally had to stand up and act like everything was cool. I don't know how I hopped on my board, how my foot found the pavement again and again, how I wheeled right up to the death scene with Fang, pretending I didn't have a clue.

The 7-Eleven is pretty much directly across from our school, and by the time we arrived, quite a crowd had gathered. Fang weaseled his way to the front, dragging me with him. The body was already covered up, but the puddle of blood around what was left of Stan's head kept growing. Staining the white sheet, running off the sidewalk, spilling over the curb, screaming its redness into the street. As if a little thing like being dead was going to stop Stan from making sure that anyone who'd been in the basement the night before and was staring down at his body just then would never forget my prophetic little tale. And the guys who'd been at Fang's were all over it. They looked at the puddle of blood and they looked at me, jaws slack, bodies tense. They dragged their gaping eyes from my face to the skateboard cracked in two in the middle of the street. The red van with the unforgettable Canadian plates? They practically nailed me to its bashed-in grille with their silent, stupefied accusations.

Fang's fingers bit into my upper arm. He yanked me toward him, into the heat of his breath and body, and never mind the crowd, never mind we were two inches apart, he started yelling, shaking me and yelling, "You knew. You fucking knew." I told him to shut up, just shut the fuck up, I knocked his hand from my arm, but by that time it wasn't only Fang. Chad Turner and Dwight Slater and a few of the other guys had broken through the shock and were jabbering about what I'd said, and pretty soon everyone was swinging from Stan's body to me and back again, like spectators at some slo-mo tennis match. The horrified crowd eventually set their sights on me. Silent. Waiting. Eyeing me like I'd just leapt the net and beaten the favorite to death with my racket. In the hush, even the ambulance guys paused to check out the blasted kid up front, the one everyone was gawking at. If people were expecting an explanation, I sure as shit didn't have one. If it was an apology they wanted, I knew there was nothing anyone could say that would make this right. Stan was dead. I had to bail.

I went to push my way out, but there was no need. Everyone took a neat step back, line dancers in retreat, and I sashayed up the lane they cleared for me and hopped on my board and I split, a thousand pairs of eyes pressing on my back.

I rounded the corner, was halfway up the block when I saw Faith. Stan's Faith. Riding her bike along the opposite side of the street, chin lifted just a little toward the sun, hair flowing in a wind of her own creation. Something gorgeous slicing through the madness. Someone innocent of the mess on the sidewalk ahead. She raised her hand to wave, she smiled, but I dropped my head and pushed even harder for home, my board wobbling underfoot. Still, the snapshot of the girl on the bike followed me, a haunting thing of beauty I knew would break around the next bend, sure as a glass slipping from my hand.

At my neat little house on Clive Avenue, I barricaded myself inside. I locked the doors, yanked the curtains closed, shuttered the blinds, constructed a modern-day fortress before crashing in my room. I'm not going to bore you with all the crap that went through my mind while I was lying there, but I will tell you that after a couple of hours I got up and went to the bathroom to fondle a few razor blades and check out our pill supply. (My mom was pretty anti-meds, I wasn't holding out much hope. Inside the medicine cabinet, three Extra Strength Tylenol, a box of Imodium, some Midol, and an old bottle of penicillin, which I'm mildly allergic to. I took the Tylenol but left the rest because I had no desire to break out in a rash and not shit for a week, and although I was suffering, it wasn't from cramps.)

I was on my way back from the can when I heard the noise outside. I pulled the blind on the hall window back a bit, and *fuck,* the WDFD van and its crew were setting up out front. The roving-eye guy, the one with the long shaggy blond hair who likes to pretend he's some surferesque dude (yeah, right, in Stokum), came and pounded on the door. He waited awhile, staring straight ahead while the cameraman hung over his shoulder, all ready in case anyone was stupid enough to open up. After a while of filming my front door—brown, wooden, three rectangular windows at the top, nothing special, really—they went and did their spiel on the sidewalk. One of the neighbors probably figured I'd finally committed the grisly felony they'd always known I was capable of, and they must have called my mom at the Michigan Savings and Loan where she works as a teller, because she pulled into the driveway about ten minutes later.

By that time I was back in my room, but I was still peeking out, so I saw her arrive. It made me sick the way the reporter and his cameraman crowded around so that my mom, who is really small, had to fight her way out of the car. Surfer boy pushed his microphone in her face, which was so bewildered and scared I could tell she didn't have a clue what he was even saying. She made it onto the front stoop, but her hand must have been shaking really badly, because it took her a long while to get in. Once she did, though, she kicked it into high gear. Flying around the ground floor, screaming my name, before pounding up the stairs two at a time.

My bedroom door ripped open and my mom staggered blind and breathless into the room. It took a few seconds for her to find me, crouching by the window in the half-light of an afternoon behind drapes. And man, she went all shattered pixie on me then, fingers fluttering to her throat, staggering backwards, sagging against the door frame, all the energy that usually holds her up gone. And she kind of choked up her next couple of lines.

"The radio said a boy had been killed, on a skateboard, then I got a call and … and …" She covered her face and her chest started heaving and I realized she'd driven all the way home thinking I was dead. God, seeing my mom hiding out in her hands, watching her slide down the door frame until she was at my level, well, let's just say I was pretty happy I hadn't followed through on the Midol overdose or anything equally retarded.

When she did finally lift her head, it was to quietly ask, "Who?"

I couldn't even look at her. "Stan," I said to the dark blue carpet between my feet.

"Oh, *Luke.*" My name quivered into the room on a soft push of breath. "Oh no. Not Stan." I dared to glance up. From across the room, from fifteen feet away, I could see her eyes were already glistening. Me, I wouldn't cry for days. And even then, it wouldn't have all that much to do with Stan.

MY MOM DIDN'T ASK ME about the camera crew outside right away. Even if I wasn't bawling, she could tell how shaky I was. She took me downstairs and made us both a cup of chocolate milk, although I was definitely in need of something a tad stronger, and she probably was too. Then she sat across from me at the kitchen table and carefully asked about the van out front. It took me a couple tries to get going, but I finally gagged up my tale. I told her what had happened in Fang's basement the night before, although I bypassed the bit about the skank weed short-circuiting my brain and channeling me into some psychic freak-show wavelength, which was my only theory at the time. I blamed the dope, always an easy target.

My mom didn't say much. She just fiddled with her glass while I talked, and when I was done she gave this long, kind of whistling sigh and got up to phone my dad. She ran her fingertips along the wall as she made her way to the hall, where the phone sat on a little table by the front door. I stayed in the kitchen. Normally I like the kitchen. The 1950s Westinghouse Frigidaire with rounded edges and a silver pull handle in one corner. The metal-edged Formica table with matching red leatherette chairs in the other. Last summer my mom and I tarted up the old cupboards with a coat of high-gloss white and threw down some chunky black and white checked lino. So now the kitchen has a real cookies-and-milk kind of vibe, and usually it's an awesome place to hang. But that day I just laid my head on the table and wrapped my fingers around its cold edge and held on until I heard the squeal of tires on pavement and the slam of a car door.

After my dad pushed through the media scrum outside, he and my mom whispered in the hallway for a bit. Then he called me into his office at the back of the house and closed the door. I basically went through the same drill I had with my mom, but it took a lot longer. My dad is fairly detail oriented, being the head honcho supply chain guy at the Kalbro plant where, like, everybody in Stokum works if they aren't employed by CME, Central Michigan Electric, the big coal-burning power plant south of town. (At Kalbro my dad makes sure things are lined up so that Ford and GM always get the auto fabrics of their dreams, just-in-time. You know that slick blue nubbly crap you drive around on? The tawny faux Naugahyde? The burgundy velveteen? That's Stokum, man.)

My dad badgered me all through the story, like he was going to personally present my case to the big guys in Detroit or something, and I had to tell him *exactly* what happened at Fang's, couldn't skate around anything, including the bad weed. (I admitted we'd "tried" pot, but I made it sound like it was one of the first times so he wouldn't think I was a complete stoner and get all disappointed and shit.) Still, even with him, I didn't bother mentioning anything about the weird musical shiver under the tree that morning. Even if I'd wanted to, I couldn't have found the words to explain that freakiness.

We ate leftover tuna casserole in front of the TV that night (normally forbidden given that dinnertime is "sacred"), tuned in to WDFD's six o'clock report. I was seriously hoping Stan and I hadn't become, well, big news, and we weren't the lead story, which was a happy one. Evidently the terrorists were all talked out, chatter was on the decline. John Ashcroft, our homeland security hombre with the heavy brow and the oh-so-serious, tuned-into-all-things-terrorist face, actually offered America a steady, if guarded, smile. He announced that the national threat level, which had been jacked up to orange around the joyless first anniversary of the World Trade Center attacks, was being dropped. We were now to live careful, yellow lives rather than the high-octane orange ones we'd been leading. Unfortunately, this American didn't find the news as comforting as Ashcroft had probably hoped, and I was definitely still in an orange funk when the roving-eye guy came on with the real news at the end of the hour.

He was standing in the 7-Eleven parking lot with the van behind him. Thankfully, Stan's body had been removed, but still, I felt sick just looking at the whole scene. The reporter pushed his hair out of his eyes and started in with all the usual crap. "A minor, whose name is being withheld pending notification of family members, was killed this morning when he was struck by a van turning into the 7-Eleven parking lot across from Jefferson High.

The young man had been skateboarding along the sidewalk on his way to school when he was hit." After about two seconds of this, the dickweed cameraman zoomed in on the bloody sidewalk while the reporter blabbed offscreen, building up the suspense as to why this wasn't just another "tragic traffic accident." Then the camera pulls back from the bloodstain and there's fucking Slater standing next to surfer guy, his hair all combed and his zits battered over by pancake makeup. Dwight's trying to look all broken up about Stan, but when he starts in with the story it's obvious he's totally getting off on being behind the mike, I mean, you can just sense his hard-on excitement. I will say, he stuck pretty much to the facts, but I didn't think his big dramatic pause before he got to the part about the license plate was really necessary.

"BLU 369," he said, and then he repeated it just so everyone would know it had really stuck with him. "It's easy to remember, because it's the color blue, like without the e, and then three, six, nine, like, you know, you just keep adding three." When he turned and pointed at the van and the camera panned to the plate, well, both my parents started shifting around in their seats like their gitch had just jumped a mile up their asses or something. Then, catch this, my buddy Fang climbs out of the "soundproof" van where he'd been waiting like some cloistered game show contestant. He repeated the story, only he was all nervous and everything and he messed up the license number, got the BLU wrong, which made Dwight—still standing on-camera, thrilling at the airtime, playing at sad—look like a real wizard.

I was shaking my head at the lame antics when they cut over to my place and gave what little background they could on me.

I came off as "just an average kid," which I thought was pretty decent because, seriously, I'd been expecting worse. But then the reporter raised an eyebrow and said that I had refused "all requests for interviews," and they flashed a close-up of my freshman yearbook photo and let the picture do their fucking dirty work. God! There I was with hat head (the photographer had *insisted* I take off my cap) and my eyes half closed and this pained grimace on my face because I still had braces and refused to open the lid on all that metal. Their average-teen crap was laughable next to the picture that told the real story, the story of a loser with bad skin and so little self-confidence he couldn't even face a camera head-on, whose main hobbies include skateboarding, smoking illegal substances, predicting the deaths of close friends and, oh yeah, whacking off. *Then* they zoom in on my window and there I am, all hunched up and peering out like some child molester or something, and Lance lays out his last line.

"While we were hoping that the teen at the center of this story, Luke Hunter, would come forward and talk to the roving-eye team, for now Stokum's own Prophet of Death is keeping all predictions to himself. Lance Winters, on the scene, for WDFD."

My dad turned off the television then, and my mom put her hand on my knee and said, "Well, there you go. That's over now," a couple dozen times to try to make herself believe it. We were still sitting there, in a stunned sort of silence, when the phone started ringing. Loud and aggressive, like some mighty intruder charging in and out of our living room. No one moved. The phone kept squealing. Finally my mom got up to grab it. My dad and I listened to her murmuring in the hallway for a few minutes before she appeared in the doorway.

"It's for you," she said, holding the receiver out as far as its spiral tether would allow.

"Who is it?" I asked.

"Mick." My absent uncle. Her missing brother. My mom kept her face blank and her voice steady. "He wants to talk to you."

"Where is he?"

"Mexico."

I dropped my head and found a super-interesting spot on the carpet. No one said a word, but we all knew that WDFD's signal barely reached across the state, let alone the continent. And we all knew that Mick *never* called.

For just an instant my eyes flickered up. "What's he doing down there?"

"Helping some farm co-op locate well sites."

"Witching for water, you mean." Lots of sneer to the words.

"Yeah, witching for water." Her voice was hard now. She pointed the receiver in my direction. "Luke?"

I got up, but I pushed right past my mother, and my uncle in Mexico, on my way to my room.

But I'd only made it halfway up the stairs when it happened again.

THREE

My hand was on the banister, I was mid-step, and this flash hit me, clear as the newscast we'd just been watching. By the time I put my foot down, I knew that Mr. Bernoffski, the old Polish guy who lived two doors down, was going to get crushed under his John Deere riding mower when it rolled on the steep part of his backyard, where the lawn slopes down to the cedar hedge. His chest would be crushed by the weight of the mower, a broken rib would puncture his left lung. He would be unable to breathe or call for help and would die from lack of oxygen at 3:18 P.M., October 9, 2002.

I think I went into some sort of preprogrammed self-survival mode right then. I made it to my room and collapsed on the bed. I stared at the ceiling—mind gone, body wiped—before fading out completely. I woke up around four A.M., still fully clothed, drenched with sweat, gasping for air, basically scared completely shitless. It took a long while for me to even get my breathing under control, and even then I could feel the vapors of terror pumping through my veins, refueling, getting ready to spin me out around the next corner if I didn't hold tight.

As I lay there trying to stay sane, I saw my running shoes sitting neatly beside my bed. Toes lined up with the edge of the carpet, laces worked loose. I knew that one of my parents—my dad probably, he was the neat freak—had come in and, seeing me crashed, had bent down and slipped off my shoes, carefully, so he wouldn't wake me up. Like I was still just a little kid he'd carried in from the car after some late night drive home. I stared at those shoes and my heart slowed beat by beat by beat until I was finally able to think about Stan and Mr. Bernoffski and what the hell was going on. The only thing I really came up with was the importance of preventing the close encounter between my Polish neighbor and his John Deere from happening. I figured if I saved Mr. Bernoffski, if he just didn't die, then maybe my life wouldn't completely derail. The glowing green numbers of my alarm clock crawled toward seven o'clock, by which time I couldn't take it anymore. I got up, snuck out the kitchen door and headed for the house two doors down.

I cut through the Connellys' backyard before the Bernoffskis' fence pushed me out front onto the street. It was a bit of a mind melt to see the roving-eye van still parked in front of my place, a nasty reminder that this nightmare was way real. I pulled my hood down as far as possible, hopped the porch railing and rang the bell, one eye on the van, one eye on the door. When the old guy finally opened up, he looked crabby as hell and I could tell he was all suspicious and shit. He was tugging at this ratty blue bathrobe, trying to cover his gut, but I was so revved up I just started rambling.

"Hi, sorry to bother you. I don't know if you recognize me, I'm Luke Hunter, I live just up—"

"Jesus Chrrist, you tink I'm stupid? I know you. You Doug's boy. Of course I know. Jesus Chrrist, what time is it?"

"Ahh, yeah, it's early, sorry, but I go to Jefferson High and I have to do community service work, you know, like help out an old person or a kids' soccer team or something like that. It's mandatory for my civics class, and I was wondering if I could cut your lawn for a couple of months, for free of course, and I could come whenever you want me to, but I've gotta start right away, and—"

"What you be say?" His voice was loud. He looked confused. So I repeated the whole thing, really slowly, which practically killed me, what with the van on my ass and everything. Still, I could see that, second time around, Mr. Bernoffski was catching my drift, because his face sort of relaxed and he started nodding, following along.

"So you want to cut my grazz," he said when I'd finished, and by this time we were both bobbing our heads at each other like two of those bobble-head, spring-necked dolls, and I was thinking I'd just saved this guy's life when he says, "No one touches my tractor. No one. I cut my own grazz. I no need no help," and he starts to shut the door.

I just about went crazy then, threw myself inside and insisted he let me cut the grass *today*. I'd bring my own mower, I'd hand-trim his monster of a lawn, edge the fucking sidewalk, whatever, but he had to let me do it. I think I scared him a bit, because he was clutching at his robe like he thought I might try to rip it off, and he started pushing me toward the door and saying something like, "Okay, okay, you crazy keed. You cut the grazz, but I watch you. And not today. I cut it yesterday."

"You cut the grass yesterday?" My mouth a mile wide.

"Yes. Yes. You blind or what? Look, look." He pointed out the front door and I turned around and, sure enough, the lawn was completely shorn. I could have laughed out loud. "You come next week, okay? You come Tuesday. Always Tuesday, I cut the grazz. Today Wed-nes-day."

I jumped off the porch, landed right on the grass, the beautiful, pubic-short grass. I flipped the bird at the van as I went by, didn't give a shit if the roving-eye team got a good look at The Prophet, because it was Wednesday, and Tuesday was the day, man, Tuesday was the day.

My parents let me stay home, although they both headed to work. I basically hung out in my room, listening to tunes and trying to catch some zees after the four A.M. wake-up call. I finally drifted off after lunch, woke up around three o'clock feeling like shit. I headed to the bathroom, started getting dizzy in the shower.

I rested my cheek against the wet tile, fiddled with the tap to cool down the water. From that weird angle, through the gap between the wall and the shower curtain, I could see a slice of our backyard out the little window over the toilet. The sky was gray and I could tell the wind had picked up by the way the branches of the oak tree next door were jumping. Then I saw the wheel. Hanging dark and steady against the green of the Bernoffskis' cedar hedge. An evil black moon rising from the undercarriage of a toppled riding mower.

I was still pressed against the wall, staring out the window, when I felt him pass through me. It was different than it had been with Stan; it wasn't as clean somehow, and it lasted longer. I closed my eyes and felt the hardness and the happiness of my neighbor shivering through me. Power chords of love dropped me to my knees, spiraled into rhythm and melody, exploded in a fearless white crescendo.

Then it was all over for Mr. Bernoffski, and I was left kneeling, naked, under a stream of water that was slowly running cold.

BACK IN MY ROOM, it went something like this. I couldn't sit down. I couldn't relax. My fists were rock. I picked up my toes-to-the-carpet shoes and hurled them at the window. A crack split the glass. I tossed my chair across the room, took a swing at my fern. I ripped the concert posters off the wall, kicked the bedside table over, trampled the light, smashed the shade, pulverized the bulb pretending it was Mr. Bernoffski's head—Mr. Bernoffski the fucking liar who didn't cut his whole lawn on Tuesday, oh no, he liked to cut the steep part at the back on Wednesday. The fucking stupid immigrant fucking liar. Now he was dead and I was fucked because I'd been too stupid, too lazy, to take a look over his fucking back fence. What the fuck was he thinking with his only-Tuesday bullshit? FUCK. I jammed my face into my pillow and screamed and screamed and screamed.

IT STARTED GETTING DARK around 4:30, started to frigging pour at 4:45, and I just lay there in my warm, dry room trying to ignore the glass in my feet and the thunder outside and the images flashing through my brain. Mr. Bernoffski, his lungs flattened, his cold white body pinned to his freshly cut lawn. Mr. Bernoffski in his shabby bathrobe. "Jesus Chrrist, you tink I'm stupid?" Stan, head split wide, puddle of red, sky of blue. Stan in the La-Z-Boy. "Oooh, you're really freaking me out, *Luke.*"

Yeah. Freaking me out. Really.

FOUR

I sat in the back seat on the way to my friend's funeral, staring out the window as if I'd never seen the streets of Stokum before. All the town's east-west roads dead-ended into Erie, and that day I glanced down every one to watch the lake spit chunks of dirty foam onto the beach like some angry, stalking beast. Even behind glass, I could hear the water roar.

Closer to the car, houses floated in the middle of soggy lawns, trees had been stripped, there were branches down everywhere. We passed an Olds, its roof crumpled beneath an uprooted tree. I figured the car had been empty when the tree hit, because seriously, I probably would have been in the loop if someone had bitten it inside. As far as I knew, there'd only been the one in-town casualty the night before.

It had taken a while for someone to notice the dead man under the mower. When the hammering on the back door finally started up, we'd just finished dinner. Which had been painful. First off, my parents and I had sat around the table acting like we were on the set of *That '70s Show* or something, and we didn't want to disappoint, we had to keep it light. Our shiny retro kitchen turned into some sick joke, with Mom and Dad jabbering about the weather, how the sewers had backed up, how the cars were shooting speedboat-sized wakes onto the sidewalks along Main Street.

The branches of our birch tree were bashing the window, clawing to get in, the rain was hitting the glass like buckshot, the lights were flickering, and it felt like the wind was trying to suck the house into fucking Kansas, man. But my parents just kept talking and I just kept choking down my spaghetti, pretending to be enthralled by the storm chatter, pretending my room wasn't completely trashed, pretending my feet weren't cut to shit, pretending my legs weren't jittering under the table like some ADD kid high on Big Gulp, pretending no Polish neighbor of mine was getting all crunchy under his old John Deere two doors down.

Pretending I didn't have a clue why Mr. Connelly, the guy who lives beside us, was pounding on our door, all soaking wet and madman frantic.

Apparently he'd been watching the storm when, in a burst of lightning, he'd seen the overturned tractor. He'd rushed right over, but couldn't budge the mower. He wanted my dad to come and help him lift it. Connelly must have been in shock or something, because I don't think he even realized Mr. Bernoffski was, like, way dead. He and my dad hauled ass out of our place like two puffed-up rescue heroes, armed with a Swiss Army knife and a Maglite they scrambled out of a cluttered kitchen drawer. My mom called 911 while I sat there trying to look surprised about the whole thing, feeling like a cowardly loser for having let it happen.

They didn't have much luck with Mr. Bernoffski, who'd already started to stiffen up, but they had no problem tracking down the missus—they simply hit the redial button on the kitchen phone and voilà, Mrs. Bernoffski was back from her sister-in-law's before the body had been bagged. My mom had gone down to stay with her for a while and I'd hobbled upstairs and tried to soak the shards of light bulb out of my feet in the tub. I ended up having to use my mom's tweezers and I got most of it out, but I'm not that flexible and a couple pieces still stabbed into the soles of my feet as I headed to my room.

I forgot the glass when I saw my bedroom door swung wide open. I'd definitely left it shut. I pictured my dad pacing inside, repair estimate in hand, but it wasn't like that. The room was empty. The furniture, upright. Transparent packing tape snaked along the crack in the window. The fern was back on my desk, its broken stem topped with a healing blob of sap. The Chili Peppers and the White Stripes had been returned to the wall, pretty much intact, but Papa Roach was beyond repair. He lay crumpled in the garbage can with what was left of the lamp.

And that morning at breakfast, no one had said anything about the damage, which was pretty cool. What wasn't cool was picking Fang up on the way to the funeral. After his big prime-time television appearance, I wasn't in the mood for him, or any of the boys from the basement for that matter. Regardless, my dad pulled up in front of Delaney's and gave the horn a blast. I figured it was my mom who'd offered him a lift, knowing there was no way his own mother would crawl out of her boozy swamp just to take her son to some kid's funeral.

Fang slid into the back seat and gave me a careful nod that I didn't return. I just narrowed my eyes and stared out my window, trying to figure out why someone with so little to offer was sitting in my car while Stan, who'd had it all, was stuffed inside some box.

To be honest, at that moment, I couldn't have said why Fang and I were even friends. Lack of worthy alternatives probably had a lot to do with it. And habit, I guess, one that started back in kindergarten.

I haven't got the greatest memory, don't remember a whole hell of a lot from when I was little, but I do remember the first time I saw Fang. Standing on the top rung of the purple elephant jungle gym at school, all stretched up on his toes, hands over his head, a fearless smile plastered across his face—this in the days before he grew the tusks. For a kid in kindergarten, that top rung was brain-damage high, and he'd been jerked down pretty fast when our teacher, Mrs. Spielman—the one with the blue mole on her chin—caught sight of him. It was right afterwards that I got my mom to call up his mom to invite him over, and pretty soon Fang was at my place every day after school. His mom would pick him up on her way home from work, and back then she wasn't so bad, just kind of skinny and quiet and pale and always being extra-polite because my dad was her boss at Kalbro.

I know we probably watched TV and played Hot Wheels and Lego, probably battled over Pokémon cards, but the purple elephant escapade wasn't a one-time deal. Because what Fang really liked doing was climbing. For a while I tried to keep up. We started in the backyard with the fence and the trees, then moved on to the drainpipe that ran up the side of the house. I could never make it more than a quarter of the way up, but it didn't take long before Fang could shimmy to the top. When we got older, we'd bike around Stokum looking for stuff to climb—the fifty-foot maple behind the library, the water tower (he didn't take the stairs), the flagpole at City Hall, City Hall itself. Fang was so good, I tried to convince him to set up some stunt to get into *The Guinness Book of World Records*, but he was super-shy around other people and he threatened to quit climbing altogether if I didn't stop bugging him about it. I remember he got all pissed off and kept saying that it had to be *just the two of us*, it was something only *we did*, that the whole thing would be wrecked if anyone else even knew about it. So I quit with the record thing and Fang got what he wanted—an audience of one.

Fang was always completely stoked after a climb. We both were. We'd jump around, talking right over each other about how high he'd gone, how awesome it was, how hyper-human he was. Fang would goof around, flexing his muscles and shit, posing so I could take his picture with the Polaroid camera I always brought along. I'd put the date at the bottom and the estimated height of the climb, but when I showed Fang the pictures afterwards, he'd be all pissed off. He was usually smiling, full out, and he thought his teeth ruined the shot. We'd get into this big charade, with him threatening to rip the thing up and me convincing him not to. I'd tell him how good he looked—"Seriously, man, it's an awesome picture, you're totally cut"—and he'd get this weird smile on his face that he always tried to hide.

He never did trash the pictures. He kept them in a Converse shoe box under his bed along with a list of scalable targets around Stokum that we planned to hit once one of us had a license and some wheels. We made the list when we were, like, thirteen, but almost right away Fang lost interest. At first I just ignored his lame attitude and I kept dragging him out to all the high shit in town so I could get one more glimpse of his fearlessness. And he'd still climb, he wasn't nervous or anything, it just seemed like all of a sudden I was way more into it than him. Until he started to jump, at least. The jumping was something else altogether, and it was just one more dark, crazy thing I tried not to think about as we wound our way toward the New Life in Christ Church where Stan's funeral was being held.

None of us had ever heard of the place and we got lost on the way there. When we finally found it, we were late and there were no spots left in the parking lot. I got jittery as hell, circling around the block, watching the other latecomers filing through the doors of the crappy little whitewashed box, which had practically no windows at all. We finally left the car in front of the fire hydrant right across from the church. As I crossed the street, I had to curl my toes and walk on the edges of my feet, courtesy of a couple stubborn slivers of glass. I did my best not to look too much like a hunchback; still, I was definitely moving slowly, and my mom and dad, confusing pain for dread or despair, flanked me up the stairs, which I thought was a bit much. But I tell you, I was happy I had a parent either side once we stepped inside.

The church had one of those low, dropped ceilings with the fluorescent lights, which made the room feel instantly tight and obscenely bright. There were only two windows topping each sidewall, narrow rectangles of pebbled blue plastic that gave a bit of a death-glow pallor to the faces around me. And there were a lot of faces.

Although it was a nice tribute to Stan, we had zero hope of slipping into a back pew unnoticed. It didn't take long for a black-suited usher to latch on to Fang. Another one hooked my mom, and we were forced up the aisle, funneled toward the flower-stacked coffin at the front of the church.

There were no seats. None. We kept moving past row after row of Sunday best. I tried to remain calm, but every time we passed a pew there'd be a ripple of noise, a barely subdued wave of gawker excitement. People were covering their mouths and leaning over to whisper to their neighbors, before doing these close-chested little points at me. I stopped even looking for a seat. I kept my eyes fixed straight ahead, silently cursing my parents for stopping to pick up Fang, for getting lost on the way to the church, for being late, for putting me through this shit. Still, my mom held her head high and I knew I was probably the only one who noticed how her hand, the one not clasped around the funeral guy's arm, trembled in the still air of the church.

My dad put his hand on my shoulder and guided me forward, but by this time folks up front had been alerted to the fact that The Prophet was in the house, and pretty much everyone cranked around to stare. Except for the buzz of the tubular lights, the place went completely silent. I mean, it wasn't like the church had been rocking before we showed up, but at least people had been breathing and shit. I can tell you, it was a long, painful, freaky walk up the aisle that ended right at the front, one notch behind Stan's blasted parents.

We nodded our condolences and the Millers nodded blindly back, sort of staring but you just knew they weren't really seeing. I sat down, and right away someone tapped my shoulder. I had to swing around because, regardless of circumstances, it's pretty much impossible to ignore a tap. It was Faith Taylor, as in *the* Faith Taylor, looking all weepy and gorgeous, the only mourner whose honeyed brown skin hadn't paled under the harsh lights. She started to say something and, despite everything, I felt myself being drawn into her perfect pink lips like they were the only comfortable spot in town. But right then the organ wailed and Faith's gaze flew over my shoulder to the front of the church.

Behind the pulpit a big man in black robes gave the signal and everyone rose to sing "Amazing Grace," which had apparently been one of Stan's favorites. I stood up and pretended to follow along even though I didn't know half the words.

All I really remember about the funeral is the thick, sick smell of too many flowers lodged at the back of my throat, Faith's soft, steady crying behind me and, of course, what happened when the electricity cut out near the end of the service. The church suddenly went dark and this collective whisper rolled through the congregation. There was a bit of blue light seeping in the windows and a red emergency exit thing going on by the doors, but what really powered the place were the previously subdued altar candles. Only the coffin and the first couple rows were hit by their yellow glow. Seeing how I was right up front, the candles went searchlight on me.

As the rest of the church faded out, the Pastor seemed to double in size. With his oiled-back hair and his smooth preacher voice intact, he leaned in close to his bible and kept chugging along, completely unfazed by the power outage. Like I said before, I hadn't exactly been taking notes, but all of a sudden the atmosphere was supercharged and from here on in the sermon got fairly hard to forget. (In case anyone did, the Bible references were on the back of the funeral pamphlet that had been lying on our pew, and they came in handy when writing this out, so thanks for that, Pastor Ted.)

"'Believe not every spirit, but try the spirits whether they be of God; because many false prophets are gone out into the world.'" (1 John 4:1.) "The unrighteous speak evil of things they understand not and shall perish in their own corruption!" He never looked up, but his voice shot through the church and straight on into my dirty soul. "Only Jesus can show us the way. And only those who speak for Jesus can know that way. Remember, while we see not yet all things put under man, we see Jesus, who 'by the grace of God, might taste death for every man.'" (Hebrews 2:9.)

Right then, the lights flickered back on and the Pastor raised his arms in a showy V. I was starting to wonder if the janitor or some loyal churchgoer wasn't playing God with the old fuse box, when the big bastard lifted his eyes from his bible and shouted, "Yes, it was Jesus and only Jesus who tasted death for every man, so that we might know eternal life, as our Lord himself confirmed in that most blessed of benedictions revealed to us in chapter 11, verses 25 and 26 of the Gospel According to John. 'I am the resurrection and the life, he that believeth in me, though he were dead, yet shall he live, and whosoever liveth and believeth in me shall never die.'" He paused and dropped his arms, then looked at the Millers and said softly, "Stan lives. Stan lives."

As if that wasn't a-fucking-nuf, the Pastor cornered my parents outside the church for what looked like a super-uncomfortable, one-sided heart to heart. And Lance Winters, who'd kept his distance before the service, was on my ass, but I jumped into the car real quick, snapped the locks and put an end to him. When my parents, shadowed by Fang, finally ditched the preacher and piled into the car, they definitely looked a bit bent.

"Holy Christ," my dad said, gripping the steering wheel, all white-knuckled and breathing hard. His eyes flicked to the back seat. "You okay?"

I nodded.

"We're all fine. We're all just fine," my mom said, but I wasn't so sure because her head was bobbing around like she was in the early stages of some shaky disease or something. Fang, on the other hand, sat motionless beside me, trying his best not to exist.

"So, what did the pastor guy want?" I leaned forward to ask the question.

"Nothing," my dad said, real fast and real flat.

My mom looked at him like she wanted to add something, but in that same tight voice he said there was nothing worth talking about, and my mom suggested it might be a good idea to get the hell out of there.

We practically ran Lance and his cameraman over, wheeling onto the street, and from the back seat I mouthed a nice clear "fuck off" at them, right before we got stuck behind the hearse and were forced to head up the funeral procession. Oh yeah, one good thing—Pastor Ted slipped in behind us. I think he leaned on the horn accidentally. I don't really know. Either way, he was hard to ignore. Even Fang couldn't resist. At the beep, we all turned to gape at the big man, planted behind the wheel of this old beater of a K-Car. Except for the enormous glow-in-the-dark Jesus dangling from the rearview, I thought the vehicle really put a dent in the Pastor's smooth guy-of-God image. Still, he saw us staring and he gave us a confident nod before we all started rolling.

Being wedged between the Pastor's rusted-out shit box and Stan's luxurious last ride was a fairly uncomfortable place to be. It went without saying that we had no plans to venture out to the graveyard. When the hearse went left at the end of Highland, we hung a discreet right. Unfortunately, Ted followed us and then half the fucking congregation followed him, until my dad finally had to get out and wave everybody off. There was a general brouhaha as a couple dozen cars tried to back up or U-turn their way in the proper direction. My dad ended up directing traffic for the next five minutes while people gawked at me and my mom and Fang, trying hard to look cool inside the Taurus. By this time I couldn't help seeing the humor in the whole twisted situation, and I started to wave at the onlookers and my mom started laughing at my dad flailing around on the street. Fang just rested his head against the back of the seat and closed his eyes, no doubt wishing he'd walked home even if it was all the way across town.

Despite my father's best efforts, we didn't manage to shake all the hangers-on. When we stopped to let Fang off, the roving-eye boys were right there, idling behind us, and they were already parked solidly in front of our place when we scrambled out of the car. My father said he'd take care of them and made a move for the garage while my mom and I dove inside. It took a couple of minutes before my dad emerged from the garage armed with my old pink and yellow Super Soaker. He did this Terminator march across the lawn, Soaker cocked, and when he got to the van he stuck his foot inside, pushed the sliding door wide open and blasted the news team. Ammo spent, he threw the water gun onto the lawn, said a few choice words to his wet friends and headed inside.

We had a surprisingly laid-back dinner before I crashed in my room. Lying on my bed in the heavy afterglow of my friend's funeral, you might guess I'd be thinking about Stan, but I wasn't. I was thinking about me, what had happened to me, how crazy the whole fucking thing was, how impossible, how insane, and suddenly there she was, this dying stranger girl floating around my brain. It wasn't like it had been with Stan and Mr. Bernoffski. It wasn't an instantaneous, straight-from-the-gut kind of deal. It was a hazy and distant sort of knowing that settled into me, one part freaky premonition, one part doomed daydream. There were no times, no dates, no license plate numbers. Just a flutter of dark, lifeless eyes and long, lifeless hair. Just a set of pale lips that would never "say cheese," and two pupils rolling to white above a necktie of blood.

Just a flash of red razor. Then nothing. But massive amounts of confusion and dread and disbelief.

FIVE

I hadn't been to see a doctor since I broke my wrist attempting a spectacularly unsuccessful front side nose grind off the Stokum library railing. Still, given that a) Stan had died, and b) it seemed I'd known about it beforehand, my mother thought it might be c) prudent to talk to someone with a couple of university degrees, so d) she hooked me up with Dr. Cramp (dig the name). It had been two years since the busted wrist, but the same lame mags still littered the waiting room, the same bogus sailing art still clung to the walls, and the whole place still had that gross wart-remover smell.

Cramp himself was an okay guy, if you're into the golden-haired, completely mainstream, totally successful type. He wasn't from Stokum (no kidding), had been in town maybe five years max. Before ending up in this shit hole, he'd apparently been over vaccinating kids in Africa for free, saving entire villages from Ebola and whatnot. There were two pictures on his desk: one of the good doctor squatting in the middle of all these smiling black faces, the other of a gorgeous yet wholesome-looking woman with nice perky tits. (Normally enough to give me a huge boner. Unfortunately, over the last couple days, my boner blood had leaked out the gashes in my feet, which were fucking killing me by this time. However, my brain was still being supplied and I was pretty certain photo number one captured the African experience and photo number two the beginnings of a bouncy family life.)

My mom was with me in the office, and Dr. Cramp listened to her rambling psychotically about my destructive tendencies (so she *had* noticed my room), my stage one drug addiction and, oh yeah, the premonition. Cramp played along, said he'd seen the story on TV, said he was friendly with the Millers, said it was a real shame about Stan. He checked out my eyes, took my blood pressure, listened to my heart, then asked my mom to step out of the room. He wanted to have a few words.

As soon as she left, Cramp hopped up onto the other end of the examining table, all friendly and relaxed. "So, the story's true, then?" he asked in this real low-key kind of way, like we were talking about the Red Wings or something.

I nodded.

"And it happened the way your friends explained on TV?"

"Yeah, pretty much," I said, trying to sound equally casual.

"In that much detail?"

I nodded again and he whistled, utterly impressed.

"Anything like this ever happened to you before?"

He was playing it so straight I hesitated for only a second before I told him about Mr. Bernoffski and the weird flash of the girl with the razor. I explained how I had the premonitions a day prior to the deaths, how I'd felt both Stan and Mr. Bernoffski sort of pass through me when they died; and God, it felt good to tell someone the whole deal. Dr. Cramp just sat there, taking it all in, stopping me a couple times to clarify. When I finished, he went to his desk and started making notes in my file. I got a bit freaked imagining all the bent shit he was jotting down, and it took a while for me to get the nerve to ask him if he'd mind checking out my feet.

"Your feet?" he said, looking up.

I kicked off my shoes, started yanking at my socks, but he held up his hand, gave me the wait-a-minute wobble, so I stopped. Cramp stood up behind his desk in total slo-mo, with his eyes locked on my feet like he'd never seen a pair of bloody socks before.

He came over, lifted one foot and then the other. Then he did it again. He was acting so astounded, I was pretty certain the Ebola rumors had to be false, and I didn't see how the leg calisthenics were helping, so I finally yanked off my socks and stuck a foot in his face so he'd take a look at the actual wound.

"Glass," I said. He didn't respond, so I felt obliged to offer a bit of an explanation. "Stepped on a light bulb."

He nodded, but his face was all blank and he still wasn't saying anything. But at least he started moving at regular speed again. He opened the little cupboard over the sink and took out a couple brown bottles, threw some stuff into one of those metal, kidney-shaped trays and stuck his miner's light on. He knelt on the floor and cleaned the cuts before numbing the soles of my feet with some sort of anesthetic. It still hurt like a bitch when he started digging, and it took a while before he managed to work a piece loose. He held the little red shard up so I could take a look, then dropped it into the metal pan, where it clinked like a bullet, man. Cramp ended up pulling four splinters out, and one of them was pretty long, too; it was a wonder I'd even been able to stand with that fucker wedged in my foot for the last couple days.

With my feet wrapped in white, gauzy bandages, I started to put my socks back on, but they were a complete mess. I asked if I could toss them in the garbage, told him I really didn't feel like getting into a deep discussion with my mom about my feet, if he caught my drift. He said he did, pointed at the garbage can in the corner, and was already back behind his desk when something nasty, something totally nasty, started brewing inside me.

It started out small and heavy—a slow beat pounding my stomach to stone—but it grew bigger and darker and faster, until waves of hopelessness and helplessness and fear were rolling through me like a black symphony. Afterwards, I vomited in the sink, couldn't stop vomiting. Cramp came over and put a hand on my shoulder, wet a cloth and laid it across the back of my neck as I clutched the edge of the counter and waited for my gut to quit quivering.

It took a good five minutes before I was steady enough to rinse out my mouth and make it back to the examining table. Dr. Cramp suggested I lie down, said the nausea was probably brought on by the pain of removing the glass. Maybe he was right, maybe the nastiness was just a reaction to the pain, but I don't know, right then I was thinking some girl might be dead. I closed my eyes and asked Cramp if he could leave me alone for a couple of minutes. I could hear the shake in my voice and I knew he could too. He said he'd be back after he'd seen the patient in the other room, if that was okay with me. I may have nodded, I don't know. The door closed and the tears rolled. There was no stopping them. I didn't even bother trying.

Dr. cramp had given me plenty of time to sort myself out before he'd called my mom back into the office. She'd looked worried as hell because I'd been in there for like an hour, but Cramp told her he thought I was going to be just fine, I was shaken up a bit, but overall I was handling everything pretty well. I nearly shit when he said that, but then again, I guess you'd probably have to show up with your head in a box or a chicken shoved up your ass or something to get a bad report in Stokum. He did hand me a prescription for Trazon—apparently just the thing to keep me cool for the next few weeks—along with a bit of doctorly advice. Cramp warned me to "stick to the recommended dosage—two pills, three times a day—otherwise you'll be completely stoned. Okay?"

Yeah ... *okay*. It took me about thirty seconds to hustle my mother into the car and straight on over to Burton's pharmacy. She wasn't too pleased, but I was. I downed four pills as soon as we got home, another four after dinner. And I spent most of the weekend holed up in my room, pleasantly wasted. At some point I did scan the obits section of the *Stokum Examiner,* and I also took a couple minutes and googled the Net for chick suicides. It was impossible how much shit came up—page after page of desperation and gore, a dozen dead girls that could have been mine—but there was nothing, no one, I could really pin down.

It was pretty sour reading, but the Trazon made it easier. The Trazon made everything easier. I barely had to think. And I was sleeping like a corpse, got blasted from the depths Monday morning by Sum 41 screaming about the state of the world on my clock radio. Right away I chugged some pills, and I stuffed another fistful in the pocket of my jeans before heading downstairs for breakfast. It sort of registered that at the rate I was going my two-week supply would be gone in about five days, but I wasn't worrying about that. I had other things on my wobbly mind.

My parents had decided four days off school for predicting the death of a close friend was enough, and after we ate, they drove me to Jefferson. Seeing how I was trapped in the car, my mother took the opportunity to harass me.

When she wheeled around in her seat, her bank makeup looked all bright and tight on her pale face, which had gone insta-old in a few short days. "Have you got in touch with Mick yet?"

Mick. I'd only met him once or twice, but I'd heard his story about a million times. Whenever my mom talked about the guy, I could just tell that, despite everything that had happened, she still loved her delinquent brother, or at least her memories of him. "Our phone would ring," she'd say, her eyes all wide and sparkly, her voice all thin and trippy, "and if Mick was in the room we'd all look at him, and he'd say, 'It's Uncle Steve,' or 'It's the man across the road,' or 'It's Miss McMillan from school,' and sure enough, when we picked up the phone, it was. It always was. He was only around four or five when he started doing it, and at first my parents and I, and Mick too, we were just so shocked. But after a while we got used to it. But still, there was this unspoken rule that he never did it if there were guests in the house."

My mother's arm was thrown over the seat, and her hand bit into the fake leather upholstery behind my father's head. "Well, have you called him? I put his number on the fridge for you."

"Listen," I said, the drugs making me cocky, "I don't see why you want me to call the jerk who bailed on you, like, three days after your dad died. When you were, what, seventeen and freshly orphaned? He doesn't give a crap about you or me or any of us, okay?"

My mom's face fell, but she kept up the staring to nail me with her next inquiry. "Do you at least want to know what he said on the phone? Why he was calling?"

I turned my head to one side and let my eyes glide out the window, although I made sure my mother could still see the slippery I-don't-give-a-shit smile I'd wrapped my mouth around. She didn't say anything. She just watched me, watched me until my smile had hardened up and I was staring through the glass at absolutely nothing. Then she turned to face the front. Out of the corner of my eye, I saw my dad reach over and put a hand on her knee.

WHEN WE GOT TO JEFFERSON, my father threw the car into park and asked if I wanted him to come with me. But seriously, I couldn't imagine it, so I said a quick farewell to my parents and floated in solo. Despite my mom trying to hammer me flat in the car, I still had a pretty good buzz on, like the good doctor had promised. I could sense everybody taking a step back as I cruised by, could hear the halls go quiet, but it didn't really bother me. I just kept my eyes straight ahead and let the Trazon carry me through.

The teachers welcomed me back as smoothly as they could. Mr. Thorp, my math teacher, gave his huge head a stiff nod and we both tried to ignore the empty seat near the window where Stan should have been. Mr. Wood, the guy I had for tech, said he was glad to see me, but I knew he was full of shit because I could see how nervous I was making him. Mrs. Hayward, the only halfway decent teacher I had, was pretty cool. It was the second year in a row I'd had her for English, so we were pretty used to each other and she treated me with easy indifference, the way she treated everyone until they did something exceptional—good, bad or otherwise.

Mrs. Hayward lived on a farm, always wore black rubber boots to class, often smelled of manure and probably wasn't the most popular teacher in the staff room. So it wasn't really all that surprising, then, that she'd taken a liking to me, especially after we discovered our common love for Dr. Seuss.

At the beginning of last year she'd assigned an essay and an oral presentation on a novel we'd read over the summer. Given my fairly light holiday reading schedule, I had to go to the library and grab the first thing that fell off a shelf. It turned out to be horrible. Getting through it was painful, like dragging myself over page after page of broken glass. I'm not even going to tell you what it was, it was that bad. Anyway, I wrote the essay, trashed the book in a hostile but humorous sort of way. For my oral presentation I didn't want to torture the class with the lifeless details of what I'd actually read, so instead I gave a snappy little intro to *Horton Hears a Who!*, highlighting the Gaudíesque influence apparent in Seuss's zany artwork. (My parents took me to Barcelona that summer. While visiting the Spanish sights, I also managed to lose my virginity—a huge, unexpected bonus that hadn't been mentioned in any of the travel brochures I'd read beforehand. I'm not going to get into that here, however, because right now I'm discussing the purity of Seuss.) I went on a bit about the doctor's unparalleled ability to turn simple language into poetry, and for my big finale I read his story of the elephant and the Who-inhabited dust speck. I figured I'd get a failing grade, but I didn't care. Funny thing is, it turned out that Mrs. Hayward had read the same unnamed, un-Seuss piece of shit I had and she'd completely despised it too. She gave me an A on the written report, saying she liked my tongue-in-cheek approach to criticism, but warned me to clean up the language and watch my run-on sentences. I got an A-plus on the presentation. My only A-plus ever, which totally reinforced my belief that if I just set my sights low enough, even I could do well.

After English class, lunch was particularly desperate. There was no way I was going out to the back parking lot to hang out with the media-savvy stoners I'd once called friends, and I certainly wasn't going to put myself on display in the cafeteria. I gagged down a sandwich and some pills at my locker, then headed for the library, the safe haven of freaks, geeks and small-town prophets.

I crashed on the floor at the end of one of the stacks and was just sitting there, balled up inside my hoodie, when Ms. Banks, the librarian, tripped over me. Her armload of reading material came crashing down, and there she was, bookless, towering over me in all her Pamela Anderson-ish glory. Tight white jeans ran up, way up, her slim legs to a perfect round ass. A flowery top that would have looked like hausfrau shit on anyone else was just begging to be ripped off her. It was truly a sight to behold.

Ms. Banks pressed a lucky hand to her chest. "You scared me to death," she said, all flustered. "Are you okay?"

I flipped her a rigid thumb, indicating I hadn't been seriously injured. She bent down to retrieve the books and I could see this lacy thong underwear peeking out the back of her jeans as she crawled around, so it probably goes without saying that I just sat there, enjoying the show.

"Thanks for the help," she said once she was stacked back up. She was looking fairly annoyed as she tossed her head toward the open area in the center of the room. "There are tables available." Her blonde ponytail bounced enticingly, but I didn't move. "Look, can I get you something?" She sounded very irritated.

"Like what?" I dared to raise an emboldened eyebrow at her, all suggestive and shit. (I know, I know. Don't even talk to me. It was the meds, man.)

"Like a book. This is a library." Snit for snat.

"I'm fine." The syllables slid slowly from my mouth.

Ms. Banks settled her load of literature onto a nearby shelf, crossed her arms over her chest and leaned up against the book stack. "Is that right?"

I could see she was trying to get a look inside my hood, trying to check out my eyes, tightening up my Trazon looseness in the process. "Yep, that's right." I concentrated this time, spat the words right out. I figured she'd get the hint and take off, but she didn't.

"Find something to read," she said firmly. By this time it was evident neither of us was in a flirting sort of mood, so I told her I'd prefer to be left the fuck alone as I wasn't bothering anybody. She pulled her shoulders back and put her hands on her hips, and although she looked even better with her tits sticking out like that, I knew she was completely pissed.

"Get out."

"Oh, for Christ sake." I started to get up, but it took, like, way too much effort, so I plopped back down and cranked my low-wattage charm up to one. "Listen, I'm sorry ... really. I was rude. Sorry. But I need to hang out here for a while, okay? I'm going through a bit of shit right now."

"Are you really? Well, you know what they say—God will not look you over for medals or diplomas, but for scars. That's Elbert Hubbard, an American essayist, if you're interested."

I pulled up the cuff of my shirt and displayed the quarter-sized disk of raised flesh decorating the inside of my wrist. The neat stitches ringing it transformed what would have been an otherwise ugly lump into a shiny little sunshine of a scar.

"Got one," I said, giving her what I hoped was a winning smile. And then, to impress her, I rotated my arm so she could see the identical twin on the other side. "Impaled myself on a fence spike."

"Ouch." Her face pulled into a golden grimace.

"If you think that's bad, you should have seen the fence."

She sort of laughed at that.

"Listen, if I pretend to read something, can I stay?"

"No. Either find something to read, and I mean really read, or leave." She took a deep breath. I tried not to notice her breasts heaving beneath her blouse, really I did. "Now, because I'm in a hospitable mood and you've got that scar, I'll start again. What do you like to read?" she said, trying unsuccessfully to hide the I'm-about-to-change-your-life edge of excitement in her voice that proved, despite being a hottie, she'd picked the right line of work.

"I dig music."

"Music?"

"Yeah, alt-rock, rock."

"Well, this isn't MTV, but let me think." She headed into the stacks, jingling her ear with her finger, tuning in her internal Dewey decimal system, another sign she was a born librarian. She was back in a flash with a book and a smile. "Here you go. *Come As You Are: The Story of Nirvana*. I had to look up the author. I haven't read it. My husband said it wasn't well written but it was interesting. You'll have to be careful, the binding's weak."

She handed me the book. Three scungy, long-haired freaks glowered at me. I liked it already.

"I assume you've heard of Nirvana?" Ms. Banks asked. "Kurt Cobain? Dave Grohl? I forget the bass player's name, but he's really tall."

"Krist Novosic. Or Novoslick. Or Novoselic." I sounded like I was on Novo-something, trying to get my mouth around the name, but it didn't matter. Ms. Banks knew I was a bit wasted and it was apparent she was prepared to tolerate it, especially since she'd booked me up.

"That's right," she said. "Krist Novoselic. Well, enjoy." She picked up her pile of books, was halfway up the aisle when she turned and came back. "You know, I was devastated when Kurt died. I'd had such hope for the music, such faith in him, you know? But when you mess around with heroin, well, you know. Live by the sword, die by the sword. Or in this case, the gun. If you're smart," she said, looking me head-on, "you'll stick to something a little tamer. Anyway, at least Dave Grohl has moved on."

"Foo Fighters rule." I gave her the extended forefinger, pinkie rocker salute.

"You got it." She offered up a nice, if somewhat charitable, smile. "You're not a library regular. Care to remind me of your name?"

I pulled off my hood and let her have it. "Luke. Luke Hunter." I tried not to flinch.

She raised both eyebrows and went into a bit of an extended nodding session. "Right. I know your mom. From Friends of Lake Erie."

"Yeah? My mom loves Lake Erie. All the Great Lakes, really." At least the Trazon hadn't impeded my ability to be a complete moron.

Ms. Banks let me off easy, however. "Yeah, me too. Anyway, don't forget to sign the book out before you leave."

"No problem. Uhmm … sorry about being rude, before."

"Sure. As you said, you're going through some shit. It was nice meeting you, Luke. Say hi to your mom for me, okay?"

I told her I would. Then the lovely Ms. Banks took her luscious self up the stacks and I opened the book.

SIX

The phone was ringing when I got home from school. This wasn't surprising. Since becoming Stokum's hottest freak-show attraction, it had been going pretty much nonstop. My parents handled most of my new fans. Apparently, I didn't have an overabundance of concerned friends, but some Michigan media, along with a few psychic hotline types, were interested in hearing from The Prophet. Shit, there'd been calls from as far away as, well, Minneapolis. Regardless of point of origin, everyone got the same no-comment comment, before being asked politely to bugger off. I don't know why we didn't just unplug the phone. I guess we were all secretly waiting for some super-important call to straighten things out. Or maybe that was just me. My parents probably wanted to be sure they could get in touch when they were at work, and seeing how my dad was too cheap to spring for an answering machine, the phone just kept wailing.

I grabbed a snack and, ignoring the latest caller, went to the living room to watch some videos. That worked for a while, the jerk on the other end finally hung up, but the ringing started up five minutes later and again five minutes after that. Normally the Trazon got me through these annoying moments pretty easily, but for one reason or another—it might have been the chat in the stacks with Ms. Banks—I'd skipped my after-school meds. So I was a tad straighter than I'd been the last couple days, and the ringing sounded a tad louder, a tad more persistent and, yes, maybe even a tad friendlier than usual. Finally I grabbed the phone off the front hall table and carried it as far as the cord would permit, which left me at the entrance to the living room. I muted the White Stripes, which hurt ("Hotel Yorba" video), and picked up the receiver.

"Hello, I'd like to speak with Luke Hunter." I recognized the big voice right off.

"This is he."

"Hello, Luke. This is Pastor Ted Bradley, from New Life in Christ Church. I'm a good friend of the Millers. I knew Stan very well."

He paused, waiting for me to make things easy for him, but I wasn't in a particularly cooperative mood. I concentrated on Meg and Jack, jumping around the hotel room, silently banging the drum.

"Did your parents mention I'd spoken with them after the service?"

"Nope." I slid down the wall, settled myself on the thick green carpet, kept my eyes on the screen.

"Ahh … well, I did. I was hoping they'd pass along my message. I wanted you to know that we, all the parishioners, are confident that Stan is in good hands, so to speak. He had accepted Jesus as his savior some years back, and although he hadn't been attending church regularly for a good while, we firmly believe he remained committed to Christ. I thought you might want to know this. Thought it might make things a little easier for you."

I wasn't sure what to say to that, so I mumbled something about Stan being a good guy and Ted seconded the motion and we seemed to be getting along nicely, before he turned his attention to yours truly.

"Now, Luke, how are *you* doing?" he asked, sounding all concerned.

"Fine." Looking for a bit of distraction, I started testing out the elasticity of the phone cord, seeing how many times I could loop it around my neck. I held the receiver a couple inches from my ear, so the springy plastic cord could slip smoothly around the back of my head and down onto my throat, but the Pastor was still coming in loud and clear.

"This can't have been easy for you."

"I'm fine." I kept looping.

"I thought you might like to come down to the church so we could talk about what's happened."

"I don't think so." The cord had done seven loops. I tried for an eighth.

"So ... you're sure you're fine?"

"Positive." By this time I was kneeling and I'd sort of tipped forward, and my head was at a horrible angle. The receiver was jammed into my cheek and the rest of the phone was dangling off my neck and the whole elasticity experiment was beginning to feel a little stupid and tight.

"Well, eventually you'll need someone spiritual to talk to. I have no doubt about that. Are you currently affiliated with any Christian organization?" he asked.

"Nope," I gasped.

"As I thought." He puffed a big sigh into my ear. "Well, I want you to know I'm here for you in that capacity. I believe I can help. I'm worried about you, Luke."

He had reason to worry. The cord had twisted itself into a bit of a knot, and for a second or two I actually panicked, thinking it might be irreparably tangled. I imagined myself choking to death and leaving everyone thinking I'd killed myself over a phone call from the Pastor, which would have been a really sorry way to go. I finally had to drop the receiver and claw the goddamn cord off my neck. I'm not sure what I missed, but Ted was still going strong when we reconnected.

"… a real gift. I am hoping you'll reconsider."

"Yeah, well, thanks. Listen, I've gotta go." I massaged my neck, trying to get the blood flowing back to my brain.

"All right, then. But if you change your mind, please feel free to call me. Can I leave my number?"

"Don't have a pen."

"Right." Another sigh. "Well, I hope you'll drop by sometime. When you're ready to talk. You know where to find us."

"Sure," I said, being completely agreeable because I figured he was ready to pack it in. He wasn't. He was one of those people who really liked to have the last word.

"One final thing. Luke, I want you to know that I think you are a very unique person. I know you might not believe it right now, but you are. What's happened to you is very special. I want—"

I didn't wait for the Pastor's blessing to hang up. I hit the volume on the TV. The White Stripes had already checked out.

Standing in front of the hall mirror, I admired the welts on my neck. I kept my eyes on the narrow tracks ringing my throat so it was easier to pretend the call hadn't pried me open a bit, that it hadn't made me think. I trailed my finger along first one thin red groove, then the next, attempting to hold off the why-me's and the holy-shit-how's and the what-the-fuck's-going-on's rattling around my brain. It was trying, I mean really trying, ignoring all the questions I had no answers for. And I started to get pissed—at Ted for thinking he could just call up and shove me into such dangerous territory, at myself for dropping the Trazon barrier low enough that this shit could get to me. Yeah, I was definitely headed for some serious anger—the only emotion I was really any good at— but I short-circuited the surge with a fistful of pills and some screaming videos.

My favorite of the set was definitely Papa Roach. He was mad, madder than me, he was raging, and every chick in the video, well, they looked just like my flickering suicide girl. I mean, I could see that's where she'd come from, that "Last Resort" girl with her dead eyes and her pale face and her smileless lips. I'd ripped her off from Papa then let my imagination hand her a razor blade so she could finish what he'd started. It wasn't even a stretch; I mean, I'd seen the video a hundred times, and if you listened to the lyrics, she'd been contemplating suicide anyway, right? And the black symphony in the doctor's office? I figured it was like Cramp said, inspired by pain.

Funny how, along with the drugs, that settled me down so by the time my parents arrived I was feeling pretty okay, although they were looking fairly distressed. They turned down the television, went upstairs and changed out of their good, dark clothes, then crashed beside me on the couch. According to them, there hadn't been a whole pile of people at Mr. Bernoffski's funeral. A few relatives, the Connellys from next door, a couple old guys from the plumbing place where the corpse used to work. Apparently, Mrs. Bernoffski was barely standing by the time they pulled up to the gravesite.

My mom was just about to get up to pour drinks for herself and my dad when she noticed the marks on my neck. Usually I'm a good liar, can make up extraordinarily impressive shit when put on the spot, but right then I couldn't think of anything remotely feasible to explain the welts.

"I wrapped the phone cord around my neck," I said, picking at a loose thread on my jeans.

I could feel my father receding into the ugly floral cushions beside me as my mom pushed herself forward to perch on the edge of the sofa. Resting her elbows firmly on her thighs, she twisted round and stared at me in this incredulous manner. Her hair was tucked behind her ears and her face was very pale. "And why did you do that?"

"I wanted to see how many times it would go around."

She leaned forward a little more and exchanged a long raised-eyebrow look with my dad.

"Listen, it was just this completely retarded thing I did."

"I'd say."

My father tried to bail me out. "Mary, Luke has been doing stupid things like that all his life."

My mom, looking seriously skeptical and fed up, pushed herself off the couch and started for the kitchen. On her way out, she paused, nailed me with some real killer eye contact, and said that personally she'd had enough of funerals for a while and was thinking about pouring herself a double.

I RAN OUT of Trazon on Sunday about three o'clock. I was pretty cool about it until the effects of the last dose actually wore off. By seven P.M., I was all geared up, bouncing around my room, trying to avoid contact with any heavy, haunting thoughts. With the prescription drugs finished, I figured a course of alternative therapy might be in order, so I rooted around until I found an old bag of weed stashed in a running shoe at the back of my closet. I went through the usual drill: rolled a joint, cranked up the Offspring, opened the window, shoved a towel into the crack at the bottom of the door to avoid smoke seepage, crashed on the bed and sparked up. Almost right away I could feel my body sink just that much further into the mattress and a smile slap itself across my face, thick as cold paint. I lay there for a while, completely relaxed, listening to tunes, feeling groovy. A couple scary images tumbled through my brain, but they were just loose background stuff barely resonating behind the throb of the music and the steady lick of cool air caressing my skin.

What with all the licking and throbbing, it didn't take long for me to realize I'd just puffed myself into a state of hypersensitivity, which I knew was not a good place for me to be. Soon the easy vibe tightened down. The padded edges turned hard. And surprise, surprise, death crept in close. So close, I could feel suicide girl hiding under my bed, and Stan crouching in the corner beside my desk, blood puddling at his feet. My ears filled with a vacuous roar, my eyes locked onto a square of ceiling above my bed, but still I knew Mr. Bernoffski was in the closet and Mexican Mick was leaning against the door, watching the whole scene, an amused smile plastered on his face. And pretty soon I was positive it was going to happen again, that we were all just waiting for somebody else to show up dying, my mom or dad, say, or maybe another kid from school, someone close, someone within arm's reach I wouldn't be able to save.

But no one died. No one even flickered. What happened was the weed wore off. The CD ended. And I was left alone, very alone, in my very quiet room.

SEVEN

When my dad dropped me at school on Monday, I gave him a wave, waited until he turned out of the driveway, then took off. I wasn't too groggy or sick to head into school or anything like that. It was just that I had shit to do.

I hopped on my board, pulled my hoodie up against the raw morning and, avoiding the bloodstained sidewalk in front of the 7-Eleven, I headed downtown. Like most things in Stokum, it wasn't far. It only took me about five minutes to make my way out of my ugly little oatmeal subdivision. Once liberated, I hit Water Street and from there it was a straight trajectory to the fibrillating heart of town.

The houses on Water were nice. Big old redbrick jobbies, with wraparound front porches and stained glass windows, set way back from the road. Even this late in the year, the lawns were still a fresh-looking green and flowers hung on in the gardens. I figured Dr. Cramp and his sweet-looking wife probably rolled around in one of those places, probably had Sunday barbecues with the neighbors, all of them stupid enough to live in Stokum despite their big bank accounts. I knew for a fact that Mr. Kite, the main man at Kalbro, lived in the choicest house on the street. He'd invited his managers and their families over for a party this one time and my dad, being the supply chain guy, said we *had* to go.

Kite had been odd. He'd given us this endless tour of his house and we'd all had to pretend to be amazed by the ceiling moldings and the walk-in closets and the TV in the can (which was cool) and the wood-paneled library with the fake books and the purple living room that had just been "done" by a Chicago decorator and the lounge with the hand-carved pool table which none of us were allowed to touch. Then the equally odd Mrs. Kite, wearing this tight gold dress, fed us crappy Costco lasagna off paper plates before forcing all the kids to go swimming even though it was a cock-shrinking sixty degrees outside. I'd silently protested by pissing in the pool and have since refused to attend any of the Kites' other functions. And seriously, unless my dad is a completely different person than I think him to be, I have no idea how he manages to work with Mr. Kite day after day. No idea.

A couple blocks past the boss's place, the stately houses came to an abrupt halt at McCreary Park. The rich people pressed enough cash into someone's hands to keep it lush and vagrant free, and a new, all-American bandstand stood whitewashed against the greenery at the back of the property. However, Water Street turned a little sour on the other side of the park, where things went retail. The redbrick buildings were still standing, but all the decent stores had either shut down or moved out to the mall when Wal-Mart set up shop on the outskirts of town. Downtown was left with the little branch of the Michigan Savings and Loan where my mom worked, the doughnut hole, the two-screen Royal Cinema, Burton's pharmacy, a pawnshop and, of course, Hank's T-Shirt Shack.

I slowed up to check out Hank's window display—all tacked-up Ts, glass pipes, bongs and black velvet boards of jewelry—then

ground to a halt at the entrance. The door was shedding thick
curls of lime green paint and, like every place in town, there was a
flyer taped to the glass. ASTELLE JORDAN. MISSING, announced the
big black letters at the top of the poster. Underneath the catchy
title, a pretty, smiling face afloat in a sea of long, wavy curls. Below
that, in smaller letters, the stats: Sixteen years of age, five feet three
inches, 110 pounds. Brown hair, brown eyes. Last seen, Subway
Restaurant, October 3, 2002, 4:15 P.M. Lace-up Mavi jeans. Dark
gray Nike running shoes. Red "Fantasy" shirt. Blue Adidas
backpack. Seen Astelle? Better give the Stokum police department
a ring.

I didn't know her. She went to the Catholic school on the other
side of town. I might have seen her at a basketball game or two, I
wasn't sure; there were a lot of hotties at St. Pete's. Still, I recognized her from the onslaught of media exposure her smiling face
had received since her disappearance. And I couldn't help thinking
about the weeping older version of that same face standing behind
a quivering flyer, pleading for help on the evening news for the
past few weeks. It was probably just a couple dead men doing
their voodoo death whisper in my ear, but I definitely wasn't
getting a good vibe from the girl on the glass. I gave the tail of my
deck a kick. My board jumped into my hand. Avoiding contact
with the poster, I pushed my way into the Shack.

I shoved my board in the battered umbrella stand inside and
checked out the dude behind the counter. Shaved, various piercings,
fat tribal tattoo around his left arm—the usual tough-guy shit. I'd
never seen him before and, seeing how I wasn't in the mood for
chitchat, I toured the store, hoping Hank would presto soon.

The new guy behind the counter stared at me, probably thinking I was about to stuff some product down my pants and split, but I didn't care. I was in no rush, so I just holed up in my hoodie and fingered the merchandise, worrying the dude behind the counter. And for just a minute, and for the first time since he died, I let down the gate and I thought about my buddy Stan.

Last year was the 150th anniversary of Stokum becoming a town or some such nonsense, and Mr. Tanner, the principal at Jefferson, had gotten all jissy about it. He'd declared September Community Spirit Month, decided everyone at school *would be* involved and started assigning all the projects he'd cooked up over the summer. Most of the kids in my homeroom class had to work with this old bag from the local museum setting up a display in the school foyer, laying out the history of our great town, which was just as boring as it sounds. Stan and I got assigned the fund-raising gig for the sophomore year, going head to head with the other grades to see who could raise the most money for the new wetlands park the city was throwing up on the outskirts of town. The park was going to be littered with wild grasses and bulrushes and ponds for frogs and migrating ducks (since all the natural habitats within a thousand miles had been destroyed by unfettered development, as my mom pointed out that evening at dinner). According to Tanner, who'd leaned across his desk with his eyes ablaze and a determined finger pointed at me, Stan and the other fund-raisers/hostages, this watery utopia deserved our most committed efforts.

Stan and I weren't really friends at this point, but we'd locked eyes that day in Tanner's office, exchanged an in-sync what-a-complete-asshole look, and I guess we just moved forward from there. I think Stan appreciated my low-key wit and I picked up on his enthusiasm for kicking the competition. We settled on the T-shirt idea pretty quickly and I came up with the slogan in about five seconds. While I was in my room designing the logo on the computer, Stan completely chatted up my dad, convincing him to get Kalbro to donate two hundred dollars to the cause. Seed money in hand, we'd headed to Hank's to make a deal.

Hank was a middle-aged guy with a wig of wiry black hair and a largish, slogan-slathered gut. The first time we went into the Shack, he was sporting a neat white shirt emblazoned with a distinguished-looking crest announcing his membership in the Eastern Seaboard Pervert Association. He'd been cool with us at first, but Stan had warmed him up fast, telling him what we were up to, stressing our desire for the cheapest shirts available—any color, any size, any vintage. Sensing a business opportunity, Hank escorted us into the back room and grabbed a couple beat-up boxes from a top shelf loaded with similar-looking cardboard refugees. (When I told my dad about this later, he got a glint in his eye and said this was a perfect example of the problems associated with supply chain management, albeit on a much smaller scale than the ones he dealt with at Kalbro. Christ.) When we opened the boxes up, we found a payload of raunchy, orangey red T-shirts faded out in places and with the odd ripped seam adding character. One box was all XLs, which would do for the guys, the other all XSs, which Stan and I imagined wrapping nicely around the Jefferson girls' tits. We settled on a buck a shirt for two hundred shirts, and after Hank saw our logo, he said in the name of community he'd print them up for free.

It was already near the end of September when we set up our booth (the two boxes stacked one on top of the other) in the school foyer, right beside this wooden statue of Stokum's founding father, Mr. R.J. Stokum, inventor of the then new and improved Red Stokum wheat, a hearty fall strain which was more resistant to insects and cold than any other wheat at the time. Yee-haw! By way of advertising, Stan wiggled into one of the XS shirts and I threw on one of the XLs, and charging twelve bucks a shirt we sold out our *Stokum Sucks* Ts before the end of the lunch hour. I think every kid at Jefferson bought one, and although we never saw her wear it, we definitely outfitted Mrs. Hayward, our English teacher, with an XL model, and rumor had it that Ms. Banks slipped one of the library regulars some dough to buy her one too.

Of course, there were complaints. My mom rolled her eyes when she saw the shirts and called me an idiot, and once our customers started sporting their new garb at school, some of the teachers got to grumbling. Needless to say, Principal Tanner wasn't pleased. He dragged us into his office and gave us this long speech about how we'd sullied the spirit of the campaign, how we should be ashamed of our smart-ass cleverness, which wouldn't get us far in life, whang, whang, whang. When we plopped the $2,400 down on his desk, he kind of shut up. Still, it nearly killed him to hand over the fund-raising award at the assembly at the end of the month. Stokum's mayor was on hand to receive the loot and, despite all the organizing of dunk tanks and bottle drives and bake sales, the entire school only raised $4,363, which demonstrates just how hard Stan and I had spanked everyone's asses with our one lunch hour of work.

When we went up on stage to get our certificate, the whole auditorium, a virtual sea of pukish orangey red, erupted into a "Stokum sucks, Stokum sucks" chant. Tanner went all red and hid behind the big cardboard check he was about to hand over, but the mayor, trying to demonstrate his hipness, joined the chorus, pumping his fist in the air campaign-style, trash-talking his city, while Stan and I laughed our asses off.

I was sort of lost in all this, probably even had a smile lighting up my gob, when a loud voice slapped at me. "Hey, are you gonna buy something or just fondle the shirts or what?"

I looked up. I'd forgotten the tough guy behind the desk. "I'm here to see Hank. I'm one of the … Is he going to be here soon or what?"

A shrug of shoulders. "He's the boss man, not me."

"Yeah, no kidding. What time does he usually get here?"

"What's it to you?"

"What's it to me?" My bright-light face went dark. "I need to fucking see him, that's what."

"I'm not allowed to give out details about his comings and goings."

I shook my head at that. "Hank will be pleased his new employee has boned up on all the shop's privacy rules and regs."

The dude crossed his arms over his chest and his mouth pinched into an anal little pucker, causing his nose and lip rings to do a mating dance sort of thing right there on his face. "Listen, I don't know what your problem is, but—"

"I don't have a problem." I planted my hands on my hips and widened my stance.

"Yeah, you do. You have a completely fucked-up attitude, for one thing."

"Really? *I* have a fucked-up attitude? Maybe you should give me the name of your charm school, asshole."

He pushed himself off his stool and came around the counter. Unfortunately, he was a lot bigger than he'd looked sitting down. I stood my ground and, so he could see how scared I wasn't, I stepped away from the rack of shirts and yanked my hood down.

He totally pulled up. "Holy shit! You're that kid." He ran his hand over his bald head and, despite the tattoos and the protruding hardware, his facade cracked, leaving him looking all pierced and pathetic. "I saw you on the news. I mean, I saw your picture. It was a shitty shot, but seriously, you look like total crap. Are you okay? You an addict or something?"

"Working on it."

"Yeah, like, who isn't?" he said, laughing, but in a real shaky sort of way.

He was already back behind the counter by the time I settled myself into the window display. He kept staring at me, though, checking the clock, staring at me, drumming his fingers on the display case, rattling the gear inside. Then more staring, more clock checking, more drumming. The whole thing was fairly painful, and I was thinking about going over and smashing his noisy fingers into the countertop when he suddenly sparked up a conversation.

"The Prophet of Death," he said, shaking his shiny head. "Goddamn. Death predictions. Goddamn. Stuff like that *really* freaks me out."

"Really?" I mean, the air was thick with his nervousness. "If it makes you feel any better, I'm not expecting you to bite it anytime soon."

He shook out a laugh, recommenced with the finger tam-tams. "I believe in all that stuff, though," he said in this confidential tone, like I might have cared. He was full-on gaping at me now, obviously no longer concerned with the time. I could practically see his gears grinding, just knew he was going to come up with something good. "So … how'd you do it?" he finally asked. Like it was some sort of trick.

I offered a "No fucking idea" and pulled my hood back up. He went quiet for a while and I thought he was going to leave me alone. He wasn't.

"So, like, did you know for a long time the other kid was gonna die? Or did it, like, come to you all at once, or what?" The fact that I wasn't responding didn't seem to slow him down. "What I can't figure out is, if you knew it was going to happen, why didn't you do something? That's what I don't get."

I'd had enough of his stream-of-consciousness crap. I headed for the door, had almost escaped when Hank came out of the storeroom. When he saw me, he sputtered to a halt. Yeah, an eyeful of me had old Hank totally stun-gunned, and I could just tell it had been a stupid idea to drop by the Shack. Like I could just go up to people, like some regular person, like someone who hadn't known his friend was going to die, and say what? Jesus. What an idiot. I grabbed my board and threw the door open. But before I could bail, Hank kicked it into gear and he was right there, outside, beside me.

"Sorry about that, Luke. I was just—just surprised to see you," Hank said quietly.

His T-shirt wasn't as reserved. *Tact is for people too dumb to be sarcastic,* it announced in huge white letters. Except for the shirt— one of my favorites—I did not like what I saw when I looked at Hank. His mouth was a hard, tight line. His eyes were liquid. And he kept swallowing, trying to gag down a whack of big sloppy emotions. Right away I could see he was dangerous. And he was contagious. Just one gulp of him had my throat, my chest, my gut so tight. Then he tried to talk, another mistake, because his voice was all quivery and weak.

"I was just thinking about Stan, in the back room there." He hitched a thumb over his shoulder. "It's all I *can* think about. It's really hit me, Luke." He ran an arm under his nose, half smother- ing a wet-sounding snort. "It's just so terrible. I mean, he was so young. He was so, so—"

I held up my hand, straight-armed his words like some nimble running back, so he'd stop and I could escape before the monster wave of guilt and grief and whatever else was rising inside me completely wiped me out. But Hank was quick. I'd dropped my board, already had one foot on deck, when he grabbed my arm and pulled an envelope from his back pocket.

"These were for you. For you and Stan. I've been carrying them around for days, wondering what to do with them. Take them." He shoved the envelope into my hand, then bolted for the store.

I took off across the street. I only glanced back once. Through the pane of glass, Hank was watching me roll away, looking all white and scared behind the smiling face of the dead girl on the door.

I ripped into an alley down the block to reconstruct myself and to shake off the aftershocks of Hank. It took a while, a good long while, before I could even deal with the envelope. Inside, a folded sheet of paper and two tickets. The Chili Peppers, in Detroit, in December. *Got these as a promo.* The words scrawled across the page. *Thought of you guys right away. Have a blast. Your buddy, Hank.* I sat on my board. I laid my head in my hands. In that narrow alley, with everything looming large, I felt so small, small enough to be crushed by the weight of a couple goddamn tickets.

AFTER THE PATHETIC BACK-ALLEY DRAMA, I headed to Burton's pharmacy, which had been the real purpose of the trip downtown. The Shack had been a stupid detour, one that had only reinvigorated my quest for Trazon and the necessity of putting as much distance between me and myself as possible. I was hoping I could talk my way into a refill, although the empty bottle I'd jammed in my pocket that morning clearly indicated none was available. I mumbled my problem to the pharmacist, some young, clean-cut guy in a lab coat who, one step up, had a good twelve-inch height advantage on me. Peering up, I explained how I'd somehow lost or dropped some or most of the pills into the toilet and/or sink and that I was in need and would he mind very much phoning Dr. Cramp to see if he could refill the prescription over the phone.

The guy behind the counter shoved his hands into his deep white pockets and leaned back like he was trying to distance himself from a particularly stale fart or something. He gave me a tight-mouthed look, making it clear that he was disappointed by my lack of originality while at the same time revealing himself as a master spotter of prescription junkies. He shook his head at me, just in case I was too out of it to pick up on the look, before turning around without saying a word.

He went and chatted up some lady loitering amongst the drugs, clipboard in hand. She took the bottle, read the label, moved her glasses down her nose and checked me out. Then, heads in close, the two of them started whispering and the dickweed who'd been harassing me suddenly turned to stare, and I knew The Prophet had been fingered. I thought about just taking off, figured I was out of luck anyway and that I'd have to track down Dwight Slater between press interviews to see if he had anything stronger than skank weed stashed in his locker. But the lady started flipping through her clipboard, tugged a sheet out and handed it to the guy. A couple minutes later he returned, carrying a neat white and green Burton's pharmacy bag, which he efficiently stapled closed.

"That'll be $18.65," he said, handing it over. I must have looked a bit stunned or something, because as he dumped my change into my hand he added, "The refill was faxed in this morning."

I was thrilled. I didn't give the mystery fax a second thought. What I did was give the asshole in the lab coat a big fuck-you smile, making it clear I was pleased by the power shift that had just taken place while at the same time revealing myself as a big Dr. Cramp supporter. And just in case he was too out of it to pick up on the subtlety of the smile, I gave him the finger, then left without saying a word.

EIGHT

With a locked-down supply of drugs, I managed to wipe out the rest of October and the first half of November. The days sort of ran together, with me floating through a blurry obstacle course of worried faces, a multitude of moving mouths, everything safely on the other side of my Trazon bubble. I knew it wasn't the best way to be spending my precious teen years, but hey, the premonitions, my aura of freakishness, the absence of Stan, all felt murky and distant, and that was the mission, man, that was the mission. Still, heading into the second half of November, the Trazon started to fail me. I couldn't get the dosage quite right and shit started slipping through.

For one, I started to notice just how much school sucked. I hadn't really spoken to Fang and the boys since that last time at Delaney's. I was still pissed at them for spilling to the media, but mostly I didn't want to brush up against anyone who'd been within earshot of the story I'd told in the basement that night. Fang did attempt to make contact, and for a while there he tried to get in my way at my locker after school, looking all pathetic and confused, asking *me* if I was okay. I had nothing to say to that. I had nothing to say to him. Eventually he got the hint and stopped showing up.

Having no friends except for the dead one following me around wasn't great, but still, there were other, braver kids who wanted to be my pals. They'd come up to me at my locker or corner me in class and at first they'd act really nice, like we were old friends and they gave a shit about how I was doing, but even on high doses of meds I could smell their desire for answers dripping off them like busybody BO, could see them lining up their real questions just like Baldy had that day at Hank's. *So, how'd you do it? If you knew it was going to happen, why didn't you do something? That's what I don't get …*

Things weren't much better outside of Jefferson, although I had found a friend in Jesus, or one of his spokespeople, anyway. Pastor Ted was a persistent bastard, and like some revved-up game show host, he kept calling, trying to get me to *come on down*. He claimed he was concerned, and it wasn't only him: God was concerned. They were both there for me, they could help, they'd seen cases like mine before. Ted didn't really worry me; he seemed harmless enough with his promises of salvation and spiritual gifts and everlasting life and whatnot.

On the home front, my parents and I weren't exactly hitting it off either. I'd been spending most of my time in my room, and I knew they were worried—that much was obvious—and it wasn't because they thought I was surfing the Net for porn or injecting shit into my veins or getting blisters from jacking off, all the usual things parents buzz about outside their teenagers' closed doors. Their worry was cord-around-the-neck bigger than that—but seriously, parents freaking about teens, it's kind of part of the deal. I couldn't help them out, was pretty sure they couldn't do squat for me, so I avoided them as much as possible, fell into monosyllabic communication mode whenever we did come face to face.

Of course, my mother wasn't having it. She kept chipping away, trying to crack me open. Coming up to my room, throwing the door wide like she was totally welcome, settling onto the bed. Wanting to talk. About what had happened. About how I was. Upset she had no answers for me, nothing that might make it make sense. All she had to offer was Mexican Mick. Yeah, she yapped about him a lot, and it was always the same old crap. How she thought I should talk to him. How when Mick was little and the phone ...

One day I just shut her down. Forget the Trazon. Forget the hazy, lazy buzz. I was instantly angry. "Yeah, I *know* about Mick," I snapped. I'd been at my desk, eavesdropping on my old friends' moronic instant messaging session, but I got to my feet pretty quick. Because it's easier to freak, easier to flap your arms and raise your voice and charge around a room, when you're standing up. My mother was leaning against the wall just inside the door. Arms folded across her chest, mouth knotted up, she watched me go to it. I think I was only about two inches from her face when I told her I was sick of her implying that what had happened to me had anything to do with some nothing, psychic call-display talent her loser brother had twenty years ago. To pretend that it did, to make it seem like Mick and I had something in common, felt like a fucking insult. What happened with Stan and me wasn't anything, *anything* like the freaking phone thing with Mick, okay? OKAY?

"So, what was it like, then, Luke?" she asked, countering my red-hot rant with a cool white calm.

I could only shake my head. As if, *as if,* I could explain that. To her. To anyone. I sat down on the bed, spent from the outburst, knocked out by one question.

"I know you don't think much of my brother. I know you think he's a coward who left when he shouldn't have. But can I tell you something, Luke? Mick was an amazing boy. He was the kindest, most sensitive kid. There was really something special about him. I adored my brother, and yeah, he's let me down, and yeah, he's had his share of troubles as an adult, but I still love him. And can I tell you something else you *don't* know about him?"

I didn't bother giving my consent and she didn't bother waiting for it.

"Mick did leave me on my own when I was seventeen. But he didn't leave three days *after* our dad died. He left three days *before*." She paused, knowing the critical change in information, the after time-warping into before, would grab my attention.

"When my mom died"—she did a couple quick loops with her hand, rolling past the cancer part of the story—"my father went kind of crazy. Right away he made us get rid of all her things, everything. And a month after she died, he sold our house, and a month after that, we packed up what was left and we moved. Mick and I hadn't even seen the new place, we just climbed into the cab of the moving truck and drove across town. But when we got there, Mick wouldn't go inside. There was a big scene on the lawn, my father and my brother were screaming at each other, and Mick just kept saying there was no way he could go into that house, there was no way *any of us* could go into that house. My father kept telling him not to be silly, to grow up, but nothing he said would change his mind. Eventually Mick just walked away. He didn't even take a suitcase. He was sixteen years old, and he walked away with nothing." She took a long drag of air, turned it into a big windy sigh. "Three days later, my father was up on the roof, fixing the aerial so he could watch some football game on TV, and he fell off. And he died."

When my mom sat down on the bed beside me, the mattress shifted, but I didn't. I was rigid. I was a statue, staring blind out a window held together with packing tape.

"I don't know why I never told you this before. I've never even talked about it with Mick. Or your dad. Not really. I guess I thought I was protecting him somehow—from inquiry, or guilt, or implied responsibility—I don't know. It always just seemed easier to say Mick left after Dad died. But now ..." She put her hand on my stony shoulder. Without even moving, I blasted her with coldness, gave her the old back-to-the-face blow-off, until finally she pulled her hand away.

I didn't see her get up. I didn't see her put the scrap of paper, the one that had been stuck on our fridge since the day Stan died, the one with my uncle's phone number on it, onto my desk. And I didn't hear her say she loved me, she'd do anything for me, her life circled around mine. No, I definitely didn't hear any of that.

MIDDLE OF NOVEMBER, November 15, the first day it hadn't warmed up at all. I was heading home after school, underdressed in the latest fall fashions—Converse kicks, T-shirt, jeans with a ripped-out ass, unbuttoned Levi's jacket with the standard-issue black hoodie underneath. There was frost on the ground and the pavement was slick in all the shadowy places. I hunched into the bitter wind whipping across Erie to scream up the Stokum streets, but as soon as I picked up any speed, my wheels would sideslip on me and my forehead was icing up. After a couple cold blocks, I called an end to my boarding season and started to walk. I was semi-frozen by the time I turned onto Clive Avenue. Still, I slowed up in front of the Bernoffskis' to take in just how shitty the place looked.

The house was all shut up, curtains pulled tight, letters and papers hanging from the black metal mailbox. The once-perfect grass was brown and the parts that weren't buried under piles of rotting leaves were about six inches long. I was thinking about how Mr. Only-on-Tuesdays would flip if he could see the old homestead now, and about the John Deere in the garage— probably untouched since my dad and Mr. Connelly had wrestled it inside and closed the door. I didn't even notice the station wagon parked across the street from my place. I was halfway up my front walk when I heard a car door open and someone calling my name.

"Luke? Luke Hunter?"

I turned to watch a lady stumbling out of an old Volvo wagon, clutching something pink to her chest. She rushed toward me, looking off balance and sort of battered with her dark hair limp and stringy as if she'd forgotten what a shower was for and her coat hanging open despite the nipple-erectus weather. She looked sort of familiar, but I was pretty sure we'd never met. I yanked the cuffs of my sweatshirt down as far as they would go, picked up my board and turtled into the collar of my jacket as the lady hurried across the street.

She stopped at the end of my walk, introduced herself in a nervous voice. "I'm Mrs. Jordan. Astelle's mother." She shifted in front of me, holding what I could now see was an Old Navy sweatshirt in her tight hands, waiting for me to clue in, but nothing registered. "The mother of the missing girl."

That registered, big-time, like a well-delivered kick in the nuts. Just to be sure, she pulled a sheet of paper from her pocket and forced it into my hand. I didn't even look at it. I knew what it was.

"I saw you on the television. I'm awfully sorry about your friend. I wouldn't be here if I wasn't, if I didn't think you could help." She held the sweatshirt out and shook it a little. Behind the light pink cloth, her face was rigid and gray. "It's Astelle's." Her voice was barely there.

I took a step back. My teeth were chattering.

"It's Astelle's," she said again, her voice rising as a blast of frigid air whipped up the street. The flyer snapped against my leg.

I took another step back.

"No one's been able to help, it's been forty-five days now, I thought you might ..." She shook the sweatshirt at me. It fell open, trembling between us like some faded bullfighter's cape. "Please. Take it. Please."

She was crying now, wringing the sweatshirt in her hands, begging me to touch it, just take it, please, please, maybe I'd feel something, maybe I'd know ... I turned and I ran. I don't really remember how I got my keys out of my bag or what happened to my skateboard or how I got inside. I do remember my heart hammering against the stiff wood as I leaned against the front door and stared out the little rectangular windows at the top.

Mrs. Jordan pressed the sweatshirt to her face and held it there for a long time, her body shaking into it, shaking like her coat. In the heat of my front hall, with my teeth clattering together, I watched the lady and her coat flapping out there in the cold wind. Finally she dropped her arms and folded the shirt into a neat package. On upturned palms, she carried it back to the Volvo and drove away.

I only saw Mrs. Jordan that once. Nonetheless, I think she deserves an honorable mention for her intense, best-supporting cameo in the *Luke Hunter: Death Prophet* saga, although I came off as a bit of a wimp in that particular episode. Too cowardly to touch a sweatshirt. Too pathetic to deal with a desperate mother. Offscreen, I'd tried to be braver. I crumpled the Missing poster up, tossed it into the garbage can in my room, cranked the music, tried to get angry with System of a Down. But it didn't work. I finally had to pick the goddamn thing out of the garbage. The paper was wintery cold, despite all the hot details. Only sixteen years old. A mere five feet three inches tall. A feathery 110 pounds. Heaps of brown curls. Big brown eyes. Sexy lace-up jeans. A Fantasy tight shirt. Shit, I barely glanced at the neatly written address, phone number and plea for help on the back. I folded Astelle up, reduced her to a thick square and tucked her in my wallet, so she could ride around in my back pocket like some cursed charm.

Besides Astelle, there was another girl giving me a bit of trouble, but trouble of a different flavor. She was alive and sizzling and could usually be found in the library, where I was still spending most of my lunch hours. And to be honest, those lunch hours had started to feel less like hiding out and more like waiting—for Faith to show up and claim a seat. Preferably close enough for viewing yet far enough for comfort.

To keep Ms. Banks happy, I'd given up my spot on the floor at the end of row *H* through *J* for a back table off to one side, and was reading all her latest picks for troubled teens. This one day, it was sometime near the end of November because the Peppers concert was only, like, a week away, and I was half wondering what to do with the extra ticket and half reading *Cannery Row,* which was nice and short and pretty good, too, when I felt someone watching me. And I looked up.

Faith's emerald eyes were upon me, but I don't think it was me she was seeing. She was sitting, perfect and still. Her hair was pulled away from her face, which was this incredible golden brown—mulatto, Eurasian, Hispanic, some exotic foreign blend. It took a couple seconds for her to realize I was watching her, and I know this sounds completely lame, but in those few seconds I could see right into her. And God, it was sweet—beauty and sadness and mournful grace lit the fucking library, man. I couldn't look away. Then she blinked and focused and there I was, gawking, looking like the creep I was. I dropped my eyes fast, pretended to read, but I could feel her getting up, could feel her coming closer. The gorgeous girl on the bike. What I dreamed. The broken girl in the church. What I dreaded. I clutched my book in my hands like some fat kid clinging to the last Krispy Kreme in town.

A pair of black, shiny Doc Martens topped by dark jeans appeared beside my table.

"Hey," she said. Her voice was low for a girl's, but soft.

I managed to look up. She was even more delicious up close. My mom would have made note of her good posture and lack of makeup, but my eyes wandered to her shirt. It was one of ours, and Stan and I had been right—the XS did wrap nicely around this particular Jefferson girl's tits, which were small but nice, although I was sort of disgusted with myself for even noticing.

"Hey." Now it was me sitting perfectly still, it was Faith seeing right into me. I held on, maintaining eye contact, bruising my book, threatening my heart.

"I miss him," she said.

I looked away.

"I miss him." She said it again before she turned and headed for the door.

I could see the empty spot beside her where Stan should have been as I watched her go. Still. I watched her go.

AND THAT NIGHT, the night after Faith, the funniest fucking thing happened. I was alone in my room, right, just listening to tunes, mellow shit mostly—Limp Bizkit's "Behind Blue Eyes," Pearl Jam's "Better Man." Some old stuff that came to me through my parents. R.E.M.'s "Man on the Moon." Elvis Costello's plea not to be misunderstood. The entire Nirvana *Unplugged* CD. Turns out it wasn't a good idea. Even with the Trazon—one too many or one too few, I'm not really sure—the songs made me soft. Which was stupid, because I knew I had to stay hard, I knew I had no other way to do this. *This* being life, mine in particular. Still, that night, I didn't, couldn't, turn off the music.

And all of a sudden, there I am thinking about this old dude, dying. Bits of feeling and knowledge and song mixing together to become a flashing picture, a low-res MPEG video flickering on the gray screen in my head. It wasn't particularly outstanding—just an old man dying an old man's death—but afterwards I dropped to the floor. I mean, really dropped. Death fantasy or death flash— either way, the old guy completely felled me. And once down, there was no getting up. Once down, I lay there with the music going and my cheek pressing into the carpet and stared at the dust beneath my bed. I could find no way to stop or to discuss or to figure anything out. Shit, at that moment, I couldn't even see a way off the floor. I dragged air into my lungs. I expelled it. I stared at the dust. In the dangerous stillness of my own room, it took everything I had just to do that.

I lay there all night.

Like that.

And in the morning, I got up and went to school. Because that's what every teenager in America has to do, pretty much every day, September through June. No matter what. No matter how. And if the kid happens to be of the male variety? You've gotta know there's no one waiting at the front door to hear his tale of woe. Even if he had a willing listener? Or, say, a blank page right there in front of him? Real words wouldn't come. He'd tell you everything was cool. He'd tell you it was just an old man dying an old man's death.

NINE

Another night, a Friday night, end of November, the beginning of yet one more dull weekend at home. I was so bored, so blasted from hanging alone in my room, I risked heading downstairs after dinner to cozy up with the folks. They seemed pleased to have me join them for the last of the six o'clock news, which proved to be interesting viewing.

Lance Winters was all over our living room that night. I'd been wondering about him. He'd disappeared from my life a month or so back, but before that, surfer boy had been making a real effort to be there for me, after school, once, even twice a week. He'd acted like he had no hard feelings about the Super Soaker incident, was all smiles when he fell in beside me, promising to turn me into the biggest thing to ever hit town. He'd tell me how good, how profitable, it would be for me to share my story with the country, because it would be the country. Man, just the license plate thing was priceless! The exposure could change my life, and his too, could get us both out of Stokum, because he agreed with me, this place sucked, ha ha ha. But the window was closing, let's face it, we were going to be blown out of the water by the boys in Iraq if we didn't act fast.

Seemed he'd been right. Because there he was, plastered across the screen, spewing about his upcoming series on the local guys who were headed to the Gulf. He showed a couple highlights from the interviews (eight guys and their families, one per night). Judging from the clips, it seemed like everyone was pretty confident the war, if it happened, would go well. The boys were ready, were proud to be able to help out the U.S. of A. and whatnot, although the chubby girlfriends and mothers admitted they'd be pining for their men. I couldn't really get into it, even when they showed a clip of Dwight Slater's older brother Dwayne (full interview Tuesday). He'd enlisted after graduating from Jefferson last year, was only a couple years older than me, so I probably should have cared, but seriously, I just couldn't get past Lance.

Unfortunately, it was a big night for the roving-eye boys, and Lance was still in the spotlight for the next bit o' news. What with the darkening sky and his hair flapping unprofessionally in the breeze, it looked like he was coming to us live from the bandstand in McCreary Park, the chunk of green space separating the big houses on Water Street from the stores downtown.

"Oh, here we go," my mom said, with a sharp edge to her voice.

"What?"

"You missed this at the beginning. Listen."

Lance chitchatted with the station anchor for a while. I'll summarize. Apparently, a bunch of gay guys, driven out of the rest stop on Interstate 75 near the Rolland/Stokum exit, had been tooting each other's horns in the McCreary Park bandstand on a nightly basis for the past few months. After complaints from locals trying to use the park for nonsexual activities like letting their dogs shit, the police had finally raided the place. Fifteen Stokum residents, including several minors, who'd been in the swing of things last night at Blow Job Central had been arrested. Odd thing was, no names had been released. Lance and the anchorman got all revved up speculating how the sting must have netted a couple big local players—guys with enough power to keep the names locked down tight.

"Jack wasn't at work today," my dad said in this slow, speculative sort of tone.

"Mr. Kite? Your boss?" Visions of Kite standing in his purple living room blabbing about his decorator from Chicago while the missus handed out crap food in her shiny dress danced through my head.

"Yeah."

"Oh, for heaven's sake," my mom said. "Don't even go there. That's just ridiculous."

"Mr. Kite's gay?" I asked.

"No!" This from my mom. "You see what you've started? Mr. Kite is not gay. Anyway, it doesn't matter if he is."

"All I said was, he wasn't at work today. He never misses work."

"That's enough," my mom said, tacking on a disgusted, "Really!" From where I was sprawled on the floor, I couldn't see my parents on the couch behind me, but I had no problem imagining the killer look my mom was using to extinguish this particular tête-à-tête.

By this time the news anchor was gone and Lance was now solidly center stage. Having an eye for detail, he and his camera guy poked around a bit, filmed a couple limp condoms shriveled up under some bushes at one side of the bandstand and an effeminate-looking guy sitting on a nearby bench pretending to read a newspaper (I guess no one called to tell him the party was over), just in case anyone doubted the validity of the story. A few concerned citizens were pressing in on Lance, all eager to be interviewed. One of them turned out to be my good doctor's wife, "Laura, Laura Cramp," who was particularly pissed at the "perverse activities" that had been taking place within ejaculating distance of her family's home. She pushed her long blonde hair over her shoulder and her big blue eyes straight into the camera. She wanted to know why the names of those arrested hadn't been made public so the citizens of Stokum would have the information needed "to ensure *our* park and *our* community are as safe as possible for *our* children." The whole time she was blabbing, she was also absently caressing her bump of a belly, drawing attention to the fact there'd soon be one more unsafe child toddling around the condom-cluttered park.

Lance assured her he was going to pry the lid off the whole sticky business before signing off. But the feed didn't cut back to the newsroom right away, and during the delay the home viewers got a couple-second shot of Lance taking a long, lecherous look at Laura Cramp's pregnant tits. And seriously, I couldn't help expressing my thoughts.

"God, that guy is a complete asshole."

"Watch your language," my dad said behind me.

"Sorry, but he is."

"Listen, if you don't have anything nice to say, don't say anything at all."

I'd heard that one a million times. It was one of my mom's favorites, and it looked like she was just getting started. She gave me a poke with her shoe. "And while we're on the subject, Luke, I can't remember the last time—"

I didn't stick around to hear what she couldn't remember. I rolled up off the floor pretty quick, hit the stairs at a trot, with my mom calling after me, sounding tired and annoyed. But seriously, I wasn't in the mood. Turns out, neither was she.

"GET UP."

Followed by a sharp click. I squeezed my eyes shut and threw an arm across my face to block out the hellish blaze flooding my room.

"Turn that off!"

"Get up."

I lifted my head. The clock flashed 7:30. A frame of bright sunlight edged my curtains. I squinted at my mom, standing beside my bed wearing an old pair of jeans, plaid shirt and baseball cap. She wasn't dressed for the bank, which made sense when I remembered it was Saturday.

I reached out and tilted the shade on the bedside light so it wasn't completely blinding me. "What?"

"You're coming with me," she said, and marched out of the room.

"Great," I called after her. "Do you wanna tell me where we're going?" She didn't answer and I just knew the destination wasn't going to be put to a vote. My hand dropped from the lampshade to the bottle of Trazon on the bedside table. I popped off the lid, and all of a sudden it was my mom with the ESP, because she swung back into the room, hands on her hips.

"And leave those goddamn pills alone," she snapped. "I think it's about time you tried making it through a day without being stoned to the gills."

"Settle. It's not like I'm doing anything illegal. Just following doctor's orders." I wrapped my fingers around the pill bottle just to bug her.

"Well, maybe the doctor is an overprescribing idiot."

"Yeah, and maybe you're overreacting."

"Luke, I'm telling you I don't want you taking any pills today. Okay?"

"Fine," I said, keeping my voice casual, letting her know how completely out of line her anger was, how her suggestion wasn't causing me any concern.

"Fine," she snapped, and stomped out of my room again.

My mom's idea for a mother–son bonding activity was a bit bizarre. We ended up picking dead fish and garbage off the Stokum "beach" as part of the fall cleanup organized by my mom and the rest of the Lake Erie enthusiasts. Even on sunny days the sky was a dark, dirty gray along the southern shore, courtesy of Central Michigan Electric's coal-burning plant, located only a few short miles from town. My mom had told me there'd been plans to replace the thing with a wind-powered facility, but the project never got off the ground. Fearing job losses, the workers, including lots of Stokumites, had fought against it. So, to the south, the sky was gray.

I hadn't been to the beach in a long while. My parents used to bring me down a lot, to skip rocks or collect shells or whatever. And I remember, when I was little, looking across the water to the horizon and thinking it was the end of the world I was seeing. Until this one night my dad threw a big map on the kitchen table and ironed the creases from the Eastern States with his palm. I was five or six at the time, I could barely read, but regardless, my dad gave me this impromptu geography lesson in preparation for an upcoming road trip or something. He'd dragged his finger along the Erie shoreline, reading the names on the map aloud. Detroit. Toledo. Lakewood. Cleveland. Then he'd moved farther east, into pale green places I'd never heard of. "Pittsburgh," he said. Then, raising his eyebrows, "New York City."

We weren't even on the map. He had to pencil Stokum in between Detroit and Toledo, and I remember going to bed all worried and confused. Even after he showed me the map, shit, even right that day, I could look at the lake and convince myself there was nothing on the other side of all that water, that we hung alone on that skanky strip of shoreline.

Quite a few people showed up for the cleanup, including the Great Lake–loving Ms. Banks, who managed to look hot in rubber boots and a baggy fleece jacket. Even with the lovely librarian lurking, I kept to myself so I wouldn't have to engage in any taxing conversation or answer any probing questions. It was a weird morning—handling dead things, being only partway there on Trazon (to keep my mom happy I'd halved my regular morning dosage, but had stuffed a few pills into my pocket just in case things got rough at the beach), surrounded by open space and dirty air, trying hard not to think about so many things.

Like ... the fact that I'd actually had death premonitions. *Actual premonitions of death.* Two for sure. More, maybe. That day, denial was difficult. The ones I couldn't nail down, the ones with no names, were harder to write off as mental backwash left behind by the Bernoffski–Miller tag team, or figments of a video-stoked imagination, or fallout from a ramped-up obsession with death. Even without the maybes, there was no getting around the brutal reality that, for a couple of days there in October, I'd known how, and when, someone was going to die. And for the few choice seconds they were actually doing it? How I'd felt their swan songs playing inside me. Aided by a medicinally mutated mind and a knack for deceit, I'd gotten so good at pretending the premonitions and their aftershocks weren't real, I'd almost begun to believe my own twisted version of the truth. Almost.

But that day on the beach, in the gray-light sky, that fantasy just wouldn't hang. And once I acknowledged the premonitions, I had to admit how truly freaked I was, how scared, how badly I wanted this shit to stop. *Then* I had to consider the possibility that maybe, just maybe, I did share some freakoid genetic mutation with Mexican Mick. See, that's the problem with stepping up to one thing: It leads to the collapse of the next untruth, and the next, and before I knew it I was pressed up against the cold hard fact that Stan was dead.

I mean, I knew he was dead. I'd seen the body on the sidewalk. I'd done the funeral. And just in case all that slipped my mind, two, three times a week Pastor Ted was there, on the other end of the line, going on about Stan's one-way trip to paradise. So, yeah. I *knew* he was dead. It's just that I didn't believe it. Not really. Maybe I was in shock or something, but until that morning on the beach, part of me had been waiting for my friend to just show up, a huge smile plastered on his face as he explained how he'd staged the cream scene at the old 7-Eleven. Laughing his ass off at having pulled off the world's sickest joke.

And once my dead friend found me, he wouldn't let go. Then all morning it was Stan slicing through town on his board, so smooth and easy you'd think the pavement had turned to water. Stan strolling out of Jefferson's back parking lot, a basketball tucked under one arm, a beautiful girl under the other. Stan clowning in the school foyer, squeezed into a *Stokum Sucks* XS T. Stan lying in the next sleeping bag, his head thrown back in a big, easy laugh.

That particular laugh came on our one and only camping trip. Having raised all that dough with our T-shirt gig, I guess Stan and I both felt some kind of claim on the wetlands and had decided to camp out, even though the park definitely wasn't designed for overnight stays. Stan had brought most of the practical gear and I'd brought the weed. We didn't have a tent, we just lay under the stars, nestled inside the Millers' fluffy sleeping bags, serenaded by frogs, the fire we'd cooked the dogs on dying out by our feet.

We were whanging it back and forth a bit, and I'd been trying hard to get Stan to talk about Faith, maybe offer up a few choice sexual details, something to sugar up my fantasies of fantasy girl, but he kept moving the conversation in a completely different direction. He kept telling me how amazing she was, what a clear, expansive way she had of seeing the world. He told me about her huge appetite for learning, how she wanted to know everything, do everything, be everything. I watched him as he talked, and man, he looked so happy, not like hard-on happy or anything, more like completely-in-love happy, and I remember being amazed at how, lying on the hard ground in the middle of a fake swamp, he still managed to look like a *GQ* model lounging on the deck of a yacht or something.

When Stan finally stopped for air, I made another attempt to knock the conversation down to my level. "Your girlfriend's also a wee bit of a hottie."

"Yeah." He reached over and gave my shoulder a shove. My sleeping bag slid beneath me. "Don't go near her, man. I just know she'd dig you."

My head flew off the balled-up hoodie I was using for a pillow. Craning my neck, I stared at Stan. "Are you fucking joking?"

"No." He rolled on his side and propped his head on his elbow. His face was all serious, and even though we were, like, three feet apart, suddenly he felt super-close. "Don't play dumb with me, Luke. Don't think I can't see you. I see you, man. Always thinking. Always trying to figure things out. In a weird way, you're just like her." The Luke Hunter he described was, like, a million shades away from any self-portrait I might have painted. And he wasn't even finished. "And you know you're funny as hell. Here's a news flash for you: Dumb people aren't funny. At least not on purpose, anyway."

"Do you have any idea who you're even talking to?" My sleeping bag was beginning to feel a bit confining, sort of tight at the bottom, having worked itself around my legs. I gave my cocoon a couple kicks to straighten it out.

"Yeah. Yeah, I do."

Wanting to change the subject and keep Stan from guessing

that my conversational repertoire didn't normally go beyond lobbing an occasional grunt or abusive insult at my friends, I put some effort into asking him a couple of questions. "How about you? What do you want to do? After high school, I mean."

"Doctor. Probably. And you?"

"Never thought about it."

"Never thought about it!" His eyes bulged. "We're graduating in, like, two years. Time to come up with an exit strategy, buddy. Seriously. You're definitely too large to be contained by this town. You blow in math, but you're good in English, right? Remember your Seuss presentation?"

"It was retarded."

"It was hilarious. There's a reason you got an A-plus, Luke. And you wrote that story. The one Mrs. Hayward read in class, about that kid growing up in a real shit town who has, like, zero self-esteem? The one who can't talk to anyone?"

"I don't really recall." The fire, which I'd thought was pretty much out, suddenly crackled before spitting a large ember my way. It landed on my highly flammable sleeping bag, suspended above my cock by a handful of feathers and two nothing layers of poly-ester. I scrambled to free my hands—tucked into the waistband of the jeans I hadn't bothered to remove—but Stan was way quicker. He reached out and flicked the ember straight back into the fire on his first try, no problem, then carried on like saving my ass was nothing, nothing at all.

"You know the story. Where the kid starts smoking after his mother gets rolled under by the paving machine? All those images of tar? All that social alienation?"

"It's starting to sound familiar." I was suddenly very hot inside the cheap synthetic sack, and I pressed my knees against the lining, trying to create a little breathing room. When I dropped my legs back down, I saw the misshapen black circle decorating the sleeping bag below my navel, its melted edge already cooled and curled.

"I'm telling you, the story kicked."

"Mrs. Hayward just read it to embarrass me. She hates my guts."

"Don't be an asshole, man. First of all, you and I both know you're her fucking star pupil. And secondly, she read your story to inspire the rest of us. To show us what was possible." Even in the dark, I could see how his eyes glistened. "So pick up a pen, dude. Write some shit down. Send it off to a few colleges. See what happens."

"What are you? My fucking career counselor or something?"

"Nope. Just your friend, Luke. Just your friend." He didn't even flinch. He wasn't the least bit uncomfortable saying the words. Then, for no apparent reason at all, he threw his head back and laughed, the big, easy laugh.

Fucking Stan. He could do shit like that. Look people in the eye and say good, true things. Fool you into believing that everything you ever wanted was so close all you had to do was reach out and grab it. Fucking Stan. Busting with laughter. Thrilling to life. Making it all look so goddamn effortless.

WHEN WE TOOK A BREAK for lunch, I ended up talking to my mom and Ms. Banks (you can call me Kate—outside of school). I found out she was married to the big black guy who owned Sam's, the independent music store in Rolland—the artsy college town just up the highway from Stokum—where I bought all my CDs, which explained her above-average knowledge of rock musicians vis-à-vis most hottie librarians.

I had half a tuna sandwich stuffed in my mouth when "Kate" asked if I'd like to design the shirts for the One Drum music festival in April. One Drum was this big outdoor event, held every spring in Rolland to raise money for local food banks. I knew Sam's was one of the main sponsors, because Stan and I had sold shirts for Hank there last year, and Sam's logo had been plastered everywhere.

My mom acted all surprised by Kate's offer, like they hadn't preplanned the whole thing. Apparently she was oblivious to my mouthful of food, because she kept nudging me and saying, "Well, Luke, what do you think? What do you think?" Finally, to shut her up, I gagged out a "That'd be cool," spitting a huge hunk of tuna onto Kate's boot in the process. Always graceful, she tipped her foot nonchalantly and the saliva-slippery fish slid onto the sand.

The day on the shore wasn't a major blast, but I have to admit it was a change from being stuffed in my room. I was pretty happy with the new T-shirt gig, and despite Stan invading my space, I'd managed to forget the pills in my pocket. But I can't give my mom all the credit for getting me to kick my prescription drug habit. I went back to the full-dosage drill on Monday, when I headed to school.

But the Trazon just wasn't cutting it anymore; no, it wasn't even coming close to stopping life from kicking the total shit out of me on a fairly regular basis. I figured I'd probably developed some sort of immunity to it, some resistance or something, I didn't really know. Whatever it was, that Monday morning I wasn't even halfway to Jefferson when the trouble started. When I came across the bird. Lying on the sidewalk, just a little fart of a thing, half-frozen, one red-tipped wing cocked at a crazy angle, one yellow eye blind. Its legs were twigs. Its legs were a complete joke. Still, I couldn't step around it. I couldn't move past it. Even with a bitter wind pushing me along and a couple fresh pills cushioning the march, I had to squat down and run a finger up the bird's soft belly. And when I did, it quivered, man, a quiver that shot up my arm like a fucking electric shock.

My hand jumped away. The bird's clawed feet contracted then released, the softest scratching noise ever, a stick-drawing scraping across cold concrete.

I don't know where I found the courage to pick the bird up, because usually I'm not good with shit like this. Normally, with only a bit of bite in my gut, I'd have pretended it didn't exist, that I wasn't leaving it behind for some neighborhood cat or some heartless dude's big boot or some practical guy's steady hands. But this time I did it, I scooped it up, cradled it in my palms. It was the bird's lightness, its near weightlessness, that got me. I straightened the broken wing then gently pressed my thumb to its toothpick rib cage. There, like some fragile miracle, a pulse, a heartbeat.

I'm not sure how long I crouched on that strip of sidewalk, freezing my sac off, waiting for that bird to croak. Thinking what? That my just being there would help it along? That I was special? That it was my duty to watch it go? To witness its death? To feel its life?

It was a strange brew of mercy and madness that had my thumb moving from the bird's chest, had both thumbs moving to its neck. And I squeezed it tight so I could press down hard, hard enough to feel the snap of hollow bone, the last beat of unsung song.

Breaking its neck was easy. Killing it was hard.

Seriously. It was pretty messed. How, after everything, one little shit of a bird felt so huge. How it blew me to pieces. How, two eyes blind, it made me bawl.

I DIDN'T GET ANY FARTHER that day. What I did was stagger back home—pitching the stiffy bird over a fence somewhere along the way—before falling into the old homestead, where, wham, I caught an eyeful of myself in the front hall mirror. I was shuffling along like Ozzy, man, all slack-jawed, with one hand trailing the wall to maintain balance, tears streaming down my face. It wasn't a good look. It wasn't a look that said "totally together" or even "completely spaced out." What it said was "freaked out." Freaked way the fuck out.

So I dumped the rest of the pills down the can and decided to take control. One of the first things I did was grab a clean piece of paper and a pen and start a list. I put Stan on the first line. To the right of his name I wrote the time and date of his death: 8:37 A.M., October 8, 2002. About a third of the line was still empty, so I made another column and jotted down a few details: skateboard, van, 7-Eleven. Underneath Stan went Mr. Bernoffski along with his stats. Then, what the hell, there was a lot more page, so I added the maybes. No names or times or good solid details, just the suicide chick, just the old dude who'd pinned me to the floor of my room. Shit, I even threw down the bird.

Sitting at my desk beneath the taped-up posters of my rock gods, holding that list in my hand, I started to see things a lot clearer. For the first time I thought I had some clue which way this whole thing was headed. I hadn't turned on any music when I'd sat down, and the house was perfectly quiet. I could hear my breathing, could feel the rise and fall of my chest, gases seeping across nothing boundaries. I watched the warm CO_2 ripple the paper in my hand and, yeah, I was pretty sure I knew how things would end up.

Still, I was a coward. I didn't have the balls to put my name on the list. Instead, I shoved the paper into my bedside table drawer, right on top of the phone number I'd never bothered throwing out. Right on top of the handout from my buddy's funeral.

TEN

I stared down the tunnel of my hands and on through the cold glass of Delaney's sliding door. I shouldn't have been surprised to find the basement still looking like an advertisement for a couple dozen of the carnal sins. Stuffing leaked from a fresh rip in the couch, a multitude of empty beer cans poked from underneath its ratty fringe and there looked to be a hash pipe resting precariously on one arm. Center stage, a bag of Lay's had spilled its guts and a halo of chip crud decorated the dirty carpet.

My breath was fogging up the glass, so I had to wipe a spot clean to see the La-Z-Boy in the corner. I wasn't expecting to see Stan sitting there. I'd gotten past that particular delusion. Still, looking at the recliner, which was occupied, I felt the pre-concert buzz that had carried me over to Delaney's evaporate.

Fang was perched on the edge of the seat with his head hanging down and his hands clenched between his knees, as if he was praying to the crusty beer stain on the floor or trying hard not to yack or something. Shit, even dead, Stan could have mustered up more energy than the body in that chair. I didn't knock. I just stood there staring. The stereo wasn't even on. Or the TV. Just Fang, hunched up alone in his skanky basement.

Fucking Fang. Fucking *Stan*. God, I swear if he'd been standing in front of me at that moment, I would have killed him all over again. I mean, how was I going to escape *this* without him? How was I supposed to become some great guy, the one he'd dangled in front of me, without him to show me how it was done? Jesus Christ. I had to press my forehead against the frosty glass, had to deep-freeze my brain and ice down my anger before I could even lift my arm and rap on the door.

When my knuckles hit, Fang's head snapped up. His eyes were wide and startled, and it took a while for him to even look behind the knocking. He finally spotted me, and a pained smile spread across his face, but he didn't make a move, he just sat there nodding. It wasn't until I grabbed the handle and shook the door that he finally clued in.

Coming across the room, Fang looked scrawnier and more heroine-junkie-ish than ever. Even with the long hair, the big dark circles under his eyes were evident, and I saw how his hand shook as he unlocked the door. I think even Steven Tyler would have been a little disappointed at just how bad Fang looked. The only thing about my buddy that wasn't completely messed was his shirt. It was new. It was a Hilfiger. Ultra-fresh, ultra-red-and-white. Ultra-sharp creases racing-striped the sleeves.

"What's with the shirt, man?" I asked as I stepped inside, but if Fang heard me, he didn't let on.

"Hey, Luke," he said, wrapping his arms across his chest and hunching up against the blast of cold that followed me inside. He watched me out the corner of his eye as I stamped around trying to warm up. If I hadn't known him so well, I'd have thought he was uneasy about seeing me after everything that had happened, but, like I've said before, Fang had looked at everyone sideways since he was a kid, trying to cover up his teeth and his shyness and his bloodshot eyes and whatever else he was trying to hide.

Besides, we'd already discussed our recent hassles. After kicking my Trazon habit, I'd become aware of just how rank it was to have zero friends and I'd finally broken down and called up Fang. I'd been pretty up-front about what I thought of him spilling his guts to Lance, told him I was super-pissed. He'd said, yeah, well, he could understand that, but about the interview, seriously, he didn't have a choice, the reporter was fucking pushy, had practically held him hostage inside the van until he agreed to talk. I knew where he was coming from, but still, I suggested it would have helped me out if he'd given a definitive no to surfer boy.

"Yeah, well, I've always had a bit of trouble saying no," he'd said, and we'd both laughed at that because it was the total truth. Then I'd mentioned the extra concert ticket and he'd said cool, he liked the Peppers, even though he probably didn't. So there I was a couple days later hanging with Fang, who, although obviously stoned, also seemed sort of tense, which was unusual. Normally, when Delaney was stoned, he wasn't much of anything.

"You okay?" I asked, trying to get a good look at him, which was never easy.

"Yeah. Why?" His arms were still locked across his chest and he was shifting from foot to foot.

"You look, I don't know, kind of tight."

"I'm fine." He gave me a rigid smile. "You want to smoke before we head out?"

I shrugged, said maybe we should just get going. I hadn't taken off my jacket and I was definitely feeling edgy in the basement with the unoccupied easy chair.

Fang didn't seem to notice. He grabbed his tin of weed, settled himself on the couch and started rolling. I sat at the opposite end, didn't even realize I was jiggling my knees until he shot me one of his rare direct looks, letting me know I was hindering his creation of the perfect joint, which was one thing he took seriously. When he'd finished, he held out his masterpiece so I could take a look— tight white cylinder, small cardboard filter inserted at one end— then sparked it up. Like usual, we didn't say much while we smoked, just settled back and let the dope work its magic like it had a thousand times before.

I did what I normally did when I was in the basement getting stoned, which was ponder all the stuff Fang and I used to do before we dedicated ourselves to drugs. Bombing around town on our bikes, looking for shit to climb. Filling shoe boxes full of pictures of ourselves high on something other than weed.

As far as I knew, the last time Fang ever climbed anything was at the end of freshman year, one day prior to this mammoth math test. He and I had been dicking around in the cafeteria, trying to study, and we'd both been in serious danger of flunking. We started going on about how much easier it would be if we just had a copy of the fucking test. We knew where the tests were: stacked up and ready to go in the supply room at the front of Mr. Thorp's class. And given that we had math last period, we also knew that, while Thorp always locked the classroom after school, he usually left the supply room open.

We waited until that night before making our way back to Jefferson. From outside the building, it took a while to figure out where the classroom was, but when we did, Fang started to climb. The school is made of this phony stone, and the mortar joints are deep and wide, and it took him all of about fifteen seconds to get to the second floor. He crawled through the window at the back of the class, the one I'd casually unlocked before final bell. A minute later he dropped the test out the window. It floated down, right into my outstretched arms, like some beautiful white bird coming in for a landing. Right away, I started checking out the questions. I never even saw Fang climb back out the window. When he called me, he was already on the roof.

"Hey!"

I craned my neck and there he was, three stories up, rocking back and forth on the ledge like he was standing on a curb or something.

"Think I should go for it?" he shouted, leaning out over the edge and glancing down.

This wasn't new. The last few times we'd been out on a climb, Fang had turned into one of those *Jackass* dudes and had started jumping from higher and higher up whatever he happened to be clinging to at the time. I guess it gave him a thrill, but seriously, it scared the shit out of me. I mean, I was used to seeing him get higher and higher and smaller and smaller. He made it look so easy, I'd never been too freaked. I didn't believe in Fang falling. But he was a climber, not a jumper, and I knew he could only leap from so high before his gravity-sensitive superpowers failed him.

"What are you doing?" I whisper-screamed. "Get down here!"

"Am I awesome or what?" His laughter came in bursts. He raised his arms above his head and howled.

"Fang, shut up! Get the—"

"Tell me I'm awesome, Luke." He was practically yelling. "Tell me I'm fucking awesome."

"You're fucking crazy! And this isn't fucking funny. Now get down, Fang."

He spread his arms wide and dropped his head so he was looking right at me. I could see the toes of his shoes, flat and dark, hanging over the ledge, but I couldn't see his face.

"I'm so fucking awesome." He laughed this weird, hysterical laugh and rocked forward, and God, I was sure he was going to swan-dive off the roof. "Don't you just love me?" He stopped rocking. "Tell me you love me." This time he said it so softly I could barely hear him.

"Fang. What the fuck … Fang."

We stood motionless, caught in a long, freaky silence, locked together across three stories of night air. Then Fang stepped off the roof.

His arms circled backwards and his knees were bent and he looked like he was jumping off the high board at the Y. He landed in a bush, was laughing in a wild, pained sort of way when I dragged him out. He got up and hobbled around for a while, all hunched over, howling and moaning like some injured werewolf. Then he collapsed on the grass, curled into a ball and started gasping. I thought maybe he had cramps from all the laughing, but I wasn't sure he hadn't punctured a lung, and I was trembling as I bent down to check him out.

He was bawling, full-out bawling. I kind of panicked and started shaking him, asking him if he needed help, but he pushed me away, told me to leave him alone, so I did. He stayed down, rocking and crying, for another five minutes at least before he got up and we walked home like nothing had happened. Except for a bit of a limp, it didn't seem like he was even hurt.

We both ended up acing the test, but that episode kind of took the excitement out of climbing and pilfering tests and pretty much everything else. Soon the only thing we had any fun doing together was getting high, which seemed a lot less dangerous than hurling yourself off a building in the middle of some mental breakdown. I guess that's how we worked our way into full-time-stoner status, how we ended up where we were at that moment, sitting in Fang's basement, smoking up on his refugee couch.

We were already passing a small roach back and forth by the time I noticed the empty shelf under the TV.

"Where's your DVD player?" I asked. Fang had been the last kid in Michigan to get a player. His mom had finally bought him one last Christmas with some of the back pay she'd received after convincing some doctor that, seriously, she had a repetitive strain injury. She was now on long-term disability from Kalbro, where she'd worked on the line for fifteen years or something like that. Fang claimed there was nothing really wrong with her and the only repetitive strain injury she had was from bringing a bottle to her lips one too many times. Still, he'd been happy with the new equipment.

Fang coughed up a lungful of smoke and shook his head, staring at the empty shelf in disgust. "Someone stole it."

"Someone stole it?"

"Yeah. One of the guys."

"Are you joking?"

"Do I look like I'm joking?" At that moment Fang looked like he could barely slide off the couch let alone come up with some convoluted lie to amuse a friend. "That's why the door was locked. Someone stole the fucking thing."

"Who?"

"Probably Dwight. I think he pawned it. He showed up with a big bag of shit a couple days later. Was in a pretty generous mood, too."

"Fucking Slater." Now it was me shaking my head in disgust. "He would." I took a minute before glancing over and asking the next question. "So, I take it he's not hanging out here anymore?"

"Nope. None of them are."

I let the news that I hadn't been missing any parties settle in. "So what have you been doing?"

"Hanging out. You know. Nothing much." Fang shook his head so his hair fell over his eyes. "Hey, did you see Slater's brother on TV the other night?"

"I saw a clip. Not the whole deal."

"Did you hear what he said when that asshole reporter asked him what the most important thing he was taking to the Gulf was?"

"No, what?"

Fang readjusted the joint between his nails, which he kept a little long for the purpose, had another toke and held it out for me. I waved him off. He took his time exhaling. "Wet Ones," he said through the smoke.

"Wet Ones?" I laughed. "I thought he might have said his gun."

"Nope. Wet Ones. To keep himself tidy."

"God, you should definitely kick the shit out of Dwight."

"Yeah, but it could have been my mom."

We guffawed over that for a while, although the idea of Fang's mom trading his Christmas gift for booze wasn't much of a stretch.

"So why don't you kick the shit out of *her*?"

Fang sucked what was left out of the joint, crushed the roach into the ashtray, then gazed at me in this really long, steady way, like he'd finally gotten up the nerve to let me take a genuine look at him in his crispy new shirt. "Luke," he said slowly, "do I look like I could kick the shit out of either one of them?" We laughed again, because we were stoned and because it was the total truth and because we both knew it wasn't funny at all.

Our hee-hawing was kind of cut short by a glassy smash from above, followed by a loud bang as something heavy hit the floor overhead. My eyes flew to the ceiling, slapped with dirty white paint and a fresh, ringing silence. "What was that?"

"Nothing," Fang said flatly, his face blank.

"That wasn't nothing, Fang. That wasn't fucking nothing."

"Fine," he said in a pissed-off tone. "I'll go check it out."

I started to push myself off the couch, but Fang, already two steps up, pointed a finger at me and told me to stay where I was. I have to admit, I was sort of relieved. For the past couple of years I'd avoided climbing those stairs, afraid of running into his wasted mother or her wasting absence in equal doses.

Fang was back in a few minutes, his eyes still blank and bloodshot. When I asked him what happened, there was no long, steady stare. He barely even looked at me.

"Like I told you, *Luke*." He said my name hard so I'd know not to push any further. "It was nothing."

ELEVEN

An hour out of the basement, Fang and I trudged along the dark corridor of road cutting through the wetlands park on the outskirts of town. Thoughts of a bigger, brighter, more musical world on the other side of the park pushed us along, until we were backing up the I-75 on-ramp, our little frozen cocktail-weenie thumbs struggling for attention beyond the Stokum city limits. It was after seven o'clock by this time and, being early December, already midnight black. The lights of the cars tooling up the ramp blinded us as we shuffled backwards through the snow that had started falling, like, two minutes after we'd left Delaney's in our lightweight concert garb. The rotten weather and the bang in the basement right before we'd left had pretty much killed the fun we'd had going on, and behind me, Fang was stomping his feet and bitching. We were never going to get a ride, he was freezing his ass off, his feet were fucking soaked—all the usual cold-weather complaints. I was less vocal about the crap weather, was more concerned with how close and how fast the cars were ripping past us.

I guess, ever since I sat down and made the list of dead men, I'd started thinking about dying. I mean really thinking about it. I hadn't had a personalized death premonition or anything like that, but I knew that sooner or later it would be my turn to go. And given the present setting—a dark, treacherous bend of blacktop—it was pretty easy to come up with something good. A car heading into the slippery curve a tad too fast. Time freeze-framing as the guy behind the wheel locked eyes with the hitchhiker—trapped in the head-lights and unable to dodge the thousand pounds of steel sliding straight at him. The scene would unlock with the quick, heavy thud of a body on a hood, then warp-speed into a scrambled collage of bent limbs and black pavement and broken glass. The driver would scream as the hitchhiker, and maybe his friend, disappeared under the car, crunching beneath the heavy snow-packed wheels.

Fang, still grumbling about the frigid temperatures, had no clue. How I'd squeeze my eyes shut and choke down a scream every time a set of headlights nailed us. How I wrestled with death on the edge of the slick winter pavement. Turns out I shouldn't have worried, because it was always just a push of cold air, a splash of icy slush and a fresh "Fuck" from Fang that hit me as car after car swept past and onto the highway.

When a big black rig finally pulled over, brakes wheezing, engine rumbling, I ran for it, leaving the nasty death scenario stalled at the side of the road. And there was no arguing over who would do the talking. That had been decided about ten years previous, so of course it was me climbing onto the running board and yanking open the passenger door.

The trucker, wearing a welcoming smile, the standard-issue baseball hat and a plaid shirt, was pint-sized behind the wheel. He leaned forward and turned down the folksy shit spewing from the radio. "Where you headed?" he asked in this weird high-pitched voice.

"Detroit."

"I'm going to Windsor. Jump in."

Fang and I climbed aboard. Pretty much right off, it was evident the driver was a talker.

"Nice weather for hitching," he said with a laugh, which, seriously, I can only describe as jolly.

"Yeah. Thanks for picking us up. We were freezing out there."

"I bet!"

He opened his window, stretched out a stubby arm and cleared the snow from his side mirror. As he waited for an opening in the traffic, I checked him out, and man, he couldn't have been over five feet. He was pulled in tight to the wheel, and it was lucky the driver's seat was split from the passenger's, otherwise it would have been a long, uncomfortable ride for Fang and me, pretzeled against the dash. Since we had some room, Fang took advantage. He stretched right out, leaning his head against the cushioned wall of the cab and pretending to nod off, a common avoidance-of-conversation-with-strangers tactic of his, one which left me to entertain Shorty.

"So what's taking you to Dee-troit on a night like this?" he asked, shooting me a friendly grin.

"Concert."

He looked pleased to hear it. "Really? I'm a music lover myself. Who you seeing?"

"Red Hot Chili Peppers."

"Never heard of them. That's probably no big surprise. Don't have any kids your age. Don't have any kids at all, for that matter. Doctors tried some experimental drugs on me when I was eight, nine years old, so I'd gain a bit of height. Technically, I'm classified as a dwarf, but I'm on the tall end of the scale. Had a hell of a time getting my commercial license, but I can drive a rig as well as the next guy, big or small. The buggers finally had to give it to me, no rule against it when I applied, although they've changed that now. Any-hoo, the drugs messed up my reproductive apparatus. Don't get me wrong, everything's still functioning, but, well, not to put too crude a point on it, I'm shooting blanks, as they say."

I pretended not to hear him. "It's Exit 81, in Auburn Hills, just before you get to Detroit, actually."

"Right." He reached forward and fiddled with the radio before snapping it off and giving me another warm grin. He went on a bit then, filling me in on the rest of his limp life history. I thought I was going to be able to settle back and just let him roll, but he wrapped things up pretty fast, then set his sights on me.

"So, what should I call you?" he asked, giving me a formal sort of nod.

"Luke. And you?"

"Little Bob. You hitchhike often, Luke?"

"Nope."

"Your parents know you're hitching?"

"Nope."

"Kid your age probably shouldn't be hitching."

"Guy your size probably shouldn't be picking up hitchers."

Little Bob let rip another jolly laugh. "You're probably right about that. But I pick up a lot of people and I'm still here to tell about it." He raised both hands from the wheel and waved them at me, demonstrating just how "here" he was, before remembering the rules of the road and grabbing the wheel. "Truth is," he said, swinging the truck into the passing lane, "I like people."

He nodded, smiling and waiting and smiling some more. He looked so pleased with himself, I felt obliged to hold up my end of the conversation.

"That right?" I said, sounding as bored as possible.

"Yes, I do."

"Personally, I think a lot of people are assholes." I managed a bit of enthusiasm for that line, backed up as it was by my experience with pretty much the entire Stokum population.

"Well, sure, there are some of those out there. But you know what I find?" He paused, beaming, and I could just tell he was getting ready to lay some impotent elfin wisdom upon me. "I find pretty much everybody has some good in 'em. You look long enough, you'll find a bit of holiness. I'll tell you something else. People who make good choices in life, they unleash that holiness on the world. Great men know how to do this, fearless men. And once in a while someone really spectacular comes along who reveals the godliness of all humanity. Once in a damn long while."

He glanced over at me, to see if I was listening. I pretended I wasn't. Ignoring safe trucking practices once more, Little Bob fixed his eyes on me. "You want to play a game?" he asked.

"A game?" I made those two words sound exactly like an "Are you fucking serious?" four.

"Yeah, a game."

Bob was starting to mildly freak me out. "You don't seem like a real trucker."

"I'm real." He lifted one hand off the wheel and held it out in front of me, palm skyward. "Take my hand," he said.

"*What?*"

"Take my hand. It's part of the game."

"I'm not holding your frigging hand."

"I don't want you to *hold* my hand. I want you to rest your hand in mine. I'm a bit of a mind reader, see? Just put your hand here and I'll tell you what you're afraid of. Then we can move on."

"Move on? Move on to what?" By this point I was fairly certain I was about to get a dose of just how much Little Bob *really* liked people.

"Just take my hand …"

"Listen, I'm not afraid of anything, okay? Can we just talk about something else?"

"Not afraid of anything?" he said, acting all surprised, shooting his eyebrows up under the peak of his ball cap. "Well, there's always a first."

"And I don't believe in mind reading and shit like that." My hands were safely stowed in the pockets of my jacket, out of reach of Little Bob, but under the dash my feet were twitching.

"Doesn't matter if you believe or not."

Fang shifted beside me and let out a low moan. I gave him a shove, trying to wake him up so Tiny Trucker would have someone else to harass, but Fang actually seemed to be sleeping.

Little Bob jiggled his hand in front of me. It looked soft and pudgy, was no bigger than a kid's. "Come on," he said, his eyes darting from me to the windshield. "It'll only take a second. And I concentrate best when I block out external stimuli, so I wouldn't waste any time if I were you." He flashed me a crazy smile, closed his eyes and started humming. The truck rocketed blindly up the snow-covered highway.

"Watch where you're going, for God's sake." My attempts at keeping the terror from my voice were unsuccessful, but Bob just pumped his hand up and down, kept his lids locked tight. The truck was still solidly in the middle lane, but through the flurry of flakes the taillights ahead seemed to be getting clearer and brighter as we gained on the car in front. And I could see my name on the list: *Luke Hunter. December 4, 2002. Killed in weather-related traffic accident.* There'd be no mention of the tall, reckless dwarf behind the wheel.

"Give me your hand," he said.

And I did. I put my hand on his. There was no freaky electric shock. It was warm and dry, just like it looked. I watched his face. His smile widened an inch or two before he gave his arm a little wobble and lifted his lids. I snatched my hand back and shoved it into my pocket.

"That wasn't funny," I snapped.

"No, it wasn't." He squinted into the storm. "Good Christ, it's coming down."

"Yeah, well, it's easier to notice shit like that when you've got your eyes open."

"Good point." He chuckled as he reached around the wheel and flipped a switch. The wipers slapped faster, trying to keep up with the fat, chunky flakes bombarding the windshield. Then, for the first time since I got in the truck, Little Bob was quiet. The cab must have been well insulated, because I couldn't hear the wind outside at all. We rode for a while listening to only the low, blanketed hum of the engine and the rhythmic snap of the wipers, until I couldn't take the fun and games any longer.

"So?" I asked. "What's my big fear factor?"

"Well," he said, dropping his voice an octave or two so he sounded all serious, "like a lot of people, you're afraid of being in a vehicle when someone's driving with their eyes shut." He let out a whoop, thinking he was quite a riot.

"You're fucking hilarious, you know that? You could have killed us." Then, in a pouty, pissed-off voice, "My friend just died, you know."

"I'm sorry to hear that." It was light and earnest, the way he said it, like he just knew there was more to come.

And I barely even hesitated. "And here's something that'll blow your mind. I knew it was going to happen. Knew everything. Every frigging detail."

"Ahh. Really?" He brightened at this bit of news, like a bulb all lit up for Christmas. "Thought you didn't believe in that stuff."

"I don't."

"But you have a gift."

"A gift?" I spit out a laugh. "It's a fucking curse, is what it is."

"Suppose, like a lot of things, it's all how you look at it."

"Yeah, well, whatever way I look at it, it sucks."

"Then my advice to you is this: Keep looking. It's like the assholes—eventually you'll find something good."

"Yeah, right. Whatever." I checked out Fang. He was snoring softly, and I knew it was for real because his mouth was unbuckled, which put the tusks on display, something he'd never allow if he was even semiconscious. "Want to give him a go?" I asked, jerking my head at Fang.

Little Bob shook his head. "No need. I could tell the minute I laid eyes on him what he was afraid of."

"What's that?"

"Everything. And nothing."

When we pulled off the interstate a while later, Fang woke up instantly and jumped right out, but for some reason I stayed put. It was warm in the truck and I guess I just didn't have any big desire to hop out into the cold night. I rested my head on the back of the seat and closed my eyes, but even like that I could tell Little Bob was smiling beside me, waiting and smiling and watching.

Finally I came up with something good. "You know, what I don't get is why. Why this is happening to me."

"Why *not* you, Luke? Why *not* you?" He put a bit of heat behind those words. "That's the question you should be asking yourself."

I rolled my head to the side and looked at him. "You think so?"

"I do." He nodded solemnly. "Now, go on. Get outta here." Tiny Trucker was back to friendly. "Go unleash yourself on Dee-troit."

TWELVE

The warm-up band, Queens of the Stone Age, already had the crowd jumping by the time Fang and I shoved our way to the periphery of the mosh pit. It was hot and smoky—every time the lights panned the audience, the big dope cloud was evident—but we had some room where we were. I raised my arms and howled, but the stoner-metal tunes must have seriously connected with Fang, because he melted into the throbbing mass of bodies and was gone. When we reestablished contact during the break, he looked pretty wiped out, was all sweaty and shit, and his breathing was kind of ragged. He said he could use a drink, but I told him there was no way I was losing my spot, so we stayed put and let the crowd fold in around us.

The Peppers' fans were crotch-to-ass tight when the first searing chords of "Give It Away" ripped through the Palace. Everyone went wild, pogo-ing up and down, both hands raised in the rocker salute. Flea, the bassist, was phenomenal, and the front man, Anthony Kiedis, was a cyclone, lunging and pacing and whirling in every direction, belting out the lyrics. Four huge screens hung above the stage, rotating flashing psychedelic images, but about halfway through the song I just closed my eyes and leaned back, pounding the killer rhythms on my gut. Standing there in the dark with the music running through me, propped up by a thousand other bodies, I disappeared into the greater, wilder, more joyful whole flooding the Palace, the perfect place to be.

Unfortunately, the band was only partway through the set, had just charged into "Can't Stop," when I was slammed from my sweet spot. Someone hit me from behind, hard, knocking me into the guy ahead. A second later, clumsy hands grabbed at my shoulders, trying to haul me down. I staggered under the weight, felt my knees buckling, before the hands slipped away.

I managed to turn around. Fang was on the floor, crumpled in a fetal ball position, propped upright on one dark leg. His face was wild-eyed scared, his mouth a huge dark oval. I could see he was choking, gasping for air that just wasn't coming. I grabbed for him, but the leg he was leaning against jerked, knocking him sideways and out of my reach. The crowd shifted. The forest of jeans between me and Fang thickened. I could see his arm stretched out on the concrete, could see the big black boot come down on his hand and then another one on his shoulder, and then everyone was pushing and tripping over him and I was screaming for them to stop, but no one could hear me above the wailing guitars and I was pushing back as hard as I could because I knew Fang was getting trampled. Finally, some guy clued in and made a dive for the body on the floor. He caught hold of the back of Fang's jacket and I shoved my way toward him and together we jerked upward until Fang was wedged between us and we started dragging him away.

We pinballed through the crowd, pissing everyone off. People were swinging at us as we pushed by. The guy helping me was taking most of the abuse because he was in the lead, turned half

to miss the ragged knuckles or the big, dusty footprint stamped on the front of his new shirt. He took a couple gulps before handing the bottle back, slick with sweat. I wiped my hands on my jeans and tried to clean it up a bit before offering it to Faith. I thought she'd wave off the raunch backwash, but she took the bottle from me and raised it to her lips. I pretended not to watch as she tilted her head back and poured the rest of the water gracefully down her throat.

"Great night, huh?" she said when she'd finished, rolling her eyes.

"Yeah, totally." I managed to keep the shake from my voice. Fang, trying his best to be social, spit on the floor between his feet.

"You guys on something?"

"Nothing much. Smoked a bit of weed."

She nodded toward the stadium. "Were you in there when it happened?"

"Yep," I said. "Right at the front." I eyed the ceiling, but I couldn't hold back the big, embarrassing sigh.

"Must have been scary."

"Yep," I said again.

Faith leaned her head against the wall and closed her eyes. Her lips were full and wet from the water, and her dark hair, which was all wild and kinky from the heat, glowed red in the exit-sign light. I couldn't not stare.

When she started talking, the band was really wailing, and she sort of had to yell and I sort of had to lean a bit closer—mint and music—so I wouldn't miss anything. Apparently she'd driven up from Stokum with her older sister, Mia. (I knew her. She was a senior at Jefferson, and was almost as delicious as Faith.) They'd met Mia's boyfriend at the Palace. Andy, or maybe Sandy, was at university in Detroit, and Mia had had a big fight with her parents right before leaving about spending the night at his place. The three of them got split up coming in and Faith had spent most of the concert looking for the other two. She'd checked the balcony, the bathrooms, the floor, etc., etc. She thought they'd purposely dumped her and were halfway to the boyfriend's place to have sex, which sounded about right.

"She's completely in love with this guy. The only reason she even came to the concert was to see him. I'm the big Peppers fan. I bought the tickets a long time ago." She paused. "For me and Stan."

"Really? My tickets were for Stan and me, too." And I shouted out the story about T-shirt-shop Hank. I hadn't told Fang where I got the tickets and I looked over to see how he was taking the news that he was second string to a dead guy, but he was still getting it on with the bag and definitely seemed more concerned about remaining conscious than being my lousy backup date.

Faith and I were both quiet for a while after that, staring at the blank wall opposite. Maybe she was just listening to the band, but I figured the talk of Stan had probably got her thinking about him and how he died and how I was involved, and I sat perfectly still, trying to melt into the concrete blocks behind me. It barely even registered that the music, distorted by the narrow corridor into thick, echoing noise, was "Scar Tissue," one of my favorite tunes.

When the song ended and the crowd started cheering, Faith stood up. I could just imagine how unworthy of applause Fang and I probably seemed to her right then, and I waited, motionless, to see what polite exit strategy she'd use to slip back into her better, more beautiful world.

She slid her fingertips into the front pockets of her jeans. "So, how'd you get here?" she asked.

I shielded my eyes with my hand, as if in that dim hallway I was trying to shade myself from the sun. "We hitched. Shouldn't be too difficult to get back," I said, making things easy for her.

She pulled a key from her pocket and dangled it above me. "Come on," she said in that low, sweet voice of hers. "I've got a car. I'll drive you home."

THIRTEEN

Fang and his bag crashed in the back of Faith's red Sunbird, parked a couple slushy football fields from the Palace. While our driver started up the engine, I did the gentlemanly thing and scraped the six inches of fresh snow off the windows. And I know it was completely insane, but when I cleared the windshield on the driver's side and saw Faith watching me through the glass, I felt like a kid who'd just pulled the wrapping off some coveted Christmas gift. I was less excited, however, when I brushed the snow from the back window and saw Fang's ass crack climbing out the top of his jeans.

By the time I hit the passenger seat, the car was already warm, and it didn't take us long to slip-slide our way out of the lot. It was a little before eleven o'clock by this time and Faith was worried. She didn't have her night license, wasn't supposed to drive after midnight, and, given the weather, we figured it was going to take way more than an hour to get back to Stokum. The plows were out and the roads had been cleared, but the snow was coming so thick and fast there was nothing but two dark grooves in an endless sea of white when we pulled onto the interstate. Most of the cars were taking it easy in the right lane, but the big rigs kept barreling by, shooting up walls of slush that hit the windshield so hard we jumped every time.

"Geez," Faith kept saying, leaning forward, squinting into the storm, both hands squeezing the wheel. "I hate those trucks. I can hardly see the road."

"We got a ride up in a truck," I said. "It feels safe sitting up there, above the traffic."

"It's sort of the opposite down here."

Unable to compete with the flurry of flakes rushing at the windshield, the brake lights ahead of us faded out, leaving us alone in a tight white blizzard. When they did reappear, they came back as big red disks glowing a few feet in front of us. Faith jumped on the brakes. The Sunbird skidded along the slick pavement as she wrestled the wheel, trying to keep us on the road and in our lane and away from the car in front. I kept telling her what an awesome job she was doing, and she was, but if anything, the storm kept getting worse. The snow had turned to freezing rain and the windshield was icing up. We crawled along for another fifteen, twenty minutes, but we were still a long way from home when another transport blew by, leaving us shuddering in its wake, and Faith finally said screw it and took the next exit off the highway.

We hardly knew where we were by that time, figured we were somewhere near Monroe, but the exit sure as shit wasn't a main one. We'd ended up on some small, nowhere road—which probably shouldn't have bothered Stokumites such as ourselves, but seriously, the thing hadn't even been plowed. Besides the lone bulb dangling from a pole at the end of the off-ramp, there weren't any lights at all. It was in this dull puddle of yellow that we figured out we did not have a phone. (My hopping social life didn't exactly warrant that kind of connectivity, cell phone bills would have seriously cut into Fang's drug fund and apparently, before going off to get laid, Mia had failed to hand over the one she shared with Faith.)

There was no way we were risking a return to the highway, so we hung a left and headed east, toward the lake, thinking there might be something that way, a restaurant or maybe a resort, where we could call for help. We crossed the overpass. On the other side of the highway, the forest straddling the road closed around us.

We tunneled into the swirling white blackness, listening to the beat of the fan working to defrost the windshield and the odd airy crinkle coming from the bag in the back. The radio spewed static. Faith kept the car in what looked to be the middle of the road, cutting her own path through the snow. We went a couple slow, dark miles without seeing another vehicle or any welcoming road-side establishment. I was thinking maybe we should just pull over and wait out the storm—which led to me fantasizing about an emergency kit in the trunk complete with blankets, candles, a couple condoms, and a small pup tent for Fang—when I saw this faint red glow leaking from the forest ahead.

"Look," Faith said, "there's something up there. Please, God, let it be open."

We putted into the light of a flickering sign announcing that we had arrived at the Red Carpet In_ and, yes, there was Vaca_cy. The unshoveled parking lot was deserted except for one snow-covered car and a couple truck cabs. We skidded to a stop in front of the office and Faith cut the engine. She was only half kidding as she made a show of prying her hands off the wheel. "God, that was fairly tense."

"Yeah. Fairly. Totally. But you did awesome," I said, hearing myself sounding like an idiot. Faith just smiled and thanked me for keeping her calm, then started massaging her neck and rolling her shoulders around, trying to work out the kinks. I watched her out of the corner of my eye and realized that, despite the deadly driving conditions, I hadn't been stressed at all.

Faith leaned forward to take a peek at the In_. "Looks pretty horrid," she said. And it did.

In front of us, a dozen little brown doors squatted either side of a little brown office. It looked like the handyman had been on vacation for the past couple centuries, and the threadbare, watery pink carpet leading to the office was barely hanging on. I was thinking they might want to change the name of the place to downplay the red carpet thing, but then I checked out the button-hole of an office and figured the rug was probably one of the In_'s best features. The good news was, there was a lamp on inside.

"Let's go," Faith said, killing the lights. She reached for her door handle, then paused and swiveled round to look at Fang. "Are you coming?"

He didn't answer. He was lying on his side with his knees tucked tight to his chest as if he was already working at not freezing to death. I reached over and gave him a shake. "Fang. Fang. Hey, man, get up."

He grunted a few times, but didn't budge. Faith got a blanket (no accompanying candles, condoms or pup tent) out of the trunk and laid it over him while I offered up a big thanks for the lift and apologized for my hyperventilating stoner friend crashed in the back seat. But the whole time I was talking, this stupid, excited nervousness was rumbling inside, because despite the circumstances there was no disputing that I was following Faith Taylor, as in *the* Faith Taylor, into a motel.

THE OFFICE WAS EMPTY, which gave us a bit of an opportunity to admire the décor. The walls, which may have once been white, were a tarry yellow, and judging from the smell and the big, brimming ashtray, smoking was definitely encouraged at the Red Carpet. Still, if I'd been in charge of the establishment, the first thing on my to-do list would have involved fixing the hole some dissatisfied customer had kicked into the cheap wood paneling on the front desk.

Faith and I exchanged a bit of a look before she rang the bell. I tried not to stare as she leaned over the counter, but the mirror on the wall behind her made the task of not looking at her perfect ass doubly difficult. In one corner of the room there was a rickety display rack—nailed to the floor in case anyone had dreams of owning such a fine piece of furniture—and I went over and pretended to check out the tourist pamphlets. The usual lame menagerie of attractions promised great times for the whole family at Santa's Petting Zoo or Wild Cat World or Aquadome, the big water park in Monroe. I gave the rack a push. It turned reluctantly until, surprise, surprise, a Gandy's Rock brochure spun into sight.

Gandy's Rock. A freakish, freestanding, 115-foot-high stalagmite-type rock that, according to the literature, sat in an otherwise completely flat farmer's field not far from the Red Carpet. Scientists believed the rock was a remnant of the Ice Age, left behind by glaciers as they pulled back up into Canada, where they belonged. A couple of years ago Fang and I had put the rock on our list of Michigan must-climbs, and not only because of its height. We were thirteen when we made the list, and we were pretty positive the retreating glacier rhetoric was bogus. Instead, we believed our own, more probable theory that the rock was extraterrestrial, that it had fallen from the sky during some ancient cosmic meteorite storm and that, once on top, Fang would be able to communicate with alien gods. (We may have made that last part up after we started smoking weed. Sounds likely, but I can't be sure.) I folded the pamphlet in half and stuck it in the pocket of my jean jacket, planning to show it to Stoner Boy later, to remind him of the only thing he'd ever been any good at.

Faith gracefully lifted her arm and gave the bell another solid ding. "Hello? Is anyone here?"

Behind the desk, a door opened. And this dude, decked out in layer upon layer of flab, a thin undershirt and a pair of tight red polyester pants, poured himself into the alley between the door and the desk. For a second I got this weird feeling that we were on the set of some low-budget thriller, or, worse, a gross-out porno flick. Either way, I was definitely an extra.

The fat guy grabbed hold of the counter, arms warbling, spread his meaty fingers across its cracked surface and gave Faith a long, leering look. "You must be real hot to be out on a night like this." The guy's voice dripped with pre-seminalish intent.

"Excuse me?" Faith said, giving him the evil eye.

He didn't flinch, just jerked his head in my direction and kept his gaze on Faith. "You and your boyfriend there need a room?"

"Actually, my *friend* and I got caught in the storm. We need a phone."

"There's phones in the rooms."

"We don't necessarily want a room. Is there a pay phone we could use?"

"Nope." The guy shot her a wide smile. She denied him entry, dropped her chin to her chest and left him face to face with his own reflection. His teeth were large and white in his loose-flesh face. In the mirror, I saw the smile slip from his eyes.

Faith leaned over the counter and pointed at the lower deck. "What about that phone there?"

"Ain't for customers." He caught her in his sights and regained his grin.

"Couldn't you make an exception?"

"For a pretty girl like you? Sure I could." He kept his hands where they were, ran his tongue across his pearly whites, making no move for the phone. Faith waited. I pretended I wasn't even there, that the hair on the back of my neck wasn't crawling. The fat man kept leering.

Faith took a couple steps away from the desk. "So ... can I use the phone?"

"Like I said, I can make an exception for you, but first maybe you can make an exception for me? Do me a little favor?" He bounced his brows up and down a couple times and flexed his pecs. Inside his undershirt, his flabby breasts danced. And before I had a chance to do anything, Faith slammed out the door. A slice of cold air cut through the office, ferreting me out from behind the rack.

"You got a real live one there." The fat guy forced out a laugh and finally looked my way. It sort of sickened me to notice his nipples, hard and erect, under the thin white cotton. Once he knew he had my attention, though, he started bobbing around, making a show of watching Faith stomp to the car. "Great ass," he said.

I'd planned on following Faith out the door, but at that, I stopped in front of the desk. "Are you fucking nuts?"

If he heard me, I wouldn't have known it. He just reached under the desk and came up with a registration form, which he slid across the counter. "Highway's closed both ways," he said, suddenly sounding all businesslike. "Just heard it on the radio. Hell of an accident. And the plows won't be down this way until mid-morning, so unless you want to freeze your butt off in the car all night, the room is thirty-three bucks."

As I filled in the form, Fatty surveyed the board of dangling keys behind the desk. Except for a few empty hooks it was full, but nonetheless he took his time mulling over the lowlights of each room. When he finally turned around, a slick white smile accompanied the key perched on his palm. "Got the honeymoon suite left."

"What a surprise. Service is so stellar, I thought the place would be packed."

"Yeah, well, Mr. Smartass, it's boring as hell out here. Sometimes I try to have a little fun, you know? Chat up the customers a bit. Can't help it your girlfriend doesn't have a sense of humor. Besides, I don't see nothing wrong with having an eye for pretty girls." He shook his head like he was all disappointed in me. "I think it's pretty goddamn normal, okay?"

I had zero intention of getting into "normal" with that abnormality. I gave him the twenty-five bucks I had on me and he gave me the key, moaning about what a big favor he was doing me, letting me come up with the rest of the dough in the morning.

I was halfway out the door when he called out, "You know what?"

I glanced over my shoulder.

"You're real lucky to have a girlfriend like that."

God. He looked so pathetic, crammed in behind the counter with the board of keys poking into his back, that for a second I actually felt for him. I just knew he'd been fat his whole life, probably crazy too, and that he'd be stuck in some tight, crappy little space for whatever was left of it.

"Listen." I rested my forehead against the door frame. The low ridge of snow that had collected against the bottom of the door collapsed onto the dirty linoleum inside. "She's not my girlfriend. I hardly even know her."

"Oh yeah?" The guy's face brightened at that. "So you haven't screwed her yet? Well, if you need any help breakin' her in, you give me a call. Just dial zero and I'll be right—"

I slammed the door, slip-slided my way back to the car without wiping out. Faith, having managed to tune in a station, already knew the highway was closed. She actually looked relieved when I showed her the key. Fang was still huddled under the blanket in the back, but his eyes were open and he was upright, and it took all of about thirty seconds for us to pile into Room 14.

FOURTEEN

The honeymoon suite was dank and cold and dirty brown. Except for the red velvet bedspreads. They really livened the place up. Faith left her coat and gloves on while she called home. Fang headed straight for the can. I settled myself in front of the heating unit and started working the knobs, but the thing was still blowing cool air when I heard water running and a rare edge of excitement in Fang's voice. "Hey, Luke, check this out." Curious, I went and stuck my head around the bathroom door. A sex-sized Jacuzzi tub, its taps blasting, took up 98.99 percent of the space, butting right up against the toilet—perfect for the legless or for those who like to soak their feet while taking a crap.

Fang pushed the moldy shower curtain to one end of the tub and started unbuttoning his new shirt, already ragged after a couple hours on my buddy's back. I squeezed inside and pulled the door shut behind me. When the shirt came off, I pretended not to notice Fang's always-impressive six-pack and his iron arms—the remnants of his climbing days.

"Do you have any cash?" I asked.

"What for?"

"For the room."

"How much is it?" Because he never had any, Fang hated discussing money.

"Thirty-three bucks."

"For this dump?"

"It's got a Jacuzzi," I said. He ignored me. "It's not like we had a lot of options, Fang."

"Did you try to talk the guy down at least?"

"No, Fang, I blew him instead and he gave it to me for, like, eight bucks. Now, do you have eight bucks? I don't want to have to ask Faith for it." I wormed into the small rectangle of space in front of the mirror where Fang was peeling off. My hair had gotten large from the snow, but for once my face was free of any major acne crops, and there were no chunks of food between my teeth. I tried my hood up, then pushed it down again. Fang was jammed in behind me, standing perfectly still. I just knew he was watching me check myself out. I pulled back from the mirror so I was no longer within zit-squeezing distance, but I didn't turn around.

Fang reached past me to put his neatly squared shirt on the counter beside the sink. Before his hand disappeared, I got another flash of his knuckles, all red and raw from being ground into the Palace floor by a black boot or two. I was going to ask him what the fuck had happened at the concert, but he got his question out first.

"Why not?" he asked.

"Why not what?"

"Why not ask her for the money?" The way he said it, like he already knew the answer, completely pissed me off.

I cleared a circle in the mist on the glass so I could meet the smirk on his face with the look of disgust I had ready for him. But in the mirror, Fang's eyes were closed and he wasn't smirking. His lips were parted and his face was all soft and pained-looking. He had, like, zero body fat, so every muscle was right there and I could see he was sort of shaking. With my back to him, he thought I couldn't see him, I knew that. And seriously, I wished I hadn't wiped off the mirror because it was really unsettling to catch Fang looking like that. I didn't know if he was experiencing God or having some sort of erotic flashback or going into seizure again or what, but whatever it was, I wanted to put an end to it, fast.

"Listen," I said loudly. His eyes flew open and I saw his face harden up before he disappeared from the glass. "I don't want to ask her for money because she gave us a ride, all right? She did us a favor. We'd be freezing to death on the side of the road right now if it wasn't for her."

"We would not," he said quietly. "We would have got a ride."

"Fang! You were a total mess. Huffing into your bag. Having a fucking *panic* attack? What's with you, anyway?"

"Nothing." Then a long pause. "I'm just sleeping like shit."

"Are you on something that's making you freak?"

"Nope. I told you. I can't sleep. It's completely fucking me up."

I heard the zip of a fly and felt body parts—knees, elbows, shoulders—bumping against me as Fang started stripping off his jeans.

"Jesus, could you get off of me, man." I climbed around him and pressed myself against the door, struggling to stay cool in the hot, cramped quarters. "Listen," I said, my voice all stern and shit so I ended up sounding just like my father, "Faith helped us out, okay?"

Fang folded his jeans, then set them on top of his shirt. "Sure. Whatever. There's money in my jacket. It's on the bed."

"Great. Thanks for being so fucking cooperative." I yanked the door open.

"You like her," Fang said in this real false-casual sort of way. I closed the door slowly and leaned up against it. The barely sanded, barely painted wood was rough against my palms.

Fang was naked now, his hands resting on his narrow hips, his elbows wide. I could give a fairly vivid description of his genitals here, but I'd rather not. I grabbed a towel from the rack at the end of the tub and tossed it at him.

"Would you get a life," I said.

He tossed the towel right back at me. "You like her." He sounded less casual, more pissed, the second time.

"What are you talking about?" The towel was thin and rough between my hands, a carpet burn of a cloth.

"I can tell."

"You can tell! Since we hooked up with Faith, you've barely been alive."

"I wasn't sleeping in the car."

Aiming for his head, I launched the towel again, but Fang grabbed it midair and dropped it to the floor. He did a rare thing then. Looked me head-on. The smirk I'd been expecting earlier slid across his face, but underneath it I thought there was a residue of the weird, wounded softness I'd seen in the mirror before. Fang kept his eyes on mine, but he raised his chin slowly, and if anything had been there, it was gone. Standing naked in the steamy bathroom, Fang looked like an unloved junkie rock star like he always had, but he looked different, too. A heel-shaped bruise darkened one shoulder and his hand was all swollen and I guess he looked tougher than normal, or maybe just more damaged.

"The money's in my jacket," he said, before stepping over the edge of the tub and lowering himself in. He stifled a gasp as his injured mitt hit the hot water, then he relaxed into the bath and began splashing water onto his chest and arms.

I grabbed for the door handle.

"Hey, Luke." Fang sounded nastier than I ever remembered. "In case you forgot, she's Stan's girlfriend."

"I didn't forget, Fang."

"Just making sure," he said, to the slam of a door.

On the other side of the slam, Faith was still on the phone. I tried not to eavesdrop on the call, which wasn't easy given the size of the place. I went and checked on the heater, throbbing away, belting out hot, dry air. I picked Fang's jacket off the bed and started rummaging through it, keeping my back to Faith so she wouldn't think I was the kind of guy who robbed his friends while they were out of the room. I imagined a mother lode of drug paraphernalia—pipes, needles, rubber tubing, a large bong perhaps—tumbling from Fang's pockets onto the bed, but except for an empty Ziploc, which I worked around, the only things I found were a pack of gum and two five-dollar bills.

I stuffed the bills into my wallet, and when the telephone receiver clattered onto its cradle I turned around holding nothing but a pack of Big Red. "So?" I said, casually sliding a stick of gum out of the pack and offering it to Faith, real gentlemanlike. She waved it off, started undoing her Docs.

"Well," she said. "My parents are happy I'm safe, not so happy I'm in a hotel room with two guys they don't know, and are very, very unhappy Mia's gone AWOL. She's over. Anyway, the highways are definitely closed. If the weather's okay, we'll drive back in the morning. Otherwise, my parents will come and get us in my grandfather's Jeep." She glanced toward the bathroom. "How's Fang?"

"He's okay. And listen." I sat down on the opposite bed. "I wanted to say sorry about that creep in the office."

"You don't have to apologize for him." Unlike Fang, Faith had no fear of eye contact, which with her was gorgeous and green.

"Well, I should have done something."

"You didn't get mad. You got us a room. That's something."

The honeymoon suite had tipped from fridge to furnace. Faith still had her jacket on and her cheeks were all red and her long dark hair spiraled around her face. There was only a couple feet of space between the beds, so our knees were practically touching, and with her staring at me, man, I felt like a sliver of ice in Fang's Jacuzzi. I took off my jean jacket, then jerked my sweatshirt over my head, taking my T-shirt with it so that I was half-naked in front of her for the few seconds it took me to wrestle my hoodie off and my shirt on, and yeah, she still had her Emerald City eyes locked on me when I'd finished, and yeah, it was my cheeks that were burning.

She picked up the phone and held the receiver out. Under the roar of the heater, the buzz of dial tone. "You want to call home?"

I blabbed something about that not being necessary because no one was worried about me. Realizing I sounded a lot like a kid whose parents don't give a shit about him, I backtracked to explain how I'd told them I was hanging at Fang's for the night, going from unloved teen to liar in about two seconds flat.

"So they don't know you went to the concert?" Cradling the receiver in both hands, she rested it on her thighs, up high, close to her crotch.

"Ahh … no. Not really. They would have made us take the bus or something." I noticed my knees were jumping and I forced them to quit, tried to assume a relaxed posture, but when I did, visions of ultra-cool ultra-Stan popped into my head and my legs started bouncing again.

"What about Fang?"

"He's having a bath." As if on cue, a shudder of engine and a sputter of jets leaked from the bathroom. "There's a Jacuzzi."

"Oh." She tried not to look surprised at the news. "Should he call home?"

"Nope. His mom's definitely not worried about him."

"You sure?"

"Positive."

She sighed and put the phone down and I started searching for a remote, located it under the bed next to someone's forgotten sock. I zapped the TV. Hissing static greeted me on every channel. I tried to ignore the zip of Faith's jacket.

"Cable's out." I flicked the television on and off a couple times, then went over and gave it a smack, hoping to jump-start the entire central Michigan cable network with a well-delivered blow, but it wasn't happening. There would be no media distraction to save me. I relinquished the remote and snuck a peek at Faith, stretched out on the other bed.

"There's a ghetto blaster," she said, pointing to a beat-up-looking box chained to the dresser. I got up, squatted in front of it and gave the power button a hopeful push. A little red light glowed and the box emitted a low electrical hum. Faith rolled onto her stomach and rummaged through her purse. Pulled out a CD case. Extracted a disc. Held it up so I could take a look. "You a Peppers fan?"

"I am."

She gave me a half smile then, just the one corner of her mouth curling up.

And when the music started, I couldn't help smiling back.

Faith sat cross-legged on the bed, looking up at me through long dark lashes. "So, hey, what's with your friend?" she asked.

"I don't know." I jammed my hands into the pockets of my jeans, hoping my explanation would suffice, but Faith just sat there waiting, expecting more. "I haven't been hanging out with him since ... well ... lately."

"You think he's into something you don't know about?"

I shrugged.

"I've heard some guys at Jefferson are into crack. That'll freak you out. Maybe you should ask him about it."

"Yeah, maybe. Fang usually only smokes pot. He's done acid a couple times. And Ecstasy. And 'shrooms. And Special K." I had difficulty stopping the list of illegal substances "my friend" had partaken of. "He says he's not sleeping," I added feebly.

She nodded and pushed herself off the bed. Smiling, she brushed past me and bent down to turn up the Peppers. The dank, dirty, brown room suddenly vibrated with sound and possibility and the sweet scent of Faith.

"You smoke crack?" she asked, turning to face me, swinging her hips to the music.

I shook my head, nervous. She felt close.

"Good, because I don't dance with guys who smoke crack. Ever."

"Yeah, well, I don't dance." To prove my point, I grabbed two handfuls of red velvet and anchored myself to a bed.

"Everyone likes to dance." And to prove *her* point, she raised her arms above her head, closed her eyes and started swaying from side to side and singing real low, like I wasn't even there. I sat perfectly still and watched her move into the music. Her black T-shirt crept up as she danced, leaving only a band of tight white undershirt ringing her belly, which lay smooth and flat and chocolaty brown above her faded, low-slung jeans.

"I love dancing," she said.

"I don't." I said it as softly as I could, so nothing would shift or change or cause her eyes to open.

"I bet you dance in your room," she said finally.

"I don't," I lied.

She stopped moving. Her eyes opened. She stood motionless a couple inches from the bottom of the bed.

She reached out and gave my shoulder a gentle push and offered me the other half of the smile she'd given me before. Her arm fell back to her side. Long fingers brushed the top of a slim thigh. "Come on. I've had a rotten night and it was supposed to be so good." She took a deep breath. Her smile disappeared completely. "And I don't like you sitting there watching me. Sooo, if you won't dance, I'll have to stop and that will bum me out and then the night will probably continue to be bad. But if we dance, well, it's hard for things to be bad when you're dancing." She held her hand out to me. "So … are things going to be rotten or good?"

And like that day in the library, I could see right into her.

"It's your choice," she said.

I didn't move. I couldn't move. The song ended. The laser crept toward the next track. Her hand hovered in front of me.

"Come on. Rotten or good?"

The first slow notes of "Under the Bridge" rolled through the room. Faith took a step back. And Stan dying on me, and Bernoffski dying on me, and Fang gasping for air on a stadium floor, and the pervert in the office, and how screwed up my life was—all of that moved through me as I sat frozen on that bed. But, there she was. Standing in front of me, beautiful and sad and full of grace. And I made my choice.

She was right. It's hard to feel bad when you're dancing.

FIFTEEN

When the CD ended, Fang exited the spa, hit me with a killer look, dove for cover under the red velvet and snapped off the rickety lamp between the beds. Either he faded out right away or he pretended to. I had no idea which and I really didn't care. Faith and I were sitting on the floor in the landing strip of white light spilling from the bathroom, talking music. Who we were listening to. Who we weren't. And man, the discussion rolled, smooth and easy as a Speed Creamed board on a freshly paved hill.

Faith was into alt-rock like me, pretty much dug all the "the" bands—the Strokes, the Vines, the Hives, the Datsuns, the Zutons, etc., etc.—appreciated some of the fringe bands like the Flaming Lips, the Dandy Warhols and the Distillers, along with some of the local talent out of Detroit (Whirlwind Heat, the Go). She also dug some of the chick stuff like Dido and Faith Hill and Coldplay, but her current favorites were definitely the White Stripes, which didn't surprise me. We were completely in sync, if I left out the thrashers like System of a Down and Rage Against the Machine and Papa Roach and all the death metal shit I listened to whenever I needed a satanic top-up. We were tight on the early influences too. Nirvana? Oh yeah. Green Day? Totally. The Smashing Pumpkins? You bet. I practically had a hard-on just sitting beside her on the floor swapping band names.

"You like Marilyn Manson?" she asked. I wasn't sure if it was a trick question, and seeing how I didn't want to derail our rock-a-thon of love with a wrong answer, I kind of hedged, although what I said was true.

"Some of his stuff. 'Disposable Teens.' 'The Dope Show.' Stuff like that."

She nodded and added a few to the list. "'The Beautiful People.' 'mOBSCENE.'"

"Yeah," I said, suddenly grinning like a fool.

"Hate his covers, though."

"Yeah. What's with those? Maybe he ran out of things to rage against."

"In this lifetime? Not a chance."

By this time Faith was sprawled out on the floor, all lovely and lanky and loose. Her head resting against the end of the bed. Her long legs stretching practically to the wall. "Hey, you know who I really love right now?" she said. "Johnny Cash."

"Johnny Cash?"

"Yeah. His last album is *sooo* mournful. It lets me release my grief in small, beautiful doses." She undulated her hand through the air in front of her. "In sad, perfect waves."

"I've never listened to him." I rested my chin on my knee, started fiddling with my shoelaces.

Faith tucked a strand of curls behind her ear, but it sprang loose again. "There's this Trent Reznor cover on his new album that's just awesome."

"Really? That greasy guy from Nine Inch Nails?"

"Yeah. You should check it out. It's called 'Hurt.'"

"'Hurt'? I don't know if I really need any more of that in my life at the moment." I thought she might laugh, but she didn't.

"It'd be good for you. Stop you from being totally washed away by grief later on." Faith gave me a long look. White teeth. Wet lips. Soft eyes.

I didn't bother mentioning that lately what was threatening to do me in didn't feel much like grief. And I didn't mention the angry, icy interlude outside Delaney's door earlier in the evening. What I did was smile, all calm and cool, and tell her, "I feel pretty okay right now."

"Right this minute?"

"Yeah, right this minute."

"Me too," she said, pushing herself off the floor and flopping onto the bed.

Fang was spread-eagled on the other double, apparently catching up on the sleep he'd missed. I tried half-heartedly to get him over to one side or the other, but he wasn't budging. Witnessing my predicament, Faith said it would be okay if I crashed with her, provided I kept my clothes on. Even though the bottoms of my jeans were still damp from the snow, I accepted her terms and conditions and crawled under the covers.

I knew nothing was going to happen, but still, lying there beside her, I could smell her sweet, minty hair, could see the bedspread rising and falling on her chest, and my cock stiffened, confident it could take over from here. I rolled onto my side and discreetly inched my hips away, trying to put some distance between my stiffy and the girl, while battling back with thoughts of old, naked chicks.

Faith wasn't making things easy. She turned to face me and propped her head on her elbow. Her breath was warm on my face. Her lips were right there. I gave up the struggle.

"You know," she said, "Stan loved doing the T-shirt thing with you. Afterwards, he always said there was something about you. He thought you were pretty cool, pretty funny, in this really self-mocking sort of way."

"Are you joking?" I said, knowing Stan wouldn't think I was pretty anything if he knew I was lying in bed beside his girlfriend harboring a huge hard-on. Still, I couldn't pretend I wasn't pleased to hear that my dead buddy had told Faith a couple good things about me.

"No, I'm not joking. And don't take this the wrong way or anything, but he also said you aren't nearly as dumb as you pretend to be."

"Listen, it's no act. My parents had me tested. I scored slightly higher than your average sheep. It was a little disappointing for them. My parents, I mean. Not the sheep. The sheep were thrilled. Anyway, my mom had me X-rayed after that. Turns out my brain is the size of a corn kernel."

"Popped or unpopped?"

"You see? I was too dumb to even ask."

She laughed, a clear, perfect laugh, then gave my shoulder a gentle push. "All joking aside, I know what he meant. About there being something about you. I can see it."

She reached over and ran her finger along my cheek, so lightly, so softly, I had to close my eyes and bite back a moan. Then her hand trailed lower to settle on my chest. For the few seconds it rested there, I lay motionless, living in the press of skin beneath her palm, sensing something big behind every beat of my heart.

Then her hand disappeared and Faith rolled away. She dropped her head onto her pillow and was quiet for so long I thought she was asleep.

It would have been nice to just lie there and think about what had just happened, but I had other matters to attend to. I reached down to straighten out my cock, bent uncomfortably inside my jeans. I had just slipped my hand inside my pants, where, seriously, it had lingered for only the briefest of seconds, when, eyes wide, Faith turned to face me.

"Luke?" she said in this real low voice, testing to see if I was awake.

"Yeah?" I said weakly, torn between the pleasant, fleshy sensation under the covers and the fear that Faith might flutter the velvet cloak to find me masturbating beside her—something I felt that, while not explicitly stated, would definitely have been included on the list of things not to be done while lying in bed beside her.

"I know this sounds weird, but do you think Stan somehow hooked us up?"

"What?" I managed to get my hand out of my pants, hoping Faith didn't hear the waistband on my Calvin Kleins snap as I came up for air.

"Well, you know how we were both supposed to be at the concert with Stan, right? So maybe tonight he was looking down, checking out the Peppers, and he just kind of …" She brought her hands slowly together, pressed them palm to palm in an innocent, prayerful display of flesh on flesh. "I don't know. The Palace is a pretty humongous place to just bump into somebody."

I was suddenly exhausted, lungs squashed flat, limbs too heavy to lift. I barely managed a shrug of my shoulders, a nothing shake of my head. "I don't know. I find that hard to believe. Then again, my life has been so insane lately, nothing would really surprise me."

"Yeah," she said slowly. "And the Palace *is* huge." I could almost see the idea rolling around her brain, like a hard, round candy, trying to find a place to stick.

"Yeah, it is," I said, not wanting to disappoint. "Good night, Faith."

"Good night. And Luke?" She lifted her head so we were looking at each other across the short, dim distance between us.

"What?"

"Thanks for dancing."

About a billion things shot through my head right then, honest, uncool, brave things I might have dared if I was someone else. But I wasn't.

"No problem," I said, like I'd done her some big favor.

I checked out the clock on the bedside table—it was 1:09— before locking eyes with Fang. It gave me a bit of a shock, really, because I'd sort of forgotten he was, like, one bed over. Staring right at me. Not even pretending to be sleeping. I snapped my eyes shut, trying not to imagine what he'd been thinking, huddled up under his red velvet bedspread while we'd been talking and laughing a couple feet away.

Regardless of the warm body beside me, or the voyeur across the runway, I must have conked out pretty quick, because when I woke up screaming, the clock read 4:17. It took a couple seconds for me to realize where I was, to recognize Fang as the lump in the bed opposite and Faith as the tangle of dark hair on the pillow beside me. Neither of them was moving. My nightmare hadn't scared them awake, so I had plenty of time to replay it.

In the dream, the elusive Astelle Jordan was no longer missing. Instead, she was tied to a bed with a pink sweatshirt stuffed in her mouth. Her long, curly brown hair hid most of her face, but it didn't matter; I knew it was her. She was so small on the bed, so light, she barely dented the mattress. Her one arm was bent the wrong way, like she had an inverted elbow, and I was on Fang's bed, with a phone in my hand and my mother's hysterical voice was everywhere and the fat guy was on top of Astelle and I watched him rape her. When he was done with that, he untied her mangled arm. It took him a long time, he was swearing and his thick fingers fumbled to work the knots loose and I couldn't take it anymore because she was choking on the sweatshirt and crying and finally I had to help him. The knots fell apart in my hands, the rope fell apart, and he wrapped his fat hands around Astelle's neck and squeezed until the room crackled with the snap of fragile bones. Then we were arguing, and I ended up throwing all this money at him, but he was never satisfied and he was getting really mad, screaming at me to check Astelle's pockets, but her clothes were all twisted up and I was on the bed, I couldn't move, I was frozen on the bed, watching as he dragged this heavy log of a plastic shower curtain trailing brown hair out one end across the honeymoon suite, pausing to give me a big white smile on his way out the door.

It didn't make for an easy night. All those vivid details were pretty hard to get past. Especially with Faith lying beside me in that bed, lost in a tangle of long dark hair. In the deep gray of a motel room dawn, with my imagination in overdrive, it was difficult not to confuse her with the dead girl in the dream. I fixed my eyes on the ceiling and faked Zen for an hour or two, until finally I couldn't stand it any longer.

I reached over, hand shaking, breath suspended. Carefully, I brushed her hair from her face. She squirmed a little and her lashes fluttered. I squeezed my eyes shut to hide my tripping heart. But before I did, I saw it was Faith. Of course it was Faith. And I slept.

SIXTEEN

Everyone in the honeymoon suite was pretty quiet that morning, which suited me just fine, being completely bagged and all after spending a good chunk of the night wrestling the wrong girl. What little conversation there was focused on the state of the roads. The cable was back up and a local station gave the all clear on highway driving. Faith yanked the curtains open on a startling blaze of light, and said it looked like the donkey track out front had already been plowed, so it was decided by one sweet voice and a couple of grunts that we'd get up and get going. Everyone took a turn in the can. Mine was brief—I mean, if I was too cowardly to reach out and touch a sweatshirt, you've gotta know I skipped the shower, with its killer curtain, altogether. Still, I couldn't help noticing how the curtain was hanging loose at one end, the holes at the top ripped right through, as if someone, sometime, had given it a good yank and pulled it down fast.

I splashed some water on my face, scrubbed my teeth with one finger, battled my mop, then bailed out of the bathroom. Faith was on the phone with her parents and Fang was already clearing off the car. I headed out to settle up on the room, using hand signals to assure Faith she didn't owe a thing.

Outside, the sun was hanging in an unblemished sky, turning the Red Carpet Inn and the surrounding woods—perfect for stashing a body—into a real winter-wonderlandish affair. It was still cold, however, and I puffed out a couple frosty clouds on the way to the office. I was hoping to leave the money on the counter and split, forget the change, but it appeared Fatty was an early riser. I could see him through the window, crammed into his polyester uniform behind the desk. For a second I considered stiffing him, but seriously, I didn't want to be involved in some humiliating fat-guy-staggering-across-a-slushy-parking-lot chase scene, didn't want to have to explain that spectacle to Faith. Besides, there was this sick trickle of curiosity pumping through me, the same stuff that has everyone rubbernecking at a crash site or devouring the details of the latest, greatest murder. I knew I was going into the office to take a look at the nightmare felon, no sense pretending I wasn't.

"Morning." The big boy smiled widely as I stepped inside. I knocked the snow from my shoes then planted myself in front of the desk. Except for a new red shirt and name tag—apparently the freak of the week would respond to the name Frank—the guy looked pretty much the same as he had the night before: weird, white, warped.

"Someone didn't get a whole lot of sleep last night," he said, giving me a knowing wink.

"Don't start with me, man." I pulled my wallet from my back pocket and laid Fang's two fives on the counter.

Frank paid no attention to the cash. Instead, he started swinging his hips back and forth, humping the desk. "So, how was she, huh?" he panted between thrusts. "Was she a good ride?" He laughed a big wet one.

"Don't," I snapped. The word bounced off the mirror, ricocheted around the room along with a sweatshirt, a rope, a rape, a shower curtain.

"Okay, okay." Frank pumped his meaty hands through the air, letting me know I should keep it down. "I was just joking." Like last night, the transition from pervert to pathetic was quick. His eyes flashed to the mirror. He checked out the door behind him. When it stayed shut, he shot me a nervous smile and grabbed the money. He had to suck in his gut to open the cash drawer.

I was about to stick my wallet back in my pocket when I saw the thick edge of pink paper inside. I glanced at Frank making change. I fingered the folded paper. A car door slammed, an engine sputtered up a roar. Out the window, a puff of blue, transparent exhaust wavered behind the Sunbird.

"You like pretty girls, right, Frank?" I asked quietly.

"I sure do," he said, chuckling. "I sure do."

"Want to see one?" I pulled the paper out of my wallet and unfolded it slowly.

"Oh, yeah!" Frank shoved my change at me then leaned over the counter, engulfing the lower deck with his rolls. "Let me see her, let me see her," he panted, reaching for my coveted piece of porn.

I surrendered the flyer.

His eager smile kind of crumpled when he saw the big MISSING at the top of the page. He threw me a worried glance, then started reading. I watched him closely, but he'd barely even skimmed the thing when the door behind him swung open and a tough, skinny old bag in a Red Carpet uniform stepped in beside him.

"Morning." She nodded at me, then at him. A red tide rose from the collar of his shirt and his shoulders crept up, like a kid expecting a cuff to the back of the head. The lady, the manager according to her tag, stopped short. There was a bit of an uncomfortable silence as we held our places. Her eyes darted from me to Frank and back again before settling on the sheet of pink paper. "What you got there?" Her voice was tight with suspicion. She snatched the paper from his hand, scanned it quickly. "This yours, Frank?"

"Nope," he said quietly, shoulders still raised.

Eyes narrowed, she thrust the flyer back at me. "I don't know what you're up to, *kid*"—she spat the last word out like some poisoned turd—"but I want you outta here." She gave her arm an angry shake. Astelle quivered in front of me. "Go on, *now*. Get out."

I grabbed the dancing girl and bolted. As I made for the car, I spun around once, took a few shuffling steps backwards through the slushy lot. Inside the office, the old broad's face was pressed in close to Frank's. Her hands flapped overhead, her mouth a dark hole, a distorted circle of abuse.

THE ROADS WERE BROWN with sand and clear of snow, the driving dirty but easy. Five minutes after we left the motel, we were on the highway. Flickering images of the Room 14 festivities, combined with lack of sleep and the sizzling winter light, were leaving me two seconds behind real time and completely out of sync with the people in the car. It didn't really matter with Fang. He had no intention of brightening up the ride with a bit of conversation. It did matter with Faith.

She was concentrating on the road and on what had really landed us in the car together. If we'd danced around Stan last night, today she put him smack in between us, like some dashboard statue of Elvis. She laid out their whole happy history, told us how life had seemed so wide open with Stan, and how even now, even after two months, she couldn't really believe he was gone. I nodded along, trying to tune in and camouflage my uneasy amazement at how goddamn freely she spoke about stuff. There was just no small talk with her. I was thinking maybe she did it by pretending Fang and I weren't there at all, but then she suddenly looked right at me—dazzling, eyes brighter than the sun—and asked, "Did you ever go to Stan's house?"

I had to think about it for a second. Stan and I had done all the T-shirt biz at my place or down at Hank's, and we'd played b-ball in the back parking lot at school and hung out at Delaney's, but I couldn't remember ever going to Stan's. When I told her this, she nodded, said she'd only been once, about six months after they started going out.

Apparently it had been a huge deal, had taken ages for Stan's parents to even agree she could come over. Then Stan's father had barely said hello and his mother was this really timid thing who'd passed around potato chips and acted like everything was cool. After a really rigid dinner, Mr. Miller had read a passage from the Bible then tried to get a discussion going. Faith had been freaked, but Stan and his mom seemed pretty used to the whole deal. Mr. Miller had listened to their interpretations of the reading with this condescending smile on his face before explaining the real, approved-by-Christ lesson meant to be taken from the passage.

"The entire time I was at Stan's, Mr. Miller acted like I didn't even exist. But right after the Bible reading, he turned to me and told me he hadn't asked me to participate in the discussion because I wasn't a *practicing Christian*. I'm pretty sure it was the only thing he knew about me, or at least it was the only thing he cared about. Anyway, after pointing out what a heathen I was, he started ridiculing my name, saying how ironic it is that someone like me, someone with 'no faith in Christ'"—she lowered her voice to mimic Stan's dad—"'should have been bestowed with such a name.' Then he asked if I'd care to tell him what, if anything, I did have faith in."

"So, what did you say?"

Faith tapped her fingers on the steering wheel and dropped her head to one side. I didn't know what she was mulling over, but I tried to think about what I'd say if some asshole put me on the spot like that. Other than the *Put Your Faith in Foster's* logo I'd seen at Hank's, I couldn't come up with much.

"I told him I had faith in myself," she said, which was sure as shit better than my masterpiece.

"And? What did he say?"

Faith shoulder-checked before swinging the Sunbird into the center lane.

"He laughed," Faith said with a tight smile, stepping on the gas. "He just laughed and laughed."

Faith was quiet after that, and surprise, surprise, Fang wasn't saying jack. Pressed against the window, he stared at the dirty cars shuffling around us like they were the most intriguing things he'd ever seen. Personally, I wanted to talk about something besides

Stan and the Millers, but everything I contemplated was either stupid or boring or both. I guess if I'd been daring I could have countered Faith's story with one about *my* family's religious rituals.

Right up front, I'd have told her that the Hunter family is not overly God. We'd never been regular churchgoers or grace-sayers or anything like that. Probably the closest I ever got to a spiritual sort of experience was during my mom's *O Brother* period, which coincided with me being about eight or nine years old.

My mother had totally loved that Coen brothers movie and she'd run right out and bought the soundtrack. And for a couple years there, it felt like our house was always filled with this old-time Southern music. She really dug this one song, this Christian revival number, and whenever it came on she'd drag me into the living room and make me dance with her. It's sort of embarrassing to even think about, because I was already pretty big by that time, but I guess my mom didn't know it, and seeing how I was her only kid, I guess I felt I owed her a dance or two.

Anyway, she'd kind of take me in her arms and I'd be all stiff, so she'd press my head to her shoulder and give me a squeeze or two to loosen me up. And she'd sing along with the soulful a cappella choir about going down to the river to pray and wearing the golden crown and the good Lord showing us the way and whatnot. She'd sing all that stuff right into my ear, and when she stopped singing I knew it was because she was all choked up by the music, and that the song, that sweet chorus of voices, had somehow become her love for me. I mean, my mom never actually said anything like that, but I could just feel it in the way she held me, in the way she sang. It may not have been the most traditional shot of spirituality, but for this kid it had felt pretty close to what I thought God might be about, what He might have had in mind for us all.

So that was kind of "It" for me. And seeing how "It" wasn't even close to something I'd ever even consider discussing with another human being, I stuck with the dead boyfriend instead.

"You know, I'd never have guessed Stan came from some whacked-out family. Was he, like, really religious?"

"We didn't talk about that a lot. I know Stan thought any story with two thousand years of staying power was one worth listening to. He also told me he went to church and took Communion"— she lifted one hand off the wheel and, curling two fingers, did the universal quotation mark thing—"'to affirm and commit to his indwelling Christ.' So yeah, I guess he was religious. Or spiritual, anyway. He told me I expanded his thoughts on God, but I'm not really sure what he meant by that because, like I said before, we didn't talk about it that much. I don't even know if he believed in the afterlife or a literal Jesus or what."

By this time we were heading into town on Highway 6, the road slicing through the wetlands park. After the drive along the sloppy highway, the snowy park looked especially clean and serene, and all conversation stopped. I think we—Faith and I, anyway—were thinking about Stan and his contribution to the scene outside our windows. The pond on my right was frozen over, and an unbroken plane of white stretched to the blue-sky horizon. I imagined all the frogs Stan and I had paid for, beneath the ice, motionless bumps on a muddy bottom, more dead than alive, hanging in a cold, dark limbo until next spring. Aboveboard, the tall grass around the pond was buckling under the weight of the snow, but the happy bulrushes stood tall under Cat in the Hat–high caps of powder.

When we exited the park, I could just tell the ride was going to end on a bit of a silent note. Turns out I was wrong, of course, because Faith still had lots to say about the old beau.

"You know, everyone loved Stan. He was such a golden boy, and I don't mean that in a bad way. Did you ever notice even the teachers at school went out of their way to get his attention? At first I thought people were drawn to his confidence, but it was more than that. You know what it was?" She paused, but I kept my mouth shut. I knew she wasn't waiting for Dumb or Dumber to come up with anything brilliant, she was just lining up her thoughts. "Stan had this intrinsic ability to see the worthiest part of a person and deal with them there"—Faith raised her hand and notched a high-water mark in the air, a couple inches from the roof of the car—"at their highest level. I'm pretty sure that's how he managed his parents. It wasn't something he worked at or was even aware of, though. It was just the way he was. And it's not like he was disillusioned or blind to the dark side of humanity or anything like that, either. But one on one, that stuff just didn't matter to him. So somehow, when you were with him, it didn't matter to you either. You knew all the darkness was there, in you, in him, in the world, but it was completely latent. And you could be good. Everything could be good."

She looked over at me, then glanced in the rearview to see if Fang was listening. Her eyes flashed green and the sun was all tangled up in her hair and it was easy to see she was the yin to Stan's shiny yang.

"Do you know what I mean?" she said in this insistent voice. "Did you see that in him?"

I wanted to tell her I knew Stan. I wanted to tell her I knew him well, but the words jammed in my throat. Instead, I dared to rip off some tiny-trucker wisdom. "Stan unleashed the godliness in people."

Faith took a good, smiling look at me then, her big eyes all impressed and opened just that much wider. "That's right. That's exactly right. I wish I'd said *that* to Mr. Miller. 'I have faith in the godliness of humanity.' God, that sounds good."

She looked so pleased, I was a bit bummed I had no follow-up and was forced to revert to my own, less impressive repertoire of replies. "Yeah, Stan was definitely a good guy."

"And Luke's a complete dick." That from Fang. It was the only fucking thing he said the entire trip home.

SEVENTEEN

Christmas Eve at the Hunters'. Normally happy, holiday times. Normally Fang would come over and my dad would throw on some mood music and my mom would whip up the eggnog and, while she was at it, a couple presents for my friend. Fang was always sort of embarrassed, but pleased, by the gifts from my mom. And I usually had some dickweed thing for him, too—a CD from Sam's, or a shirt from the Shack's sale rack, or later on something from Dwight Slater's special reserve that I'd hand over up in my room after the festivities in the living room had wrapped up. Fang never said anything, but I think sometimes the stuff we gave him was all he got for Christmas, except for maybe a dirty twenty his mom slipped him on her way out the door. To be fair, last year she had gone all out with the DVD player, the one she may or may not have stolen back later on. Still, Mrs. Delaney's holiday plans didn't really revolve around her son. She usually chose to celebrate the birth of our Lord by going on a good long bender, one that started a couple days before Christmas and ended well after New Year's.

So Christmas Eve with us was Fang's holiday highlight, and, having limited funds, he never brought over any gifts. For a while what he did bring was the Converse shoe box, and it had become sort of a tradition for us to dump the contents onto my bed and go through the pictures. Sometimes we'd pick randomly from the litter of shiny squares scattered across my comforter, and we'd laugh at Fang clowning for the camera, all pumped up after one big climb or another. But usually we'd arrange the pictures chronologically, put them in order, so we could see Fang and his achievements grow before us. His smile would get wider, his teeth bigger, and every year the estimated heights of his climbs—written in ink at the bottom of the Polaroids, along with the date—got higher. There were quite a few shots of me, too, looking as stoked as my friend, taken at arm's length by myself, or sometimes by Fang if he'd managed to wrestle the camera from me.

The last time Fang brought the box over was a couple years back. We were fourteen, maybe fifteen, and we'd headed up to my room earlier than usual, cracked open the window and smoked the holiday spliff I'd bought from Dwight. Afterwards, we'd checked out the pictures and we'd laughed like usual, but there'd been a kind of hollow edge to the whole thing and we'd shut the box up pretty quickly. We never even bothered with the "must-climb" list, the one that had Gandy's Rock perched near the top. And I think it was only a couple months later that Fang walked off the school roof, so really it was no big surprise when the shoe box never appeared again. If I recall, the next couple Eves were slow, painful affairs, with the two of us just biding time below, waiting for the moment we could sneak upstairs and get stoned.

So I was actually sort of relieved when Fang didn't show up at all this year. Unfortunately, neither did my dad. Mr. Kite, my father's probably gay boss, was on some short-term leave thing, so my dad had been working nonstop for the past couple weeks, filling in for Kite and trying to do his own job too. I wasn't sure if the old Kalbro supply chain was taut, but I'll tell you this, my mother certainly was. She and my dad had a fairly major blowout when he finally arrived home at nine-thirty. And for the first time ever, my parents decided to skip the eggnog and the Christmas tunes in the living room. I was okay with it really, but still, it wasn't a big thrill hanging out alone in my room for most of the night, listening to my parents' off-key bickering caroling up the stairs.

For a while, I filled the time by worrying. Without the Trazon it was a lot easier, and I had such a plethora of shit to choose from, it was hard to know where to start. So I got organized, I got selective and I kind of honed in on Astelle. Since getting back from the concert, she'd been keeping me company, what with her starring role in the Room 14 rape/murder saga that had started playing in my dreams on a fairly regular basis. Yeah, the whole repetitive nightmare thing had really kicked into gear, Astelle was dying on me every night, pounding every fucking detail into me again and again and again—the rope pulling on her mangled arm, the fat guy on top of her tiny body, the big hands around her skinny neck, the shower curtain trailing its wave of hair. I mean, you barely had to be psychic to figure it out.

After I burnt out on that particular worry, I had just enough energy left to stare out my bedroom window. Clive Avenue was dead, as usual. The complete and predictable lack of activity was pathetic, but also oddly calming, like looking at a really uninspired painting—a farm scene with a couple blurry sheep on a distant hill, maybe, or a poorly drawn bowl of fruit. It was snowing, chunky, wet flakes, and normally I'm with Bing and dig a white Christmas, but this year it meant I'd be busting my ass clearing out driveways.

It was my own fault, really. When Faith had dropped me off the morning after the concert, I'd headed inside and made a big show of offering to shovel out our driveway, which was really pretty lame seeing how it was my job in the first place. But I'd acted extra-nice and generous to avoid a discussion with my parents about my whereabouts the previous evening, since they were under the impression I'd been at Fang's. So the whole thing was doubly slimy really, but there you go. I'm no prize.

I'd practically finished at my place when the Polish widow pushed onto her front porch. Even though it wasn't that cold, Mrs. Bernoffski was completely swaddled—long black coat, hat, scarf, the whole bit. It took her forever to get down the stairs, turned sideways, gloved hands gripping the flimsy railing, booted feet groping for every snowy step. After the slow descent, she picked her way up the front walk, her knees coming up high under her long coat, her big boots slamming into the calf-deep powder. I mean, watching her, you'd think the earth's gravitational pull had doubled during the storm or something. When she shuffled past our place, she didn't even glance at me—the only other person out on the street—just kept her shoulders hunched forward and her head down as if she was battling a wicked wind.

It was sunny and the snow probably would have melted on its own and I didn't even know if Mrs. Bernoffski drove, but after I erased the crooked trail of footprints between her porch and the sidewalk, I hung my coat on the railing and cleared out her driveway. If that wasn't crazy enough, I went home afterwards, wrote up a note, then stuck it in her mailbox. I gave her the same line I'd given her old man about a community service gig for civics class and how, if it was okay with her, I'd be shoveling her place for the rest of the winter. It was a stupid thing to do, because it had been snowing like a bitch ever since. And I knew she got the note, too, because the next time I went over to clear the driveway, she'd inched back the drape in the front room and a slice of old, worried face had squinted out at me. When I gave her a wave, her hand had appeared, flickering for a second in the wedge of light between the parted drapes before the curtain dropped and she disappeared.

I was still staring out my window, thinking about the Polish widow, when the phone started ringing. My parents were good enough to take a time-out from arguing to answer it, and my mom hollered up the stairs that the call was for me. "And it's a *girl,*" she whispered as I grabbed the receiver. It was. It was Faith. Wishing me a merry Christmas. Asking if I wanted to catch a movie during the holidays. I tried to match her relaxed tone, said sure, that sounded good, and we picked a night between Christmas and New Year's.

"So who was that?" my mom asked the minute she saw me heading back upstairs, no doubt looking like I'd just been lobotomized or something.

I paused, one hand on the banister. "Just this girl from school."

"Do I know her?" She was off the couch by this time, standing in the hall, looking all excited. If there's one thing I can't stand, it's having my mom pry into my social activities, especially on those rare occasions when they involve a member of the opposite sex. I figured I'd put an end to things fast.

"It was Faith Taylor. Stan's old girlfriend."

"Oh," was all she could think to say as I bolted up the stairs.

I won't be a prick and use the hookup as a suspense builder, won't pump out thirty pages of crap before revealing how mightily I managed to fuck up my night with The Girl. I'll get right down to it, mention how, right off, I got myself good and nervous pondering what I was going to talk to Faith about, how I was going to act, the probability of physical contact under both a total outbreak and a clear complexion scenario—all kinds of retarded shit like that.

I mean, Faith *had* joined me in the library a few times since we'd been back, so you'd think I might have been a bit cooler, but I guess in the back of my mind I figured she'd just done it out of pity or due to a lack of alternative seating. *And* there was that one night we'd spent together in a motel. In the same bed. But that had been spontaneous, forced upon us by bad weather and strange circumstances, just some random act of God, the type of thing you can't get insurance for. There'd been no time to freak. But this was different. This was a hookup. This was very intentional, very premeditated, and I over-thought the whole thing.

I decided it would be best to leave Mr. Facetious parked on a shelf at home, because he often went too far, which tended to piss people off. However, leaving the sarcastic, mocking side of myself behind turned out to be a bad idea, because nothing really stepped in to fill the gap. No intellectual bravado, no suave charm, no superhero powers, nothing. I couldn't even think of a Little Bob line to rip off. And Faith gave it her best shot, really she did. She looked gorgeous, she smelled great, she behaved well. But I sensed she quickly tired of my stuttering replies to all her promising leading lines. I mean, you could practically hear the steam leaking out of the evening, like the hiss of a slowly released fart. I'm surprised people in the theater didn't complain.

In an effort to avoid conversation, I made a major mistake by wrapping my lips around the straw of a mega-sized Coke and guzzling the whole thing before the flick even started. (*Minority Report* ... survey says ... it sucked. It was an especially uncomfortable choice for a partial pre-cog like me who could never save the day but who knew the fucking movie should have wrapped up, like, an hour before it did.) The two gallons of pop had me squirming in my seat for the last sixty minutes of redundant nonsense, and I practically sprinted to the can when the film finally collapsed.

I made it to the blessed urinal, which was really just a long, waist-high sheet of tin screwed to the wall with a trough sort of thing below it. It was really classy, like something you might find at a semi-pro baseball stadium or some half-assed rock venue. To add to the glamour, the trough was completely plugged up, overflowing with soggy toilet paper and candy wrappers and other unrecognizable debris. So there I was, standing at the urinal, freeing the fountain drink, trying to come up with something to talk to Faith about, when I heard 1) a cubicle door creak open, 2) a chuckle and 3) a couple footsteps, before being 4) shoved from behind. Seeing how my hands were occupied, my face sort of broke the fall, hitting the wall first, a millisecond before my foot slipped into the brimming trough. I was so stunned, the voice behind me barely registered.

"You are so over, kid." I rolled my cheek against the cold tile just in time to see Lance Winters breezing out of the can, his blond ponytail bobbing behind him. He didn't even bother glancing over his shoulder to see if I might need a bit of help.

I had to jack my right leg up on the wall, had to stick my dripping foot under the hand dryer, had to stand in a crotch-splitting V for all eternity, before my shoe stopped squelching when I walked. When I finally exited the can, Faith was the only one left in the lobby. She was polite enough not to ask if I always paused to take a dump during a night on the town, which I thought was pretty good of her.

About ten quiet, painful minutes later, we pulled into my driveway—in her car, of course, because I was still too lazy and disorganized and pathetic to get my license. I mumbled a quick good night and scrambled out of the Sunbird before it started smelling of piss. And as I watched the very beautiful, very talented Ms. Taylor back onto the street, the only thing I was thinking was how completely unworthy, how utterly un-Stan, I really was.

PRETTY MUCH RIGHT AFTER imploding on the hookup with Faith, I got nailed by another dead man. There was no doubt about this one. The premonition was real, although the details weren't super vivid. Just some faceless guy, a row of cigarettes, a gun, a bang, a searing pain, a wall of blackness. Thing is, for the first time since Bernoffski died on me, I was able to identify the body. The story was in the paper the day after the shooting, on page fifteen of the *Stokum Examiner*. I recognized the victim right off. Turns out one Howie Holman from Detroit, Michigan, had been gunned down behind the counter of his own store, leaving a wife and three kids behind to clean up the mess. The guy who killed him got away with $149 and a couple of cartons of cigs. So, no big deal. Happens every day, right? But even if Howie's death had been standard-issue, he still managed to make quite an impression on me when the bullets hit.

To be honest, it was pretty fucking troubling. I mean, I'm seventeen years old. I read *Spin* or *Archie* magazines in the can. I listen to mind-crushingly loud music. I'll walk around with glass in my feet for days on end rather than admit that things aren't going so great. It takes effort for me to engage in an impersonal, thirty-second conversation, never mind getting into any sort of emotional shit. But never mind, *here's Howie*, totally stripped down, completely intense. It was like I'd asked him over to my place or something, to show me who he *really* was, what his life was *really* about, and instead of talking, he reaches inside his chest and pulls out a handful of what makes him tick, jiggles it around for a minute, filters out any pollutants, before plunging the pureness of himself into the center of my chest.

Thing is, I hadn't asked him over, didn't want to know who he *really* was. But that didn't matter. Howie wasn't waiting for an invite. I was in the bathroom, popping zits or something, when he was shot. I guess there was a part of me that was sort of waiting for him, but still, when he hit I had to grab the edge of the sink to steady myself. I tried to keep my eyes on the mirror, to watch myself as it happened, but when the dying man cut into me, my face crumpled and I dropped my head. At first it was all rage that shook me, but as I stared into the sink the anger faded and his life started playing inside me. A love song for the wife, a joyful melody for the kids, all of it backed up by the steady beat of a man marching to make a living. His echo was strong and sad and rang with a steely chord of disbelief. Disbelief that he'd had no choice in the matter. Disbelief that a stranger with a gun had made the final decision. Disbelief that everything was lost.

I opened my eyes when he was over and raised my head to meet the mirror. It took me a minute to focus, and even then I wasn't sure who was looking back. Was there a residue of Howie hanging on? Or Stan? Or Bernoffski? Was I the same person I'd been last fall, before all of this started? Was I even the same person I'd been five minutes before? I had no idea.

I know Little Bob would have said I was asking the wrong question, and my mom would have recommended a dialogue with Mick, but that day, as I stared in the mirror, I wasn't thinking about them. And after every other question faded away, I was left wondering one thing. Why? Why bother with me? Why sing for me? I was practically nothing.

I ENDED UP spending the rest of my Christmas vacation in retreat, doing research. It probably had something to do with the horror show hook-up with Faith and the intensity of Howie's visit, but mostly it was thanks to Pastor Ted. He called me up between Christmas and New Year's, and I thought maybe he'd cheer me up, tell me how goddamn special I was, how gifted, but Ted didn't even bother with the ho ho ho's. Instead, he jumped right into this aggressive spiel about how he was fully aware Stan's hadn't been the only death premonition I'd experienced. He told me he knew there'd been others. He told me he knew about the souls passing through me at the moment of death. I'd stood there in my shiny white kitchen while my lungs collapsed into black holes and my brain exploded. I mean, there was no way the Pastor could know any of the shit he was saying, but that didn't stop him. He told me about his direct line to God and said I should think seriously, very seriously, about coming down to the church for a chat. He was worried about me. Thought the devil might be involved. Told me he knew he'd be seeing me real soon. And this time it was him hanging up on me.

I'll admit Ted's call was pretty hard to blow off, and it wasn't long before I found myself picking the bible out of the drawer of my parents' bedside table where, as far as I knew, it had sat untouched for the last decade or so. But man, that little black book was packed with a billion onionskin pages crammed with minuscule writing and all these flowery let-there-be this's and let-there-be that's. I never even made it out of the Garden. Still, I didn't give up completely on finding the answers, and for a couple days there I dedicated myself to surfing the Net and reading, or at least skimming, everything I could get my hands on about the sweet hereafter and near-death experiences and premonitions and prophets and so on and so forth.

I started with all the touchy-feely shit in the *Oprah* magazines lying around the house before moving on to some Jesus-freak mumbo jumbo, got into philosophy, which eventually led me to metaphysics and creative immortality and New Age crap, and all of a sudden I was right back to *Oprah* and my brain was completely fried. It was so bad that at some point I even gave Mexican Mick a call, but a woman answered and, get this, we didn't speak the same language. I ended up yelling his name and mine into the mouthpiece for a minute or two while the lady yabbered away in Spanish, but we never got any further than that.

Eventually, I just gave it up. Because seriously, if the greatest brains in the world couldn't come up with any answers, what was some loser kid from Stokum going to add to life's big mysteries?

Having failed to convince myself of God's involvement in the mess that was my life, I used my telepathic powers to send the Pastor a mental note, telling him he could go blow himself and his pipeline to heaven unless he came up with some pretty irrefutable, divine-interventionary-type evidence to explain my whole death prophet gig. I'm not positive, but I think he probably got the message, too, because after his last, troubling phone call, he pulled a Lance Winters and quit on me altogether.

EIGHTEEN

I should have been relieved when January rolled around and put an end to my hellish holiday season. But getting back into school proved difficult. In my pre-prophetic period, I'd always managed to pull off average grades in English and most of the other subjects starting with *E,* but to be honest, my marks had never been anything to really jizz over. But seriously, coming into 2003, I was so all over the place I could barely cast a shadow. I think it was mid-month before I managed to pick up a pen. Even then, the shit I handed in usually bounced back with a big red zero or sometimes just a concerned-looking question mark at the top. Then this one day, at the beginning of semester, I came in to find a note stuck to my locker. According to the yellow Post-it, I had an appointment at two o'clock that afternoon with Mr. Tanner, the principal/guidance counselor/premonition therapist, and I figured what the hell, I'd miss chemistry, so I headed to the office at the requisite hour.

Tanner greeted me with this complete bullshit smile, looking like everything was just peachy and ripe, but underneath the phony grin I could see he was still bitter about Stan and me mocking his community spirit project way back when. He parked himself behind his big principal's desk. I slouched in the chair opposite. Tanner opened with a real quiet, concerned voice, so I'd know how sensitive he was to my situation, how he understood this was a "heavy" time for me. He wanted to talk—about things in general, or about what had happened to Stan, or "if that was too difficult" perhaps I might want to discuss what had really "gone down" that night at Todd Delaney's. Now, I wasn't expecting Tanner to have any suggestions on how to deal with the problems associated with being a teen death prophet, but all of a sudden I realized he was just like everyone else at Jefferson. He didn't give a shit about how I was "handling things." He wanted the details, man. And the whole time he was trying to rattle them loose, he was picking his nose.

He was doing it in that distracted, marginally socially accept-able way, just a thumb flicking the corner of one nostril. Still, it was distracting—even before some piece of snot got stuck on his finger and he dropped his hand under the desk really fast. I was forced to sit there, knowing he was rolling his prize around between finger and thumb, trying to ball it up so he could flick it or, worse, wipe it on the underside of his sticky desk. *Then* he had the balls to act all indignant because I wasn't opening up to him.

"Luke," he said, "if there's any hope of us getting anywhere today, you might want to actually say something."

So I obliged. "And you might want to quit picking shit out of your nose," I said, and, well, let's just say the session went down-hill from there.

Mr. Tanner got all defensive and basically laid out this theory about how my "gang" and I had gotten together *after* Stan died and made the whole premonition thing up. (Which shows how truly out of it he was. I mean, the probability of our "gang" plan-ning something of that magnitude was, like, nil to negative one.)

Then he went on to imply that we'd done it because we were such pothead losers that exploiting our friend's death was probably the only opportunity any of us would ever have to claim our fifteen minutes, which, according to Tanner, was increasingly important for a lot of talentless teens, "you just have to look at the growth of reality TV."

If I hadn't been so pissed off, I might have actually played along just to close the curtain on The Prophet, but I didn't want to give Tanner the satisfaction of thinking he'd shaken me down. So I sat there with my arms folded across my chest and my legs stuck straight out in front of me and I told him to go screw himself. Which was stupid, because after he kicked me out of the aborted therapy session, the vengeful, nose-picking bastard went around spouting his theory to anyone who'd listen, apparently in such a way that it appeared I'd actually admitted to making the whole thing up. It felt like it took about two seconds for me to make the transition from small-town freak to big-time liar.

Funny, I didn't acquire any new friends as a result of the metamorphosis. As for my old "gang," the only one I could even remotely tolerate was Fang, and, since no-showing on Christmas Eve, he hadn't even attempted to make contact. He was either too choked or too stoned or too panicked to bother, and given that the one sentence he'd uttered in Faith's car on the way back from the concert had me as the subject and dick as the adjective, I sure as shit wasn't going out of my way to track him down, either.

If Fang and I were casually avoiding each other, then I'd been actively avoiding Faith. I tried to do it in this I'm-super-busy-with-my-hectic-social-schedule, catch-you-later kind of way, which was so false and pathetic, because the truth was, I didn't have a friend in the fucking world. At the same time, I wasn't so sadistic that I'd inflict any more of my loser-boy routine on Faith, either. So I pretty much hung alone, took the liar abuse thrown my way straight-on, with an amused fuck-you smile plastered across my face, pretending I didn't give a shit what everyone was saying. Still, I have to admit, it kind of left me nowhere.

So I was definitely in a bit of a funk, a bit of a bleak period, when I did the next stupid thing. Seeing how I'm not very inventive, I had to pilfer the idea from John Asscraft, who'd recently handed out some practical advice for staying alive in an orange America. It was near the beginning of February and, poor me, I'd come home from another lonely day at school to roam around my empty house for a while, but I'd ended up in the garage. The walls were lined with tools and old sports equipment and camping gear—remnants of a happier life. The duct tape was sitting right there on the corner of my father's tidy workbench. I'd had to dig out the plastic drop sheets, spotted with glossy white dots of kitchen paint. The handy-for-hijacking box cutter I shoved in my pocket bit into my thigh all the way up the stairs.

Constructing the safe room was total cake. I sort of enjoyed the project—the whiz of slicing plastic, the scream of duct tape coming off the roll, the big speckled rectangles I fit snugly over the door and window. Afterwards, I sat on my bed, back against the wall, knees pulled in tight. Except for the dull, grayed light coming through the plasticized window and the walls of my room darkening to a deeper shade of blue, nothing seemed any different.

I sure didn't feel safer or more in control of my life. If anything, I felt more retarded and alone than ever.

It didn't take long before the air in the room started getting warm and stale, and I know it was probably just my imagination, but it looked like the fern on my desk was finished, although I couldn't be bothered getting up to check. I did lean over and let the dead men out of the drawer. I also took little Ms. Jordan out of my wallet and laid her on the bed beside the list. I tried to focus on those unlucky people—and let's not forget the bird—who'd had to say their final goodbyes to a really bad listener. I tried to get those papery slices of pain to sing for me, but I wasn't feeling much. Even when I added my name and Astelle's to the list, it just felt like more of the same. More of nothing.

Finally, I crawled into bed with my shoes on and everything. I pulled the covers up to my chin. I don't know what I was doing. I don't know what I was thinking. My thoughts probably revolved around blowing things with Stan's old girlfriend and being too lazy and thoughtless to peer over a back fence and save Mrs. Bernoffski from widowhood and people believing I was such a lowlife that I'd exploit my best friend's death and Fang calling me a dick and the brutal reality that everyone, *everyone* was going to die. Could have been an array of depressing shit like that. Probably was. Or maybe I was just feeling sorry for my friendless self. I can't really remember. I know I didn't have any plans about getting up or getting out or getting on with things. It felt more like I'd chosen a comfortable position for waiting—waiting for the next insane or dismal or completely unfair thing coming my way.

The air got staler. The room got smaller.

It was a low, insistent knock thumping through the house that finally forced me out of bed. I crouched by my plastic-coated window and peered out. The tree on our lawn was a dark, fuzzy blob. Past the wavering band of blacktop, the outline of our neighbor's house ran against the sky like watery paint. And the silhouette on my porch was muted, as if the body below was wrapped in gauze or I was seeing it from a hundred feet up. I had to press the plastic flat and lean my forehead against the glass to even recognize Faith. The warmth of my breath closed around me, and when she tilted back to scan the upper story of my house, her face was featureless. I dropped to the floor and lay frozen there, beneath the window, my cheek, my heart, pressed into the nubbly carpet. Another knock rattled the house. We both waited. The snap of a metal lid cracked the silence, and then the patter of fading footsteps. When I looked out again, the street was empty.

I ripped my way out of my room a while later and stepped onto the porch. The air was moist and cold. The house across the street cut a straight, sharp line against the darkening sky. I stood there for a long time before I reached into the mailbox. And it wasn't until late that night, when I was back up in my room, that I pulled the cellophane off Johnny Cash and let him tear into me.

WHEN MY MOM CAME breezing into my room a couple days later, she was humming as she threw her coat on the bed and started pacing excitedly between the door and the desk, where I was dicking around on the computer. It was weird to see someone in the house looking so happy. My parents had barely spoken since Christmas, my dad was still working nonstop, and lately my mom had looked like total shit—all pale except for the big dark circles under her eyes, the ones that old people get. She wasn't only pissed at my dad, she was worried about me. She kept reminding me that when she was my age she'd lost her entire family and how devastating that had been, but then, a few years later, she'd met my dad and a few years after that she'd had me, and, well ... things had gotten better. A lot better. Things cycled around. Life went on. And every time I passed her in the hall or failed to avoid her downstairs, she'd reach out to rumple my hair or to touch my arm, telling me how much she loved me, asking about the depressing music wailing from my room. "Was that really Johnny Cash I was listening to all the time?" I was pretty sure she thought I was going to kill myself. Which I wasn't. I mean, why bother putting effort into something that's going to happen on its own? Still, I didn't do a whole lot to reassure her she was wrong. I guess I liked to see her suffer, 'cause, you know what they say, misery digs company.

But the day my mom floated into my room, she was anything but miserable. She was practically bouncing as she started blabbing about the peace rally she'd been to in Rolland, how she'd marched down Aberdeen Street with the rest of Lake Erie's friends. There'd been hordes of people, she guessed well over five thousand, which she thought was impressive for a town the size of Rolland. And what a cross section! When she was in range, she'd punctuate the important bits of information with a squeeze to my shoulder. Students from the arts college, old people, veterans, politicians, businessmen, professors, housewives—you name it, they were there. She'd heard that around the globe there'd been millions, tens of millions, demonstrating! Squeeze. She was feeling optimistic about the possibility of the war being quashed by a global voice, and wouldn't that be something! Squeeze. Yes, she was definitely full of hope.

"Sounds like a regular Caravan of Love," I said, referencing an old Housemartins song my mom had played pretty much nonstop since I was a kid. It was a good, happy tune about brotherly love and living in a world of peace and whatnot, and I pretended to hate it just to bug her.

"Yes, it was. It was a caravan of love. You should have come." She grinned as she plucked her coat from the bed and Tinkerbelled it out the door, saying she wanted to watch the news to see what was happening elsewhere and oh, by the way, Ms. Banks says hi and wants to know how the shirts are coming along.

"The shirts?" I swiveled round in my chair and took a good look at my flushed-faced mother in the doorway. Her short blonde hair was tucked behind her ears and her blue eyes were aglow with a higher purpose and seriously, even though she was something like thirty-eight or thirty-nine, she looked like a kid right then.

"Yes. The shirts, the shirts. For the One Drum festival. It's in April, you know. You haven't forgotten about it, have you?"

I reassured her I was totally on it, but when I didn't turn back to my computer right away, she waved impatiently at me. "Get to work. Get to work," she said before flitting away. But seriously, I didn't feel like starting on the Let's Save Luke project she and Ms. Banks had concocted for me, so I waited a few minutes then headed downstairs and flopped onto the couch beside my mom.

"So, are you a star or what?" I asked.

"The local news isn't on yet. I'm watching CNN. They just showed London. The rally is already over there, but it looked huge." Her eyes never left the screen. She had the remote cocked, ready to fire.

The protest in New York was on at the moment, but let me tell you, it didn't look like a love train chugging through the Big Apple. Instead, the crowd, pressing up against metal barriers and jostling with cops in riot gear, was a whole lot rowdier and angrier and wetter—once the water cannons were opened up—than the caravan crowd my mom had described. The coverage only lasted a couple minutes before the station flipped over to this pretaped feature about how the average Iraqi was gearing up for war.

I got up and went to the can, and when I came back and crashed on the floor they were already interviewing this one family. There must have been about ten or fifteen people packed into a crappy-looking apartment, which, according to the reporter, was in the heart of Baghdad.

"Nice digs," I said, trying to strike up conversation. My mom gave me an annoyed look and kept watching, remote still primed.

Onscreen, the man of the house was doing most of the talking while the rest of the clan nodded around him. According to Pops, everyone was mainly worried about the youngest daughter, a diabetic. The camera zoomed in on this kid hiding out behind some lady in a head scarf. She looked about six or seven and her flowery summer dress actually reminded me a lot of the ugly couch we were sitting on, although I didn't mention this to my mom, who was oohing and aahing over the diabetic.

After the sympathy-generating close-up of the kid, the father, dressed in a shabby suit, took us up onto the roof of the building. He showed us this little metal bucket thing and explained how he'd made it from a can and a piece of wire. He ran his fingers proudly along the makeshift handle, demonstrating how he'd bent the wire and attached it to the can. I was thinking he was definitely going to have to upgrade his craftsmanship if he wanted to sell his feeble-looking creations in the States, but it turns out it wasn't exporting he had in mind.

He tied a spool of fishing line to the handle and lowered the can down a pipe leading from the roof. When he retrieved the contraption, it was filled with water from a well beneath the building. He smiled nervously as he explained to the reporter that this was how he planned to keep the girl's insulin cold if and when the power went out in Baghdad.

By the end of that cheery little number, my mom's post-rally euphoria seemed to be slipping. She was sort of sagging into the couch and the remote in her hand wasn't quite as pert. Still, she flipped to the local station, but I bailed as soon as I saw Mrs. Jordan onscreen, weeping over her daughter's 141-day absence, begging for anyone with information about Astelle to please, please come forward.

My mother barreled up the stairs a couple minutes later. She stopped outside my room, looking completely pissed, to inform me that, "There wasn't one word, not one damn word, about the rally on WDFD." And she took a second to agree with a comment I'd made a while back. "That roving-eye guy, well, he *is* a bit of an asshole." Then the slam of a door. Hers for a change, not mine.

NINETEEN

The February 2003 weather roundup for Stokum went something like this: cold, sunny days, with snow every fucking night. It had definitely not been a good month to volunteer for shoveling duty. But hey, slipping the note into the widow's mailbox had always been more about self-flagellation than brotherly love. So really, I'd gotten what I wanted, seeing how I'd practically become a lawn ornament over at my Polish neighbor's pad. Even the grief-stricken widow seemed to have gotten used to me. In fact, given the timeliness of Mrs. Bernoffski's appearances at the front window, I suspected she was actually keeping an eye out for me, and brief waving sessions now preceded the clearing of the snow. And while I wouldn't exactly call her animated, as of late her arm actions had been fairly unrestrained during the pregame greeting.

Still, it must have been close to the end of February before we finally came face to face. I remember I was about halfway up the front walk when I heard the squeak of hinges and the whoosh of a door being pushed open. I looked up. In a pair of what looked to be her husband's boots and a long black coat, Mrs. Bernoffski shuffled onto the front porch. She raised a hand. I raised one back. Without the double-paned glass between us, we were both a little nervous, and our waves were low, stiff, halfhearted-type deals. I started nervously tapping my shovel against the paving slab I'd just uncovered. The metal blade striking the frozen cement sent a steady, high-pitched ping through the cold air which reminded me of that one, tuneless *Eyes Wide Shut* note ringing out again and again when Tom is about to get nailed for sneaking into the high-class sex orgy.

Although I felt my sound effects heightened the tension, Mrs. Bernoffski didn't say a word. With a heavy sigh she settled herself down on the porch steps, her sturdy calves poking out the tops of the oversized boots. I went back to shoveling. When I lifted my head to toss a load of snow onto the bank, I saw her watching me. Pretty soon, though, she'd shifted on the step, and with her big, beefy hands on her knees she turned to face the sun. By the time I moved over to start on the driveway, I was pretty relaxed about us being outside together, so I sort of jumped when she started yelling.

"No, no, no." She waggled her hands at me. Her fingers were thick and red. "You leave it. You leave it. I no be drive."

I was a bit relieved to hear it, but, pretending to be a better man than I am, I threw the shovel into the heavy fold of snow left by the plow at the bottom of the driveway. "It's okay. I don't mind," I said.

"You get in trouble with da school if you no shovel da road?"

"Ahh … no. No trouble." I'd almost forgotten about the civics class charade.

She pushed herself off the steps. "Okay, den. You leave it. Tank you for da good work. With the snow." She stamped her boots a couple times then reached for the door handle. I was already disappearing behind the hedge separating the Bernoffskis' yard from the Connellys' when she called out, asking if I wanted a drink.

I couldn't even imagine going into the kitchen and chatting up Mrs. Bernoffski while she took a couple hours whipping up some crummy European substitute hot cocoa. "Umm, I'd better be getting back," I hollered. "I have to go someplace." I should have just pushed off right then, but the widow was still on her porch, watching me, and I felt I had to add something. "So ... thanks anyway. Next time, maybe."

"Okay, den. Next time," she said, and shuffled inside.

WHEN MY DAD and I headed out a while later, my mother didn't even say goodbye. She'd been in a shit mood since, I don't know, forever. That day at lunch, she'd attempted to create a bit of a family moment by reading aloud from the local paper, something of a Saturday ritual in the Hunter household. Thing is, she chose to bring us up to date on all this depressing shit—the debate around Colin Powell's recent WMD speech at the UN, the shiny blue-green, half-inch ash borer beetle intent on gnawing its way through all 700 million of Michigan's ash trees, the ten-game losing streak of our local hockey team, the Stokum Stingers. Still, the worst part of the Saturday morning story hour was the update on convenience-store Howie, the guy who'd made such an impression on me when he was shot.

Apparently, the police had a suspect in custody, but Mrs. Holman, the loving wife, was the impatient type. The paper said she'd gone down to the courthouse and fired off a few shots of her own. She got the guy accused of killing her husband, nailed him in the head and chest, seriously injuring a policeman and a court recorder along the way. Now she was in jail and her kids were wards of the state. I couldn't help thinking how sickened Howie would have been if he'd seen the pathetic unraveling of the family he'd worked so hard for. When the missus was asked why she'd done it, the reporter claimed she'd given him a steely look and said that Howie had been her whole world, she'd loved him with all her heart, and when that son of a bitch had killed him, well, it all just turned bad. She said it was pure hate that had driven her to the courtroom and pulled the trigger seventeen times. She also took a moment to mention how pleased she was the bastard who'd killed her husband was dead himself.

I think it was at this point that my father had peered over the page and told my mom he had to go to work. It wasn't good timing.

My mom folded the paper and set it down on the table before she started bitching. About how we hardly ever saw him anymore. About him having his priorities backwards and jeopardizing their marriage and ignoring his health (his exercise bike had been completely stationary for the last couple months) and neglecting his son. Didn't he know how precious his family was? Didn't he realize he only got one chance at this? He might not know what it felt like to lose a family, but she did, by God, she did. My dad told her not to blow things out of proportion; we'd all survive his half day away. Besides, he didn't have a choice, there was a pile of contracts on his desk that had to be ready for Monday. And there were rumors of layoffs, big ones, trickling down from head office, and talk of moving the entire production facility to China, so keeping on top of things was doubly important at the moment. My mom quieted down a bit after that, but she still looked glum as a kid without a party invitation in hand. My dad reminded her the situation was temporary and as soon as Jack got back, things at Kalbro would settle down.

At that, my mom gave him a bitter smile. "Their house is up for sale," she said.

"What?" My dad looked genuinely surprised by the news.

"The Kites' house is up for sale. I saw the sign yesterday on my way to work."

WHEN I'D EXITED the kitchen, my parents were still at the table, sitting in what sounded a lot like hostile silence. And in the car on the way downtown, my dad was all distracted and really miserable-looking and I couldn't help feeling sorry for him. I mean, it wasn't his fault his boss was gay and cowardly and failing to report for duty. Still, I wasn't about to put in a huge effort to cheer up Dad.

I was sort of edgy about seeing Hank again. I probably shouldn't have worried, because when I called to see if he'd be in that afternoon, he'd been his old self—tolerant, kind, with a whiff of regret in his voice but nothing more. I'd always imagined the whiff had something to do with owning a small-time T-shirt shop in a small-time town and dealing with messed-up small-town teens, such as myself, during most of his waking hours. Then again, maybe he was just tired all the time.

My dad slowed down on Water Street and we both checked out the brown and yellow Century 21 sign planted firmly in the middle of the biggest lawn on the street. The Kites' place was definitely looking for a new family.

"So, do you think you'll get his job?" I asked.

"His job? Oh, I don't know about that. And besides, just because his place is for sale doesn't mean he's leaving Kalbro." He didn't sound very convincing and I thought I'd push him a bit.

"But he loved that house. Remember the tour? The Chicago designer? The purple living room?"

"Yes, I remember."

"He's gotta be gay." I wasn't sure how my dad would react to me propagating the rumor, but he just shook his head, looking all dazed and confused.

"Maybe. Doesn't matter. All I know is that if Jack does leave, he'll certainly be missed at the plant."

It surprised me to hear my dad say that. I'd always thought Mr. Kite was such a dick and I guess I'd just assumed my dad shared my opinion. "You could do his job, though, right?"

"I guess so. I'm doing it now, but it's not easy. And the supply chain is getting all buggered up. That's really been bothering me. I've had to advance-order from our overseas suppliers because I just don't have the time to stay on top of things every hour of the day, which is what you absolutely have to do to keep things running smoothly. So now our inventory is up, which is going to be costly, and we were late shipping to—"

"You can let me out here," I interrupted. We were still a couple blocks from the shop, but I wanted to put the brakes on the just-in-time lecture. My dad pulled up to the curb and I threw the door open. I was already starting down the sidewalk when I heard the toot of a horn and the buzz of an electric window.

"Luke?"

I went back to the car and bent down. My dad was stretched halfway across the front seat with his head a foot or two from the open window. A bald spot, the size of a condom, shone from the top of his thick brown head of hair. His jacket was undone and there was a wedge of fat trapped between the top of his pants and the seat belt. "Don't take what your mother said about our family falling apart too seriously. She's just upset. About a lot of things. But we'll be fine."

"Yeah, okay."

"You know, she's worried about you. Taping yourself in your room and whatnot."

"What?" I gave him a shocked look, but he was so not buying it.

"There are chunks of paint off the wall around the door and strands of duct tape on the windowsill. And you left the drop sheets in a heap in the garage."

"Oh."

"Oh?" He raised his eyebrows. With the proof he'd laid out, I think he was expecting more.

"Yeah, oh." I stood up, crossed my arms over my chest and took a step away from the car.

"So, do you want to tell me about it?"

"No. Not really. I did it. It was stupid. End of story. I'll fix the wall."

"We're not worried about the wall, Luke. We're worried about you."

"I'm fine."

"You're not still taking all those drugs, are you?"

"What? What drugs?"

"Your mother told me Burton's pharmacy called the other day. Something about having some prescriptions waiting for you."

This was news to me, and I told him as much.

He dropped his head and let out this big sigh, then craned his neck up again to meet my eye. He gave me a weak smile. "Luke, you're not thinking about doing anything stupid, are you?"

"Well, not too stupid."

"If things really weren't okay, you'd tell us, right?" He was trying to look confident, but it came off as sort of anxious.

"You'd be the first to know." I jammed my hands in my pockets and stamped my feet on the sidewalk a couple times.

"That's what I told your mother. But she thinks you're keeping things from us. Thinks you're depressed. About Stan. And everything else that's happened." He edged closer to the window. "Listen, Luke, I'm not going to tell you life's easy. I'm not going to tell you it's simple. But I will tell you it's worth living. Every minute of it. You hear me, Luke?"

I didn't answer. I pressed my lips together and stared at the sky, clear and bright.

"You hear me?" Voice firm. Voice no longer anxious. Voice fucking authoritative.

I looked his way. "I hear you."

"I'll see you tonight, then. The Red Wings are playing." My father had never accepted the fact that I wasn't a big hockey fan. I was pretty sure he still fantasized about us getting crazy together over some highlight reel or something equally lame. But man, he looked sad, sitting there in the car with his briefcase bulging beside him and his new roll of fat. So I said great, terrific, I'd meet him in front of the big screen for a bit of bonding and bodychecking.

I thought he'd pull away then, but when I stopped in front of Hank's my dad was still parked up the street. I waved. I couldn't see if he waved back or not. I figured he was probably watching to see if I headed for the pharmacy, but if the old man really wanted a clue about one thing that was eating me, he should have tailed me to the Shack and watched my face turn gray as the girl of my nightmares floated me a faded smile from the sun-bleached poster taped to Hank's door.

And I guess it was my unlucky day, because inside, the same bald-headed dude who'd been working the last time I'd come down to the Shack was propped behind the counter.

He gave a snort when he saw me. "Well, if it isn't the Prophet of Death."

My special ESP powers kicked in right away, and immediately I sensed two things: One, my mere presence no longer impressed the tough guy, and two, he and I were just never going to be friends. I laid my hands on the glass and we faced off across the counter.

"Hey, Fuckface," I said, giving him my winningest smile. One side of his nose was red and tight-looking, and there was a yellowy crust decorating his gold nostril ring.

A corner of his mouth pulled tight, and he shook his head at me. "I heard you made the whole fucking thing up. What a fucking lowlife."

"And I heard you got the big Employee of the Month award. On account of your sparkling personality."

"That first time you came in here, I just knew you were totally full of shit."

"I heard the leper with Tourette's syndrome who works weekends gave you a good run for your money."

"You are one twisted, lying, mother—"

"Your nose ring is infected. But don't get me wrong. It looks good."

His jaw slackened. He couldn't help reaching up to finger the inflamed nostril.

"Yeah, that's the one," I said, and headed for the storeroom. I opened the door just as Baldy lobbed a nice clear "Fuck you" at my back. Its amplified echo accompanied me into the small concrete box of a room.

Hank, down on his knees between two shelving units, looked up. "I see you're making some new friends, Luke."

"Who, him?" I jerked a thumb over my shoulder as the door slammed shut behind me. "Oh, he wasn't talking to me. He was talking to one of the other customers. Some old lady and her granddaughter."

"Very funny, Luke." He pushed himself off the floor with a grunt and brushed the dust from the knees of his jeans, creating a fine, powdery cloud around his legs.

"That guy is a goof," I said, hoping to get a bit of conversation going.

Hank made his way down the aisle and I could see right away his shirt had a message. *Jesus is Coming. Look Busy*, it said, which

I guess is what he'd been doing before I showed up.

Hank forced his fingers through his wiry hair. He went right down the center, where the part would have been if the Brillo pad could have been tamed, then settled both hands on his hips. "Bobby is okay," he said, nodding toward the store.

"Bobby? Okay? His nose ring is infected, for God's sakes."

"I'll get him some rubbing alcohol."

"You're too nice, Hank."

"Yeah, don't you know it." He gave me a bit of a look before asking about the Peppers concert.

"It was excellent. Awesome. Thanks."

"Glad to hear it." Hank pursed his lips and gave his head a little shake. "I'm just sorry Stan wasn't there with you."

I kicked at the floor and neither one of us said anything for a couple long seconds. I was worried Hank was going to go all soft on me again, but his voice was solid when he asked what I had for him. I pulled two sheets of paper from my back pocket and handed them over. Hank unfolded one, the mock-up for the front of the One Drum shirt—a simple *Rolland Rocks* in the same font as our award-winning *Stokum Sucks* design.

"I see you're sticking with a catchy two-word slogan."

"Yeah, well, I don't want anyone to get bored and quit reading halfway through."

Hank laughed and unfolded the second sheet of paper. "Artwork," he said, raising his eyebrows at me. "Very nice."

Using a felt-tip pen and some charcoal, I'd sketched out a Native-inspired drum for the back of the shirt. Crosshatching a thick birch-bark cylinder, thin strips of leather held the skins in place at either end of the drum. If you looked closely, you could see that the leather twine was actually a finely written list of the festival bands, interspersed with the concert date—April 27, 2003. (I'd added the date on the second go, because on my first attempt the band names alone had only been enough to lace up half the drum, which had looked kind of stupid.) I thought the whole thing was pretty sweet, and I guess Hank did too, because he gave me a good deal on the shirts. We settled on a dark, mossy green, same two sizes but with no ripped seams this time. I told him I'd get him some clean copies of the slogan and the final sketch and he wrote up an invoice, which I had to hand over to Ms. Banks at school for final approval.

We headed out of the storeroom, were standing by the front door, and I was all prepared to shove off, but Hank had kind of parked himself in front of the door. He was staring out the window and right on into the next galaxy, it seemed. "You know what I can't figure out?" he said finally. "Stan was the most alive kid I've ever met. I just can't understand how you can kill that kind of energy. I mean, where did it all go?"

Now he was staring right at me, looking all confused and anxious, like he was expecting me to come up with some concrete mathematical equation to explain the dissipation of life force into the cosmos or something. Drawing on all the knowledge I'd gained over the past couple months, I gave it my best shot. "You're asking me? Man, I don't understand dick."

The dude behind the cash was totally eavesdropping on our conversation, and besides, the intimate theme of the discussion was making me uncomfortable, so I said a quick thanks and catch-you-later. But when I headed out the door, Hank was right on my ass. Outside, the February weather was refusing to budge. It was still sunny, but thick dark clouds were gathering on the horizon, no doubt preloaded with the evening's standard dump of snow.

Hank sat down on the narrow windowsill and stretched his legs halfway across the sidewalk, apparently oblivious to the cold. "I was thinking about you the other day, Luke, when I was reading this article. About this scientific study. There were these doctors, see, and they got these distant healers from all different backgrounds—Muslims, Christians, Jews, Buddhists, Native Americans, the whole shebang—they got them to pray for these people with this incurable brain cancer, right? So they split the cancer patients into two groups, right, and one gets prayed for and the other group, what they call the control group, doesn't."

Hank's hands were going by this time, like an Italian's, and you could tell by his face that he was working hard to come up with the facts. I just let him blab away, but given the research I'd done over the Christmas holidays I already knew where he was coming from. I'd read the article. I knew about the study.

The healers had been sent a name, a picture and a list of symptoms and had prayed for the person for an hour a day over a couple-month period. Results hadn't come in, but a similar, smaller study with AIDS patients had given a big thumbs-up to the effectiveness of distant healing. Surprisingly, Hank finished off his synopsis with the as-yet-unpublished findings. According to him, a majority of the cancer victims who'd been prayed for were out whooping it up on the town, while their counterparts in the control group had shriveled up and died.

"So anyway, for some reason I thought about you when I read the article. About what happened with you knowing about Stan. About there being this other dimension."

"Do you get all your info from *Oprah* magazines, Hank?"

He laughed in an embarrassed sort of way. "What about you? You a fan of the big O?"

"Not really. I picked it up one day in the can. My mom has a subscription."

"I was at the dentist," Hank confessed. "Root canal. And a crown. Now that's a sign you're getting old—bad teeth. Jesus. Anyway, the article got me thinking."

"Seriously, Hank, a couple pages in some chick magazine aren't enough to make you a believer, are they?" A beat-up-looking electric guitar in the window of the pawnshop next door caught my eye. I knew I had no musical talent, still I took a couple steps up the sidewalk to check it out.

I guess I'd been shading Hank, because suddenly he was sitting in a beam of low winter sunlight. He raised a hand to shield his eyes. "Well, there's more going on out there than we know. Shit happens that we just don't understand."

I had to agree with him on that.

"Man, I should have gone to college," he said, shaking his head in disgust at his vast ignorance.

"I don't think that would have cleared things up for you, Hank." I went to stand in front of him again, offering him some relief from the glare. "You want to know the part of that article I found really interesting?"

"What?" Hank folded his arms across his chest.

"The doctor in charge of the study, the one who'd started the distant healing research—she was the daughter of some chess champion or something, remember?"

"Yeah, Bobby Fischer. His niece, I think."

"Well, she ended up getting brain cancer—the exact kind she was doing the study on. The probability of that was like one in a million or something. How's that for a coincidence?"

Hank shook his head again, looking more confused than ever. "Behold the inexplicable," he said, not sounding a whole lot like himself. "I bet she signed herself up for the prayer group."

"Yeah, she did. It said so on the Web."

"And?"

The sun slipped behind the Royal Cinema building across the street. The light around us deepened to dusk and it felt like the temperature dropped ten degrees.

"She died," I said. "Before the magazine even came out."

TWENTY

It was already the beginning of March before I finally worked up the nerve to thank Faith for her Mr. J. Cash offering. I found her at lunch, in the library, at The Table, the one that, for a few golden weeks in December—after the concert, before the movie—I'd dared to think of as ours.

She was looking as hot and heavenly as ever. I approached from the stacks, sort of wandering out and casually bumping against the table to make it look like the whole encounter was completely random.

"Oh, hi," I'd said, acting all surprised. She smiled and gave a graceful, game-show-babe sweep of her hand toward the empty chair across the table. I slipped right into the hot seat. We chitchatted for a bit about safe stuff—how many days in a row Mr. Switzer, the science teacher, had been wearing the permasuit (forty-one), the upcoming release of the new White Stripes album (April 1), what she was reading (a play the drama group was thinking about doing; as proof, she dangled a copy of Tennessee Williams's *The Glass Menagerie* in front of me). She squared the book up in front of her, then, as usual, quickly swung the conversation in a more sensitive direction.

"Have you been avoiding me?" she asked.

"No," I said, noticing how that one syllable climbed at the end.

I said it again, keeping it low and steady. Even so, Faith kept up the questioning.

"Don't you like me?"

I swallowed hard. "No ... I mean ... yeah ... I like you."

She leaned in a bit to deliver her next inquiry, and I got a soft, staggering whiff of her peppermint scent. "Do I make you nervous?"

"No," I said nervously. I pulled her book over and started skimming the pages. "Any coma victims in the *Menagerie*? Because, seriously, I'd be perfect for a role like that, if you're looking for new talent, that is ..."

She took the book from my hands and set it back on the table in front of her. "Is it because of Stan?"

"No." Jesus.

"So, it's just me?"

"No," I said again. Nervously again. "I've just been really, sort of, busy." I picked a pen from her pencil case and twirled it on my thumb and middle finger.

"Doing what?"

I concentrated on the pencil and groped for something. "Ahh, hanging out and, ahh, shoveling snow, mostly. My neighbor's driveway. For free. Her husband died a while ago." I was trying to impress her, so I skipped the part about my passive, but integral, role in the man's death. "And I'm doing the shirts for the One Drum festival."

"Really? That's great!" She looked enthusiastic and I decided it probably wouldn't kill me to be a little straighter with her.

"Listen, I should have stopped by earlier to thank you for the CD."

"Do you like it?" She nailed me with her emerald beams. The pencil clattered onto the table, but I hung on, maintained eye contact, let her come on in.

"Yeah. I love the Reznor song. It's so painful." I took a chance. "Kind of like our Christmas hookup. Only shorter."

"Much shorter," she said, laughing. "What was with you that night, anyway?"

"It was probably the electric shock treatment I had right before we went out. I should have rescheduled."

She laughed again. "Next time," she said, and my whole body throbbed at the implication.

I was still sort of lost in that throb when Faith, always thoughtful, asked about Fang. I told her I hadn't seen him lately, which wasn't really true. I'd seen him in the back parking lot a couple of times, but he always gave me this weird look, like he was some wounded animal I'd just tried to run over or something. I had, like, zero time for his bullshit, so I'd just glide on by, holding on to his Luke's-a-complete-dick comment, pretending he wasn't even there.

"He's in my history class," Faith said, "but he hardly ever shows up. When he does, he looks so bad. Yesterday he fell asleep on his desk. Mr. Howard totally freaked on him."

"Yeah, well, to be honest, I'm sort of pissed at him."

Faith didn't look impressed. "Really? Well, I think it's time you got over it. Seriously, Luke, you should talk to him."

To demonstrate what a good, reliable, always-there sort of friend I was, I reluctantly agreed to track down Fang.

"Promise?" Faith asked.

I flashed her a peace sign. "Scout's honor."

I could see she was pleased, and she didn't press for details, which was just as well since I had no intention of actually following through. And I don't really know where I found the balls to throw out the next couple things, but they were pressing at me, I mean really pressing, and I didn't think I could just keep coming up and sitting with Faith if I didn't get some answers, and since I was interested—incredibly, highly interested—in sitting with her, I opened my mouth and let the first thing loose.

"So, hey, you've probably heard what everyone's saying, you know, that I made it all up."

"Yeah, I've heard the rumor."

"And?" I couldn't even look at her here. I concentrated on my hands, holding tight to the edge of the table.

"And what?" she said. So light and easy, there was room for my eyes to flicker to hers.

"Do you believe it?"

"Luke, I know what happened. I've talked to Fang about it."

My hands dropped from the table. "And it doesn't freak you out?"

"No."

"Or scare you?"

"*No.* Luke, you don't scare me. I know you and Stan were really close and I figure you were, like, connecting on some other level or something. So somehow, somehow, without even knowing, you knew."

I could have straightened her out right there, told her that me knowing Stan was going to get nailed by that van had nothing to do with us being tight. I mean, I barely knew Mr. Bernoffski, had never even met convenience-store Howie, and they'd both made my list. But seriously, I couldn't get anywhere close to being that honest. So instead, I nodded and said, "Okay, then. All right." And when Stan's closest pal boomed a big, joyful smile at his old girlfriend? She boomed one right back.

I guess it was my day to be studding it up with beautiful women, because as I was heading downtown after school to finalize the One Drum shirts, I bumped into another hottie, hanging on the sidewalk outside McCreary Park. And this one came straight for me, clipboard in hand. I recognized her right off, before she even told me her name. Laura, Laura Cramp, looked even better in person than she did on TV, despite the volleyball-sized bump popping out the front of her white down jacket. Laura definitely had the hit-upon-Heidi thing happening, with two long blonde braids poking from a pom-pom-topped ski hat. Still, even knocked up and bundled up, she managed to look fresh and innocent and sexy, and when she started blabbing, I acted interested.

Apparently she was a member of some group, Concerned Citizens Against Fudge Packing in the Park or something like that, who wanted to out the names of the men arrested in the bandstand. She went on about how it was "for everyone's safety" and how "men like that can be helped" and "freedom of information" and "constitutional rights," and when she pushed her clipboard toward me and mentioned the petition she was going to personally present to Police Captain Deeks and Judge Harvey, I noticed her breath was just-brushed fresh. Still, when she tried to hand me the pen, I just smiled and walked away. First off, I just wasn't the proactive, petition-pounding type. Secondly, I really didn't give a shit about who was doing what to who in the homo hangout. Thirdly, if my mom ever got wind that I'd signed Laura's list, she would have kicked my ass. I'll admit I was curious to know if my dad's missing boss was gay, but I figured, hey, there were enough small-minded folks in our small-minded town to push Kite out of the closet without any help from me and my John Hancock.

So even though I sort of blew off Laura, my streak with the chicks wasn't totally done. I ended up hanging out with Faith a fair bit over the next couple weeks. I never worked up the nerve to actually ask her out or walk her home or anything that bold. Still, it was a pretty stellar time for me. In fact, if I disregarded the recurring Astelle nightmares and a couple more dead men dropping by to sing me their songs and some random, disturbing thoughts about the call from Pastor Ted and the Amish-like shunning I was receiving from a majority of the Jefferson student body, I'd have to say March 2003 was one of the best months of my life.

I can't really say the same for my mother. She seemed to be having a fairly shitty late winter/early spring season. She'd developed an especially bleak outlook on life and was dragging her depression around the house like a dirty blanket. I tried to avoid her as much as possible, but the day I came home after school and found her sitting at the Formica table crying, I couldn't pretend not to notice.

In fact, when I'd seen her car in the driveway that day, right away I'd felt a pang of concern. It was three-thirty. On a weekday. She should have been at work. I'd gone inside quietly, had stopped in the kitchen doorway when I saw her. Her face was half hidden by the arm she was leaning on, her eyes shielded by the fingers of one hand. A ragged Kleenex poked from her other hand, which was tucked in front of her, balled into a tight fist.

"Hey," I said tentatively. I reached out and pressed a palm against either side of the doorjamb, pinning myself in the entrance to the kitchen.

My mom swiped at her eyes with the Kleenex and glanced at me quickly, forcing out a shaky hello. She was still dressed in her bank clothes and her purse and keys were in the middle of the table. I got the impression she would have preferred to be having her breakdown in the privacy of her own room, which definitely would have suited me, but by this time it was too late for that.

I headed for the cupboard and grabbed a bag of mini rice cakes, an inspired-by-sawdust snack food that my mom tries to pass off as a worthy substitute for chips. The sack opened with a puffy fart. As I leaned back against the counter and tucked one leg up beneath me, I saw my mother's coat lying on the floor. It was her good long winter jacket, the one with the fake fur collar and cuffs. I knew it had probably just slipped off a chair, but it still bothered me to see it lying on the floor like that.

I stuck a handful of rice cakes in my mouth and started munching. "So," I said. Filtered through the mouthful of fake chips, it came off very casual. "Is it the whole deal in Iraq?"

My mom's face pulled into a stiff grimace, as if she'd just stubbed her toe or something, but she shook her head. "No. It has nothing to do with Iraq."

"You mad at Dad?" This time my question was quieter, less crunchy.

"Yes," she said with emphasis, and then a noisy sniffle, "but it's not that." She rattled out a long, quaking sigh. "It's the lake."

"The lake?"

"You know, the lake." She waggled her hand in the general direction of Erie. "It's dying. Again." The "again" was very sad and dramatic-sounding. "Only this time they don't think it can be saved. I was at a meeting last night and Helen Shaunessy, our president, presented this EPA report. And today ... at work, I don't know what happened." She stared at me desperately. Her eyes and nose were all red and sloppy. "I was at my window, handing money across the counter to some customer I hardly knew, and it just hit me. *The lake is dying. It's dying.* I had to leave." Another quivering sigh escaped her. "The dead zone in the middle of the lake just keeps getting bigger and bigger ..."

"Why?" My hand was motionless inside the bag.

"The goby. The zebra mussel. The Quagga mussel. Pesticides. Aging sewage treatment facilities. Dropping water levels. Acid rain. Fertilizers. Global warming. Who knows?" She shook her head at the anoxic list. "I'm sure you probably think I'm nuts sitting here crying over a lake. I know it's not a person. It's not Stan. It's just that we're so *careless,* and ... and ..." She dabbed at her eyes. "I feel so *powerless.*"

There was a bit of an uncomfortable silence then, and I wasn't sure what to do with my distraught mother and her dying lake. I suggested calling Dad, but she gave that a quick thumbs-down, saying he was "too busy" for her. And when she snagged another tissue, I told her, "Hey, go easy, it takes ninety years to grow a box of those babies," one of her favorite stats, but she didn't even crack a smile. Flailing for something, I poured a glass of milk and set it in front of her, but I didn't join her at the table. I did pick her coat off the floor and hang it on a sturdy wooden hanger in the front hall closet. And I did stop in the living room to dig out our *O Brother* CD. I skipped right to track four. A chorus of healing voices accompanied the soggy "Thanks" that wavered from the kitchen as I headed for my tear-proof refuge upstairs.

When the war started up a few days later, we were all there, watching from the comfort of our living room, along with the rest of America. As the line of tanks started rolling across the screen on its way to Baghdad, neither my dad or I were really surprised when my mom said, "You'd think by now we could come up with something better than ... than *this*," before she got up and left the room.

TWENTY-ONE

Something in the Spirit of One T. Williams

to Break the Monotony of War and My Mother's Shit Mood

A Play in Three Acts

Written by: Luke Hunter

* * Based on a True Story * *

(A heads-up here: Any misrepresentation of conversations or characters is entirely the fault of the author, who, seriously, did his best to get things right.)

Setting: A table in a nondescript high school library.

The Players

Faith: extremely beautiful, racially mixed, 17-year-old girl who Luke dreams of nailing (let's be honest) despite the inappropriateness of such, given the recent passing of Stan, a good friend to Luke and, more importantly, a boyfriend to Faith

Luke: a bit of a loser teen; for specifics, see above. Close to six feet tall—okay, five ten and a half—with good, straight teeth thanks to some expensive dental work. Luke has

longish, wavy blond hair that curls out from beneath his
baseball cap, which is always worn backwards. Faith,
conflicted by the death of her boyfriend, has confused
Luke for someone special.

Act 1

At the rise of the curtain, Faith and Luke are onstage, seated
across from each other at a book-stacked table.

Faith: Hey, did you ever see that movie Stigmata?

Luke: Yeah, a couple years ago. I loved the part on the subway.
The whipping scene.

Faith (shaking her head): Really? I liked the part right at the
end of the movie. That quote from the Gospel of Thomas. I
checked it out on the Web afterwards—this at the height
of my spiritual conflict with Stan's parents. Apparently
Thomas had some really twisted ideas, but I did like the
quote from the movie: "The Kingdom of God is within you,
not in temples of wood and stone. Touch a piece of wood: I
am there. Turn a stone, and you will find me."

Luke: Oh, yeah. That part. That part was good too. Definitely a
close second to the whipping scene.

(Faith laughs.)

Luke (smiles, doing his best impression of charming):
Actually, it reminds me of this thing Steinbeck wrote.

Faith (obviously impressed): Really?

Luke (cool, but secretly pleased with himself): From Cannery

Row. He revised the first bit of the Lord's Prayer to "Our
Father, who art in nature ..."

(Faith beams, no doubt weighing the probability of ever being
lucky enough to bed the genius across the table.)

SHOCK AND AWE were already playing on the night skies over
Baghdad by the time my mom unplugged the television. In fact,
she not only unplugged the set, she rearranged the entire living
room, pushing all the furniture into the center of the room, covering it with old blankets and bedsheets, so that from a certain angle
it looked kind of fort-ish and fun, really, like the whole space had
been taken over by some sturdy, industrious kid. When
confronted, my mother claimed she was planning on repainting
and, while she was at it, having the couch recovered as well. She
said she wanted my help picking out the color for the walls and
doing the work. I said sure, but I never saw any paint chips, let
alone a can or a brush. The living room sat empty, with a big ghost
of furniture crowded in the middle, and whenever I passed by, I
imagined the severed television huddled somewhere in the scrum.

We have a little set in the office at the back of the house, and if
I'd been really eager I could have gone in there to claim my front-
row seat for the war. Instead, I gave up watching altogether, which
was a bit of a relief really. When I had been partaking of the action,
it had been sort of difficult for me to pretend there weren't any
musical people underneath those smart, falling bombs, and I'd had
trouble convincing myself all the exploding buildings were vacant.
I couldn't even imagine how the rickety insulin bucket might be
faring.

My dad was still tuned in, however, playing sofa soldier from the pullout in the office, the one with the metal bar underneath the seat cushions, specially designed to ensure maximum discomfort. He'd limp out of the office, rubbing his ass, to provide updates on the 507th Maintenance Company mishap or the new POWs or the unorthodox guerrilla tactics being used by Iraq's Elite Republican Guard. My dad fed me all the highlights, really, so I figured I wasn't missing anything but the pain.

Act 2

Faith (looking particularly gorgeous, but slightly melancholy): You know, until Stan died, nothing really bad had ever happened to me. I had this perfect life. Nice family, nice boyfriend, nice life. I really believed the world was good, people were good. But after Stan died, I sort of lost sight of that. Everything got very dark and confusing. For a while I hardly stepped out of my room. I had, like, zero energy. But now (pauses to give Luke a smile, although later Luke thinks he may have imagined it) I can kind of see the goodness again. I think I have to. It's who I am.

Luke: It's who you are? You're goodness?

Faith (taken aback): I didn't mean it like that, I mean I see the—

Luke (interrupting): It's okay. You don't have to be embarrassed. (Joking, to mask his seriousness) It's okay to be good. Personally, I think I'm something a lot closer to indifference or ineptitude or, I don't know … slime mold.

Faith (raises her eyebrows): You're slime mold?

Luke: Yeah. But the good kind. The kind they make penicillin from.

Faith (laughs): Well, at least you're useful.

Luke: I don't know. I think the antibiotics are all synthetic these days. I'm probably obsolete.

Faith: Well, can't you be synthetic slime mold?

Luke (considering): I don't know. It feels kind of cheap.

Faith: How about botulism, then?

Luke (feigning shock): Botulism? Man, you really have a low opinion of me, don't you? Botulism. Now there's a force to be reckoned with. Perhaps I should switch tables.

Faith (teasing, hopefully): I don't think anyone else would have you.

Luke (quickly shaking off the truth behind Faith's last statement): And you're not worried about the possibility of contamination, O Goddess of Goodness?

Faith (laughs): I think I'm immune, Botulism Boy.

Luke: I hope so. For your sake (makes eye contact with Faith, face softens up, honesty reigns) … and mine, I truly hope so.

TAKING A LEAD from me, which is almost always a bad idea, my mother was now spending a fair amount of time holed up in *her* room. I knew it was probably because of the war and the lake and a whole host of other catastrophic shit I didn't want to know about, and really, I probably shouldn't have cared. Still, with my mom flattened upstairs and my dad working all the time, the house did feel a tad quiet and the fridge a wee bit empty. It gave me some appreciation for what my parents might have been going through back in the fall when I'd spent a majority of my time in private retreat.

I tried my best to coax my mom back into our lopsided family circle. My efforts at ferreting her out involved pounding on the door, yelling that there was no milk for my cereal and that I'd appreciate her getting her ass out here so she could start worrying about me again, thank you very much. It was no big surprise when my father, having the dough to throw at the problem, came up with a far superior strategy for getting some food back in the fridge.

He arrived home one night, late again, but armed with plane tickets. He came and got me so I could watch him march into their room and drop those babies into my mom's lap. She gave my nervous father, then me, a suspicious look before setting her book on the bed beside her. I didn't even want to know what depressing thing she was reading, so I kept my eyes on my next vacation. She picked the tickets off the comforter and fanned them across one hand. My dad, doing his best imitation of firm and in control, stood beside the bed and said he didn't want any arguments, didn't want to know how many tanker trucks of fuel a plane burned during a transatlantic flight, they were going to Paris.

My mom slapped the tickets against her palm. I could see there were only two. When she looked at my dad, a slow smile crept across her face. "Well, it's not the hottest destination at the moment," she said, no doubt referring to France's poor showing in the recent Friends of America poll, which had resulted in the drastic renaming of the french fry here at home. "Still," she said, her smile growing, "I've always wanted to go to Paris."

My dad huffed out a big sigh and pursed his lips. And God, for a second there I thought he was going to cry or something. He managed to get a grip, but still, he sounded pretty choked up when he started talking. "I know you have. They're for your birthday. In April," he added, in case she'd forgotten when she was born.

"I've always wanted to go to Paris too," I said hopefully, from my third-wheel position just inside the door.

My mom dropped her chin and raised her eyebrows. "Not everything's about you, Luke."

Apparently not, I thought, but, remembering the Erie-inspired bawling scene I'd witnessed a few weeks previous, I stayed cool, didn't say a word. I told them to have a great time and headed down the hall, thinking about the unsupervised opportunity coming my way. It was almost enough to block out the obscenely soft sound of my parents' bedroom door closing behind me.

And a week or so later, I wasn't actually eavesdropping or anything, I was just passing by, really, when I heard my parents talking in their room. My mom sounded upset, *again,* which was a drag, because ever since the plane tickets arrived she'd been behaving so well. She wasn't 100 percent or anything, I mean the

TV was still buried in the fort, but at least she'd been keeping my cereal wet, going to work, preparing dinner, attending Friends of Lake Erie meetings without ensuing emotional collapse. So, it was really just concern for her that made me stop on the other side of her closed door.

The first thing I clearly overheard was something about canceling the trip to Paris. That freaked me. Given my recent studdish streak between the book stacks, I was ready to take things up a notch and had been fantasizing about having Faith over while my parents were away. I figured once we were alone on my turf, she'd probably be all over me. To be honest, I'd sort of pictured us going at it in various locations in and around and on top of the house, and the fact that the imagined sex settings might not be available was very bad news. I pressed my ear to the door.

"Everyone at work says we shouldn't go." This from my mom.

"Why?" My dad, sounding tired, frustrated.

"Why? It's unpatriotic. French hostility toward Americans. Too many people taking time off in April. Our plane will be blown up by terrorists. I could go on."

"So … what do you want to do?"

Long pause.

"I say fuck it. Let's go." It shocked me to hear my mother use the word.

"So … we're going, then?" My father sounded unsure but not at all surprised by his wife's foul mouth.

"Absolutely. We're going. We're fucking going." She laughed.

I laughed. They were fucking going.

Act 3

Luke rushes into the library, then slows to a swagger and slides into his regular chair across the table from Faith, who is looking extremely happy and excited by his mere presence.

Faith (as soon as Luke is settled): So, did you get it?

Luke (confused, then—realizing what she's asking—mimics the opening guitar riff of "Seven Nation Army," the first single on the freshly released White Stripes album): Ba-ba-ba-ba-ba-ba-ba ... (Faith smiles, then does a version which is way better than Luke's.)

Faith (laughing): Isn't it great?

Luke: Awesome. And Meg sings.

Faith: Yes! Isn't it sweet?

Luke: Very.

Faith: And you saw the video?

Luke (nods): So cool. So red and white triangles.

Faith (laughs): That's what's great about the White Stripes— they're cool and sweet. Definitely not an easy combo. Especially when the flavor of the month is shock and awe.

Luke: Yeah, no kidding. (Long pause. Luke and Faith look at each other intently. Smiles creep across both their faces. Luke is first to look away.)

Faith: So, where were you, anyway? Lunch is almost over.

Luke: Mrs. Hayward kept me after class.

Faith: What have you done now? Made some crack about her rubber boots?

Luke: Nooo. For your information, she gave me a present.

Faith: A present? Really!

Luke (pauses, then reaches for his backpack): Want to see it?

Faith: Of course.

Luke (pulls a leather-bound book from his bag and pushes it across the table): It's nothing much, just a journal sort of thing. (Faith runs her hand over the cover, admiring the book.) You know ... to write in.

Faith: Yes, I know what it's for. It's really nice.

Luke: So, ahh, Mrs. Hayward thought it might be good for me to write down some stuff.

Faith (quietly, sincerely): People can be so nice, can't they?

Luke: Yeah, once a year or so. And only if they're Seuss fans.

Faith (pushes the book back): Come on. Just admit it, without any qualifiers: People can be nice.

Luke: Okay, okay. People can be nice. There, are you happy now?

Faith: Very. Very happy. (Gives him a sexy, satisfied smile. A bell rings. Luke and Faith stand to collect their things.)

Faith (glancing at Luke): So ... are you going to the dance?

Luke (freezes): The dance?

Faith: Yeah. There's a dance this Friday.

Luke (forcing himself to move again, he sticks a book in his
        backpack): I heard the dances are completely lame. The
        music totally sucks.

Faith: I'm thinking about going.

Luke: Yeah, well, I was thinking about, maybe, going. Too.
        Maybe. You know. For something to do. Maybe. (Faith and
        Luke move to the exit, rear center stage.)

Faith: So, I might see you there?

Luke: Maybe. Possibly. Probably.

Faith: Good. Then you might, maybe, possibly, probably, see me
        there, too.

Luke holds the door for Faith then follows her, heart tripping,
offstage. Scene fades to black.

THE END

TWENTY-TWO

The weather in February may have been brutal, but March rolled by as a bright and beaming thirty-one days. It hadn't snowed the entire month and, seeing how we were well into April, I was confident the dreaded drink with the neighbor was going to be a no go. But that Mrs. Bernoffski, she's a tricky old widow. It was way above zero and the skies were perfectly clear the day I turned unsuspectingly onto my street to find my Polish taskmaster daringly positioned at the end of her walk. Like me, she was still wearing her winter jacket, open down the front. She waved when she saw me, then shuffled up the porch steps and sat down.

"Come," she said loudly, patting the empty space beside her. On her other side sat a big bottle of something clear. "Today, we have our drink." I moved slowly up the walk, watching as she fished two shot glasses from her pocket. She set them on a little silver tray and uncapped the bottle, which I could now see was some foreign-looking vodka. Surprised, I settled myself on the stoop as Mrs. Bernoffski, using two hands, carefully filled the small gold-rimmed glasses. As she passed one to me, I noticed how thick and red and sausagey her fingers were and wondered if that was a common Polish trait.

She raised her drink and gave me a solemn nod. *"Nosdrovia,"*

she said. Pressing the glass to her lips, she snapped her head back
and downed the shot in one neat gulp.

I raised my glass, gave a cheer and, following suit, slammed my
drink back. It raged going down, and when the fiery liquid hit my
gut, my shoulders shot upward and my whole body quaked. But
the second shot was smoother, and by the third I was really
looking forward to getting plastered on the porch with my
wonderful, drinking-age-oblivious neighbor on what was proving
to be a truly glorious day. I felt myself relax inside my feather nest
of a coat and, settling in, I accidentally kicked my backpack,
forgotten beside my feet, a couple steps down. The backpack
toppled down the stairs in an awkward but amusing sort of way.
I was fuzzily contemplating picking it up when Mrs. Bernoffski
wiped the back of her hand across her mouth and wrapped her
thick fingers around my knee.

"So," she said, turning to look straight at me. The sharp smell
of alcohol wafted from the pocket of commingled breath hanging
between us. Her deep-set eyes were wet and glassy in their dark
hollows. She gave my knee a squeeze and for a second I kind of
tensed up, fearing the boy-fondled-by-drunken-depressed-widow
worst. Turns out she only wanted to chat.

"You have some troubles, no?"

I nodded at her, but to be honest I wasn't sure which one of my
problems she might be referring to, so I kept quiet. I figured if
anyone was unaware of my prophetic talents it was Mrs.
Bernoffski, given that she wasn't the most plugged-in personality
in Stokum. I mean, her husband *had* died the day after Stan, so
she'd probably missed my whole WDFD coming-out party. And

unless she had Pastor Ted–type powers, she couldn't be asking about Astelle or Fang or the bevy of other folks I had difficulty dealing with, so I just kept my head bobbing and my mouth shut.

"You have da funny feelings?" I had no idea where she was heading, but sitting on that spring-drenched front porch I was suddenly roasting inside my winter jacket.

Mrs. Bernoffski squeezed my knee firmly again, and by this point I couldn't even keep up the nodding. But after a bit of a wandering start, she finally headed straight for the point.

"You think you kill my Johnny." She waggled a plump finger at me. "Dat's why you shovel my snow."

Blood rushed to my cheeks, so they burned hot as the vodka racing inside me. I couldn't think of a thing to say. Luckily, the liquor-lubed Mrs. Bernoffski was in a talkative mood.

"Listen," she said, "I know 'bout you. Johnny, he phone me dat day and he tell me how Doug's boy come and is all crazy to cut da grazz, cut da grazz. Den Johnny die. Cutting da grazz." She folded her arms across her chest, leaned back a little, and gave me a shrewd look. "And your friend, da boy on the wheely. I know about dat too."

I was managing to maintain eye contact, but I knew my mouth was hanging wide and my face was all stricken and shit. Mrs. Bernoffski gave me a firm poke, leaving a tiny divot in my down-filled chest. She held my eyes with hers, and it was probably just the booze, but as I looked into those old-world orbs, the spin of the new world seemed to slow. The wind dropped and the sun narrowed to a single beam, bright enough to light just one small front porch in one small town.

"What you think?" Mrs. Bernoffski said, her voice quiet. "You think I don't know things? I'm Polish, not stupid. I know things. One thing I know, we all have funny feelings. And we all die. Nothing no one can do. Another thing I know, it's God who decide when we die, not da little boy up the street."

I had to look away when she said that. I clenched my jaw and hung my head. I could feel the tears pooling. Beside me I heard a couple clinks and the slide of liquid from a bottle. Mrs. Bernoffski nudged a shot glass into my hand then plucked the other one from my lap. We both stared out at the peacefulness of our street, and she gave my hand a solid squeeze.

"My husband, he is a stubborn man. He let no one cut his grazz. When he die under his tractor, he die a happy man." She lifted her drink and gave me a nudge. I held my glass high. Inside, the liquor flashed silver.

"To Johnny," she said. *"Nosdrovia."*

WHEN MY MOM CAME IN and plopped down on my bed, I was digging through boxes of T-shirts. I was still a bit wasted from the after-school drinking binge with the widow, but if my mom noticed, she didn't mention it. She plucked a stray shirt off the floor and, holding it by the shoulders, flipped it front to back a couple times. Trying not to appear eager, I rooted through the box I was kneeling beside, pretending to check sizes, but covertly I kept an eye on my mom.

"Wow." She was frowning in a surprised but impressed sort of way. "They look great. Nice drum."

I cocked my head. "You like it?"

"Yes. It's really good. You're very talented."

"Thanks." I laughed off the compliment, but I had to admit the shirts did look pretty awesome. "They're fifteen bucks if you're interested."

"I'll take one for me and one for your dad." She folded the T into a neat square and set it on the bed. "Too bad we can't go."

My parents were big fans of One Drum, and as far as I knew they'd never missed a festival. For the past couple years I'd gone with my friends, and last spring I'd sold shirts there with Stan, but before that One Drum had always been a fresh-cut-fields-and-candy-floss sort of family affair. Although I never remembered much about any of the bands, I always remembered coming back from Rolland with my parents. The drives home were kind of surreal. No one ever said much, but it was always a good, peaceful kind of quiet invading the car. After a day's worth of music, I'd be feeling tired and happy and cushioned from the world outside the windows by the ringing in my ears. I think my parents were too, and for a couple days afterwards the happy beat would hold. We'd smile easy smiles as we passed, humming, in the halls, until we all eased back into the harder rhythms of life.

This year, however, my mom and dad would be cancanning it around Paris instead of listening to the bang of our American drums. They were taking the red-eye to France the next day, the Saturday before the festival, which was always on a Sunday (Sunday, April 27, to be exact, if the info crisscrossing the back of the shirts was accurate). My mom had arranged for Ms. Banks to pick me and my shirts up early on the morning of the festival, seeing how my regular drivers were going to be way, way out of town.

My mom reached over and gave the peak of my baseball cap a tap. "I'm sorry you're not coming with us."

"It's okay. Besides, I've got the T-shirt thing happening." I didn't mention anything about using the house for sex.

"Remember how much fun we had in Barcelona?"

Oh yeah, I remembered that. My mom was no doubt referring to all the tapas bars we'd visited, all the Gaudí-inspired sightseeing we'd done, which had been cool. But when I thought about fun in Barcelona, what sprang to mind were my clandestine evening encounters with Nuria, the Spanish chick who'd staked her claim on me the second night of our trip, when I'd opted for a stroll along the beach rather than a night at the newly refurbished Opera with Mom and Dad.

Nuria wasn't all that gorgeous or anything, and she could barely speak English, but her long skirt had swayed pretty enticingly when she'd headed my way across the soft sand. And man, when she opened her full lips and said, *"Hola,"* I was glad I was already seated. Her voice was magic, like a lilting silver flute or something. Yeah, Nuria and her vocals were definitely worth a lie and a nightly sprint to the beach. And on my last night in Barcelona, Nuria kept running her hands through my hair and kissing me and whispering that I was so big and blond and beautiful and that she was going to miss me, and when she pulled a condom out of her pocket I'd been quick, very quick, with my big *"Si, Si."*

I got a letter from her about a month after getting home to sexless Stokum, and unfortunately the Spanglish that had spilled so musically from her mouth lay flat as stones on the page. I never even bothered writing back. Still, I had her letter in my desk drawer in case I ever needed proof a girl had actually dug me. And despite the grammatical errors and the fact she'd misspelled my name, I was particularly fond of the PS, which went something— okay, exactly—like this: "PS. Luk, I love fuck you on the sand."

I gave my mom a big smile. "There's no way Paris could live up to Barcelona, anyway. No way." I paused and took a quick peek at my mom. She was still dressed in her work clothes, a white blouse and dark dress pants, but she looked pretty chilled, and I decided to risk the next line. "Besides, everything's not about me, right?"

My mom leaned forward, elbows on her knees, and sighed. "Listen, I'm sorry about that. But it's important that your father and I get away on our own right now. I could have been a little gentler with you, but I haven't been in the gentlest of moods lately."

"Really?" I feigned surprise.

"Really," my mom said flatly. "Still, it's true. Not everything is about you. Or anyone else for that matter. That's something you learn growing up."

"Yeah, well, thanks for the heads-up."

"Luke, could you cut the sarcasm? It gets annoying." She took a minute to slip off her shoes, then flopped over on the bed and curled up, one hand between her knees, the other slipped under the pillow. "So, how are you, really?"

"Pretty good," I said. "Pretty tired." My mom looked so comfortable lying there on the bed, I had to get horizontal. I stretched out on the floor, balled up a One Drum shirt and stuck it under my head. I closed my eyes. I knew my mom was watching, but it didn't bother me. The lingering effects of the booze and a general exhaustion pressed me into the carpet.

"That's how you look. Happy. But tired. Your dad and I both think so."

"I'm sleeping like crap."

"Oh, that reminds me. Fang called last night. He sounded awful. When I asked, he said he hasn't been sleeping. So you two have something in common."

"Not much." I knew I sounded snotty, but like the first notes of a country-and-western tune, these days the mere mention of Fang gave me an uncomfortable twang. I tried to change the topic, but when my mom had a problem child on her mind she was hard to distract. She reminded me how Fang and I had known each other for ages, how important it was to "be there" for your friends, how he was the closest thing I had to a brother, etc., etc. Only after I promised to return the loser's call did she get back to more important things.

"So," she said, "you're having trouble sleeping?"

"Yeah. Nightmares. Wicked nightmares." I closed my eyes again.

"Do you want to tell me about them?"

"Not really. They're bad. About bad stuff."

It was sort of weird, but it seemed the looser things got with Faith, the tighter they got with Astelle. Ever since the Red Carpet In_, Astelle had been a dream-cast regular, but for the last little while she'd turned into a total dominatrix. She showed up every night and she'd pulled the pink sweatshirt from her mouth and pushed the fat guy off of her and she'd started screaming, clutching at her mangled arm and her twisted clothes, her head was flopped to one side, dangling from her busted neck, and she was screaming at me to do something, do something, why didn't I do something? Obviously, dream girl didn't know that doing nothing was way more my style.

"Are you dreaming about Stan?"

"NO. *No.* Just forget it, okay? I'll get over it."

"Do you think it would help to talk to someone?"

"Talk to someone? Like who?" The vodka vapors had started to evaporate.

"Like a psychologist."

I gave that motherly suggestion a quick thumbs-down. I couldn't even imagine delving into my "issues" with some shrink. Besides, I'd already had that super-effective session with the principal, Mr. Tanner, and I'd started writing shit down in the journal Mrs. Hayward had given me, was listening to Johnny Cash on a fairly regular basis. I figured that was all the therapy this boy needed.

My mom, however, was not going to be put off. "You know Kate? Ms. Banks? Well, she volunteers at the hospice in Rolland and she suggested talking to one of the grief counselors there. So I called. The man I spoke with was very nice and he said it's often about six months after a death that people really start having trouble dealing with things. And it's not unusual to be preoccupied with death. Or to feel especially vulnerable."

I jerked my head off the floor to stare at my mother. "You called the hospice? You talked to a grief counselor? Jesus. Don't you have the lake to worry about?"

"Luke ..." My mother sounded frustrated. She pushed herself upright and gave the pillow a few soothing pats. "It's something you should think about."

I didn't say anything, hoping she'd figure out the conversation was over, but she stayed where she was, perched on the edge of the bed, watching me intently. She'd definitely lost her relaxed-but-in-touch vibe, was now shooting out gamma rays of straight worry, the kind that aren't easy to deflect. I had to remind her several times that it was Friday and, oh look, it was already quarter past five and, seeing how we were both heading out for the evening, it was probably a good idea for her to get going on dinner.

"Your father's bringing home pizza."

Well then, didn't she have some packing to do or something?

She admitted that yes, she did have to pack, which she added was something she hated. Then she sighed and, stretching out her leg, poked me gently in the ribs. "Luke?" I looked over. She gave me a quick smile, but her eyes screamed anxious motherly love. Her foot was resting lightly on my chest, rocking just enough so I could feel the slide of skin over bone. "Can we talk more about this when we get back?"

"Mom, I'm fine."

She wasn't buying it. I had to promise I'd think about what she'd said while they were away, had to promise we'd talk again when she got back from France. Only then did my mother take her foot off my chest, slip her shoes back on and exit my room.

TWENTY-THREE

Despite talk of me needing mental rehab, I was feeling pretty light and airy as I headed out of the house that Friday night. The bottle of bubbly I'd lifted from my dad's special reserve and choked down in my room after my mom left probably had something to do with it. But as I stepped out into the big bright world outside my front door, I knew that what I was feeling was more than just some cheap wine buzz, because the crazy mood had been building over the last couple weeks. Somewhere, somehow, sometime during those weeks, without even realizing it, I'd started thinking there was more to the madness than just *everyone* was going to die. And somewhere, somehow, sometime during those same weeks, I'd started to realize the premonitions were fading out. Since convenience-store Howie hit back at the end of December, I'd only had a couple dead men flicker through, and they'd been pale, tame, barely-even-there affairs. I mean, I didn't want to get too excited, didn't want to even think about it too much, in case I screwed things up. But honestly? I knew the threat of future attacks had dropped to a low, lemony yellow.

And man, as I headed to Jefferson that night, I was feeling good, so good it felt like someone had cranked the volume of life up to eleven. Maybe even twelve. The trees beat their budding branches at me, the new grass screamed green, the robins howled. Shit, even Erie looked good, hanging at the end of every street like some promising navy seduction. And when I passed other people on the street? Behind every face I heard the beat. Yeah, if I remember correctly, on that springiest of Friday nights, the roar was deafening.

Not even Dwight Slater could get me down. He was doing business in the back parking lot at school, eyes red, lids heavy, lost in a cloud of sweet smoke. As I glided by Slater and his cloud, it kind of hit me that my favorite trucker might have been right when he'd said even a curse could start looking pretty shiny if you just paid attention long enough. I mean, suddenly the last seven months of my life didn't look so grim, because I could see how far a few doses of life and death had taken me from all things Dwight, from the Luke of last fall. Shit, I could even see how the big why had kind of worked itself around. I mean, why not me? I wasn't so goddamn bad.

Inside the gym, I climbed the bleachers and took a seat near the top. The place looked like it had been made over by some love-stricken fool who didn't know Valentine's Day was way over. The basketball court bobbed under a ceiling of pink and white balloons, twisted streamers and blood-red hearts. The dancers shaking their booties on the floor flashed white light as the obligatory mirror ball spun overhead. If the music hadn't been so completely MTV verging on VH1 pseudo porn-star pop smarm, I wouldn't have been able to hide the smile trying to glue itself to my face.

Most of the chicks were tarted up for the evening, poured into hip-hugger jeans and strappy T-shirts with their navel rings and thong underwear proudly on display. The guys were hanging, trying hard for cool in their crotch-to-the-knees jeans and Eminem-inspired undershirts. Couples were grinding away on the floor, but there were also some big groups doing a kind of free-for-all, rave parade sort of thing. I imagined joining one, introducing myself as the new kid in town, cracking a few jokes, starting to groove. It might have been nice, but I knew it wasn't going to happen for the misfit in the stands no matter how good I was feeling. So I stayed put and watched from afar.

When Mr. Switzer, the science guy, entered the gym, he was pretty hard to miss. He was sporting the same ugly brown suit and thick brown glasses he'd been born in, but he'd spruced up the ensemble with a pair of yellow, industrial-strength ear protectors, the kind the jackhammer guys wear. The ear protectors served a dual purpose, because not only did they look pretty natty, they also kept Switzer's slick comb-over in place. The science enthusiasts quickly gathered round, trying to get a peek at the heavy-looking metal box he was holding—his notorious decibel counter. Between songs Mr. Switzer competed with the DJ for attention, calling out noise level readings and the probability of sustaining permanent hearing loss from the evening's festivities.

When Ms. Banks, looking luscious and lean in a long flowered dress, appeared beside the metal box, the group of geeks gathered around Mr. Switzer all tumbled aside. He took a huge chance then and pushed one side of his ear gear up so he could chat up the librarian. A couple minutes later, he carefully set the decibel counter on the bottom bleacher, patted down his pockets, then followed Ms. Banks onto the dance floor, smiling broadly. With his ear protection firmly back in place, he started to boogie, throwing his wide brown hips out awkwardly to one side and then the other, while Ms. Banks swung smoothly in front of him. Watching that spectacle, I couldn't help but laugh.

After the Banks/Switzer dance duo left the floor, I studied this one group of kids that sort of stood out, where everyone looked particularly happy, especially hip. One guy had these rectangular black glasses—definitely not standard Stokum issue—dark, narrow pants, plaid jacket with the sleeves jacked up his arms. He looked sort of cool, sort of retro. Same went for the girl beside him, who was clad in some pink and white *Ghost World* kind of dress. She kept leaning over and yelling in the guy's ear, and every time she did, he'd throw his head back and howl at the balloon sky. I was trying to come up with a theory on what those two found so frigging funny when Faith slipped into their circle.

She was wearing this loose white blouse that pulled in tight under her tits and these faded yellow bell-bottoms that shimmered when she moved. I forgot all about the shitty music. Everyone in the circle threw her a wave or a smile, and she started swaying to the music, slow and easy. She closed her eyes and, just like that night in the motel room, she danced for me, sitting motionless at the top of the gym.

I don't know how long I sat there watching her, don't remember when she looked into the bleachers, can't say exactly how she ended up beside me, close and sweet and glistening like a page torn from some scented magazine.

I watched as she stretched herself out across a couple rows of seats. Her pants looked soft as summer butter. Her hair was flipped up in a ponytail kind of thing, and when she rested her head on the bench behind us, her long neck curved to a perfect arch.

"Hey," she said, smiling at me, real loose and easy.

"Hey," I said, returning the smile, imagining what it might be like to run my tongue down her sugary neck, and then, if she was obliging, how sweet it would be to just keep moving down the goody trail from there.

"I didn't think you were going to come," she said.

"Me? I'm a dance fanatic. I never miss an opportunity to groooove." I reached over and dared to run a knuckle up her corduroy thigh. "Your pants are sparkly."

She lifted her head and looked at me. "Are you drunk?"

"No. Just bubbly."

"You're bubbly?"

"Yes. I'm bubbly."

She gave me a slow, slippery grin. "Me too."

"Really?" I feigned shock, but truthfully, since I'm so sick and opportunistic, I was happy to hear it. "Has Faith Taylor been drinking?"

"You got it, Pontiac."

"That surprises me. A nice girl like you. Drunk."

"Listen, I'm not perfect or anything. What do you think? Besides, there's nothing wrong with changing your perspective occasionally. It's nice." She stumbled over "perspective" and "occasionally," and I was about to suggest she stick to words under three syllables when the rapid techno beat of Justin Timberlake's latest affront to all things rock throbbed through the gym. We both groaned.

"Is the music always this painful?" I asked.

"It usually gets better toward the end." She nestled back into the bleachers, trying to get comfortable. Up front, under a thin layer of white cotton, her breasts jutted out a bit more.

I stretched my leg over and rubbed the toe of my shoe against her ankle. "So, I have to work at the One Drum festival on Sunday, selling the shirts that I, ahh, created."

"Really. Will they offend as many people as the last ones?"

"Probably not. They're kinder, gentler, more George Senior sort of deals." I paused. "I'm looking for a beautiful assistant to help me out."

"Hmm, how about a hungover partner?"

"You'll be fine by Sunday," I said, grinning. "Ms. Banks is picking me up. We could swing over and get you at, say, eight-thirty?"

"Or we could tell Ms. Banks that I'll get you." To highlight her "you," she stabbed me in the arm with her pointer finger.

"Even better," I said, and the big grin spread right through me.

We let the mirror ball dance over us for a while, not saying anything, reclining in the stands. Faith's eyes were closed and her hands were clasped on her stomach, and the more I stared at her the more certain I was that she was falling asleep.

I gave her another poke with my toe. "'And there she was,'" I said, "'like double cherry pie.'"

She laughed, kept her eyes closed. The bass quivered through the bleachers.

I leaned close so my lips were brushing her ear, and started singing. "'And there she was, like disco superfly.'"

"More, more," she said in this mock-begging sort of way.

"'And there she was, in platform double suede, yeah, there she was, like disco lemonade.'"

"You're *sooo* nineties."

"Jesus," I said, reluctantly pulling away. "Do you know everything?"

"Marcy Playground," she said, all slow and sleepy. "One of my first CDs. My sister wanted it, so she gave it to me for Christmas. Do you always resort to plagiarizing song lyrics to impress a girl?"

She really should have skipped the word *plagiarizing,* but I didn't mention her poor pronunciation. "First off, I'm not trying to impress you," I said. "And secondly, it just so happens I wrote that song."

She laughed. "What? When you were, like, ten?"

"Ten and a half. What can I say? I was advanced for my age."

"I thought you had the IQ of a sheep."

"Not when I was little. That was later. After I hit puberty."

"Yeah? Same thing happened to my cousin Dan," she said, and it was my turn to laugh. A current of air slipped through the gym, fluttering the sleeve of her shirt and carrying her sweet peppermint scent my way.

"You know, your hair always smells good."

She pulled a thick, dark curl to her nose and inhaled. "Aveda Rosemary Mint Shampoo. And cream rinse. I love it." Then she sat up, leaned over and took a whiff of my mop. I kind of tightened up, thinking BO and heavy, repugnant grease, but she came away smiling. "Very nice. Very you," she said, and man, right then I wanted to live in the lofty heights of those fragrant bleachers.

Faith, however, was stirring. She was eyeing the dance floor, and I tensed up a bit because I thought she might be contemplating reentering her circle of friends below, and I think we both knew I wouldn't fit in.

I hoped a bit of witty, bullshit banter might keep her where she was. "So, do you want to hear how I wrote the Marcy Playground song, or what?"

Faith looked over and rolled her eyes at me, but I could see she was interested in what I might come up with.

"See, first I cut you out of our grade six class picture, you know, when you were still really ugly, and I blew the picture up on the photocopier we have at home. Then, for inspiration, I tacked that super-big, super-repulsive picture of you onto my bedroom wall, and I wrote it. I wrote the song."

She gave me an amused but skeptical sort of look. "I didn't move to Stokum until grade eight."

"Are you sure? It feels like I've been in love with you for way longer than that." The last part just slipped out. I didn't even mean it. Afterwards, I couldn't think of anything to say. I kept my eyes locked firmly on the balloons. It felt like a long while before Faith reached over and threaded her fingers through mine.

"Come on," she said, giving my hand a squeeze. "Let's dance."

We were halfway down the stands when the first ba-boomps of "In the Cold, Cold Night" sounded and Meg White's schoolgirl charm turned the Jefferson gymnasium into a velvet underground.

"See," Faith said, "I told you the music got better."

The gym was pretty crowded, and as we pushed past the other couples I was aware of my body brushing against other bodies, was aware of my feet picking a careful path across the varnished wooden floor. But mostly I could feel the way my hand was wrapped around Faith's and the gentle pull on my shoulder as she led me to the center of the dance floor. And when she stepped into my arms, so help me God, I nearly wept.

TWENTY-FOUR

I bit the inside of my cheeks as I moved up the hallway, grinding tender slabs of flesh between my teeth. I stopped in the doorway of the office and silently watched my father watching TV. Bad news screamed around him, so he couldn't hear me breathing, hot and hard, behind him. He couldn't see my rage tumbling through the room, couldn't taste the blood in my mouth, couldn't feel how tightly my fists were clenched.

It took a while for him to finally swing his head over his shoulder. "Hey, how was the dance?" His happy question thinned to a whisper as he looked at me, standing in the doorway, menacing and mean, a pitchfork pointed straight at him. "What's wrong?" He sounded scared. "What happened?"

With a narrow glare, I threw everything inside me at my weak, fat, balding father. "Nothing fucking happened."

His jaw dropped. "What did you say?"

"Are you fucking deaf? I said nothing fucking happened."

I left him frozen on the sofa, head twisted round, eyes bulging. I pounded up the steps. I slammed the door to my room. I shook the house.

I waited for him to come, listened for his heavy footsteps on the stairs. When he stepped into my room, his arms were stiff at his sides. "What the hell is the matter with you?"

"Get the fuck out of here." I spat the words at him.

"Are you drunk?"

"Fuck off."

I watched the anger rip through him, spark from his eyes. He stepped forward and slapped me, hard, across the face. My head snapped sideways. My cheek burned. The room reeled. It was just what I wanted. I grabbed his shoulders, bit into his flesh with my nails, threw him away from me. He stumbled backwards, bounced against the wall. His shoulders hit first, then his head. He was halfway down. I moved in to tower over him.

My father pressed both hands against the wall and splayed his fingers. He pushed himself up, regained his height. He took a minute to steady himself before he raised his head. When he did, his gaze was hard and unbreakable, his voice a dagger. "I won't do this, Luke. I don't know what happened to you tonight, but I won't do this. So back off."

My heart, my blood, pounded, pounded.

He stepped away from the wall. He pushed his face close to mine. His breath was hot on my face. His eyes gleamed. "I said, back off."

My chest heaved. Everything closed in on me. My father trembled in front of me. I trembled in front of him, split down the middle by fury and shame, hate and love, understanding and darkness, a frantic tide pulled by a wild moon. And then my fists loosened. My hands flew to my face, everything crashed inside. My father's hands found my shoulders. A moan shattered the room, knocked us to the floor, where my father put his arms around me and held me while I bawled.

Afterwards, he wouldn't leave until I told him what was wrong. I stood in the center of my room, trying to figure out what to say. I knew the choice I made could tear my world further apart or pull it back together. For once, I wanted to be honest. I wanted to tell him how Faith had stepped into my arms. Pressed her mouth to my ear. Shattered me with one word. But that story was too fresh and too raw, it just wouldn't come. So I offered up the last seven months of my life instead. My sentences tangled and twisted together, every word I said had my father looking more startled and more confused, until finally I just pulled the list from my drawer and shoved it into his hands.

His face went white as he read the page. I knew right then I wouldn't be saying anything about the people living behind those names. Besides, even if he'd been strong enough to hear it, I had no way to really describe Stan or Mr. Bernoffski or Howie Holman to my father. How to explain that music? How to explain those songs?

My father stopped halfway down the page. "You're on here." His voice was so tight, the words barely made it out. He kept his eyes on the quivering sheet of paper.

I thought back to the day I'd renovated my room with duct tape and plastic, how nothing I'd felt when I'd scratched myself onto that page. But now I could see how careless I'd been, how stupid, because one look at my dad told me what a son's name on a list of dead men could do to a father.

"I was wrong. It's not going to happen."

He stared at the paper for a long time before he spoke. "You're sure?"

"Yeah," I said, wrapping my arms tightly across my chest. "I mean, I know it'll happen one day, whenever. Like it does for everybody. But right now, right here, I know putting my name down was a mistake."

My father nodded. "What about her?" He pointed to the name below mine. His finger shook under *Astelle Jordan*. My eyes trailed the list. At the top, a dead friend. Next, a dead neighbor. Below him, a dead girl, a dead man, a dead bird. And Astelle. Astelle Jordan, who'd been shaking her own brand of music into me for the last hundred nights.

And I said it. I finally said it. "She's dead."

My father did two things then. First, he told me I had to talk to Mrs. Jordan, because if it were me, he'd want to know, he'd need to know. Then it was his turn to break apart.

WE BOTH AGREED not to tell my mother. Not before the trip, at least. Or there would be no trip. And the tickets to Paris were nonrefundable. My father was pretty frantic, but he'd always been a bit of a tightwad, and I told him again and again I was fine. Really. I'd been living like this for months now, right? This was only news to him, right? I was used to the whole crazy thing, okay? And I'd do something about Astelle. I'd talk to her mother. Seriously, I would.

The next morning, my father ran right out and bought an answering machine so I wouldn't miss any of his calls. And after lunch, when he climbed into the car beside my mom—rooting through her purse, double-checking flight times and passports and airport terminals—his face was as white as it had been in my room distracted, only half-interested when she answered. "At work, probably. I don't know. House was empty when I got back."

"You mean she doesn't know you're here?"

"Nope." She fluttered her hands by her shoulders in mock enthusiasm. "Surprise, surprise."

I tried to get my mind around this shocking bit of information, but the music and the girl and the insanity of the situation were sort of fracturing my thoughts. Still, even I knew that her mother would have appreciated a call, but I wasn't about to start telling anybody what to do.

She pushed her long, dark curls off her face. A row of studs climbed one ear. She put a hand to her nose and sniffed, her slim fingers thick with silver rings. Her skin was a lot lighter than Faith's.

"So, where were you, anyway?"

"Miami." She gave a bitter laugh. She had tons of hair. A thin white neck. "Lost in Miami."

"Lost in Miami?"

"Yeah. Lost. Totally lost. On the beach. In the clubs. On the streets. Heroin gateway to America, you know?" She started twisting her buttons again. "I *really* don't feel like talking about it, okay?" Her gaze bounced around the room before finally landing in the corner behind me. She went completely still.

I looked over. A big ivy plant spilled off a table and dangled to the floor. Astelle pushed herself off the couch and dropped to her knees beside it. She tore at the ivy, parting the long strands with her fingers, and then she pulled a backpack—a blue Adidas back-pack—from the tangle of leaves. She started unzipping zippers and digging through pockets, pausing only to tell me how bad I looked and how she had something that would make me feel better.

My head was banging. "Is it okay if I turn down the music?"

She didn't hear me. She kept rooting through her bag and then with a satisfied smile she pulled something from an outside pocket. She dropped back onto the couch, clutching a Ziploc in one hand. It was the one I'd been expecting when I'd searched Fang's hoodie that night at the Red Carpet, dirty with crushed green buds and pills and tiny white papery squares, each printed with what looked like a horned devil's head.

"Sunshine in a bag," she said in a singsong voice. She was talking to me, but her eyes, big and shiny now, were firmly on the Ziploc swinging back and forth between us.

The dance beat seemed to quicken, to get more intense. "Could you turn down the …" I pointed to the stereo at her end of the couch.

She leaned back and spun a knob. The pounding dropped a notch. "What? You don't like music?"

"No … yeah …" I shook my head.

She gave me a playful, scornful look. "You do smoke?"

I nodded.

"I figure, you fall into someone's house, puking, in the middle of the day, you probably like to party, right?"

I nodded again, even though Astelle's voice was so fast and eager it was pretty obvious she was going to "party" whether I was into it or not.

"Is weed okay?" She raised her eyebrows and her voice went up too. "Or do you want something a little wilder?"

"Weed's fine. Weed's good."

When she folded herself into a cross-legged position, her skirt stretched across her thighs, putting the crotch of her underwear on display. I tried to concentrate on her hands as she rolled a spliff—she was as good at it as Fang was—but the strip of white cotton between her legs was distracting. She sparked up a minute later, took a quick toke, then shuffled along the couch and held the joint to my lips. I took a drag. It was potent, and it hit fast. So good, so familiar. I relaxed into the cushions as Astelle held the spliff up again.

By the time we'd each taken our last puff, her toes were tucked under my leg.

"Feeling better?" she asked, giving me her first steady smile.

I smiled back sloppily and sank deeper into the couch.

"You look better." Her toes pressed into the back of my thigh. "You're very cute. Very sexy."

A snort shot from my mouth. "Try very fucked-up. My life is a fucking joke."

"Yeah, well, I know what that's like." She tilted her head to one side and stared right at me. "So, who are you? What are you doing here?"

"Luke Hunter. Asshole. Here, look, I'll show you." I was laughing, a stupid, stoned, bitter laugh, as I fumbled my wallet out of my pocket and dropped the reason for my visit into her lap. She gave me a curious look, then slowly unfolded the paper. Her mouth thinned to a tight white line as she read her own Missing poster, and time may have been sort of warped by the weed, but it felt like it took a long time for her to react.

"God, one hundred and ten," she said finally, rattling the paper. "I only weigh, like, ninety-seven pounds. My mother doesn't have a clue about me. Not a clue." She tried to iron the flyer flat over her bag of magic, but the creases wouldn't straighten. She looked up from the paper to sneak a glance at me. "So, what, you thought I was pretty, so you carried my picture around like that?"

"Actually, I thought you were dead. I was positive you were dead. So I finally *did something* about it, I finally came over here to tell your mom all about it. What a fucking idiot." I stretched my arms along the back of the sofa and tried to hold back the sharp slaps of laughter that were bursting out of me. Her toes slid from under my leg. She fidgeted beside me, tugging at her skirt and her buttons, watching me laugh. I tried to stop, I really did, but it took some time for my sick amusement to fade. When finally nothing felt very funny, I let my head drop back onto the couch, between my outstretched arms.

"So what, you don't think I'm pretty, then?" Her little-girl question floated over. The cushion beside me tilted and shifted and she bumped against me.

I should have told her she was kind of missing the point, but I was too dopey and exhausted and disgusted to bother. It was easier to nod and laugh and tell her I thought she was fucking gorgeous, thought she was a fucking babe. She stood up then, asked me if I wanted anything to drink, anything to eat. I said I didn't. She gave the peak of my baseball cap a gentle tap and told me not to go anywhere, she'd be right back.

My eyes followed the swing of her skirt, the swing of the Ziploc, to the hall. When she disappeared, the room twisted around me. The green velour darkened. Jesus spun on his cross. The long grass quivered. The music got louder, then faded away completely. Waves of panic kept trying to knock me over, but I pushed them back, fighting to stay mellow, fighting to still my thoughts and stay on the good side of the high.

When Astelle came back five or ten or fifteen minutes later, she stood in front of me. I watched her sideways, barely raising my head from the back of the couch. She looked way dreamier than she had in any of my nightmares, and I couldn't really remember why I'd been afraid of her for so long.

"My boyfriend OD'd in Miami," she said, pushing her hair away from her face.

"My friend got hit by a van."

She nodded before she climbed onto me, straddled me, settled into my lap. She gave me a remote smile, then started rocking gently back and forth, moving that white crotch of hers against me. I wasn't even surprised. I just closed my eyes, kept my arms stretched along the back of the couch. But she tugged at the sleeves of my shirt, carried my hands to her belly, slid them under her shirt. Her breasts were soft and warm. I brushed the tips of my fingers across her tits. She sighed. I tugged on her nipples and she moaned. She lifted up and wiggled her hand inside my pants. She undid my jeans and pushed them low on my hips. And then I was inside her and she was moving up and down on my lap, we were moving and moaning together and my hands were under her skirt, wrapped around her, and the panic was there, pressing into the pleasure, and her hip bones were sharp under my thumbs, her ass a smooth, bobbing curve beneath my palms. I bounced her up and down, harder and faster, and harder and faster. I squeezed my eyes shut and let myself go.

Afterwards, she slid off me, slid onto the couch and curled into a ball. She pulled me down behind her, wrapped my arm around her, and we stayed like that for a while, pressed together with my face buried in her long dark hair, thick with the smell of dope and some cheap flowery shampoo.

I think Astelle fell asleep or passed out then. But my worry over her mother coming home and finding us there wrestled a million other troubling thoughts, and I couldn't relax. If I'd just left then, I might have been able to rationalize the whole messy afternoon, blamed it on the drugs or the shock or whatever. But when I tried to bail, Astelle woke up and followed me to the front door. And when I lifted her up and fucked her right there, against the wall, there was no excuse for that. I knew exactly what I was doing, exactly who I was doing it to.

the night before. The car roared to life. My mom paused to give
me an excited, worried grin and to wave goodbye. My father
couldn't even manage a hint of a smile. He backed the car down
the driveway, looking scared and shaken and small.

IT WAS THE FIRST TIME that year I'd taken my board out, and I
just hung out in front of my house for a while, far from the phone,
tightening up the shaky trucks and replacing the grip tape on the
deck. I concentrated on the spring tune-up. Nothing else. The feel
of the skate tools in my hand, the rough scratch of the tape, the
spin of the freshly Speed Creamed bearings. When the board was
running smooth, I did a couple warm-up ollies before waxing the
curb and practicing some grinds. It was close to four before I
rolled off my street. The hum of the deck as the wheels moved
along the pitted pavement felt good under my feet. I took long,
hard pulls to pick up speed. The wind tugged at my baseball cap
and ballooned inside my hoodie as I raced down the streets of
Stokum trying to outrun my life. But it followed along, ten feet
behind my board, and when I finally stopped across town, it
plowed right into me, practically knocked me down.

I was breathing hard as I pulled the pink paper from my wallet
to check out the address on the back. *232 Highland Avenue.* I
groped around a bit, found Highland a couple blocks down. One
beat and I was there.

I picked up my board and walked slowly down the street:
274 … 268 … 252. The neighborhood was quiet. Nothing but
chirping birds and the bang of a distant door. I was surprised to
see the New Life in Christ Church halfway down the block. I

stopped in front of the crappy little whitewashed building. Images of a flower-choked coffin, a silent congregation and Faith crying softly behind me flickered. I turned my back on the church and snuffed out that scene. Number 232 was across the road and two houses down. A desperate-looking lady with limp, stringy hair, her coat flapping in a cold wind, and a white-faced father holding a paper announcing his child's death whispered to me then, and I had to snuff them out too.

Mrs. Jordan's cruel life was housed in a small redbrick bungalow. In the center of the yard, a doomed ash tree was green with new leaves. Behind the branches I could see the curtains on the bay window were closed. Low, muffled music leaked across the lawn. My heart thudded in time. My board swung like a metronome in my hand. I forced myself up the concrete path, climbed the porch steps slowly, pushed a glowing white button. The ding-dong was barely there against the pulse of music and the rush of blood in my ears. I pressed my hand to the door. A vibration moved up my arm, into my chest, down my legs, making them tremble. Jesus Christ. I thought I was going to faint. I closed my eyes. I dropped my head.

The door disappeared from behind my hand and the music crashed into me and I lifted my head and it's then that I think I sort of collapsed. I remember falling forward, and a warm hand on my arm, dragging me inside and pushing me onto a couch, and pounding, pounding dance music and a glass being thrust into my hand. I remember a voice telling me to drink and a trickle of water running down my throat and my stomach hardening and a burning sourness filling my throat, and gagging, gagging and staggering off the couch, small hands resting on my hips, steering me toward the bathroom at the end of a hall, my mouth full of puke.

Afterwards, I rinsed my mouth out with some Scope that was on the counter and sat down on the toilet. I held my head in my hands, rocking back and forth, making the plastic seat creak. God. God. God. Superman Stan couldn't even make it to school. My Polish neighbor couldn't even make it around his lawn. The old man couldn't get through a day, the bird through a flight, Howie through a shift at work. There was no way some waif of a girl could survive months on her own in this brutal world. No way. I mean, I was the Prophet of Death, right? Dead people were my thing.

I'd known Astelle Jordan was dead the second I saw her face decorating Hank's door; I hadn't had to reach out and touch a sweatshirt or grab hold of a shower curtain to figure it out. And I understood the details on Astelle had come at me from a different angle, I understood that, but so what? She'd found her own way to pound them in. And she'd been good at it, too, she'd been fucking fantastic. Next to the reality of the nightmares, my premonitions felt like toothless bedtime stories. Next to the Jordan women haunting me day and night, the dead men felt like friendly ghosts. I mean, Astelle had a poster campaign and screamed through my dreams. Her mother shook articles of clothing at me and begged me for help on the six o'clock news.

But Astelle and her mother hadn't been haunting me. I'd been haunting myself. Freaking myself out. Killing off missing girls. Turning fat freaks into felons and dreams into lies. Beating myself up for being too cowardly, too scared, to say what I knew—what I thought I knew.

But I didn't know a thing.

When I staggered out of the bathroom ten, fifteen minutes later, Astelle was leaning against the wall, one leg tucked up under a short plaid skirt.

"Are you all right?" she asked. Her voice was high and light, a little girl's voice struggling to be heard over the thud of the bass. I just shook my head and wobbled for the front door, but she steered me back to the couch and told me to chill out for a while, to make sure I was feeling okay before I left.

"Besides, I could use some company," she added, giving me a weak smile. I stared as she flopped down beside me. Her hands twisted in her lap, her gaze flickered around the room—to the blaring stereo, the black television, the dark green velour chair, the cross over the door, decorated by an anguished Jesus and a few long grassy stalks. It took a minute for her to come back to me. "So ... who are you, anyway? Do you know my mom or something?"

"Sort of." I sat frozen on the reeling couch, watching her move and breathe beside me.

"Sort of?"

"Not really." She was small, tiny, pretty. Dance music closed around us.

"Lucky you." She glanced at me. Her eyes were brown, like the poster said, but the whites were red.

"Where is she, anyway?"

She shifted beside me, started scratching at her arms, fidgeting with the buttons on her tight white blouse. Her eyes kept darting over my shoulder, to something behind me, and she seemed distracted, only half-interested when she answered. "At work, probably. I don't know. House was empty when I got back."

"You mean she doesn't know you're here?"

"Nope." She fluttered her hands by her shoulders in mock enthusiasm. "Surprise, surprise."

I tried to get my mind around this shocking bit of information, but the music and the girl and the insanity of the situation were sort of fracturing my thoughts. Still, even I knew that her mother would have appreciated a call, but I wasn't about to start telling anybody what to do.

She pushed her long, dark curls off her face. A row of studs climbed one ear. She put a hand to her nose and sniffed, her slim fingers thick with silver rings. Her skin was a lot lighter than Faith's.

"So, where were you, anyway?"

"Miami." She gave a bitter laugh. She had tons of hair. A thin white neck. "Lost in Miami."

"Lost in Miami?"

"Yeah. Lost. Totally lost. On the beach. In the clubs. On the streets. Heroin gateway to America, you know?" She started twisting her buttons again. "I *really* don't feel like talking about it, okay?" Her gaze bounced around the room before finally landing in the corner behind me. She went completely still.

I looked over. A big ivy plant spilled off a table and dangled to the floor. Astelle pushed herself off the couch and dropped to her knees beside it. She tore at the ivy, parting the long strands with her fingers, and then she pulled a backpack—a blue Adidas back-pack—from the tangle of leaves. She started unzipping zippers and digging through pockets, pausing only to tell me how bad I looked and how she had something that would make me feel better.

My head was banging. "Is it okay if I turn down the music?"

She didn't hear me. She kept rooting through her bag and then with a satisfied smile she pulled something from an outside pocket. She dropped back onto the couch, clutching a Ziploc in one hand. It was the one I'd been expecting when I'd searched Fang's hoodie that night at the Red Carpet, dirty with crushed green buds and pills and tiny white papery squares, each printed with what looked like a horned devil's head.

"Sunshine in a bag," she said in a singsong voice. She was talking to me, but her eyes, big and shiny now, were firmly on the Ziploc swinging back and forth between us.

The dance beat seemed to quicken, to get more intense. "Could you turn down the …" I pointed to the stereo at her end of the couch.

She leaned back and spun a knob. The pounding dropped a notch. "What? You don't like music?"

"No … yeah …" I shook my head.

She gave me a playful, scornful look. "You do smoke?"

I nodded.

"I figure, you fall into someone's house, puking, in the middle of the day, you probably like to party, right?"

I nodded again, even though Astelle's voice was so fast and eager it was pretty obvious she was going to "party" whether I was into it or not.

"Is weed okay?" She raised her eyebrows and her voice went up too. "Or do you want something a little wilder?"

"Weed's fine. Weed's good."

When she folded herself into a cross-legged position, her skirt stretched across her thighs, putting the crotch of her underwear on display. I tried to concentrate on her hands as she rolled a spliff— she was as good at it as Fang was—but the strip of white cotton between her legs was distracting. She sparked up a minute later, took a quick toke, then shuffled along the couch and held the joint to my lips. I took a drag. It was potent, and it hit fast. So good, so familiar. I relaxed into the cushions as Astelle held the spliff up again.

By the time we'd each taken our last puff, her toes were tucked under my leg.

"Feeling better?" she asked, giving me her first steady smile.

I smiled back sloppily and sank deeper into the couch.

"You look better." Her toes pressed into the back of my thigh. "You're very cute. Very sexy."

A snort shot from my mouth. "Try very fucked-up. My life is a fucking joke."

"Yeah, well, I know what that's like." She tilted her head to one side and stared right at me. "So, who are you? What are you doing here?"

"Luke Hunter. Asshole. Here, look, I'll show you." I was laughing, a stupid, stoned, bitter laugh, as I fumbled my wallet out of my pocket and dropped the reason for my visit into her lap. She gave me a curious look, then slowly unfolded the paper. Her mouth thinned to a tight white line as she read her own Missing poster, and time may have been sort of warped by the weed, but it felt like it took a long time for her to react.

"God, one hundred and ten," she said finally, rattling the paper. "I only weigh, like, ninety-seven pounds. My mother doesn't have a clue about me. Not a clue." She tried to iron the flyer flat over her bag of magic, but the creases wouldn't straighten. She looked up from the paper to sneak a glance at me. "So, what, you thought I was pretty, so you carried my picture around like that?"

"Actually, I thought you were dead. I was positive you were dead. So I finally *did something* about it, I finally came over here to tell your mom all about it. What a fucking idiot." I stretched my arms along the back of the sofa and tried to hold back the sharp slaps of laughter that were bursting out of me. Her toes slid from under my leg. She fidgeted beside me, tugging at her skirt and her buttons, watching me laugh. I tried to stop, I really did, but it took some time for my sick amusement to fade. When finally nothing felt very funny, I let my head drop back onto the couch, between my outstretched arms.

"So what, you don't think I'm pretty, then?" Her little-girl question floated over. The cushion beside me tilted and shifted and she bumped against me.

I should have told her she was kind of missing the point, but I was too dopey and exhausted and disgusted to bother. It was easier to nod and laugh and tell her I thought she was fucking gorgeous, thought she was a fucking babe. She stood up then, asked me if I wanted anything to drink, anything to eat. I said I didn't. She gave the peak of my baseball cap a gentle tap and told me not to go anywhere, she'd be right back.

My eyes followed the swing of her skirt, the swing of the Ziploc, to the hall. When she disappeared, the room twisted around me. The green velour darkened. Jesus spun on his cross. The long grass quivered. The music got louder, then faded away completely. Waves of panic kept trying to knock me over, but I pushed them back, fighting to stay mellow, fighting to still my thoughts and stay on the good side of the high.

When Astelle came back five or ten or fifteen minutes later, she stood in front of me. I watched her sideways, barely raising my head from the back of the couch. She looked way dreamier than she had in any of my nightmares, and I couldn't really remember why I'd been afraid of her for so long.

"My boyfriend OD'd in Miami," she said, pushing her hair away from her face.

"My friend got hit by a van."

She nodded before she climbed onto me, straddled me, settled into my lap. She gave me a remote smile, then started rocking gently back and forth, moving that white crotch of hers against me. I wasn't even surprised. I just closed my eyes, kept my arms stretched along the back of the couch. But she tugged at the sleeves of my shirt, carried my hands to her belly, slid them under her shirt. Her breasts were soft and warm. I brushed the tips of my fingers across her tits. She sighed. I tugged on her nipples and she moaned. She lifted up and wiggled her hand inside my pants. She undid my jeans and pushed them low on my hips. And then I was inside her and she was moving up and down on my lap, we were moving and moaning together and my hands were under her skirt, wrapped around her, and the panic was there, pressing into the pleasure, and her hip bones were sharp under my thumbs, her ass a smooth, bobbing curve beneath my palms. I bounced her up and

down, harder and faster, and harder and faster. I squeezed my eyes
shut and let myself go.

Afterwards, she slid off me, slid onto the couch and curled into
a ball. She pulled me down behind her, wrapped my arm around
her, and we stayed like that for a while, pressed together with my
face buried in her long dark hair, thick with the smell of dope
and some cheap flowery shampoo.

I think Astelle fell asleep or passed out then. But my worry over
her mother coming home and finding us there wrestled a million
other troubling thoughts, and I couldn't relax. If I'd just left then,
I might have been able to rationalize the whole messy afternoon,
blamed it on the drugs or the shock or whatever. But when I tried
to bail, Astelle woke up and followed me to the front door. And
when I lifted her up and fucked her right there, against the wall,
there was no excuse for that. I knew exactly what I was doing,
exactly who I was doing it to.

TWENTY-FIVE

When Faith stepped out of her car the next morning, I could barely look at her. She stood on the driveway, with her hands on her hips, watching as I stuffed boxes of T-shirts into the Sunbird, which turned out to have zero room for cargo. I could feel her behind me, mad and confused, all ready to get into it. I concentrated on loading the boxes, giving the last one a couple crushing blows before cramming it into the square of floor space on the passenger side and folding myself around it. When Faith joined me inside, I told her we had to get Fang before I cranked up the radio. She turned the DJ down immediately, but still, between my directions to Delaney's she had time for only a few curt questions. What happened to me at the dance? Why did I take off so suddenly after—what?—one dance? I shrugged her off before Fang, so skinny and pale he looked like he'd just climbed out of a coffin, squeezed into the box-packed back seat and put an end to all conversation. I stared straight ahead, mesmerized by the strip of blacktop leading to the Rolland fairgrounds. I didn't say anything about Fang's knees jittering against the back of my seat, although I felt like turning around and punching him in the fucking face the entire time we were trapped in the car.

It had been my mom who'd insisted I hook up with Fang when she'd called from the airport the night before. After staggering

home from Astelle's, I'd wrestled the TV out of the pile of furniture in the living room. I'd plugged in the set, turned it on full
blast. I couldn't be bothered putting the rest of the shit back
where it belonged. I just parked myself on the sheet-covered
couch, smack in the center of the room, and surfed between bad
music and bad sitcoms and bad movies and bad commercials
and bad war. Hey, look at that! There'd been no fucking power
in Baghdad for six weeks. I bet that guy with the insulin bucket
was pissed! When the phone rang, I'd been tempted to leave it,
but I'm such a nosy, sick, twisted bastard, I couldn't. I guess I
thought it might be Faith. Or maybe even Astelle. Before I left,
she'd asked for my number, and for obvious reasons I'd felt
obliged to give it to her. So my hand was sort of shaking as I
picked up the receiver, but turns out it was only my parents,
calling from Detroit.

My mom had been in charge for the first couple minutes,
reminding me for the hundredth time to take out the garbage
Tuesday morning, that if I needed anything I was to call Ms.
Banks, that there were labeled dinners in the freezer, one for each
day except Wednesday, when Mrs. Bernoffski was bringing something over, that the number for the hotel in Paris was on the
fridge, that there was a six-hour time difference, that I should have
fun at One Drum and, oh yes, had I called Fang and asked him to
help me at the festival yet?

What I'd really wanted to say was no, I hadn't called him. What
I really wanted to tell my mom was Fang should have been the one
creamed by the van instead of Stan because then my life wouldn't
be quite so fucked-up; I'd have a decent friend and Faith would

have a decent boyfriend, and no one would give a fuck if Fang died anyway, right? But I didn't say any of that. Instead, I told my mom I'd be sure to call.

When my father took over, the conversation was all long, stilted pauses and pathetic small talk; until my mom whispered over my dad's shoulder that she had to get some gum so their ears wouldn't pop on the plane and blew a kiss into the phone.

My father waited until she was gone before telling me he wanted to call the trip off. He didn't think he could keep my news from Mom. He didn't think he could get on that plane. When I told him Astelle was alive and well, for a while nothing but an occasional muffled loudspeaker announcement came down the hollow line holding us together. When my dad did finally speak, his voice was thick with emotion and he kept saying, "What a relief, oh what a relief, oh my God, Luke, that's good news, you must feel so much better." He laughed nervously. I could just picture him, all weak-kneed, propped up in the phone booth, rambling away. "Oh God, that's great news about the Jordan girl, and here comes your mother, and I guess we'll go. And Luke? I love you. You have no idea how much."

Although it was the last thing in the world this piece of shit son wanted to do, he did phone his piece of shit friend, who agreed to help him at the festival. And just so there's no confusion about what a piece of shit the son really is, I'll tell you that the only reason he even made the call was because he knew the piece of shit friend would serve as a nice conversation buffer during the ride to Rolland with the solid gold girl.

And he did. With Fang in the car, no one said a word.

When we arrived at the fairgrounds, the lot was already littered with beat-up-looking VWs and box trucks and old station wagons. Of course, the WDFD van was there, on the edge of the grass, close to the main stage. Faith parked the Sunbird and Ms. Banks must have been watching for us, because she hurried right over, looking slutty in a pair of jeans and an old Nirvana T—both definitely tighter than the gear she wore at school. It was hard for me to be civil, and seriously, she couldn't have missed the tension spilling out of the car alongside the battered boxes. She tried to infuse a bit of enthusiasm by pointing out how great the weather was (I hadn't noticed) and where we would be setting up (in a prime spot just inside the front gates).

Our table was tall with shirts when the first concertgoers started arriving around ten. The uncomfortable silence from the car was holding, however, and Faith and I were having only the briefest exchanges, to discuss prices and sizes, to make change or to ask for "The cash box, please." Fang stood two feet behind us, leaning up against the chain-link fence that circled the fairgrounds. He looked pathetic as he fumbled to slide the T-shirts into the cheap plastic bags Hank had supplied, but he also had a bit of a subdued grin and I knew he found the friction between me and Faith pretty goddamn amusing and every time I turned around to give him a shirt, the urge to knock his big pointy teeth down his throat resurfaced.

There was really no musical relief for our motley sales crew, either. The bands were scattered around the fairgrounds, well back from the front entrance, and whatever they were trying for sounded like tuneless noise and echoing feedback by the time it reached us. We were left with this fucking one-man band, parked opposite our table, on the other side of the gates. He was welcoming the crowds with folksy numbers he played on the instruments—washboard, harmonica, drums, cymbals—lashed to various parts of his body. The kids dug him, and he posed for pictures between songs. I found him amusing for all of about five seconds. Mostly I felt like shoving his little honking horn up his ass, but I knew that would probably cause trouble. Especially when Lance Winters showed up to film him. I held myself as far away from that media scumbag as possible, curled my fingers around the chain-link and tried to blend into the backdrop beside Fang. I know Lance spotted me, though, because when he turned around to check out the shirts, he gave Faith a roaringly wide, white smile, which disappeared pretty fast when he saw the roadkill plastered against the fence. He didn't bother trying to kick-start our old friendship or anything, but he did give me a nice scowl and proclaimed the shirts to be the ugliest fucking things he'd ever seen before heading out in search of his next prime-time victim.

The only other entertainment available was Pastor Ted and his throng of religious fanatics, who were wedged into sandwich boards and parked just outside the entrance. Seems the New Life in Christers were pissed about the concert being held on a Sunday, "the seventh day, the Lord's day, a day for quiet prayer and reflection." No one seemed to be paying them much attention, and most of the literature they were handing out turned into a big One Drum welcome mat at the front gates. There was this one voice, though, loud and sure, that buzzed in my ears like a trapped fly, reminding me of once-upon-a-time phone calls and hotlines to God. Yeah, the Pastor's all-knowing, I'll-be-seeing-you-soon sound cut straight into me, and I have to admit I was pretty goddamn relieved when the Jesus freaks called it quits before noon and went home to give thanks for the rest of the day.

Despite everything, our merchandise was selling well and a pretty steady stream of customers distracted us from our personal problems for most of the morning. Still, I was hyper-aware of Faith's every move, knew exactly where she was, exactly how far she was from me at all times. I pretended not to notice that she didn't have a bra on under her tank top, pretended not to notice the slim silhouette of legs under her long white skirt. And we were careful not to touch, so careful it felt like some repulsing magnetic field had settled between us. Still, we were in tight quarters, with Fang and the fence behind us and the table in front, and every so often the magnets collided. She'd reach for a shirt and her hand would graze my wrist, or her elbow would bump mine, or her shoulder, her tits, would brush against my back as she slid by. Then the contact was supercharged and for a fraction of a second the push became a pull that shot through me like a couple hundred volts. When the connection broke, when Faith's hand or elbow or shoulder disappeared, I was left holding my breath and my skin tingled where she'd been.

It was pretty difficult to concentrate on the customers, even harder to chat up the visitors who came by to say hi. Ms. Banks kept checking on us, making sure we had enough change or, one time, dropping off some cold drinks. Hank stopped by too, and he bought a shirt, which was pretty decent seeing how, if he'd wanted to, he could have just printed one up. And, oh yeah, just before noon my buddy Dwight showed up looking like he'd used the concert as an excuse to spark up a little earlier than usual. He hung with us for a good five minutes, trying to talk his way into a free shirt. I ignored him and kept glaring at Fang, trying to get him to do the same, seeing how he was the one out the DVD player. But Fang was passive, as usual, returning the lowlife's stupid smile and nodding along as Dwight blabbed about his brother over in Iraq, "kicking serious ass, and, well, fuck, that totally warrants a freebie, Prophet man."

Just watching him bob around on the other side of the table made me sick. Because with Faith sizzling beside me and the sun sky-high overhead, there was no denying it: Dwight and I looked alike. Even with him stoned out of his mind, I could see how people might confuse us for brothers. I'd been an asshole to think we were so fucking different. I finally just whipped a shirt at my skank twin and told him to get lost. Dwight grabbed it, smiled and stumbled into the crowd, completely through with us now that he had what he wanted.

Things at the table slowed down after noon, when Brown Bag took center stage. I remembered them from the previous year. They'd played a lot of decent covers—everything from Elvis Costello to Puddle of Mudd to Linkin Park—and a few less impressive numbers of their own. The lead singer was ripped and ripe, the chicks had freaked, so it was no surprise there'd been a lot of tit-tight Brown Bag Ts coming through the gates that day. A large crowd had gathered around the stage at the far end of the fairgrounds to hear what the band had in store for them this year. I took a couple tens from the cash box and handed one to Fang and told him I could look after the table if he wanted to go get something to eat or listen to some tunes. Fang took the money and split, probably to find Dwight and hit him up for some weed.

I held the other ten out for Faith. Avoiding eye contact, I made her the same offer, said I could handle things on my own for a while if she wanted to take off.

"I don't want your money," she snapped, slapping it away. The bill fluttered to the grass. I took my time bending to pick it up, but when I came up with it, she was waiting for me. "Tell me what's going on," she said, her voice hard.

I could see how tense she was, and for some reason that calmed me. I settled back against the table and looked her in the eye. In my most don't-give-a-shit voice I told her nothing was going on, and watched her coil even tighter.

"Listen, did something happen at the dance?"

"Nope." I smiled steadily, meanly.

"Luke, what's the matter?"

"Nothing." I dropped my eyes and brushed my foot back and forth across the trampled grass.

"Nothing? Give me a break. Something definitely happened."

"If you say so." I was holding on to the nasty smile, but I could feel the cool giving in to the heat creeping up my neck.

"So, you're not going to tell me?"

"Nothing happened, okay?" I fought to keep my voice steady, but I knew she could probably hear the bitter, angry edge. "Why? Were you expecting something to happen?"

"No. I don't know. I just thought you might, I don't know, walk me home or something."

"I never said I'd walk you home, Faith."

I tried not to watch as she marched across the golden fair-grounds, glowing like a fucking angel in her white skirt, because I just knew that was pretty much the last I'd see of her. I wrapped my fingers around the chain-link fence then and kind of bashed my forehead into it for a while. When I finally unhooked myself and turned around, the guy opposite stopped mid-toot to stare. His muted instruments flashed nothing but sun, until a gaggle of noisy kids showed up and he got back to minding his own business.

Fang never did come back, but Faith really surprised me by returning an hour or so later, with her face back in place and ready to sell more shirts. I sort of wished she hadn't bothered, because I was feeling really pathetic and my forehead was still probably smacking red and I definitely didn't have the energy to be mean anymore. When she was back beside me, I kept bumping into her and dropping money all over the place, and I couldn't get the fucking cheap pieces-of-shit bags open and the handles kept ripping and the shirts wouldn't slide inside and I seriously thought I was going to start bawling, except right when I was about to have my breakdown Brown Bag stopped playing and this weird hush settled over the fairgrounds. I think Faith and I both looked up at the same time to see what was going on.

We watched the crowd ripple, then part to spit out the lost girl. Everyone's mouths hung wide as Astelle wobbled across the fair-grounds. At first she didn't appear to be headed anywhere in particular, she just zigzagged across the open field, a thousand pairs of eyes following her along. Then she set her sights on the front gates, and as she got closer and closer a new band started up and distorted music swallowed us all whole. I'm not sure when Astelle spotted me. I do remember this strange, vacant smile spreading across her face, and completely freezing up as she came around the table and slid past Faith, slid her fingers right into the front pockets of my jeans. She pressed herself up against me and she was sort of laughing about how she'd escaped and her pupils were huge and I was pretty sure she'd forgotten my name because she kept calling me Fantasy Boy. She was tugging at my pockets and bouncing her hips against my thighs, sort of yelling at me about coming over tomorrow night, tomorrow night, because her mother would be out and we could party because after that she was off to rehab and she wanted another night with Fantasy Boy, Fantasy Boy.

Then, through the shock and the blare of noise, a bright, blinding white, and Lance Winters sticking his microphone across the table and shouting, "Astelle, Astelle!" She turned around and the light hit her and I could see how gray her skin was and how dark the moons were ringing her eyes. She slumped against me as Lance spread himself across the table and practically shoved the microphone down her throat, firing off a round of frantic questions. I felt her knees give out, and when I grabbed her under the arms to hold her up I could feel how frail and slivery thin she really was.

Faith did a brave thing then. She stepped in front of me and Astelle and told Lance to "turn the camera off," each word crisp and clear. I guess she looked so fierce and so sure, he did it. When he'd backed off, I scooped Astelle up and carried her out the front gates, relieved that Pastor Ted wasn't around to witness my latest satanic fuckup. Faith must have tracked down Ms. Banks, because she showed up a couple minutes later. Astelle was passed out and

I was holding her on my lap, doing a shit job of keeping her dangling limbs, her hair, out of the dirt of the parking lot. When Ms. Banks squatted down beside us, she barely looked at me.

She pulled back Astelle's lids, checked out her eyes, pushed up one sleeve of her shirt, then the other. We both saw the trail of bruises wandering from wrist to elbow, decorating her pale skin like some sort of primitive tattoo. Ms. Banks flagged down the ambulance, already on hand for the event, and the medics loaded Astelle inside. They asked us a couple questions we had no answers for before they took off, lights flashing, kicking up a cloud of dirt and gravel, dusting up the sun.

"SHE DEFINITELY LOOKED SWEETER in the pictures."

This from Faith. I was back behind the table, but I stared straight ahead. I had absolutely nothing to say.

"I thought she was missing." Faith sounded aggressive.

I didn't look over, but I knew she had me locked in her sights. I watched the guy opposite strumming his washboard, watched him blowing his horn.

"Where was she?"

It took a lot of energy for me to work up a sigh. "I can't get into this, okay?"

"I asked you where she was."

I managed another sigh, then, "Miami."

"And now she's back?"

"Yeah."

"Did you know her before?"

"No." I leaned on the table, let it hold me up, let my head drop.

"But you know her now?"

"No."

"She seems to know you."

"She doesn't."

"It looked like she knew you."

I could tell Faith wasn't going to stop. But I needed her to stop. So I turned and faced her and told her what she had to hear. "Listen, I can't be your boyfriend. I can't. You had a boyfriend, you had this fucking great boyfriend, but he's dead. He died. And your life isn't so perfect anymore and you can't handle that. So you came up with this crazy idea that Stan brought us together or something and you think your life will be all wonderful again if you hang out with me. But it won't. Stan didn't bring us together. We bumped into each other at a concert one night because I'm a stoner and my friend is a stoner and he had some stoner panic attack. Okay? I'm just this fucking loser who hangs out with other fucking losers. Okay? Do you get it? Do you get it?"

Her face was all white and stricken and I thought she'd quit then, but she kept it together, she kept it coming, although she sounded sort of shaky. "I thought we were talking about Astelle. What does this have to do with her?"

"Nothing. Everything. Fuck, I don't know, Faith. All I know is that you have no idea who I even am." We were head-on now, voices raised, concert over, bodies quaking. The one-man band had stopped to watch.

"Really? Really? You know what I think? I think *you* have no idea who you are."

"I told you who I am. I'm a fucking loser."

"Yeah, well, that certainly takes away all expectations, doesn't it? What a fucking cop-out."

Faith scooped her purse from under the table and started fumbling through it. She was breathing really fast, and when she finally pulled her keys out I could see she was crying. Her arm slammed into mine as she pushed past me. Her minty scent practically felled me.

She stopped on the other side of the table, both hands clinging to the strap of the purse she'd flung over her shoulder. The sun was streaming across the field so one half of her was lost to the low, blinding sunshine, the other half to shade. As we stood there facing each other, I had this flickering thought that I looked the same way to her, split down the middle by light and shadow. For some reason that one stupid, stupid thought made everything tighter and harder and clearer and sicker.

"You know what, Luke? Maybe you're right. Maybe that first night we met, maybe I did think Stan had something to do with it. But it was just this deranged idea. This momentary belief in a magical fate. Don't you ever have weird ideas? Don't crazy things ever occur to you? Anyway, it doesn't even matter. I liked you. I had fun with you. I felt good when I was with you. I don't see anything wrong with that. I don't see what's wrong with wanting things to be good." Her voice, usually so lovely and low, was high and desperate behind her tears. "You tell me what's wrong with that."

She waited. She put a hand to her forehead and shaded her eyes so she could see me, and she waited. But I had no answer for that quivering question.

Finally she dropped her hand and shook her head at me. "You'll have to find your own ride home. Maybe when your girlfriend comes to, she can give you a lift."

She turned and disappeared through the front gates, and I knew. I'd made her stop.

I DON'T KNOW what happened to Fang. He never did come back to the table. It was Ms. Banks who helped me pack up and drove me home even though the concert wasn't over. She didn't ask me a lot of questions, said we could work out the finances later, which was really nice of her. And she didn't say anything about me gagging back the sobs as we headed out of the fairgrounds and through the wetlands park and right on into Stokum, which I thought was pretty decent of her too.

Only two things worth mentioning happened once I was home.

First thing. I was getting one of the dinners my mom had left in the freezer, and an envelope with my name on it fell out. Inside, a cold, mushy card from my parents and a couple White Stripes tickets. Masonic Temple Theatre. Detroit. End of May. I should have been thrilled, but all I could think about was who I wouldn't be going with. I threw the tickets onto the kitchen counter. The envelope bounced off the toaster and dropped to the floor.

Second thing. Another soon-to-be-dead man. And this time the details were pretty clear. There was no missing the taut rope around the skinny neck. There was no missing the teeth.

TWENTY-SIX

After the shock of rope and teeth, I admit it, I was a bit messed—madmanning it around the house, reeling from room to room, brain gyroscoping inside my cranium. I'd thought the premonitions were fucking fading out! I'd thought the wormhole connecting my subconscious to the deadly nether regions was shutting down. I mean, since convenience-store Howie, I'd only been hit by a couple hazy flashes, had only had to listen to a couple sacred swan songs. But man, all of a sudden the wormhole was ripped wide open. The Prophet was back onstage.

Because the skinny neck, the pointy tusks, well, they were Fang's, man, they were his. Apparently it was my buddy who'd be hanging tomorrow, or at least that's what my mutant mind was telling me. FUCK. Flying off the school roof. Bawling in the bush. Panicking at the Peppers. Graveyard white at One Drum. Kicked dog in the Jefferson parking lot. Crash bang boom from above. When I thought about that shit, it was easy to believe Fang was up for it. Then again, I'd magicked myself into believing Astelle was dead. She wasn't. But Stan was. Bernoffski was. And the handful of nameless folks on my list? Well, I wasn't 100 percent on them either way, but the bird was definitely history. I mean, I'd *killed* the fucking bird.

Talk about fucked-up.

I tried kicking a couple holes in the bathroom door, but I was too shattered to inflict any real damage. Instead, I sort of staggered downstairs and started tearing through my parents' liquor cabinet, searching for an escape route. It came in the form of a big bottle of Southern Comfort hiding near the back of the cabinet. With a shaky hand, I twisted the cap and took a long, sweet, burning gulp of whiskey, one that would have made the Polish widow proud.

Half an hour later, the bottle was empty and I was starfished on the hall floor, admiring the crystal chandelier spinning slowly overhead. When the phone rang, I didn't even think. I reached up and fumbled the receiver to my ear.

"Yeah?" It came out all slippery Southern drawl.

"Luke?"

"Yeah?"

"This is Mick."

I sputtered up a laugh. *"No fuckin' way. My favorite uncle!"*

"I take it this isn't a good time."

"A good time? A good time? What's that?" The words were sloppy. I'd always been a pathetic drunk, which was why I totally preferred drugs.

"Are you okay?"

"I'm *perfect.*"

"I take it your parents aren't in."

"You take it right."

"Anyone else there?"

"Nope." Now the light fixture was solid; it was the floor that was spinning. I didn't mind. I was just biding time, waiting to pass out.

"Listen, Juanita just got hold of me. Said some kid had been trying to get in touch. I thought it might have been you."

"Thought it might have been me? Didn't you know? Isn't the phone, like, your speciality?"

A bit of a snort came up the line, but nothing more.

"What? Aren't you Mr. Call Display anymore?"

"Listen, do you have someone you could call?" Mick asked, sounding flat and tired. "A friend who might swing over and keep an eye on you?"

"A friend? All my friends are either dead or dying."

A long, stern pause, then, "Yeah, well, that's sort of why I was calling. Feel like talking about it?"

"I *never* feel like talking about it," I said, but it was all slur and no edge. Still, I wasn't too tanked to switch topics. "Hey, so where are you, anyway?"

"Texas."

"What, witchin' for oil now?" An idiot laugh. My eyes slid shut. The chandelier disappeared. The world went still. I felt safer in the dark. It was a place I could be braver. With one palm, I anchored myself to the floor. "So, listen, since you called, I have a question for you. Did you know your father was going to die, or what?"

I didn't get an answer. What I got was a bunch of heavy breathing in my ear.

"Hey, Mick? I'm talking to you, man. You're the one who called. You want to talk, or what? Did you know your dad was going to fall off the roof and die?"

More silence, more heavy breathing, but I didn't really mind the wait because, even though I was drunk, even though I wasn't a huge Mick fan, I really, really wanted him to answer that question.

Finally, he spoke. "I had a feeling, Luke." Just hearing him say it put a quiver in my belly. A flutter in my chest. A pound in my heart. "I had a strong feeling something bad was going to happen."

"Strong enough to make you bail on your whole family?"

"Yep." He was getting mad, it was him yepping me now, but I was used to mad. Mad didn't scare me.

"You think if you'd stuck around you might have saved him?"

"I don't know. You tell me."

I huffed up a sad, little snort. "I haven't saved anyone, yet."

For a while there was nothing but telephone hum holding us together. I could feel my body softening into the floor, my mind getting weak, the darkness getting scary, the booze turning from mean to messy. A flash of Stan. A flash of Bernoffski. A flash of bird. I opened my eyes and stared at a hundred cuts of crystal sparkling overhead.

"Listen, Luke," Mick said quietly, "maybe it doesn't work like that. Maybe it's not about intervening. Maybe it's just fate momentarily revealed."

"Maybe it's not." A flash of Fang. "And you think about it, right? What might have happened if you'd stayed?"

"Every day. Every day of my life."

Another long pause, stretching from Michigan to Texas and back again, was finally broken by my next dangerous question.

"Have you ever heard music playing inside you?"

"Music?"

"Like, when someone dies."

"No."

"Not even when your dad—"

"NO."

"Maybe if you hadn't run away, maybe if you hadn't …" A drunken, mystery tear slipping from my eye, unharnessed, unhinged, running into my ear. "I hear music. I hear music, and it's so fucking beautiful it's terrifying." The receiver fell from my hand.

"I understand fear." Mick's voice crept across the carpet. "I understand terrifying."

I SHOULD HAVE BEEN completely bagged the next morning, but I wasn't. The blanket of Southern Comfort had hardened into a killer headache, a raunchy gut, but neither one was anywhere near big enough to touch the panic. When I scraped myself off the floor that morning, I was right back to wild. And I knew I had to get to Fang because, Jesus Christ, if either one of us was going to survive this fucking ordeal, people had to quit dying on me. I staggered out of the house in yesterday's clothes, with only one thing in mind: No matter what, no matter how, I was going to make sure my buddy didn't wrap a rope around his neck that day.

Still, it must have been fate that made me grab my jean jacket—untouched since the Detroit road trip—on my way out the door that morning. I was halfway to Delaney's, body wired, brain tripping, when I slipped my hand into the pocket and found the forgotten Gandy's Rock flyer, tucked inside the denim folds. Yeah, I guess it was fate, because when I opened the pamphlet and saw the picture of the jagged, towering rock sitting alone in the middle of my glacier-flattened state, the plan was revealed.

I changed course, retreated to my house, looked up an address, pounded my way out again, this time headed in a different direction.

I pushed right past the getaway car parked in the driveway. I ripped up the front steps, raised a fist and rapped on the door, shining under a fresh coat of ruby red paint. A green-eyed, mocha-skinned woman opened the door. She looked a little troubled at finding a strange, anxious boy darkening her front porch.

"Yes?" she said. Her voice was low and worried.

I said I was there to see Faith, that I needed to see Faith.

"Are you Luke?" she asked.

I nodded. She hesitated for a second before disappearing inside, and it took a minute for the beautiful daughter to show up. When she saw who was paying her an early Monday morning visit, she stopped well back from the door. She crossed her arms over her chest. I could tell she wasn't impressed. But she didn't mention the rumpled shirt, the dirty jeans, the unbrushed hair, the unbrushed teeth, the crazy eyes. A flat "What?" was all she said.

As I stood there staring at Faith in the hall, the high tide of emotion that had carried me to her place kind of trickled away and I sounded nothing but weak and whiny when I told her I was in trouble and needed help.

"Phone 911. That's what they're for."

"I really need a ride somewhere."

"Call a cab, Luke."

"Are you working for the phone company now, or what?" It was lame, I knew it, it was the wrong time for humor, but I so wanted to see her smile. She didn't. And I thought about yesterday, how I'd *needed* her to stop pretending I was someone I wasn't and how I'd watched her walk away and how I'd thought I was going to fucking die right there because my heart was so pierced and my hope was so pierced and my life was so pierced and making her walk away was the last thing in the world I *wanted* to do.

And there I was, one day later, standing on her front porch, desperate for her and her help. But Faith just reached for the door and it looked like she was going to close it and that had me spewing frantic words all over her until finally I managed one clear, crisp sentence.

"I think Fang is going to do something really stupid."

She paused and stared at me intently then. I stared right back.

"You think he's going to do something stupid … or you *know* he is?"

I put a hand over my eyes and squeezed my temples hard. "I know," I whispered. Then, louder, "I know."

"Like you did with Stan?"

Behind my hand, I nodded.

FAITH GOT THE KEYS. When I asked her what she'd told her mom, she looked at me and sighed and said, "The truth." I handed her the Gandy's Rock pamphlet, told her that's where we were going, and we drove the rest of the way to Fang's in silence. I went around back and banged on the sliding door leading into the basement, screaming for Fang to let me in until I thought to actually check the door. It was unlocked. It practically slid open on its own.

I stepped inside and let my eyes adjust to the dim basement light. The place still reeked of smoke and beer and forgotten snack food, but there was no one dangling from the chin-up bar. I pushed Fang's bedroom door open. There was just a lump under a ragged-looking bedsheet. Everything was still. Everything was dark. My hand shook as I yanked open the curtain. Sunlight painted the walls, flooded the bed.

And the lump, why, the lump threw an arm across its beautiful, ugly, pinched-up face and all my fear over Fang dying, about him being dead, turned to disgust instead of relief. Lying on that bright, dirty bed, he looked so skinny and white and squinty and scared, I could practically hear his silent screams about having nothing to live for. I stepped close to the bed and jerked my elbow back. I slammed my fist into his shoulder. Knuckles crunched bone.

"Get up."

"What the—"

I hit him again. As hard as I could. "Get up."

He was all eyes then, the sun wasn't bothering him then. He watched me carefully as he swung his legs over the side of the bed and sat up, cradling his shoulder. "Is it just me, or is someone in a shit mood?"

Fang could be really fucking funny, but I ignored him. I issued another command. "Get dressed." We shared a long, steady look that told me Fang and I were reading from the same tragic script.

He pretended we weren't.

"What are you doing, Luke?" he asked. He sounded tired. He kept rubbing his shoulder.

"You know exactly what I'm doing. Are you so fucking stupid you thought I wouldn't know? You fucking idiot."

He dropped his eyes to the floor and wrapped himself in his own arms and started rocking back and forth. His weakness, his distress, only made me surer.

"You were here when I told everyone Stan was going to die. Remember? Remember that? But still, you're so stupid"—I jabbed my finger into his chest—"you thought you could just go ahead and kill yourself and I wouldn't know about it?"

Fang swung his eyes from the floor to me. "What are you talking about?" he asked quietly, but I wasn't really listening. His talking wasn't part of my plan.

"You think this is a joke? You think life is a fucking joke? Get dressed!"

He didn't move, so I kicked him in the side, real cool, real kung fu—style. My shoe skidded off his ribs, hit the soft spot below. He fell sideways on the bed.

"Get dressed!"

Fang slowly picked his jeans off the floor, finally realizing we'd be doing things my way.

I dropped down beside the bed and shoved one arm under the crippled box spring. I swung wildly until the tips of my fingers brushed against a smooth surface and I heard the soft rub of cardboard on carpet. I pressed my head to the floor. In the tangle of balled-up socks and dust and ratty magazines sat the Converse shoe box—the glimmer of red star on the lid, the march of thick blue letters along the side.

I didn't even want to know what Faith might be thinking as I pushed Fang toward the Sunbird, my hand slamming into his bony back every time he tried to stop or ask a question. I squeezed the cardboard box and I squeezed Fang's skinny neck as I shoved him into the car. Inside, I locked the doors with a sharp electronic snap.

Once we were on our way, I thought I'd lighten things up by pulling the lid off the shoe box and trying to get the old Christmas vibe happening right there in the car. Of course, I found a stash of dope polluting the box, so I hit a button and threw all Fang's problems right out the window. The Ziploc, a dirty camouflage green flashing glassy sparks of pipe, tumbled along the highway before being obliterated by the car behind us. Fang laughed at that. Since he was enjoying the theatrics, I swiveled round to face him and started whipping the pictures at him, one by one. I'd take a picture, a smiling, happy picture, a former-Fang-at-his-best picture, and I'd put one corner between my knuckles, and with a snap of my wrist I'd make the picture fly. I'd make it spin through the air, make it crash into Fang's miserable face, screaming at him to "Look, just look at yourself." I sensed Faith shifting around beside me and I could see how white her knuckles were against the black steering wheel, but I didn't look any further. I needed all my energy for Fang.

It was pretty obvious he was no longer amused, but, surprise, surprise, he didn't fight back. The stupid prick didn't even put his arms up to try to stop the flying photos or the empty box I threw into the back seat. He just sat there with his head against the seat and his eyes closed, ignoring the proof of better days that littered the floor and the seat and the crotch of his jeans.

The rest of the ride to Gandy's Rock wasn't great, either. I'd run out of party tricks, so I just concentrated on keeping everything simmering inside. I stared straight ahead, glued my eyes to the road, and if I felt my anger trying to morph into something else—fear or panic or doubt—I'd throw a little lighter fluid onto the glowing embers. A splash of Stan dying on that sidewalk, a swallow of Faith whispering in my ear, a page of dead people fucking up my life, using me, *using me*. My eyes would narrow until all I could see was the blacktop racing under me, and I'd hold on to the rage. When we exited the highway, you can bet I pretended not to see the old Red Carpet Inn, scene of my latest, greatest mistake.

I had no idea what Faith and Fang were thinking. We were like three separate spheres jittering through space, not touching, not talking, for fear of knocking our little red capsule off course, having it crash, ignite, burst into flame. It was a bit of a shock, then, when Fang jeopardized our fragile flight pattern by leaning forward and slapping a picture against my left cheek. He jammed it in hard, ground it into my face for a couple seconds, before dropping it onto the front console, below the gearshift.

"Look at this one, asshole." He spat the words out before fading into the back.

I couldn't help myself. I stared at the picture. Baseball cap already on backwards, shaggy blond hair already poking from under the rim, the kid who danced in the living room with his mom grinned up at me. His smile cut ear to ear. His smile said complete happiness, total abandon. Unquestionable faith.

My throat tightened. I knocked the Polaroid to the floor.

But Fang wasn't finished. There was more unsettling shit coming from the back seat.

"You've got no clue what's going on, Luke," he said. He caught my eye in the spacecraft's rearview. I could see he was just as scared as I was. I knew Faith was, too. Fang shook his head at me. "No fucking clue."

FAITH SWUNG THE SUNBIRD into the parking lot and cut the engine. We all ducked forward, craned our necks and stared. The rock dwarfed the car, blackened the windshield, killed the sun. Fang was the first to get out. Faith moved next, but when she tried to escape I reached out to stop her. Her arm was warm and soft under my hand.

"Don't touch me," she said, jerking away. Her shoulder banged against the door before she centered herself in the driver's seat.

"You have to stay in the car." I said it as firmly and evenly as I could.

"Luke, what's going on?" Her voice was desperate.

I gave her a bold smile. It was tight and phony, stretched Saran wrap thin. I knew I probably looked like a crazed maniac, but I kept smiling. "Listen, I know what I'm doing, okay? But this is something between Fang and me. Something we do, okay? Just stay here. Everything will be fine."

"But I thought, I thought …" She looked from me to the rock to Fang, standing off to the side of the car, his back to us, hands on his narrow hips.

"Everything will be fine. This is going to help." I looked her right in the eye. "This is going to be good."

Faith put a trembling hand over her mouth. "Oh God, are you sure?" Her voice rose to a high whisper. "Are you sure?"

I steadied my gaze and, because I was such a good liar, because I had so much practice lying, it was easy to tell her, "I'm sure. Just stay in the car."

"I don't want to stay in the car." She choked on frustrated tears. She rested her forehead on the steering wheel and closed her eyes. "I don't understand. I don't understand anything anymore."

I tried to convince her that I knew what I was doing, but she was still clinging to the steering wheel like some wilting life raft when I got out of the Sunbird. It was pretty fucking troubling to see what a couple months with me had done to her, but I had to slam the door on that thought if I was going to do what came next.

Things were calmer outside. The sun was shining, fields of grass surrounding the parking lot swayed in a light breeze, bright little bird chirps ruffled the air. Fang seemed relaxed, happy even, as he stared up at the rock. I pretended he was formulating a strategy, planning his ascent, and when I stood beside him I could almost feel the energy building between us, like it used to when we were younger and we'd stand at the bottom of the next big thing. As we walked across the field, Fang and I kept our eyes on the ground, watched our feet kicking up dust and trampling down grass, so when we reached the rock it felt like it had sprung from the earth to block our path.

Fang looked up the hard gray wall, damp and dark at the bottom where the sun hadn't hit. Ribbons of white cut across the face, going up, across, down, disappearing suddenly. I watched him kick off his shoes, tug off his socks. He picked up a handful of loose soil and rubbed it between his hands. The dirt fell to the ground with a sharp, dry rattle.

"So, this is it, then?" Fang asked. "This is how it happens?"

"No. NO."

I told him to concentrate, to pick a route, but he just tilted his head up and arched his back until it seemed like he was staring at the sky, not the rock, not the rock, but I wasn't even sure about that, because I *was* looking at the rock, man, and the fucking thing was high, way higher than anything Fang had ever climbed. I tried to focus on the mission, but the whole thing suddenly seemed blurry and illogical, as if we'd skipped a couple critical planning steps along the way.

But when Fang finally turned around to ask a few questions, he looked calm.

"So, what do you want, Luke? You want me to fall? From, what, halfway up? The top? What? You want me to jump? You want me to jump from the top?" He swung from me to the rock. "Yeah, that would be pretty fucking spectacular." He was smiling, sounding friendly, but his eyes were tight slits.

"I want you to climb up." I could barely hear myself over the bang of my heart. "Then I want you to climb back down."

"Whatever you say. You're the one playing God here, Luke."

"Listen, Fang, you don't have to do this, you know."

He howled at that. "You went and got your girlfriend, you beat me out of bed, you dragged me out here. So spare me, Luke."

"You'll be fine. You go up. You go down. No sweat. We walk out of here. Everything's different. Everything's better."

"No sweat." Fang was smirking, a sad, knowing smirk, his big pointy teeth refusing to be contained. And in the face of that smirk, in the face of those teeth, the sun felt too bright and the air too warm. The wind was gone, the birds silent, the fields frozen in time. Fang was the only thing moving.

He took a step toward me. "What's the matter, Luke? You scared? You scared?"

I couldn't answer. I was having trouble dragging oxygen into my lungs. I couldn't understand where all the anger had gone. I tried thinking about Stan, or Faith, or my mess of a life, tried reclaiming my rage, but it didn't work. It was Fang, fucked-up, stoner Fang in front of me. No one else. I stretched out my arm and leaned against the rock. It was cool beneath my hand, immune to the sun's touch. Its permanence radiated through me. I couldn't pretend it had come to us. I had brought us to it. I'd traded a rope for a rock. A huge, fucking killer of a rock.

"You want me to die for you, Luke?" Fang's voice roared in my ears. "Is that what you want? You want me to die for you?" I shook my head. The ground ran in front of me, thinned beneath me, became a spiderweb of truth and lies. Fang's hands were on my shoulders, shaking me gently. "Because I'm going to die anyway, right? You said so, right? So let's go. I'll do it for you, man."

Only my hand against the rock and Fang's hands on my shoulders kept me from falling.

Fang was shaking me harder now, and his fingers were biting into me, bruising me, and when I dared to lift my head to meet his eye, God, there it was, everything, everything I'd ever known of him was right there, just waiting for me. I knew what was happening. It had happened to me before, with Stan and Mr. Bernoffski, with Howie Holman, with the nameless people stuffed in the drawer of my bedside table. The difference was, Fang wasn't dead. He was standing right in front of me, doing this to me, making me feel everything he did, singing me his brutal, wanting song.

And right then it hit me. I suddenly understood I was doing it to him, too. I'd always played so close and so small, I thought I was hiding from everyone, all the time. But in that tangled-up moment I could feel my friend looking into me, listening to my tortured tune, knowing my thoughts, knowing *me*.

I was the one who pulled away first. I stepped back, out of Fang's reach, air rushed into my lungs, pushing him out, he was back outside, just a desperate boy, no, two desperate boys, standing at the bottom of a towering rock.

"You know what I want, Fang?" I cut every word cleanly from my throat. "I want you to go up. I want you to come down. I want us to walk away. To get in the car. To drive home. Okay, Fang? I want things to be better. Things can be better than this. You understand that, Fang? You understand?"

He nodded. His face was white, set, hard as stone. He turned and reached for the rock.

Fang was halfway up when I heard the slam of a car door. Faith's long skirt ballooned around her as she sank into the grass beside me. She pulled the white cotton in tight, pulled her legs to her chest, made herself as tiny as possible. She alternated between burying her face in her hands and staring at the body on the wall in front of us.

Fang was small on that broad face of rock. But he moved with ease. He looked brave and strong. His path was straight. His movements sure. He climbed farther and farther from the ground, farther and farther from us.

"Oh God, Luke." Faith's eyes sparked green terror. "He's going to fall."

All my *No, no, he's not*s didn't calm her. I had to shuffle over and pull her against me. She pushed me away, once, twice, but the third time she didn't resist. With a resigned shudder she let me put my arm around her, press her head to my shoulder, lay my fingers across her lips to stop her deadly chant. She let me hold her like that, and we huddled together in the silent grass and the shadow of birdsong and we watched Fang climb.

In the months since Stan died, I thought I'd known fear. But sitting there with Faith leaning against me, and Fang far above me, I realized I had not. The fear I'd tried to drug, ignore, embrace, was an adrenaline-charged, high-speed fear that shook me awake at night and kept me running during the day. Real fear, honest fear, was chill and motionless. And in that field it hollowed me out, turned the girl beside me to glass, nailed Fang to a black tower of rock. Then it carved my thoughts into crystal wedges that would not be ignored.

I knew whatever reasons I'd had for dragging Fang out there no longer applied. I knew any plan, any power, I'd believed I had, had been given over to God, gravity and the boy on the wall. I knew that he could fall. And if he fell, I would fall with him.

I buried myself in Faith's sweet, rosemary scent and held on tight.

"HE MADE IT." The relief in her voice broke all over me. She threw my arm from her shoulders, knocked my face from her hair and scrambled to her feet. "He made it."

She pointed up at the dirty feet dangling over the lip of the rock. The rest of Fang was missing, tipped back, lying flat on top of the safe, dark shelf. I pushed myself from the ground before he could even think about standing up, spreading his arms, screaming desperate, crazy screams, stepping into nothing, killing us both. I flew to the bottom of the rock and stood a hundred feet below my friend.

"Fang?" I hollered. "Fang, can you hear me?"

High above, his legs bounced.

"You're awesome, Fang. You're fucking awesome."

His legs stayed put, hanging limp, refusing to respond. I pressed my cheek to the cold rock. The soles of Fang's feet, grayed by powdery stone, were all I could see of him. Then they disappeared. I stepped back from the wall and watched my friend get up. He didn't scream. He didn't say anything at all. He was as silent as me. I watched him step to the edge of the cliff. I watched him lift his head and arch his back and stretch his arms so wide it seemed he was hanging on nothing but blue sky.

Only then, when I'd taken him a millisecond from death, did I open my mouth.

"I love you, Fang." I yelled it as loud as I could.

And then, again, that one good, true thing. "I love you."

TWENTY-SEVEN

I cleaned up the Sunbird a bit before we all got in, plucking pictures from the seat and the floor and the back window, dropping them into the battered shoe box. Fang must have trampled the box on the way up, because when I put it on the seat beside him, its dented lid was the only thing holding the whole cardboard mess together.

The car radio was on low, and a staticky version of "Seven Nation Army" accompanied us down the I-75. All the highs and lows of the song were lost, hammered flat by the Sunbird's shitty speakers. Not that I really cared about the quality of the music at that moment, but still, it was what I noticed.

I let my head drop onto the headrest and kind of melted into the seat. The sun-baked car didn't have air conditioning and the back of my shirt turned into wet adhesive, binding clammy skin to black leatherette. I didn't bother trying to adjust the air vents or play with the fan or anything that might have provided a bit of relief. I used all my energy to stare blankly out the window. I wasn't sure, but I think Faith was sort of suffering from the same limp-rag syndrome I was, too wrung out to even give the gas pedal a bit of shit. We cruised along in the right lane at a steady forty-five miles per.

Only Fang seemed to be charged up by the climb. He had a lot of enthusiasm for big windy sighs and jittering around on the rear seat. And I couldn't believe it was even him when he poked his head between the bucket seats and in a real authoritative tone told Faith to "turn off the radio." He pulled all his anxious energy up front with him, and when he disappeared into the back he left it hanging there, thick and heavy in the now-silent front seat. The Sunbird seemed to pick up speed, draw closer to the car ahead. I sat up a little straighter, waiting for whatever fucking thing was coming next.

It didn't take long.

"They're going to publish the list of names in the paper. Tomorrow."

My mind leapt to my bedside table drawer. Fang couldn't, *couldn't*, be talking about that list. Only my dad and I knew what was hiding in my drawer. Still, I was squirming. I glanced at Faith, who was looking very tight, very tense behind the wheel. Her eyes, cautious and guarded, bounced off mine before locking onto the strip of highway.

When I turned around, my shirt pulled off the seat with a sucking smack.

Fang was white again, pure white, wringing his hands between his bouncing knees.

"What are you talking about?" My question was edged with accusation.

"You know. The men in the park. The ones who got arrested. In the bandstand. In McCreary Park."

"Oh." My panic eased, shifted. My mind jumped again, but it jumped to nowhere. "So—so what?"

Fang closed his eyes. He swiped at a ribbon of sweat on his upper lip. "Jack called me last night after One Drum. He told me the names would be in the paper tomorrow."

"Jack? Who the fuck is Jack?"

"Jack Kite. Mr. Kite. Your dad's boss."

"My dad's boss? Why would my dad's boss call you?"

Fang gave me a pleading look.

"Why would he call you, Fang?" I was like a knife now, rigid and straight, stabbed into the passenger seat.

"Because we know each other, okay? Because my name is on that list, Luke. My name is on the fucking list."

"Your name is on the list?" I heard myself sounding like a retarded parrot, but what he was saying just wouldn't sink in.

"My name is on the list."

I turned around and stared through the windshield. Stunned. Fang's name was on a list. But a different list. A different fucking list. Fang. My friend. My friend. Always wanting it to be just me and him. His sulky dislike of Stan. His weird, trembling moment in the motel bathroom. His crispy new Hilfiger shirt. Jesus Christ. Fang curled in a ball, bawling after stepping off the Jefferson roof. Fang down on all fours at the Palace, gasping for air, not because he was having a bad trip, not because his mother was a fucking alcoholic, oh no, because he'd been busted in the bandstand before the concert. Jesus Christ. The desperation I'd seen at the bottom of the rock, so real and so deep and so big. The truth behind it all.

Fang was right about one thing: I hadn't known, had refused to know, didn't want to know now.

We exited the freeway, were heading along Highway 6, cutting through the wetlands park, when Faith reached up to adjust the rearview and looked into the back.

"Fang?" Her voice, her eyes in the mirror, were ultra-careful. "They don't print minors' names."

He pursed his lips and shook his head at her. "Birthday's in February. Just turned eighteen."

I'd missed the big coming-of-age party, but still, it didn't seem like a good time to offer up any belated congrats. I was trying to think what to say when something crunched under the Sunbird's wheels. It was a soft, wet, sickening crunch, and it got everyone's attention.

"What was that?" I spun around and stared out the rear window. There was nothing on the road, nothing but long grass either side. But when I turned back around, the pavement was alive, blanketed green by bouncing frogs.

Faith hit the brakes. I hit the dashboard. Another couple dozen frogs, paid for by me and Stan, exploded under us before we skidded to a slippery stop.

"What the ..." Faith's question trailed into nothing.

I pushed myself back into the passenger seat. We all stared at the frogs, the hundreds of frogs climbing out of the pond on our left, fighting their way up the bank, leaping for the hot pavement. It took about ten or fifteen real, decent jumps for one to make it to the other shoulder, where they disappeared into the thicket of tall grass edging the road.

"Did you ever see that movie?" Faith's voice was shaky. "Where the frogs fall from the sky."

"*Magnolia*. Aimee Mann soundtrack. God's wrath raining down upon us." For some reason, I laughed.

Then a car jerked to a stop behind us. The driver beeped impatiently before swinging into the oncoming lane, giving us an annoyed flap of his hand as he came alongside the Sunbird. We heard the snap of fragile bones, the pop of bursting skin as the car rolled by, leaving a trail of collapsed green sacs in its wake.

I stopped laughing. There was nothing coming from the back seat, either. I looked over at Faith. Her face had completely crumpled. She swung her head toward me. "Does God hate us, or what?"

"No, Faith. God doesn't hate us." But I wasn't so sure.

A Jeep came barreling toward us, heading out of Stokum. It never even slowed down. Some of the frogs sat stunned and motionless as the 4x4 flashed over them, hot and fast. Others kept jumping, smashing mid-leap into its charging bumper or disappearing under the tires skinned green, spotted red.

Another fifteen or twenty cars almost rear-ended us, sitting motionless in the middle of Highway 6, before Faith started edging the Sunbird forward. She did her best, she drove slowly, trying to avoid as many frogs as she could. But they kept moving, jumping, they were everywhere, and our slow-motion journey through the bouncing wetlands only seemed to prolong the slaughter and make the crunch of bodies seem sharper and more deliberate.

By the time we made it through the park, I wasn't sure Faith could even see past the tears streaming down her cheeks and falling like fat drops of rain onto her long white skirt.

FROM THE COMFORT of the passenger seat, I watched Fang slouch up his front walk, the battered Converse box pinched under his arm. The shoes he'd never bothered to put back on dangled from the fingertips of his other hand. Faith, still disintegrating behind the wheel of the Sunbird parked alongside the curb, managed to give me a wet, worried look that pushed me out of the car.

Fang was already heading around the side of the house when the slam of my door stopped him. He stood motionless, staring down at the path of dirt we'd worn into the grass between his place and the neighbor's. I leaned up against the car. The warmth of the metal seeped through the ass of my jeans.

"Fang?" In the crook of his arm, the shoe box buckled. "Are you okay?" I asked, sounding all hesitant, like I didn't really want an answer.

"Fucking-A, Luke." He turned around and gave me a heartless smile. "Fucking-A."

"Listen ..." I tried to come up with something, but ran out of gas after one word. My arms suddenly felt apishly long, knuckles threatening to scrape the pavement. I shoved my hands into my pockets, balled them into fists.

Fang kicked at the ground a bit. His dangling shoes brushed against his leg. I was pretty sure he didn't want to step back into the craziness any more than I did. He looked up, his head tipped to one side, watching me out the corner of his eye.

"You know what I can't believe?" he said.

"What?"

"Those frogs. What the fuck was with that?"

"No clue. No fucking clue."

Fang gave a bit of a snort, then shifted the shoe box to his other arm. Other than that, he didn't make a move. He just kept watching me, glued to the side of the car.

"So, you want to hang out or anything?" My offer was lame and late in coming, and Fang knew it was insincere as shit.

"Naw, it's okay," he said. "I guess I'll see you at school ... tomorrow." He kind of choked up the last word, seeing how it was tomorrow that he was going to be shoved out of his closet. But I didn't want to think about that, and I sure didn't want to follow him inside, and, like the coward I was, I jumped at the out he'd given me.

"For sure. Tomorrow. At school. And hey, give me a call if you want me to come over later or anything like that. I'm serious, okay?" The false enthusiasm in my voice kind of sickened me, as did my hand fingering the door handle behind my back. I dropped my eyes. The Sunbird's mud flap, flecked bloody green by the wetlands massacre, was impossible to miss. I concentrated on the curb instead, the straight, narrow sidewalk. When I finally looked up again, Fang was gone.

AT MY PLACE, I convinced Faith to wait while I got a brush and a bucket and scrubbed the car. I cleaned the tires, polished up the front bumper, practically licked the mud flaps clean. Then I dragged the hose out and washed the roof, the trunk, the hood. Faith sat in the car the entire time, staring straight ahead at the water streaming down the windshield.

When I was done, I stood behind the dripping Sunbird. I don't know what I was thinking, really, what I was expecting. All I knew was, I didn't want her to leave. That I'd given her no reason to stay. I stood there clinging to my bucket of dirty water until she finally turned around and looked at me.

I held her eye as I set the bucket down in the middle of the driveway. Then I went and opened her door. It was hot inside, steamy almost. I squatted down and, to steady myself, pressed one hand against the door frame. The other one crept for her ankle. I rested my forehead lightly on her thigh.

"Luke, don't." She pushed at my shoulder.

"Faith, please …"

"I have to go. Let me go."

But I couldn't. I kept my head on her leg and my fingers wrapped around her ankle. She started crying, man was she crying, and I could tell it wasn't just about the frogs. And instead of feeling sorry, I felt a flicker of amazement that someone like me had been able to touch a girl like her. To hurt her. To make her weep. I wondered what else I could make her feel.

Her leg jumped beneath my forehead, she squirmed in her seat, but I just tightened my grip on her ankle and searched for some way to keep her in my driveway a bit longer. I finally thought of one small thing, and I begged her to come into the house with me, said it would only take a second, that it was important and that after, she could go, if she wanted. I was tugging at her arm while I talked and I kind of pulled her out of the car and clamped her hand in mine and dragged her up the stairs and onto the porch and into my house. I took her by the shoulders and pushed her against the wall inside the front door and told her to "Wait, just wait" while I ran to the kitchen.

I grabbed the envelope off the floor and sprinted back to the hall. My hand shook as I pulled one of the tickets out and held it up so she could see it.

"The White Stripes. Come. With me. Please." I pressed the ticket into her hand and curled her fingers around it. And I was so close then, I could reach up and push her hair back from her beautiful, destroyed face. "Please." I could lean right up against her. "Please."

She closed her eyes. I settled myself into her and her into the wall. I pressed my lips to hers. She turned away, so I kissed her neck, her cheeks, her hair. I took her head in my hands and licked tears from her eyelashes while her breath rushed hot across my skin. Finally, she kissed me back. Slowly at first, just a slide of wet lips on mine, but when she wrapped her arms around my neck and opened her mouth, God, I devoured her. I ground my hips into hers, I pulled up her skirt, I ran my hands up her thighs, over her ass, while a thousand *I love you*s poured from my mouth.

Faith was fumbling with the button on my jeans when the phone rang. Shrill and insistent, it choked the hall. She tightened up. Her hands fell away. I tried to ignore the phone, tried to keep going, but when the ringing stopped, a sharp click cracked the air and a weepy voice fluttered from my father's new answering machine.

"Luke? If you're there, can you pick up? Please pick up."

Everything—my hands, my lips, my brain—everything but my breathing stopped. My testosterone-charged panting was accompanied by sobs snuffling out of the machine. Faith was perfectly still against me.

"Luke? Please pick up. I thought you could come over and maybe we could—"

That "maybe we could" sprung me loose. God, I freaked at what might be coming next. I leapt up the hall, crashed into the table. With a muted thud, the receiver bounced on the carpet, dangling from its springy cord. The voice disappeared from the hall. I snatched up the phone and hunched over the table.

"Hello?" I tried to sound normal, but I didn't. Most of me was still with the girl up the hall—my fingers were still between her legs, my heart still pounded against hers—as Astelle whispered in my ear.

"Luke, can you come over?" She'd stopped crying, but I could tell she was fighting to speak. "My mom's gone. To work. But she found my backpack. She took everything. Luke? Are you there?"

A hard, stifled "Yes" was all I could manage.

"I'm locked in. And I'm sick. I'm really sick, Luke. I need you. To come over here." Her voice rose. "Can you bring me something? Anything? Okay? Please? Okay?"

"I thought you were in the hospital." I tried to keep my voice low and steady, but it echoed through the silent house.

"No. No. Can you come?"

I said what I had to to get her to hang up.

I set the phone down gently, squared it up on the hall table, before I turned around. Faith was still there. I wasn't sure she would be. Her skirt was hanging neatly in place and her eyes were hard. Lying mute on the floor between us, a crumpled envelope and two concert tickets.

When she slammed out the door, I followed. I followed her right to the car. I thought she'd just get in and drive away, but she spun round, her hair, her teeth, her eyes flashing in the sun.

"Can you tell me one thing, Luke?" She was quivering mad. "I want to know what I ever did to you."

I put my hands on my hips and hung my head. The button of my jeans was still undone. I closed my eyes. After Astelle and Fang and a couple of deadly lists and a road full of frogs, the answer to her question seemed stupid and weak even to me, but I said it anyway. "You called me Stan."

Faith waited until I got up the nerve to look at her before asking, "When?"

"At the dance." The gym, dark and crowded and full of Meg's sweet voice. "When we were dancing." Her lips moving up my neck, leaving a trail of wet kisses behind. I'd pulled my hips back so she wouldn't feel my hard-on. And then her mouth was against my ear and everything else—the gym, the crowd, the music— disappeared.

As I stood there on my front lawn, I tried to keep my voice factual, emotionless, so I could finish, but the anger that had abandoned me at the rock came back to turn my sentence mean. "You kissed me and you said, 'I love dancing with you, *Stan.*'"

Faith looked away then, but only for a second. "Listen, Luke, I know you're not Stan. I've *always* known that. But that night I was drunk and I made a mistake. Probably because I was happy and I felt good. Like I did when I was with him. And I'd felt like that before when I was with you. You know that? I'd felt *so* happy." The breeze rushing across my front lawn shook her skirt. "But that doesn't matter now. I'm not happy now." She yanked the car door open, was halfway in before she stopped and narrowed her eyes at me. "You were right about one thing. I don't have a clue who you are."

My face burned at that. My heart burned at that.

"Just some fucking loser, right?" She gave me a tight smile and slid behind the wheel. When she slammed the door, a wedge of white cotton dangled from the door onto the wet pavement and an engine roared to life.

She ran right over the bucket. Dirty, soapy dead-frog water splattered her skirt and trailed the Sunbird down the driveway, down the street, out of my life.

I WAS VERY POPULAR for the remainder of the afternoon. The phone just wouldn't quit. First my parents from Paris. They were having a great time, *bien sûr,* were on their way to the Loire Valley and might not be able to call for another couple days, so if I was there would I please pick up. I did. They didn't seem to notice I could barely speak, didn't seem to hear me gag when they asked if I'd found their little gift in the freezer. Then Astelle called back, sounding truly, desperately sick. Every time the phone rang, I prayed it would be Faith, feared it would be Fang—bawling, rope in hand—but it never was; it was Astelle, always Astelle. Finally, I decided it would be easier to just do what she wanted than to go slowly insane at my place.

So I grabbed my board and headed out, but to be honest, I was a bit of a mess. I was a mess when I went into Burton's and picked up one of my unclaimed Trazon prescriptions and I was a mess when I came out. It definitely wasn't a good time to run into Slater. I wasn't exactly feeling sociable, and when he started bitching about his free One Drum shirt being the wrong size, well, it felt like the most natural thing in the world to smash my fist into his fucking face. I heard the bone in his nose pop, felt it crack, slip sideways. Still, he was lucky—seriously, he had horseshoes up his ass that day, man—because I was so fucked up it would have been nothing to beat him to death with my skateboard right there on Water Street.

Instead, after one punch, I dropped my arms and let the kid who'd tried to kill me back in grade three do it again. He didn't disappoint. He hit me over and over again. He knocked me to the ground and kicked me in the ribs and banged my head against the sidewalk a couple times, while the SUPPORT OUR TROOPS banner strung across Burton's fluttered overhead and Astelle's faded face smiled from the front window. Dwight had his hands around my neck, he was already squeezing, by the time a few concerned customers finally came rushing out of the pharmacy and dragged him off me. Everyone started pressing in, trying to get a look at my injuries, but I pushed them away and jumped on my board and took off, fast.

So I wasn't just a mess, I was a fucking bloody mess when I got to my new girlfriend's house. I decided to shove the pills through the mail slot and split, hoping she'd take the whole bottle at once and never call me again, because, let's face it, her timing was pretty fucking bad. I think I was bawling by this point, there was probably a lot of blood and snot and tears all over my face, and I was staggering along that empty street past blank brick walls and mute birds and dying trees when, like a bolt of cool lightning, another death flash hit.

I dropped to my knees and disappeared into a burst of light, of life, of joy, a single breath, a lone heartbeat, one pure and fearless note. Then suddenly the life was over. The note was gone. And the silence left behind was overwhelming. Infinite. I searched for some kind of echo, for a residue of sweetness or strength or grace, but there was nothing. Nothing. Nothing but me.

I lifted my head then and screamed, a terrified, horrified scream.

I guess the only person who heard me was Pastor Ted. He's the one who found me, crying and bleeding and screaming to God. He's the one who helped me to my feet, who led me up the stairs, who guided me into his windowless church.

TWENTY-EIGHT

When I stepped into the church that day, propped up on the Pastor's arm, I thought I was stepping through a couple of sloppily painted, standard-issue doors, the kind they sell at Home Depot. I didn't know those doors were actually some sort of portal into a narrow, parallel universe where rules are carved into tablets of stone and ideas haven't changed for a couple thousand years. Had I known, I would have worn a toga.

Instead, I was sporting a tattered T-shirt, courtesy of Dwight Slater, and while I might not have realized I'd just left the Technicolor world behind, I did know one thing: I wanted my life to change. Which was lucky, because hey! Pastor Ted wanted exactly the same thing. In fact, while I'd been fucking things up over the previous seven months, he'd just been waiting for me to show up so he could realign my life. His strategy for change was fairly major, too. I'm not talking a bit of tweaking here and there, a couple heart-to-hearts and I'd be on my way, walking in the light. No, Pastor Ted was thinking mega-overhaul—mind, body, soul—deliverance, repentance, immersion. The whole shebang.

He started out slow, though. He settled us into the front pew and I think he was probably following standard preacher guidelines for dealing with breakdowns here, because he left an optimal amount of space between us—a comfortable but compassionate couple of feet. I knew he was there, but I could pretend he wasn't. Welding my fingers to the smooth wooden seat and planting my feet on the floor, I tried to get a grip. But no matter which way I turned, I kept running into this Gandy's Rock wall of despair. And every time I hit that wall, a desperate, choking cry got knocked out of me.

A teenage boy bawling into the silence of an empty church—now that's a pretty horrific sound, right up there with the moans of a freshly castrated hyena. Thankfully, it's fairly hard to sustain that kind of anguish, and the noisy drama wrapped up pretty quick.

Afterwards, I tried to clear some of the mess off my face with what was left of my shirt, but I must have been doing a fairly poor, shaky job of it, because Pastor Ted, who'd been sitting motionless beside me, finally sprang into action. He slid from the bench to squat in front of the pew, and I have to say, at that moment, he looked very calm, very concerned, with a soft but in-charge sort of smile stuck between his weak jaw and his watery eyes. He was probably about forty, forty-five, but he was dressed younger, in a pair of loose jeans and a Red Wings sweater.

"We need to get you cleaned up." When he spoke, his voice filled the church like Sunday. He made his way soundlessly to one side of the pulpit and slid through a half-opened door leading into what looked like some sort of office. A minute later he reappeared, damp towel in hand. The cool cloth felt good against my face, and even though my nose was thick and painful and my right eye was all swollen, I could tell that up front I'd sustained no serious injuries. However, when I swiped at the back of my neck, the towel came away red.

"Mind if I take a look?"

I swiveled round and the Pastor started poking through my hair, which was as warm and sticky as my neck.

"You've got a good-sized cut back here," he said. "May I?" He held out a hand and motioned for the towel. The ends of his fingers were bright with blood.

Resting a knee on the pew, he moved in tight so he was crouching over me and pressed the cloth firmly against the back of my head. I closed my eyes and tried to ignore his closeness, the way his crotch was, like, two inches from my right arm.

When he moved away, a warm trickle of blood slid down my neck.

"Looks like you'll need stitches. Here, hold this." I reached for the towel. "Press hard, now. I'll be right back—see if I can't find someone to patch you up." And before I could get up the energy to tell him not to bother, I'd be fine, he'd disappeared again.

I stretched out along the pew, closed my eyes to shut out the burn of the overhead lights and took a deep breath. There was a mustiness in the air, a hint of damp cellar, a whiff of stale sweat left behind by a rowdy congregation. It didn't bother me. I let go of the towel pillowed under my head, and my arm drifted off the bench to float weightless in midair. It was probably the hysterical bawling that had wiped me out, or the fight, or maybe I was just slipping into coma. Either way, thoughts of Faith and Fang and Astelle and how I'd just been slain outside by a single note seemed distant, muted by the church's shadowy stillness and the Pastor's lingering calm. And after all those months flying solo, it was a bit of a relief to be with someone who knew about my premonitions and wasn't completely freaked. No, the Pastor wasn't freaked. He was ready to take charge. Better yet, he came complete with God-given answers.

My lips curled into a dumb sort of smile, and I barely even registered the clatter of a receiver leaving its cradle or the rattle of buttons tapping out a number. But, rolling from the office, the Pastor's voice was strong as ever.

"Hello, Michael?" A short pause, followed by a dramatic-sounding, "He's here." I rolled my head to the side. In the gap left by the half-closed door, I could see a telephone cord stretching from a wedge of cluttered desk. "Yes … finally. He's come. I'm bringing him right over." Another pause. "Yes, judging by the looks of him, I'd say he's ready."

And that was it. No need to explain who "he" was. No mention of the gash in my head. I swung my legs off the bench and sat up slowly, the last breath of stale air caught in my throat.

THE PASTOR strode toward an old silver K-Car parked at the side of the church. I shuffled along behind, head spinning, feet kicking up dust. Ted was good enough to hand me a fresh towel before opening the back door and instructing me to lie down. I climbed in and tried to stretch out, but the seat was too short and my head got all cranked up against the door. Given the position, I had this weird high-level view of my surroundings as we left the lot. No horizon, no foundations. Just naked treetops and peaked roofs and a band of darkening sky wrapping around the car, pressing against the window.

Pretty much right away I started feeling sick and confused and disoriented, and the armrest was cutting into my neck, and I was trying not to think, but it was hard, harder than it had been in the church. I dragged my eyes inside the car, found the glow-in-the-dark Jesus dangling from the rearview, but he was bobbing and weaving on me, bobbing and weaving. So I fixed on the steady, domed light in the center of the roof and told myself to hold on, just hold on. I told myself Pastor Ted was going to help me, over and over again I told myself that, because, lying in the back seat with my head pounding and my heart bleeding and that strange slice of sky ripping by, I believed he was all I had left.

THE K-CAR'S INTERIOR LIGHT turned out to be a fairly shitty compass, and when we slowed to a crawl, swung into a driveway and slid along a redbrick wall, I was totally lost. We might have still been in Stokum. We could have been in Rolland. Shit, we could have been in Kansas. I had no clue, which I guess is what happens when you zone out and put your trust in the hands of the man behind the wheel. You can end up anywhere.

When I pushed myself up, my brain gave a mighty black throb, but still, I recognized the luxurious lawn and the cold in-ground pool behind the big house right away. I have to admit, I was kind of surprised that the Pastor had come to the Kites for help. First off, Kite was a Kalbro man, and as far as I knew the plant was still on a three-years-without-injury streak, so I didn't think he'd be the guy to patch me up. Secondly, I didn't think the Pastor would be too keen on a man who spent his evenings cruising our city's parks for same-sex action. What I figured was maybe Ted had said screw the head wound, screw the medical attention, and kicked into some two-for-one fags-and-freaks salvation mode.

I followed the Pastor up the driveway, but I was moving pretty slow. My gut was shaking and I was kind of having trouble swinging one leg past the other. Besides, I was in no big hurry to meet up with Fang's partner in crime, wasn't sure I was going to be cool in the face of that. I shouldn't have worried, though, because the Pastor threw me a curve by turning left and heading directly for the big place *beside* the Kites', the one without a Century 21 sign planted out front.

Now seriously, this shouldn't have been all that surprising, seeing how all the driveways on Water Street run along the sides of the houses, making it hard to tell which strip of asphalt belongs to which house. But, looking back, I see that's what the kid tagging Ted up the driveway was like. Head injury aside, hanging a left never would have occurred to him. He wasn't very good at turning around and taking in what was on the other side. With him it was always Astelle is evil/Faith is golden. Fang is a fuckup/Stan is God. I'm empty/you're full. There was nothing in between, no happy medium, no shades of gray. In that way, the kid in the bloody T was a lot like the guy he was following across the well-tended lawn of the Kites' next-door neighbors.

Ted and I climbed the steps onto a swank front porch, a semicircle jobbie with lots of sturdy-looking white pillars. I did my best to remain upright while the Pastor rang the bell. It only took a second for the polished brass doorknob to turn, and surprise, surprise, if it wasn't the handsome Dr. Cramp opening the shiny black door. He ushered us into this big foyer, where a red carpet staircase swept down to a black and white floor. It looked like real marble, but still, what really hit me was how warm the place was and how my head was swimming in the heat. As I bent to take my shoes off, my stomach lurched, my vision tunneled. Somewhere above me, the Pastor boomed robust greetings and explanations, leaving little room for the doctor's understated replies.

Cramp must have finally looked over and been alarmed by the way I was wobbling or something, because he suddenly moved in and helped me up out of my crouch. He guided me through his beautiful house and I remember trying to stay away from the walls so I wouldn't get blood on them. We ended up in a big bright kitchen, where a wall of windows overlooked a landscaped backyard. The doctor's wife, his beautiful wife, was there, smiling worriedly from behind a chair, the only one pulled away from a long wooden table that ran the length of the room.

Laura was wearing this plain white top, her honey hair was long and loose, and despite the big belly she looked pure and sweet and clean, and I knew what I looked like—the bloody shirt, the broken face, the matted hair—weaving my way across her shiny kitchen. So even though she and her Concerned Homophobes campaign had unknowingly contributed to the rancidness of my day, the rancidness of my buddy's life, it was me giving her the apologetic smile as I settled into the chair she offered.

Dr. Cramp put his bag on the table and Laura squeezed my shoulder gently before stepping aside to make space for her husband. She started talking quietly with Pastor Ted, but I couldn't really hear what they were saying, couldn't hear them at all once Dr. Cramp tipped my head forward, parted the sticky hair and started firing off questions. I kept my voice low and my answers brief. A fight. I hit my head on the sidewalk. How many times? Two, maybe three, maybe five. And was I still taking the Trazon? When I said no, a look of surprise flickered across his face and his eyes slid over my shoulder.

I was uneasy about the Pastor and Laura, especially Laura, standing right there behind me. I didn't want them to know about the fight, about what had happened, which was stupid really, because I think religious zealots are usually pretty happy if their converts have taken a good shit kicking prior to conversion, because hey, it just makes their job that much easier.

The doctor flashed a light in my eyes, took a look at the cut lip, the swollen knuckles on my right hand, and I have to admit that even with the unwanted audience I was relieved that someone with a medical degree was checking me out. My shirt was completely stuck to my back by this time and I was feeling brutal—dizzy, sick to my stomach, my thoughts slow and sticky as flies in Vaseline.

"You have a mild concussion." Dr. Cramp put his flashlight back into his bag. I struggled to keep him in focus, but he was bobbing around, sporting a grin that looked too wide, too excited, given the way I was feeling. "You're going to be fine," he said. "There's nothing to worry about." He pushed his sandy hair, which he wore a little long, off his forehead and gave my shoulder a quick shake. "You're in good hands. You'll need a few stitches, and we'll have to keep an eye on you for a while afterwards, okay? Laura will prep the cut, right, Laura?"

I pictured a nodding head, long blonde hair fluttering, somewhere behind me. A smile as bright as the sun.

Ted and the doctor left me alone with Laura then. I watched her take a large silver bowl from a cupboard, place it under the tap and turn on the water. In the last of the daylight flooding through the windows, she became a wavering silhouette, smudged at the edges by the steam rising from the sink. She only turned real again when she walked toward me holding the bowl carefully in front of her. Setting it on the table, she dipped in a crisp cloth and started gently wiping my swollen lips and dabbing around my eye. The water felt good, warm and good, and when Laura came close I could smell clean sheets or spring flowers or something that fresh. But then the smell became the choke of flowers at Stan's funeral, my face buried in a girl's long dark hair, a field of grass swaying around two terrified boys, and my stomach tightened and I had to fight back the sting of bile that climbed my throat.

Laura just kept sponging my face and wringing out the cloth until the water turned from pink to red and I thought I was going to bawl.

"Okay, now," she said with a gentle smile. "We'll get you out of that shirt."

I bent forward, put my arms up, and she wrestled my shirt over my head, discarded it in the sink, while I shivered in her bright kitchen, feeling cold and dirty and sick. Returning with fresh water, she began cleaning around the cut on my head, moving the cloth in small, hot circles through my hair, onto my neck, over my shoulder blades, down onto the flesh above my jeans. I rounded my back and held my head in my hands, and I started searching for one thing, one good thing I could tell her about me, about my life, one thing that might stop me from crying. But when I opened my mouth, all that came out was a pathetic-sounding "Thank you" before the tears started to roll.

She put her cloth down and for a few long, still seconds she laid her palms, her fingers, on my back. And when she came around front her eyes were lit with such passion, such knowing grace, she knelt in front of me and took my hands in hers and told me everything was going to be fine, God would see to it, everything would be okay, she understood, she'd been where I was, she'd been that low before Pastor Ted had saved her, and he would save me too. I wanted to say yes, yes, but instead I pushed her away and vomited in her beautiful kitchen, puking foul brown puke into a bowl of tainted water.

I thought she'd make a run for it then, press herself against a far wall or flee the room to avoid being contaminated, but she stayed close, put her hand right on my shoulder as I retched over that bowl.

"That's right," she said quietly. "You let it out. That's right, Luke. Let all the bad stuff out."

TWENTY-NINE

"So, you're feeling better?" Dr. Cramp asked.

I watched the reflection of the beaten-up kid nod tentatively from the far end of the kitchen table. Night had fallen. The windows had turned black. The landscaped yard had disappeared. As had Laura.

After the puke-a-thon, Dr. Cramp had stitched me up and lent me a clean shirt—a mustard-colored polo kind of deal—that his wife had helped me into. It was big in the shoulders and ugly as corn-covered shit, but when Laura had straightened the collar and told me I looked great in it, well, there was no arguing with that. Then they'd settled me into a leather-clad den/recovery room with strict orders not to fall asleep. Laura had kept coming in to check on me, and this one time she'd sat down on the edge of the couch, and with her so close, with her big belly barely brushing my side, I'd managed to come up with a couple brilliant questions about the fetus. Was it her first? (it was) followed closely by the super-original, When is it, ah, like, due? She rolled her eyes and laughed before telling me the baby was a week late already, but she didn't mind, she loved being pregnant.

At some point she offered to call my parents for me, so they wouldn't be worried, but I told her not to bother. The folks were in Paris—yeah, Paris, France—celebrating my mom's birthday. I tried to sound casual, like flying to exotic destinations was something we did all the time, so maybe she'd think I was more than just some loser kid who'd dropped by to spew body fluids all over her house. It kind of worked, too, because her eyes got all big and impressed and she gushed about how she'd always dreamed of going to Europe.

By the time I made it back to the kitchen, the clock on the microwave read a cool 9:26. I twisted the time around, personalized it into two and a half hours left for Fang to make good on my premonition. So far his suicidal song hadn't hit the airwaves, and with the good doctor on one side of me and the Pastor on the other I could feel my tension around all things Fang easing and my thoughts stretching toward a new and better day.

"Your head feeling all right?" Dr. Cramp asked.

"Yeah. Thanks. Thanks for patching me up."

"My pleasure." He pushed away from the table. "Laura made some soup. Do you feel up to that?"

I watched as he served up dinner. He had broad shoulders, strong pipes, no gut at all. He looked athletic, like a tennis player maybe, or a serious pickup b-ball player, although he was too short to play under the basket. It was pretty easy to see how a babe like Laura would go for a guy like him.

And the bowl of soup he set in front of me definitely hadn't come from a can. It was hearty-looking stuff, lots of veggies floating in a thick brown broth. The first spoonful was hot and delicious, and I was suddenly starved, couldn't remember when I'd last eaten. Being careful of the mangled lip, I dug in, but stopped when the Pastor laid his Frisbee-sized hands on the table, took a few deep breaths and started into this long, rambling prayer.

Despite my jumping the gun on the big soup blessing, the mood in the kitchen was fairly relaxed as we ate, the chitchat mundane—no, I wasn't really a Red Wings fan and yeah, the folks were in Paris, and school? it was okay. When I casually asked where the missus was hiding, the doctor said she was upstairs resting.

I was only halfway done my meal when the Pastor wiped his mouth on his napkin and nailed me with a real direct, real unwavering kind of look. "So, Luke, I want you to know how happy we are that you finally decided to come to see us. As you know, we've been worried about you."

I didn't know what to say to that, so I gave him a weak smile and kept eating.

"And I imagine you didn't come to my church today looking only for medical attention, did you?" My spoon stopped mid-flight.

I thought about telling him I hadn't come looking for anything, that it was a total fluke I'd crashed right in front of New Life in Christ. And in a way it was. I mean, the only reason I'd even been in the vicinity was to drop a "present" off for a "friend." But there was a part of me that didn't quite believe it. Maybe it was the death premonitions finally taking their toll, or one too many blows against the sidewalk, but as I sat there with a chunky spoonful of soup hovering between me and Ted's question, a part of me believed I was probably where I was supposed to be. That the ride I'd stepped onto seven months earlier had been rolling toward that moment of emptiness in front of the church sure as a runaway train on a clear stretch of track. That it was more than just coincidence I'd been delivered into the Pastor's hands like some package of damaged goods.

I set my spoon neatly beside my bowl, raised my eyes to his and said yeah, I was looking for more than just help with the head wound. My weak acknowledgment set Ted free, and he got pretty enthusiastic telling me how, ever since Stan's death, they'd been waiting for me, praying for me, and how God had told him my premonitions were ongoing and that when the time was right I would come to him for help.

For a million uneasy reasons, this news had me squirming on my hard wooden chair. "Look," I said, "I don't really know what you're talking about. But if you want to know why I'm here, what I *need* ..." I stopped and took a deep breath. I tried smiling, so they'd see I wasn't worried, but the smile was totally forced and probably came off all psycho despite my best efforts. "I tried to handle things by myself. I tried to just ... just ... live with it, you know?" My voice was embarrassing, quivering with emotion and shit, but I made myself keep going. "For a while I thought I was doing okay, I thought I was sort of getting it. But then my life got so messed up, *so messed up* ..." I picked up my spoon and rolled it between my fingers. The handle, etched with narrow, parallel lines, was surprisingly cool. I glanced at Ted. "I need the premonitions to stop. You told me you could help me. But can you make them stop?"

"Yes." The Pastor's voice was thick with confidence. "Yes, I can."

Both Ted and the doctor beamed at me then, and I admit I sat up a little straighter, started listening a little harder. Unfortunately, the Pastor jumped right into a pile of crap I didn't want to hear.

"Now Luke," he said, leaning close, getting bigger, "there are some people who are very open to spiritual processes. Obviously, you're one of them." Pressing a mitt to his chest, he did a pretty shitty impression of humble. "As am I."

"Laura, too." It was Dr. Cramp piping in here, plugging his wife.

"Yes. Laura is an extremely gifted member of our church. A crucial member. As you could be." He offered that up like some promising, sugary treat. When I didn't bite, he carried on, totally unfazed. "Laura's talent is for discerning spirits, as opposed to your gift of prophecy. Which is the reason we're here, isn't it? You have a gift, Luke. A powerful spiritual gift."

I'd heard it before. From the dwarf. This time, like then, I wasn't exactly charmed by the news. The Pastor didn't seem to notice.

"You have a gift, but you've made some bad choices—failing to accept Christ into your life, for one—which have left you vulnerable."

"Vulnerable?"

"To Satan's influence. Listen, Luke, I know for a nonbeliever such as yourself what I'm saying may sound strange. But considering what's been happening in your life, I think it's very important that you hear me out, all right?"

My eyes swung for the clock. It wasn't even ten o'clock. We'd only been in the kitchen, like, twenty minutes and the guy was talking Satan. I lowered my eyes and, avoiding the bowl of lukewarm soup, concentrated on the smooth tabletop. Oak. Walnut. Maple. Shit, I didn't know.

I was thinking about leaving, about just standing up and heading out. But when I imagined stepping back into my life, all I could see was a parade of people living and dying on me. The impossibility of Faith. Fang dangling from a rope. Astelle at the head of a million more mistakes. I didn't want to admit that coming to Ted for help was turning into just one more fuckup to add to an already impressive list. I had to believe I was there for a reason, that I was safe where I was, that I'd be okay, that if I made it to midnight Fang would be okay. I reminded myself that Ted knew about the premonitions. Inexplicably, im-fucking-possibly, he knew about them all. He'd told me he had answers. He had solutions. Maybe even a happy ending.

The Pastor cleared his throat. "Was Stan a boy you admired?"

Jesus Christ. From Satan to Stan in ten seconds flat. I gave Ted a sideways look, one I'd learned from Fang, and nodded.

"And why was that? What did you admire about him?"

I shifted around a bit, shrugged my shoulders a few times, hoping to dodge the question. But the Pastor folded his arms over his chest and kind of stretched out in his chair, all ready to wait me out till fucking Sunday if he had to.

So I gave it a shot. "I don't know. I guess I admired pretty much everything about Stan. He was cool, funny, smart. He was just a good guy, you know? He wasn't afraid of being good."

The Pastor jackknifed forward, leaning in so close his soupy breath pressed at my face. "Is that what you're afraid of? Being good?"

I pulled back. I turned away. I couldn't even hold on to the sideways thing.

Still, I'm pretty sure Ted sensed he'd hit a nerve, and he kept coming at me. "You know, Luke, Stan was the boy he was because he had Christ in his life. And do you know who guided Stan to Christ?" He stabbed a finger into his chest. "I did. *I* was Stan's pastor. *I* helped him become the boy you so admired. I can do the same for you. I can give you what he had, and more. And I can make the premonitions stop." He paused, letting the drama grow in the silence of the kitchen. "Now, I'll ask you again. Considering what's been going on in your life, don't you think it's important for you to hear what I have to say?"

I wanted what the Pastor was offering up, I wanted it so bad. I wanted to be brave enough and good enough and normal enough to reach out and grab what he was dangling in front of me. I wanted to be like Stan. So I lifted my head and, avoiding the scared-looking kid plastered onto the pane of glass at the other end of the table, I told Ted I was listening.

He'd been sitting stiffly, but he settled back in his chair when he heard the news, looking all relaxed and happy, like he'd just gotten the world's best hand job or something, instead of the nod from me.

"You know, Luke," he began, totally in the groove now, "even as we sit here, there is a war being waged. A war of good and evil. As it stands, having failed to accept Christ's protection, Satan has been able to hijack your spiritual gift. Right now you're on his team, so to speak. You're on the wrong side of the fight. That's why your premonitions, *all* your premonitions, relate to death.

Without Christ as your savior, there can be no wisdom, no light, in your visions."

The whole time Ted was spewing, I could feel the anger flickering, churning, growing bigger, getting hotter, turning my hands to fists under the table. Why was he doing this? He looked sane. Why couldn't he say something sane? Was this the shit he'd sold Stan? I couldn't believe it was. I glanced at Cramp, who hadn't said dick, thinking he'd be all bug-eyed from trying to choke down what Ted was serving up, but he was nodding along, lapping it all up.

"Listen," I said when Ted finally stopped for air, "can we just talk about making the premonitions stop?"

The Pastor carried on like I hadn't even spoken. He blabbed about the three stages of salvation—repentance, baptism, a strict diet of Godliness. And his voice got really loud when he started explaining how, first, he'd have to say a special prayer to deliver me from the evil residing within me.

"Deliver me from evil? Isn't that, like, Our-Father-who-art-in-heaven's job?" It was a stupid joke, meant to lighten the crazy-heavy mood in the kitchen, but neither of my dinner pals even cracked a smile.

"We are God's foot soldiers," the Pastor said firmly. "It is our duty as Christians to lead you to the Lord. Without deliverance and healing, the Gospel is just good advice, not good news."

Now, if someone had forced me to predict what we were going to talk about when we'd sat down at that table twenty-six minutes earlier, I would have guessed that God would come up a couple times. I wasn't that out of it. I mean, I was suffering from a wicked case of otherworldliness and there was a preacher dude present. I'd have guessed that Ted would tell me his views on what The Man had been hoping to achieve by pouring death down my throat, by filling me with the music of a half-dozen dying souls. And maybe if I'd admitted that, yeah, those songs had felt *holy*, like they had been touched by God, that's all it would take.

An acknowledgment of His existence. Inside Stan and Mr. Bernoffski, inside the others.

Twenty-six minutes earlier, I would have guessed the Pastor might nod and smile, lay a hand on my head, utter a few *Praise the Lord*s and send me on my way. Lesson learned. Premonitions over. Walking in the light.

But as Ted spoke, I knew the God giving him his answers lived in a whole different wonderland than mine. His God didn't do sing-alongs for the dying. His God wrestled Satan. His God didn't want vague acknowledgment. His God required deliverance and repentance and full-immersion baptism.

I shoved away from the table. My chair hit the floor. And I was on my feet, saying thanks for the soup, thanks for the stitches, but I've gotta bail. I was pushing through the comfy den, heading straight for whatever was on the other side of the front door, when I bumped into Laura.

She looked paler than she had before, and she moved slowly down the stairs as if she'd finally noticed her load up front. "You're not leaving, are you, Luke?" She sounded concerned. "I was just bringing you this."

She stretched out the piece of white cloth she was carrying, held it by two corners, flipped it front to back a couple of times before I even recognized my shirt. The blood was gone, washed away.

A neat line of stitches ran from the collar halfway down the front of the shirt, which looked freshly ironed.

"Good as new," she said. "I bet you thought it couldn't be fixed, huh?"

I didn't answer. For some reason, that impossibly clean, carefully mended, perfectly pressed T-shirt struck me dumb. Even when Pastor Ted and Dr. Cramp charged into the front hall, I didn't move. I stared from Laura, to the shirt, to the front door and back again. The care taken. The miracle worked upon a worthless rag of cotton.

Laura's eyes bounced from face to face. "What's happened?"

"It appears he's leaving us, Laura," the Pastor said. "I believe he's uneasy about the deliverance prayer."

"Oh, Luke." Laura came down the last few steps and stood in front of me. Tilting her head to one side, she gave me a little smile—a hint of challenge, a touch of disappointment. "You're not afraid of a simple prayer, are you?" When she pushed the T-shirt into my hand, I could feel how fresh the goddamn thing was, could smell a sting of bleach, a hint of lemon. The seam of stitches pressing into my palm.

"Come on," she said, taking my other hand. Dr. Cramp and the Pastor remained motionless as Laura led me across the marble foyer and opened the door of a shimmering white bathroom.

In the mirror, a shock of black eye and busted lip and wild hair.

"You can change in here." She pressed gently on my back. "Go on."

A battered hand squeezing the shit out of a perfect shirt.

A door closing softly behind me.

WE SETTLED INTO THE DEN, me on the couch, Laura one
cushion to my right, her husband across the way in a fine-looking
chair—brass tacks, burgundy leather, matching footstool. As for
Ted, well, he was pacing the room, all robed up in his black
preacher gear—I guess he didn't do prayers in the hockey jersey—
and ready to go. And I was more relaxed than you might think.
The good doctor had slipped me a little something after I'd exited
the can in my resurrected T. Even though I was pretty sure that
drugs and concussions weren't a kosher combo, Cramp hadn't
seemed worried and my head had been pounding. So I'd downed
the little blue pills he'd offered before following him into the den
and claiming the seat beside his beautiful wife.

In case the drugs weren't doing their job, the Cramps tried
loosening me up with a few comforting tales of Ted's prior salvation successes. I didn't really listen—at this point I was just sort
of playing along, figuring yeah, a prayer was nothing to worry
about, and afterwards I'd find an excuse to split—but Laura's
story really blew me away. Apparently, pre-Ted, she'd been
broken and empty—addicted to OxyContin, living on the street,
doing whatever it took to get money and stay high *(Laura? No
fucking way)*. On the hunt for her next prescription, she'd stumbled into the Stokum clinic and found her future husband. I
guess he'd hooked her up with some methadone and taken her
straight to Ted, who'd been quick to drive out her evil, forgive
her sins and usher Jesus into her heart. Now she was filled with
Christ's love, devoted to her community, a gifted member of the
church.

The whole time she spoke, she massaged her belly. The whole

time she spoke, she fucking glowed. She was turned toward me, we had some serious eye contact going on, so it sort of felt like Laura and I were the only ones in the room.

"Remember when I was cleaning you up in the kitchen?" she asked.

Like I could forget that semi-erotic rubdown. I gave her a smile and settled back into the couch, getting comfortable as the little blue pills started pillowing my thoughts.

"Luke, when I laid my hands upon you, I felt Satan dwelling within you surely as I felt the glory of God."

That sort of wiped the dopey smile off my face.

"That is my gift. Discerning spirits." She picked a sheet of paper off the coffee table and shook out its folds. In very pretty, very Laura writing, I saw my name at the top of the page. And, sitting on the first line, a single word. *Fear.* On the second line, *Rage.* Then *Envy.* Then *Lust.*

I didn't get any further before Laura handed the paper to Ted, who, in his long black robe, was looking very large and steady and sure.

Surer than I'd ever been in my entire life.

I glanced around the room, from one intense face to the next. Even with the pills puffing up the edges, I could see things weren't going to be so easy. I couldn't just play along. I could feel how scared I was. How vulnerable—as vulnerable as I'd been when I'd dared to open myself to the possibility of Faith loving me. Loving *me.* And she'd done me in with one word. Yeah, I understood the danger lurking in the soft spots.

And there I was, on the Cramps' couch, so soft and so scared

I'd have made a blob of whipped cream look tough, and Ted's towering over me.

"Let us pray." His big voice boomed in my ears.

He and the Cramps bowed their heads. I just closed my eyes so I wouldn't have to watch. The Pastor asked for God's guidance and protection before I heard the rattle of paper. "In the name of Jesus, I remove you evil spirit of fear and send you to the Cross." There were a couple long seconds of silence, then, "In the name of Jesus, I remove you evil spirit of rage and send you to the Cross."

When I'd seen it, I'd thought Laura's list was some one-sided character profile, a Luke-Hunter-at-his-worst sort of deal. But no, it was the Pastor's guide to my salvation, and he was using it to battle evil.

The first couple were easy. When he said "fear," I thought here and now, me and Fang. Nightly nightmares of a dead girl gift wrapped in a shower curtain. A half dozen people dying inside me. A hollowed-out boy kneeling in front of a church. When Ted said "rage," I saw my father slamming into a wall, posters being ripped to shreds, Fang hunched up in the La-Z-Boy. Envy? Wonder boy Stan sprang to mind. Lust? Faith, beside me under a red velvet bedspread. Faith, across from me at a library table. Faith, against me, against a wall, her skirt lifted. Faith, anywhere. Sexual perversion? Ms. Banks's mammoth tits. Astelle Jordan's beckoning white crotch. Blasphemy? That one was a fucking no-brainer.

Most of them bit deep, and I have to admit being pretty impressed by how well Laura had nailed me on just one try. "Cowardice" brought to mind images of me fleeing a Mexican phone number and a trembling pink sweatshirt, me bailing on my gay friend Fang. Self-pity? Some jerk taped up in a safe room playing at life. Deception and deceitfulness? I gagged that one down, like a fucking horse-sized pill, because it was me. My whole life. The way I dealt with my parents. And Faith. And pretty much everyone else. The way I tried to fool even myself, to shade myself from what I felt, what I believed. Who I was.

By the time Ted got round to asking God to heal my brokenness and to fill me with joy, I was feeling pretty low. Whatever you tagged it—a roll call of evil or a litany of character flaws—Laura's list had pressed into all my dark places. But nothing had been cut away. Nothing had made it to the Cross. The joy Ted spoke of didn't exist for me. I had no sense of God. I had never felt further from the truth.

THIRTY

So it turned out the prayer wasn't so simple. It wasn't cake. And in combination with a couple of wicked blue pills, it stole the energy I needed to get myself out of the den. After the deliverance prayer, when Laura suggested that it might be best if I just crashed on their couch for the night—seeing how my parents weren't around and there were both a doctor and a pastor in-house and more healing to be done in the morning—I barely managed to tip over. She tucked a down comforter around me and stuck a feather pillow under my head, but I didn't even look at her. I just sank into the makeshift bed and the blanket of dope and passed out.

When I woke up, the den was dark. Just a small reading lamp on in the corner, lighting up the chair where Cramp still sat, reading a newspaper. He must have felt me looking at him or heard me stirring or something, because a second after I opened my eyes he was right beside me, perched on the heavy wooden coffee table, playing doctor. He checked out the stitches, checked out the face, asked about the head, gave me a couple of pills I recognized as Tylenol for the pain.

With a snap, he recapped the bottle and dropped it into the black doctor's bag by his feet. He leaned forward, his elbows resting on his knees, his hands dangling loosely in front of him. Even at—what?—three, four in the morning, even this close,

Cramp looked all chiseled and alert as he eyed me keenly. "That's quite a shiner you've got there," he said lightly.

I didn't respond. I just threw an arm over my face and let out a sigh. I wanted to be left alone. I wanted to go back to sleep. But more than that, I wanted out. It took effort—my head was thick and pounding, my body stiff and sore—but I pushed the comforter onto the floor, swung my legs off the couch and sat up. Cramp stayed where he was, sitting on the edge of the coffee table, not giving me a whole lot of room to maneuver.

"So," he said quietly, "besides the headache, how are you feeling?"

I gave him a hard look. "Shit. I'm feeling like shit."

His lips pinched into a tight line. "Listen, I know what happened earlier was heavy stuff. The deliverance prayer can be pretty draining. But can I tell you something that might counterbalance what you heard here last night?"

At that, I gave a bit of a disgusted snort, which Cramp must have translated into a yes.

"Do you remember the first time we met?" he asked. "In the helicopter? Right before they airlifted you to Children's Hospital in Detroit?" I stared at him blankly, although I knew exactly what he was talking about. "You were on a stretcher. Your arm was loose at your side. The paramedics who cut you off the fence couldn't use a stabilizing board because of the spike, which they left in place to prevent blood loss."

He shook his head, remembering, and I had to admit, he'd picked a good place to start. I *loved* the impaled-on-the-fence story and, never having heard his version, I stayed put, pressed his take up against mine to see how it fit. To be honest, my memories of that day didn't include Cramp, but he must have been there, because he had all the dirt.

"The spike had to be an inch in diameter. Was clear through your wrist. There wasn't much blood, just a trickle running from the wound to the curve of your elbow."

His eyes moved to my wrist and, shit, that's all it took. I rolled right over. I rotated my arm so we could both see the raised circle of flesh on the one side and, with a flip of the wrist, the waxy white twin on the other.

Cramp was perfectly still, and his eyes gleamed with a weird hypnotic glow. "I was very struck by your injury. And when I took your arm in my hands to examine it—" He paused, as if he was suddenly unable to go on. And despite everything, I was deep in his story, I wanted to hear the rest. When he did start up again, his voice was all low and hushed, like he was talking in a church or a hospital or some other sacred site. "You know, Luke, when I touched your arm that day, something very ... very strange happened. And it happened again, during your last visit to my office. After Stan died."

Again, my recall of that visit was fragmented, and what was left behind had nothing to do with the doctor. What I remembered was getting hooked up with a Trazon prescription and the suicidal symphony. The one that had painted me black in his office. I remembered vomiting in a corner sink, and being alone, bawling on the examining table. It was like all my memories of those first days after Stan died: Against the shock of the premonitions, the roar of the people dying inside me, everything else disappeared.

Cramp leaned over and started rooting through his bag. The clink of surgical steel, the crackle of sterile paper and then, dangling in front of me, a freezer-sized Ziploc. Inside the bag, two flattened strips of white cotton, each banded with black and carrying a dark brown stain.

"Remember these?"

I shook my head. Through the plastic, behind the dirty lumps, the doctor's face slid into a distorted smile. Cramp gave the bag a jiggle. The cotton shifted, took shape. The pocket of a worn heel. A thick elastic seam. A hardened circle of blood. The edges pulled back, let in some light, and suddenly I could see more of that visit to the doctor's.

Those were my socks inside that bag. The socks I'd worn to Cramp's office. The ones I'd bled all over after the old no-shoe on the light bulb. Jesus Christ. *He had my socks. In a bag.*

An icy sliver slid through me, as chill and motionless as the one that had claimed me at Gandy's Rock. I mean, sharing space with a man who carried my bloody socks around with him was freaky enough, but I could feel something else lurking behind those socks. I forced myself back to that day at the doctor's. I watched him pull the shards of glass from my feet. I heard the clink as they hit the metal pan. I'd forgotten the glass. I saw myself dropping my socks into the garbage can next to the sink. I'd forgotten the socks. I forced myself back further, and there was my distraught mother leaving the room. I'd forgotten my mother. And there was the doctor. Sitting at the end of the examining table, casually asking me questions. I saw myself, white, sick with dread, scared shitless by my own life. I watched my mouth open. I heard myself tell the doctor about Stan. And then, there it was, the deadly, dangerous thing crawling out of my mouth.

I told him about Mr. Bernoffski.

I told him about the flash of suicide.

Before the list, before my father, before anyone else, when everything was still scary and crazy and raw, I told him.

Then I fell into a bottle of Trazon and forgot.

But Dr. Cramp didn't forget. Oh no, *he* told Ted.

Stunned. Stunning. Stunned. Me. Gaping at Cramp. His lips quivering. His eyes gleaming blind faith. His voice still holy. "When I saw the circles of blood, when I took your feet in my hands, I was overwhelmed by a vision of Christ on the Cross. It was incredibly powerful, just like that day in the helicopter. And it confirmed my belief that you're—"

I think it was about here that the shock lifted. And about ten milliseconds later I hit the street running. The only noise to be heard: bare feet slapping pavement and my name being hollered into the night.

I was a good six or seven blocks up Water when the K-Car caught up to me. Ted was behind the wheel. Fucking Ted. I just kept sprinting in and out of darkness, hoofing it through puddles of streetlight, legs pumping, gut cramping, lungs burning, brain screaming.

Ted rolled down his window and trolled along beside me. "Hold up," he ordered, and "Calm down," and "Would you stop for a minute." A lot of shit like that.

Finally he swung the car into a driveway up ahead and blocked the sidewalk and as much as he could of the road. But it wasn't until he hopped out and threw his arms up like some horned-up traffic cop that I really paid him any attention. "Get the fuck out of my way," I snapped, heading for the front of his shit box, but he was right there, stepping in front of me. I tried going around back, but he shuffled sideways, arms out, doing this blockade dance sort of thing so I couldn't get by. I tried pushing past him a few more times, but shit, I was burnt. After the sprint I was huffing for air, and the stitch in my side felt like another fucking fence wound. I leaned over, dropped my head and grabbed my knees.

The Pastor hung over me, watching me gasp. "What are you doing, Luke?"

I lifted my head and managed to spit out some words. "Catching my fucking breath. What's it look like?"

"It looks to me like you're running away from God."

"Yeah? Well, I'm not. I'm running away from you, you fucking liar." I sucked down more air, felt my breathing slow.

"I never lied to you, Luke."

"Like fuck you didn't. Your lies are the only reason I'm even here."

"Did something happen in the den with Michael?"

My chest was still heaving, but I was upright and Ted was two inches in front of me. Even in the dull yellow glow of a streetlamp I could see the bags under his eyes, the push of paunch distorting the front of his tacky hockey sweater, the loose droop of skin along his jaw. I could see how stupid I was to have ever believed he had something to offer.

"Yeah, something fucking happened in the den with *Michael.*" I twisted the name into a sneer. "He showed me my fucking socks.

He showed me the fucking light. He showed me you have no *in* with God."

The Pastor's hands found his hips. "Yes, well, Michael has a habit of talking too much. All I can tell you, Luke, is the Lord works in mysterious ways."

I gagged up a big, hateful laugh for that lame biblical cliché. "Yeah, and so does Dr. Fucking Cramp."

This time I was too quick for Ted. I darted onto the street and started jogging. The Pastor fell in beside me, taking long, hurried strides.

"Do you even know where you're going?" he asked. "Or what you're doing?"

"No. But don't worry, I'm used to it."

I kept charging along. Rushing to keep up, Ted took a while to lay the next thing on me. "Luke, do you have anything, anything at all, to believe in?"

I was so ready for that one. "The godliness of humanity," I said, getting a little more mileage out of the tiny trucker. But then something else, something original, came to me, and I stopped. And I turned to Ted. "You know what I believe in?"

He couldn't help himself. He smirked, already knowing it was going to be good, but I didn't care.

"Dancing with my mother," I said. "Dancing with my mother."

The Pastor laughed, like I knew he would, before he started preaching. "Jesus said, 'I am the way, and the truth, and the life. No one comes to God but through me.'" And his voice was calm but frustrated, as if he were talking to a moron, when he said, "That's all there is to believe in, Luke. Dancing with your mother is a nice thing to do. *Nothing more.* There is only one path to God, and that is through Jesus Christ, our Lord and savior. Now, come on," he said, reaching out to take my elbow, "get in the car."

I yanked my arm away. "I'm not getting in your fucking car, Ted. I'm not going anywhere with you."

"Listen, Luke. You're just tired. You've had a—"

This time it was me grabbing him. "Don't fucking do that to me, Ted. Don't try to tell me about myself. You don't know me. You think you do, but you don't. You decided I was evil before Laura even got near me. And you know why? You know why, Ted? Because something amazing happened to me, something completely out of this fucking world, and you couldn't explain how something like that could happen to someone like me, right? It couldn't be good. It couldn't be godly. It had to be evil. Because I don't belong to your church. And I don't believe what you do. I sure don't believe you can wave some magic wand over me, say some stupid prayer and *bam!* I'm golden. And you know what else? I don't believe you had anything to do with who Stan was or what he believed in. Okay, Ted? Okay?"

I was shaking his arm. And all of a sudden he wasn't looking so goddamn hard and sure, and I could just tell he was wishing he'd spent a little more time banishing my rage as I squeezed the shit out of his elbow.

"You want to know something else about me? I'll tell you something. I'm not evil. I'm not playing on Satan's team. I'm just a fucked-up kid who came to you because you said you could help me. Okay, Ted? Okay? And here's another bone for you. I'm not as dumb as I fucking seem. At Stan's funeral, at my *friend's* funeral, I knew you were talking to me. I was paying attention, okay? It was Jesus who tasted death for every man, right, Ted? Isn't that what you said? Isn't that what you put in your fucking pamphlet? Well, guess what? Over the last seven months, I have tasted death. Not Jesus, Ted. Not Jesus. Me." I punched a finger into my chest, hammered in the next four words. *"I have tasted death."*

The Pastor twisted his elbow from my hand and took a couple of steps back. When he was out of reach, he lifted his chin and looked down at me with narrowed eyes.

"So tell me, Luke, what was that like?"

I knew one thing. Whatever I said wouldn't matter. I could see Ted in front of me, he was standing right there, but I knew he wouldn't hear a word I said.

"You'll just have to wait and find out for yourself, asshole."

This time, when I started jogging away, the Pastor didn't try to follow. But like I've said before, he's the type who has to have the last word, and he did throw out a final farewell before I faded into the night.

"You are not worthy of Christ," he hollered at my back. "You are not worthy."

THIRTY-ONE

When I look back on that head-to-head with the Pastor, I'm pretty sure the only untruth I told was saying I didn't know where I was headed after I left him hollering up Water Street. Because that night, when I started running, I didn't even have to think. My feet carried me down familiar roads and around corners I'd turned a thousand times before. And with every step, whatever spell I'd been under at the Cramps' broke a little more, until my thoughts were clear and I was running hard and fast. Still, I couldn't get where I was going—where I should have been all along—quick enough.

I think I started getting scared a couple blocks from Delaney's place. I think it was about then that I really started to freak. Whatever the doctor had slipped me had wiped me out for the last part of what was supposed to have been my buddy's final day. We were already a good four, five hours into Fang's tomorrow, and I didn't know if he was dead or alive, if he was home lying in bed or swinging from a rope.

As I charged down one empty street after another, I thought about the flash of despair he'd shown me at Gandy's Rock, and the pained confession rolling from the back seat of the Sunbird, and I could see it—Fang chinning himself on that goddamn bar we'd installed in the bathroom doorway, biceps bulging, blue-snake veins popping, rope dangling loose. He'd hold himself there for a minute, because he could, because he was that strong, and only when he felt his arms starting to go would he bend his knees and let himself drop. Rope tight. Neck snapped. Game over. Jesus Christ.

That image chased me all the way to Delaney's back door.

The backyard was dark and silent. No streetlamps. No blue TV flicker. No white TV noise. Nothing. I pushed my feet through the grass until I hit the concrete slab by the glass door—too black to throw a reflection. My heart was slamming. My breathing ragged. I found the handle and pulled. The door jumped open. My eyes were already on the bathroom when I hit the lights.

Empty. The doorway was empty, the chin-up bar was empty, the couch was empty. When I went into Fang's bedroom, he wasn't there. I hollered his name. No answer. I climbed the stairs like a thief, slow and quiet, alert and scared, one shoulder dropped back, fingertips trailing the wall. It had been years since I'd been on the ground floor, but I knew my way around. Cupboard of a kitchen straight ahead—empty—box of a living room to the left. On the couch, a body, but right away I knew it wasn't Fang.

Lying on the sofa wearing this flimsy nightgown, Mrs. Delaney looked like a skinny little kid. A skinny little dead kid. I stared at her for what felt like a very long time, waiting for some sign of life—the rise and fall of her chest, a rasp of breath—but I didn't find one. I forced myself across the living room. My hand was shaking as I turned the switch on the lamp near her head.

In a blaze of light, Mrs. Delaney came alive. She threw up an arm, batting at the lamp, and moaned. Up close she didn't look like a kid. She looked old and scrawny and sick. Up close I could see there wasn't a whole lot left of the pretty, nervous mother who'd picked her son up at my place after work ten years back.

"Mrs. Delaney?"

She squinted at me. "Luke?" She said my name so gently it surprised me. I couldn't tell if she was wasted or not.

"Yeah, it's me."

"What happened to you? Did you get in a fight?"

I reached up and fingered the split lip, the swollen eye. I'd forgotten how I looked. "Yeah, I did. But listen, do you know where Fang is?"

With a sigh, she sat up, rubbed her face roughly with both hands. "He called me at Eddie's. Told me what was going on. He was so upset, I came right home. Jesus, Luke, he's such a nice, sensitive kid, you know? This just isn't fair." She was sounding teary and drunk.

"Listen, Mrs. Delaney, do you know where he is?" I was sounding tense and scared.

She leaned over and turned the knob on the lamp, once, twice. The glare dropped to a glow. "He's in my room. Sleeping."

I don't really know what happened to my face then—it was already busted up, but it must have shattered some more when I heard the news.

"Luke?" Mrs. Delaney said quietly. "It's okay. He's just down the hall."

FANG WAS ASLEEP in his mother's bed. I thought about waking him up, but man, I was wiped. My legs were so soft, my gut was so soft, my bones were so soft, I'd barely made it down the hall.

Curled up and breathing deeply, Fang didn't take up a lot of space, so I collapsed beside him. The soles of my feet ached from pounding miles of hard pavement. It felt like they were cut up. I wasn't sure. I didn't look. And the hall light was flooding the bedroom, but I couldn't be bothered getting up and turning it off. I just closed my eyes and sank into the mattress.

I guess it was one of the mighty sighs that kept blasting out of me that eventually woke Fang up. He didn't say anything or make any movement, but I could feel his heavy stare. I looked over. He was still balled up, but his eyes were open, although I could barely see them through all the hair.

"What happened to you?" he asked.

I shook my head. "What didn't fucking happen to me?"

"I mean, what happened to your face?"

"Slater."

"Slater? *Asshole.*"

"I started it."

"Asshole."

I snorted at that. Afterwards, we were both quiet. My thoughts tripped back and forth through the massive amount of life that had happened to me—to him—in the last twenty-four hours. I mean, it felt like a fucking decade since I'd kicked Fang out of bed and up Gandy's Rock, but it was, like, barely yesterday. I didn't want to keep lying there all mute. I knew I had shit to say to him. But like usual, I didn't know where to begin. Finally I picked someplace close.

"I saw your mom on the couch."

"Yeah." He stretched his legs out, stuck an arm under his head. "She made me dinner. It sucked."

"Still. That's cool."

"Yeah. Would have been nicer if she wasn't hammered."

More silence as I searched around for something that would take us nearer to where we had to go.

"My feet are fucking killing me."

"Your feet?"

"I ran over here with no shoes on, Fang." I sucked in some air, worked up another massive sigh. "I ran over here and ... I had no shoes and I was so scared, I was so fucking scared." I had trouble squeezing the last couple words up my throat. I didn't really know why—there were too many reasons to choose from, I guess—but all of a sudden my chest was tight and my stomach was hard and I was fighting not to cry.

Fang got up slowly and looked at my feet. "There's gravel and shit in them. And one of them is cut." He disappeared into the hall. I heard him rooting around in the bathroom, opening cupboards, slamming drawers. He was back in a minute, with a semi-fresh-looking towel, a faded green washcloth, a Band-Aid.

"Lift up your legs," he said. He slipped the towel under my heels then sat down on the end of the bed. "God, man, your feet are a fucking mess."

I didn't say anything. I couldn't say anything.

"And there's blood on the sheets."

"I'm sorry." The words flew out, a thousand pounds of pressure behind them.

"Don't worry about it. They were dirty anyway. Here," he said, holding out the cloth, "you better get cleaned up."

"I'm not sorry about the fucking sheets, Fang."

He dropped his arm, stared down at his hands. "Oh," was all he said.

"I'm sorry for bailing on you this afternoon. I'm really fucking sorry."

He gave a little shrug and started flicking the Band-Aid he was holding. With every snap of his finger the sterile paper crackled, the bandage jumped. "I know you're crazy about her."

"I've been a total dick."

"No, you haven't."

"Listen. Out at the rock, I didn't even know what I was doing. I wasn't even fucking *sure*."

"So, you weren't sure. So it would have been easier to do nothing." Fang brushed his Steven Tyler hair out of his eyes so we could get a good look at each other. "Listen, Luke, you didn't do nothing. You saved my life, man. You dragged me out to that rock and you saved my life."

And God, I was so choked up I could barely tell him, "No, Fang, it was you saving me."

MRS. DELANEY was gone by the time I got up the next day. It was past noon, so I guess I'd given her plenty of time to head out. When I asked, Fang mumbled something about her already being back at Eddie's. Until a couple hours ago I'd never even heard of Eddie, didn't know who or what or where he was, and from the dark look on Fang's face it was pretty obvious he wasn't going to tell me.

Seeing how we had the place to ourselves, we hung out upstairs for a change, eating cereal and watching a bit of mindless TV in the living room. It was already late afternoon when Fang handed me a pair of socks and some shoes and asked if I'd mind going to get a paper.

I swung over to my place, and when I pushed through the front door I practically tripped over the White Stripes tickets lying on the floor of the hall, where in some other lifetime they'd dropped from a girl's hand. I don't know why I did it. I mean, I was grabbing the frozen dinners my mom had left me, anyway, thinking they'd come in handy at Fang's, but I stuck the tickets back in the freezer, where I'd first found them. I guess, in some twisted crevice of my mind, I was thinking I could do a deep-freeze voodoo thing on them—you know, conjure a couple of cold tickets into another chance with the warm girl.

On my way out, I hunted around for our copy of the *Examiner*, finally found it in the bush beside the front porch, one of the spastic paperboy's favorite spots. Brushing off the damp leaves, I saw that Todd Delaney, Jack Kite and the rest of their bandstand buddies were front-page news. I read the article right there on the front lawn. There was a quote from Laura, letting the named men know that with God's guidance she and the other members of the Concerned Citizens of McCreary Park, which meets at seven o'clock Wednesday nights at New Life in Christ Church, were ready to help them overcome their deviancy—a brutal old word if I've ever seen one.

When I got back to Fang's, I just sort of shoved the paper at him with an awkward grunt. He sat down at the kitchen table and, head in hands, started reading. I didn't want to stand there watching him, but I didn't want to leave him alone, either, so I got busy jamming the food I'd brought over into the near-empty fridge and the iced-up freezer.

"Jesus," he said, finally looking up, "do you think everybody's going to start calling me Todd now? Because seriously, it sounds so much gayer than Fang."

We both laughed a bit, but to tell you the truth he looked pale as shit, hanging over the table, staring at his name blaring off the front page of the paper.

Afterwards, I didn't really know what to say, so I kind of wandered out of the silent kitchen, muttering something about needing a shower, and headed downstairs. The bathroom in the basement was totally skank, but shit, the chin-up bar was clean, and that's all that really mattered. I hopped right in and cranked up the hot water, and man it felt good to wash away the filth and madness of the past few days. I'd just started lathering up my hair when I got nailed by the other side of yesterday's death flash, the one that had dropped me to my knees outside Ted's church.

I pressed both hands to the wet tiles. Even then I barely managed to hold myself up. Because that day it happened again. The moment of death was a perfect repeat of the premonition itself. Clinging to the walls of that slippery shower, I felt a heart beat inside me. A breath fill my lungs. And I shook, I trembled, I lived and I died in the purity and fearlessness of a single note.

Afterwards, in the sting and rush and the steam of Fang's shower, I opened my mouth and let the water pour down my throat. I drank it in, I swallowed it down, and with every gulp all I could feel and taste and hear was that note floating inside me, filling me up, busting me open, setting loose all my music and my noise.

THIRTY-TWO

Fang and I spent the rest of the week hanging at his place. Neither one of us—but him in particular—was in any big rush to get back to school. We slept late every day, cruised around on our boards in the afternoons, and, except for some moms with little kids, we had the neighborhood to ourselves. We were always careful to be back at Delaney's before school got out, and usually we'd grab some of my mom's frozen food before crashing in the living room and listening to tunes. I think we were unofficially trying to find some common musical ground or something, because we ended up going back to all the stuff we'd grown up on, all the songs we knew by heart. I threw on some Offspring—"Pretty Fly," "Original Prankster," "Come Out and Play"—some Green Day, some Sum 41, the Nirvana *Unplugged* CD (which Fang had always loved). He chose tracks from Oasis and Sugar Ray and Smash Mouth. Still, it seemed his pick of the week was the Smashing Pumpkins' *Mellon Collie and the Infinite Sadness*. He surprised me by playing the hardest track on the album, the raging "Bullet with Butterfly Wings," aka "Rat in a Cage," about twenty times in a row one day. We both threw ourselves around the room a bit when it was on, because truly, it's an excellent tune, but I have to admit I was also sort of worried about why that infinitely sad, infinitely mad song was finally speaking to my buddy.

And we never talked about Fang being gay. I guess what we were doing that week was hiding out, but it didn't feel like that. It just felt like we'd chosen to spend a couple of easy days together, days when my list and his didn't even exist. We took a TO and did whatever we wanted to do, which ended up being a lot of nothing. Time was soft. The music good. The world distant.

We did smoke the odd joint, but it was definitely a secondary activity. And we did have the occasional visitor. Mrs. Delaney came back once or twice to see how her son was doing, but she never stayed too long, and she never seemed too sober. But the big visit happened Wednesday evening, one day after Fang's name had hit the paper. That was the night the chicks showed up.

I was the one who answered the knock, opening the front door just a crack before I saw Ms. Banks, Faith and Mrs. Bernoffski, with a big clay dish, on the other side. The two older ladies started shrieking when they got a look at my face, which had bloomed into a hellish palette of grayish yellow and blackish purple. After they finished with the face, they started talking all over each other, telling me they'd been worried, they hadn't known where I was, they'd been scared to death. Faith didn't say a word. She tried to leave almost right away, but Mrs. Bernoffski hustled her inside and insisted she stay for dinner. "Da casserole is big enough for everyone, it is delicious, and besides, I hate to see good food go to vaste."

Faith gave me a quick look as she brushed on by. "I see you managed to get yourself beaten up," she said flatly, like it was no big surprise, like it had only been a matter of time, like she was disappointed she hadn't done it herself. She headed straight for the living room and started talking to Fang, who was sitting on the couch looking all staggered by the home invasion.

I hung out in the kitchen. Mrs. Bernoffski popped the food in the oven, located a can of Ajax under the sink and tried cleaning up, while Ms. Banks reminded me that she was the one who was supposed to be keeping an eye on me while my parents were out of town. When I hadn't shown up at school for a few days, she'd been worried, leaving messages at my place, asking my friends if they'd seen me, etc., etc. She'd finally swung by my house after school to see if I was there. It happened to be the day Mrs. Bernoffski was bringing me dinner, something I'd forgotten about but she hadn't. When she arrived, casserole in hand, she'd found the lovely librarian pacing the sidewalk in front of my place. I guess one of them had finally said the word *missing* and they'd spun themselves into a bit of a panic. They climbed into Ms. Banks's van, nabbed Faith, who told them I might be at either Astelle's or Fang's.

I guess they stopped somewhere and looked up the Jordans' number. Ms. Banks told me Astelle was already tucked into rehab, but on the phone Mrs. Jordan had been quick to mention finding an empty pill bottle with my name on it beside a passed-out girl a few nights earlier—Ms. Banks raised her eyebrows here—and the resultant trip to Emergency for a quick round of stomach pumping. Mrs. Jordan had also asked Ms. Banks to pass along the message that, if and when I turned up, I was to stay the hell away from her daughter.

Still, Ms. Banks was pretty gentle with the lecture. I mean, even if she hadn't seen the paper, she couldn't have missed the buzz about Fang at Jefferson. I'm sure she knew why I was there.

We all crammed into the kitchen to eat. Mrs. Bernoffski said a little Polish prayer to start the meal, and I guess that's what got me thinking about Ted. How he'd told me I was on the wrong side of God, how he'd hammered me with my sins, how he'd proclaimed me unworthy. But, that night, in that kitchen, there were people—people who cared about me, people who might have even loved me—squashed around Fang's table, eating some tasty home-brewed chicken and rice concoction. And I thought just that, wasn't that enough to prove Ted wrong?

"What's so funny?" It was Faith, across the table, staring straight at me, all annoyed and confused. The angry edge to her voice had the rest of our dinner companions stopping to take a good look at me too.

"What?" Even as I said it, I could feel the smile on my lips, and I realized I'd probably been grinning into my plate for the last few minutes. "Nothing is funny," I said, still grinning.

She glared at me, so long and so hard everyone else dropped their heads and got busy eating.

"Listen, I'm just happy. That you're all here. There's nothing wrong with being happy, is there, Faith?" I said, throwing one of her own lines into the glare.

Forks and knives clicked around the table, but there was nothing from her.

So I leaned halfway across the table and I didn't care that there were three other people in the kitchen, I told Faith I was sorry. I told her I was sorry, really, really sorry about Astelle. I told her I'd made a huge mistake. I'd been a complete jerk. Mostly I told her I was sorry I'd hurt her, because a person like

her, a great and gorgeous person like her, did not deserve to be
hurt. Ever.

I wasn't sure about Faith, but Mrs. Bernoffski seemed moved
by the heartfelt apology. She pulled a tissue out of her sleeve and
blew her nose a couple of times, while Fang did his best impression of invisible, and between bites Ms. Banks threw quick
glances up the table.

"You drive me crazy," was all Faith had to say.

"Better than boring you to death," I said, pulling back onto my
side of the table.

"Not much better," she said, refusing to smile, "not much."

The only ray of hope Faith gave me, the only clue she left that
maybe, possibly, she'd been thinking kind thoughts about me, was
the newspaper clipping I found on the kitchen table after she was
gone. It was from the *Examiner* and concerned the Highway 6 frog
massacre. According to wetlands experts quoted in the paper, the
whole thing had resulted from the pond being too shallow and the
water too warm. Thin-skinned and sensitive to that sort of shit,
the frogs had crossed the highway in search of cooler digs. Sweet,
neat handwriting filled the right margin. "No big *Magnolia*
mystery after all. Just another homegrown calamity claiming a
thousand small green lives. Faith."

Maybe she'd left the clipping for Fang. Maybe she'd left it for
me. Maybe she'd left it for both of us. Whoever it was meant for,
I was the one who folded it in half and stuck it in my pocket,
so I could feel Faith and the frogs' true story riding close to my
skin.

ON HER WAY OUT the door that night, Mrs. Bernoffski stopped and asked me to come by her place the next day, because she needed someone to cut "da grazz." I must have looked, I don't know, stunned or something, because she'd been quick to tell me not to worry, she'd pay me for the work. So there I was the following afternoon, nervous as hell, watching the widow swing her garage door open. I was imagining chunks of Mr. Bernoffski clinging to the John Deere and the blades dark with dried blood and matted hair, which was all really stupid seeing how the old guy hadn't even been run over. But inside the garage the tractor gleamed, all shiny green surfaces and slick black tires. Not so much as a stray piece of grass decorated the cutting blade, and the garage smelled not of death but of soap and Armor All. A pail, still-damp cloths draped over its edge, sat off to one side of the tractor. I could almost see the widow cleaning it behind closed doors, her big, meaty hands moving with as much care over the hard metal surfaces as they would over the planes of a corpse.

I knew she'd done it out of respect for Mr. Bernoffski, a man I'd never really known except in the moment of his death. And I wanted to say something, something about how strong he'd been and how much he'd loved her, but when she pressed the John Deere key into my hand and wrapped her fingers around mine, she held my eyes for as long as she could, and I knew there was nothing this boy could tell her that she didn't already know.

She gave my fingers a squeeze. The rough edge of the key cut into my palm. "Be careful. At the back," was all she managed before disappearing into the house.

I admit I was pretty happy the widow was hiding out inside when I discovered just why Mr. Bernoffski had been so possessive of his mower. It only took a couple minutes for me to figure out that if I spread my legs just so, my balls rested solidly on the vibrating seat, which made for a pretty sweet ride. I had a hard-on for most of the front yard and all of the back, and the only thing that really got me down was thinking about the old dude riding around in a similar state, which just seemed twisted and sick.

The tractor was parked safely inside and I was halfway down the front walk when Mrs. Bernoffski emerged from the house, a sturdy black purse wedged under one arm.

"Hey, where you be go? I pay you. I pay you."

"Oh, that's okay," I said, trying to slip away, but she waved me over, insisting I take the money she pulled from a small, beat-up change purse and worked into my hand.

"Five dollar," she said, and I almost laughed. "And"—looking very serious, she raised a finger—"one shot of vodka." Seeing how she was obviously as unfamiliar with the concept of minimum wage as she was with that of the legal drinking age, I decided to forgo the college fund in favor of more booze. I tried to invert the equation, suggesting one dollar and five shots of vodka would be more appreciated. But she was having none of it. "I don't send you home drunk to your mommy. Last time, we have to talk. Now, we know each other, yes? So, one shot of vodka."

The only other outing I made that week that's worth mentioning was my trip to the hospital. To see Laura Cramp. Fang and I had been keeping a low-key watch on the *Examiner*, and let's just say the Cramps' announcement in the Births and Deaths section of the paper caught my attention. They'd had a son, James Michael Cramp, at 4:42 P.M., Tuesday, April 29, but they'd only had him for a minute.

If I'd been nervous going to cut my neighbor's grass, I can't even begin to explain how I was feeling pushing open the door to Laura's room. Still, it seemed like I didn't really have a choice in the matter. I'd seen the announcement in the paper. I'd known what it meant and what I had to do.

Laura was sitting up in bed with a sheet pulled over her knees. She was staring blankly at a little TV suspended from the ceiling, but she looked up when I slipped into the room.

"Oh, hi, Luke," she said, giving me a smile that didn't come anywhere close to reaching her eyes. Still, I was relieved she was alone, and when I went and stood beside the bed, I tried to ignore the missing bump, the deflated stomach.

"Looks like the war's over," she said flatly, motioning to the TV. She picked up a remote and turned up the volume, and together we listened to the President—standing on some mighty ship, in the middle of some huge ocean—announcing the end of major combat in Iraq. I mostly stared at the big MISSION ACCOMPLISHED banner flapping in the background while George W. thanked the soldiers for serving our country and our cause.

After the big "may God continue to bless America" finale, Laura pressed a button and the screen went black. Then there was just this big silence in the room, and Laura wasn't saying anything, so finally I grabbed onto the bar running along the side of the bed and, white-knuckled, told her I'd seen the announcement about the baby in the paper. She just nodded and her lips pressed into a hard white line. And she sounded sort of lifeless and disbelieving all at the same time when she said they'd had no idea the baby was at risk. If they'd known, they would have gone to Children's Hospital in Detroit for the delivery. The ultrasounds had all been normal. An autopsy was being done to determine the cause of death.

"They always said there is no disease, no sickness, too hard for God. But, but"—her voice was suddenly high and thin—"he was in my arms, I was holding *my baby* in my arms, and he took just one breath, just one ..."

Even before she started to cry, I had to look away, down at my feet, at the wall, anywhere but at her. With all the death I'd been handed over the last seven months, you'd think I would have been prepared, that I would have been tougher, but I'd never come anywhere close to the raw grief I saw on Laura Cramp's face that day.

She pulled a Kleenex from a box beside her bed and blew her nose, wiped her eyes. I kept clinging to the bar on the bed, holding on, trying to work up the nerve to tell her what I knew.

"The Pastor says it's God's will, that my baby will be waiting for me in heaven. But I want him now. I want him *now*." Suddenly she reached out and grabbed hold of my arm. "And you're just a boy, right? Just someone else's son. Just a good boy. Right, Luke? Right?" She was clinging to my arm and searching my face as if she might find an answer there, and it took a lot to keep my head up and my eyes on her.

I didn't know what to tell her. I couldn't say I was thick with good and bad and love and hate and truth and lies. I couldn't say

I am music. I am noise. I am every great and sorry thing in between. That stuff wasn't going to help her. So I leaned in close, as close as I dared, and I opened my mouth and said what I'd come there to say. "I felt your baby."

"What?" she whispered. "What did you say?"

"I felt your baby."

Slowly, she turned her face toward me. Steepled hands hid her mouth and nose. All I could see were her eyes, stretched wide above trembling white fingers. All I could hear was her breath, trapped behind cupped palms.

I had to pretend I wasn't afraid. I had to use all my strength to tell her what she needed to hear, to say the one thing I knew she'd understand.

"He felt like God," I whispered. "He felt like God."

THIRTY-THREE

My mom swiveled round and aimed a careful smile into the back seat. "So, Luke, do you want to go home? Or out to the cemetery? Your choice."

I pressed a button. The rear window slid open. Riding a blast of cool air, the chatter of birds filled the car. I stared at the hearse, idling in front of the church, and thought back to the last time my mom had asked me that same question. That day, Stan had been in the back of the long black beast and I'd been a small-town freak. That day, I'd chosen to flee the scene.

I looked at my mom, still peering at me from the front seat. "We could go to the cemetery," I said. "Avoid creating traffic chaos."

"What?" My mother's eyebrows, light and fine, drew together.

"Remember Stan's funeral? How we tried to bail and Dad ended up directing traffic?"

"Oh, right." She laughed, shook her head. "That was awful. Crazy."

My father found me in the rearview mirror so I could see his eyes roll playfully. He leaned forward and turned a knob. The radio came to life, cushioning the space between us with soft, bluesy jazz.

At home, things hadn't been quite so easy. I'd moved out of Fang's on the weekend and had been hanging at my place Sunday

afternoon when my parents were due back. After Paris, I thought they'd be all champagne smiles and caviar kisses, but they weren't. Apparently my father had told my mom about my list in the plane on the way home, and I guess the news had practically knocked her into the Atlantic. She'd still been sort of staggering as she made her way up the front stairs and into the house, and once my father told me why, once I knew she was in the loop, I hit the two of them with a brief synopsis of my week alone.

I didn't think they needed to hear about my evening at the Cramps', so I skipped the fun with the fundamentalists. And I skipped the whole Astelle/Faith/One Drum drama too. And I definitely didn't mention the trip to Gandy's Rock. What I told them was that I hadn't been at school all week because I'd had a feeling Fang was going to kill himself because he and a handful of other homosexual men got arrested in McCreary Park—oh yeah, including your boss, Dad—and Fang's name had been on the front page of the paper, and since then he'd barely stepped out of his house and I'd been over at his place keeping him company.

Even with all the shit I'd skipped, it was enough. Afterwards, my parents just sort of banged upstairs, suitcases smacking every step, and collapsed on their bed. Still, the next day, right after my mom quit her job at the bank, she did go over to see Fang. And my list had migrated from my room to the middle of our dining room table without any help from me. But that's as far as we'd gotten. My parents had been back for a good five, six days, and we were still tiptoeing around each other, like we were carrying wobbly towers of cards or something, whispering to each other

without ever moving our lips. *Are you okay? Yeah, I'm okay. Are you okay? Yes. No. Maybe.*

Oh yeah, before I forget. A few nights back, I found this appointment card for a marriage counseling session lying on the front hall table. That had been sort of unsettling, but it was another thing we weren't discussing, another thing coiled up in the Hunter household, biding its time. One thing we were talking about was my parents' jobs, or lack thereof. Like I mentioned, my mother quit the bank the day after she got back from France. I knew I was probably part of the reason, but she told me that even before Paris she'd volunteered to work on one of the EPA boats scheduled to investigate Erie's ever-expanding dead zone this summer, a dead zone that seemed to be taking its toll on the lake and my mother in equal doses.

As for my dad, well, Kalbro had announced they were moving a big chunk of their production to China, which I think he might have warned us about at one point or another. With the news now made public, most of the town, including Kalbro's supply chain manager, was trembling with the bad vibes. I wasn't shaking, wasn't really bothered at all by the impending fallout. Maybe I was just being naive, but I figured we were going to be okay, me, my mom, my dad—although I had my doubts about Erie.

I glanced out the back window as the funeral procession moved into downtown. There was no end to the line of cars behind us, and up front there were hundreds more vehicles trailing the hearse. It felt like the whole town was following Dwayne Slater, Dwight's older brother, on his last ride out to the Stokum cemetery. Pre-Iraq, Dwayne had been all proud smiles and so big on Wet Ones.

Unfortunately, his homecoming had been a lot less smiley, if not less patriotic, seeing how he'd returned to town in a flag-draped box, shot in the head while patrolling in Baghdad, like twenty or thirty other guys since the war had been declared all but over.

For a million reasons, it felt weird to be at his funeral. First off, the brother of honor had beaten the shit out of me not so long ago. Secondly, after tangoing with Ted, I'd been sort of nervous setting foot inside a church. But my mother had insisted I go, because Mr. Slater worked at Kalbro, because Dwight and I were friends (our fight was another one of the details I'd spared my parents), but mostly to show respect for a boy who'd died serving his country.

The funeral was held at Sunnyside United. With its soaring steeples, stained glass windows and chiming bells, it was a way more mainstream affair than the little white clapboard number that had spirited Stan away. And the service *was* okay. The front row had been studded with white-gloved soldiers, the whole church filled with hymns and personal tributes to the dead man— who, if you believed the guys behind the mike, had been a hell of a lot nicer than his younger brother. The word *hero* was mentioned more than once.

The string of cars trolled up Water Street through a bright spring day. The sun beamed straight through a million miles of black space to press through new leaves, to bounce off flagpoles, to land squarely on the sidewalk, painting downtown Stokum a thousand different shades of light and shadow. Everyone who hadn't shut down to attend the funeral lined the road, waving small American flags. Hank was there, hunched up in front of the

T-Shirt Shack, right where I'd left him when I'd come down to see about the One Drum shirts and we'd ended up outside, talking Stan and Oprah Winfrey. I raised my hand and waved, but he didn't see me. He just kept staring at the cars, looking all lost and confused.

McCreary Park marked the end of the somber storeowners. We rolled past the neat square of grass with its bright white bandstand, its perverted pulpit, and right on by the For Sale sign planted in front of the Kites'. All the curtains were drawn at the next-door neighbors', turning the panes of glass into blind rectangles. If nothing else, I'd have to say my evening at the Cramps' was pretty fucking memorable. I didn't know how the doctor was holding up, having just lost his son. And I hadn't seen Ted since I bailed on him that night. I know he's kicking around town, though, still looking for broken folks to save. Still believing he's right and I'm wrong. Still believing in a God who chooses sides.

If I do run into him again, I'm thinking he shouldn't have any hard feelings. I mean, I know Ted was hoping for a long-term relationship and all I gave him was an aborted one-night stand. Still, in a real roundabout way, he got what he was after. He wanted deliverance, repentance and baptism, and the way I see it, the trio happened. I was delivered the moment I walked away from him on Water Street. I repented to, and was forgiven by, my buddy Fang. I was baptized in a skanky basement shower. I know it's a long way from Ted's narrow path; still, salvation is what he wanted, and it seems to me salvation is what went down.

So it wasn't all bad. And somewhere between here and the Cramps' front door, I even managed to figure a couple things out.

One. *Yeah,* everyone *is* going to die. But first, we get to live. And that's big. That's beautiful. That's not to be missed. Two, and maybe I'm just trying to make myself feel normal here, but the way I see it, anyone, if they're paying attention, could have a list like mine stuck in some private drawer. People they know, strangers they don't, claiming a line on their page. The difference would be, the details—the whens and the hows—would have to be filled in after the fact rather than before. The difference would be, the person making the list would have to care enough, and listen hard enough, to hear the music playing in the people passing through their life. And the list wouldn't be months long. It would stretch over a lifetime, and would always, always, end with the name of its maker.

As for my premonitions, they seem to be in remission, for the moment anyway. Whether they come back or not, whether they had anything to do with some mental mutation I share with my uncle Mick, whether they're a gift or a curse, doesn't really matter. It isn't really the point. Because the list goes on. The high notes keep sounding.

The last one I heard was the one-breath wonder of Laura Cramp's baby, and it will never leave me. It sunk in so deep, it became a part of me. Or maybe it was always there, simmering inside, waiting to be recognized, waiting to join the distilled hum of a hundred million other souls that plays somewhere just beyond our reach. After being pressed up tight to life and death, it's what I believe in—a distilled hum that I plan to follow through this life and maybe the next, like my own personal anthem. Maybe it doesn't seem like a lot, but it is. If you've heard it, you know it is.

And I guess, if you pinned me down and kicked me, I'd admit that's my version of God. An all-inclusive sort of deal, without a lot of rules. Just listen for the hum.

When things get quiet, though, I still worry about Fang. I guess it's what I've done, and the real reason I've been mad at him, for half of my life. I've seen him a couple times this past week, and he seems okay, although he's still sticking close to the basement. I called him, but he definitely wasn't interested in attending the Slater funeral, soldier or not, drug connection or not. I've tried to persuade him to come back to school, and he said he would, but I'm not sure I believe him. Still, my plan is to swing by his place Monday morning so we can head to Jefferson together, arm in fucking arm if necessary. We'll see how it goes.

When I look back on things, I can honestly say that the first time I saw Fang, standing on top of those monkey bars in kindergarten, smiling that crazy smile, I knew his courage was more about despair than belief. I mean, back then I couldn't have put it into words, but even as a kid I sensed the weakness that made him strong. I knew he'd do what I wanted. And if I'm ready to confess my real sins, I have to admit that I used that info to push him to the farthest edge of fearlessness so I could watch from below. For a long time it seemed harmless enough. We both reveled in the afterglow. I have the pictures to prove it. But when Fang finally called my bluff, when he poured his desperation from the roof of the school, when he stepped into midair and forced me to witness his misery, I was the one who was scared shitless, not him. I was the one who refused the truth.

I was just lucky he gave me another chance, and that second time around I went to claim it.

WE FOLLOWED THE LINE of cars into the cemetery parking lot. The air was thick with churned gray dust. Gravel popped beneath a town's tires. A chorus of slamming doors sounded through the lot. As we made our way across the grass, weaving through the headstones, I could see the flag-draped coffin suspended over an earthy rectangle, held up by a sturdy-looking contraption made of brass and thick nylon straps. Beside the grave, a few chairs had been set up for the family. Mrs. Slater was in the middle, slumped forward, sheltering her face with one hand. Her husband sat straight-backed on the chair beside her, his eyes hard and flat, the lines of his face cut sharp by grief. Dwight was on the other side of his mother, wearing sunglasses, his hands holding tight to his knees. For some reason I felt ashamed looking at them, and I ended up staring at the coffin instead, which somehow seemed a whole lot easier.

There was already a crowd when we arrived, and more coming up behind us, but not much noise, just a bit of quiet murmuring that faded out completely when the minister began to speak. He reminded us that Dwayne Slater had made the ultimate sacrifice for his country, had died for all of us, before the white-gloved soldiers stepped forward to fold the Stars and Stripes covering the casket. When the flag was presented to Mrs. Slater, she clutched it to her chest. Both Dwight and his father nodded solemnly at the soldier who stooped down to speak to them, but Mrs. Slater's eyes were fixed on the grass a yard or two to the left of the man's polished black boots.

As the coffin was lowered into the ground, the minister recited the psalm about lying down in green pastures and walking through the shadow of the valley of death and fearing no evil. And when he asked us to bow our heads for a minute of quiet prayer, I did it, man. I did it.

When the minister gave the nod, the honor guard raised their rifles and fired three rounds. The only noise afterwards was the wail of a startled baby.

I'd been worried I might get choked up at the Slater funeral, turn it into some sort of personal weep-fest for all the people who'd checked out on me over the last eight months. But I didn't cry. The truth was, I barely knew the deceased, and the whole thing was for him, and the people who wept were the ones who'd loved him. The only time I went soft at all was right at the end, when the Pastor asked the mourners to offer comfort to their neighbors.

I guess it was a church thing I didn't know about, but all of a sudden my mom slipped her arm around me and rested her head on my shoulder. "Peace be with you," she said. Then my dad kind of draped himself over both of us so we formed an awkward triangle, a misshapen circle, and in that graveyard we held on to each other for a couple long, tight seconds. I pulled out first and turned to shake the hands of the people waiting behind us.

"Peace be with you."

"Peace."

"Peace."

It was only when the crowd started to move a bit—some drifted toward the parking lot, others went forward to drop roses onto the coffin—that I saw Faith again. She was on the opposite side of the grave, standing on the crest of the hill. Behind her, the headstones fell away and it was all blue sky above the vast grayness of Erie. I don't know if she'd been looking for me, but she raised her hand when she saw me staring. Her smile brought everything close and made everything seem possible, and for a second I believed I could have picked a pebble from the ground and thrown it straight across the lake to bounce down the streets of Cleveland or Pittsburgh or maybe even New York City.

Faith didn't come over to say hi. She waded deeper into the cemetery and, pulled by her cosmic force, I ditched my parents and followed. That's how I ended up at Stan's grave with his old girlfriend beside me, so close I could have reached out and taken her hand in mine.

"Ever been here?" she asked. I was embarrassed to say no. I'll never know what she would have done if I'd told her I'd never even thought about coming up here to say goodbye, or what she might have said if I'd admitted Stan's dying had always been more about my being abandoned than his being dead. And we would have been there until the fucking Fourth of July if I'd tried to explain all the crap I'd waded through on my way to discovering that what I'd really lost when Stan died was nothing more and nothing less than my holiest friend.

Stan Miller, Our blessed son, the tombstone read. *July 7, 1985–October 8, 2002. Trailing clouds of glory do we come, From God, who is our home.*

I was surprised the quote engraved on that thick marble slab was from one William Wordsworth and not the Bible. I'm still not sure what to think about that. Maybe, like Laura Cramp, when pressed up against the rocky reality of their son's death, the Millers' faith finally started to crack. Then again, maybe they're just big Wordsworth fans. I don't know. The only thing I do know with any certainty at all is that soon, very soon, I'm going to turn to Faith and I'm going to tell her two things about myself that she may not know.

I'll tell her I am worthy. I'll tell her I am no longer afraid. And even if it's only for one night, even if I have to throw her over my shoulder and carry her a hundred miles up the highway, we'll go to that concert in Detroit. Together, we'll push our way to the front of the crowd, so we can reach out and touch Jack, the seventh son, and when Meg strikes her cymbals and the first chords sound, we will raise our arms. And we will sing.

ACKNOWLEDGMENTS

Heaps of gratitude to:

My agent, Samantha Haywood, for her confidence and enthusiasm, and to my bold yet always graceful editor, Nicole Winstanley. It has been an honor.

The fabulous team at Penguin Canada, where truly, the fun never stops: David Davidar, Steven Myers, Jennifer Notman, Tracy Bordian, Yvonne Hunter, Don Robinson and Mary Opper.

Lauren B. Davis for her early encouragement, Barry Callaghan for accepting that first story, and Michael Helm, of the Humber School for Writers, for teaching me the value of every word.

My friends, fellow writers and first readers: Regan Orillac, Bill Marvin, Janet Richards, Anu Kanniganti and Jerome Mertz. Here's to a hundred sparkly evenings at Plaza Berri.

Carrie-Lee Brown, for the gentleness of her critiques and the strength of her friendship.

Dr. Chantal Proulx. For answering those strange questions.

Dan and Cheryl Vasiga. For loving the kids.

Kerrin Hands, for turning my story into art.

Renate Mohr, for breathing literary life into Ottawa.

Martin, for believing in me, caring for me, keeping me whole.

Brady, Cody and Behn. Men when it mattered most.

Simon, Sophia and Elise. Everything for you.

Before all else, before all others, my parents, Mary and Michael Vasiga.